THE GREAT DECEPTION

BOOK II

IN THE MAGNIFICENT

AMERICAN PATRIOT SERIES

The thundering seventeenth-century saga of Sir Richard Dunstable's evolution from English baronet to fiercely loyal American colonial . . . a heroic adventure of Indian attacks and faithful Indian companions, of loyalty and betrayal, honor and deceit, love and pain.

Here is the enthralling story of men and women and the building of a new nation. It is the epic of America.

THE AMERICAN PATRIOT SERIES
From the creators of
WAGONS WEST
and
THE CENTURIONS

Also by Douglass Elliot
Published by Ballantine Books:

THE NEW BREED

THE
AMERICAN
PATRIOT
SERIES

BOOK II

The GREAT DECEPTION

Douglass Elliot

BALLANTINE BOOKS • NEW YORK

Produced by BOOK CREATIONS, INC.
Executive Producer: Lyle Kenyon Engel

Copyright © 1982 by Book Creations, Inc.

All rights reserved under International and Pan-American Copyright Conventions. Published in the United States by Ballantine Books, a division of Random House, Inc., New York, and simultaneously in Canada by Random House of Canada, Limited, Toronto, Canada.

Library of Congress Catalog Card Number: 81-68646

ISBN 0-345-29823-3

Manufactured in the United States of America

First Edition: January 1982

I

RICHARD Dunstable felt flat, uninspired—not that he was discounting the good fortune that had come his way. Forced to flee from his native England and robbed of his title and estate by the Roundheads, who had branded him a Royalist after they had beheaded King Charles I, he had sailed to the New World to seek his fortune. Here he had acted as an espionage agent for the adherents of the young exiled Charles II, and had become entangled in a net of political intrigue that was not at all to his liking.

But here, too, he had met his own true love, Eliza Burrows, had married her, and had gone to work in the New Haven headquarters of her father's shipping business. That, he decided, was the real trouble. He was entirely too content—too happy going to work every morning, sitting at a desk, and coming home every evening to the loveliest girl in the world. Perhaps he was crazy, but he felt sluggish. As the king's forester, a hereditary post he had held in England, he had spent much of his time in the deep woods. Now, however, he was deskbound. He needed the sights and sounds and smells of the forest around him. The limitless wilderness of North America beckoned to him, and the lure was almost more than he could bear.

Walking home for his noon dinner, he saw a familiar buckskin-clad figure emerging from his own property, and recognized Roaring Wolf, an older Pequot warrior, a man of about forty, whose life Richard had saved and who had become his good friend and hunting partner.

The Indian raised his arm in a rigid salute.

Richard returned the gesture without self-consciousness.

"There are many deer at the salt lick near the red cliffs to the north," Roaring Wolf said. "If we hurry, we have much fine venison tonight."

Richard brightened instantly. Here was the opportunity he had been seeking, and he knew his father-in-law would approve of his taking time away from his desk. He hurried into the house for his weapons, taking his pistols and his rifle, which had been made to his own private specifications by an expert gunsmith, and automatically, unthinkingly, he strapped on the belt that contained his specially balanced throwing knives.

Scribbling a note to Eliza, he hurried to the stables behind the house, where he saddled Prince Henry, the jet-black stallion he had brought to the New World with him from England. Aware of his impending adventure, the great beast whinnied and pawed the ground. Richard patted him, then mounted in a quick, fluid motion and was on his way, with Roaring Wolf, as always, jogging easily behind the horse.

Heads turned as he made his way through the busy, elm-lined streets of New Haven—and with good reason. Richard made a striking figure. Over six feet tall, lean, but with a rugged build, he scorned the long, curly locks that were fashionable and tied his own crisp brown hair with an eel skin at the base of his neck. His clear hazel eyes seemed to take in everything he saw, and the confidence and seeming effortlessness with which he sat atop the powerful and spirited stallion testified to his expert horsemanship.

Within minutes they left New Haven behind and entered the wilderness. Here Richard slowed his pace a trifle as Prince Henry picked his way over fallen tree trunks and through piles of half-melted snow. Every so often Richard would glance back at Roaring Wolf, who was not even breathing hard. The salt licks were located about an hour's ride into the forest, and Richard circled so they would approach downwind from them, intending to dismount a few hundred yards before his destination.

Then disaster struck without warning. More than a half-dozen screaming Indian braves materialized from the forest to the left, and suddenly the air was filled with arrows and tomahawks hurled with deadly force.

Prince Henry reared, snorting in sudden rage, and a tomahawk struck the great beast in the forehead. Almost simultaneously, two arrows drove deep into his body.

It was impossible to survive such an assault, but Prince Henry somehow managed to stay on his feet until Richard could dismount. Then, and only then, did he topple forward and lie very still on the ground, his life ebbing rapidly.

Richard was infuriated beyond measure. His horse was near and dear to him and had served him faithfully for more than five years. Now, in a matter of seconds, the noble animal was gone forever.

Yet Prince Henry helped his master even after

death. The great beast's dead body shielded Richard as he dropped to one knee, took quick but careful aim with his rifle, and squeezed the trigger.

He felt a sense of great satisfaction when he saw his bullet bore a hole in the forehead of one of the young braves, who threw his hands skyward as he toppled to the ground.

Richard was far from finished, however. He had no time to reload his rifle, so he snatched his pistols from his belt, instinctively measuring the distance between him and the other braves, who were so confident of their coming success that they did not even bother to conceal themselves behind the trees of the forest.

The two pistols spoke almost simultaneously, and two more warriors paid for their perfidy with their lives.

Roaring Wolf, in the meantime, was holding his own. Concealing himself behind a thicket of brambles, the Pequot loosed an arrow effectively at the nearest foe, who fell to the ground and clutched at the shaft protruding from his throat. The Indians continued to concentrate exclusively on Richard, however, and this allowed Roaring Wolf to take careful aim again. Richard had no opportunity to reload, so he reached for his bone-handled, razor-sharp throwing knives. Within a matter of a few seconds, he hurled three knives, and two more braves sprawled on the ground.

Only one of the attackers was left, but not for long. Roaring Wolf cut him down with bone-chilling precision.

The battle was ended almost before it had begun. One white man in the prime of life and one overage warrior had disposed of seven young braves in less than one minute.

Roaring Wolf was delighted. Dashing forward, he claimed the scalps of the young braves—returning with seven grisly trophies, all dripping blood, dangling from his belt. The dead braves, much to Richard's relief, turned out not to be from the local Mohegan tribe, which Richard had persuaded to sign a peace treaty with New Haven. Instead they appeared to be a renegade band from the west, probably Wappinger, according to Roaring Wolf. Such isolated raids were not uncommon.

Richard soundlessly bade farewell to Prince Henry. He couldn't put his thoughts into words, knowing only that there would be a gap in his life forever that no other animal would fill. The ground was too hard for digging a grave, so he covered the body of the horse with leaves and finally turned away, murmuring only, "Good-bye, old friend, from Eliza and me."

Hoping to put the loss out of his mind, he methodically reloaded his weapons and cleaned his throwing knives, which Roaring Wolf had retrieved. Then he and Roaring Wolf resumed their journey to the salt licks. Their luck was good, and they saw a large buck, which Richard brought down with a single shot. Roaring Wolf used his tomahawk to cut a seven-foot length of sturdy young elm, and they hamstrung the buck from this pole, which they shouldered, and then started slowly back toward New Haven.

The march back was long and arduous, but in spite of the staggering loss of Prince Henry, Richard felt rejuvenated. The deep forest had worked its magic, and once again he had come alive.

Lady Celeste Murette paced the small, cramped room like a caged animal. Her wavy blue-black hair swung out wildly each time she turned and retraced her steps, and her violet eyes seemed to stare right through the bare walls of the upstairs bedchamber. Finally she sat in a chair near the one small window in the room and gazed down at the streets of New Amsterdam, her fingernails tapping steadily on the arms of the chair. The nearby marketplace had come alive with carts, horses, and bustling merchants. She envied them their activity and their freedom, for she herself was at the command of one man she hated and at the mercy of another man she feared.

The first, Peter Stuyvesant, director-general of New Netherland, would be arriving at her small house in the government compound any time now for a meeting with the French spymaster in the New World, a dour man known only as Laroche.

The second, Jules Cardinal Mazarin, first minister of France, had set in motion a series of events leading to today's meeting. It had all begun years ago, before she had met the blustery governor with the wooden leg and had been ordered to become his mistress.

As she recalled the day four years earlier, in 1646, Celeste clenched her small, well-manicured hands. Although she had worked secretly for Mazarin in the court of King Charles in England, she had never experienced firsthand the fear the cardinal's power could inspire. On that day she had been taken suddenly and forcibly from her home in England by French soldiers who had gained access to her estate disguised as gardeners. She had been set upon, bound, gagged, and spirited away across the Channel to a castle outside of Paris, where she was flung into a small, cold tower cell.

Released from her restraints, she had looked out the window of her prison in much the same way as today, experiencing the same unsettling fear and uncertainty. It was winter then, too. . . .

The drawbridge had been lowered over the moat to admit a small party of clergymen, and Celeste craned her neck to see if she could recognize the apparently important visitor now surrounded by a bodyguard of musketeers. Then, all of a sudden, she knew who it was.

He looked unremarkable, and anyone unacquainted with the man would not have bothered to glance at him twice. He wore the coarse cloak of dark gray wool that was common to parish priests. His face was pinched, ascetic, and thoughtful, the face of a devout monk. But Celeste knew that appearances were deceiving, and that anyone who regarded this man as unworldly or unimportant would have been badly mistaken.

For on closer examination, she could see that under his hood he wore the scarlet biretta identifying him as a prince of the Church, and on his finger a magnificent sapphire ring distinguishing him as a cardinal. He was none other than Jules Cardinal Mazarin, successor to the great Richelieu, and pending such time as young Louis XIV reached his majority, he was the most powerful man in France —perhaps in all Europe. Now, for the first time, Lady Celeste knew who was responsible for her abduction.

She watched the group of men cross the courtyard until they were out of sight. A few minutes later the bolt on her cell door clanked open. Then two guards, one at each arm, led her down a dark, winding staircase, through a succession of corridors, and into a large room. The room apparently was a refectory and had been filled with long trestle tables. But now, all save one had been pushed to the walls.

At the long table at the far end of the room, near the fireplace, sat Cardinal Mazarin. He stood up, walked around the table, and smiled.

Lady Celeste noticed that the guards had disappeared. Seeing no one else in the room, she advanced warily to the cardinal and curtsied deeply as she kissed the sapphire ring on his outstretched hand. She was no fool, and knew instinctively the best attitude to take with the cardinal. "Your Eminence," she said with as much charm as she could muster, "you *could* have sent me an invitation!"

Cardinal Mazarin laughed heartily, nodding as he looked her over appreciatively. "I do apologize for your somewhat primitive travel arrangements, but the truth is that the agent in charge of bringing you here is sometimes overzealous in his urge to please me. But please, sit down, sit down."

Lady Celeste tried her best to keep smiling as she seated herself in the one available chair.

Mazarin resumed his own seat, still chuckling. "For such rough handling, you certainly don't look the worse for it. Now I can see why you've become one of the most valuable agents in my employ."

Lady Celeste bowed her head slightly in acknowledgment of the compliment. She was used to flattery.

"But now, I'm afraid, I have a task awaiting you that you might not relish." His face grew serious.

She still smiled at him steadily, her violet eyes narrowing. She pulled the thin cloak she had been given more tightly about her shoulders to ward off the castle's damp chill. "I never object to any assignment, Your Eminence, providing the pay is right. And I've never had cause to complain about Your Eminence's generosity."

Mazarin took a small but exceptionally heavy purse from his belt and placed it on the refectory table. "I well realize," he said, "that you've become partial to gold." He leaned back in his seat and smiled shrewdly.

Lady Celeste opened the purse, saw the gleam of yellow metal coins inside, and nodded to indicate her readiness to listen.

"You have served France well at the court of King Charles. Now I'm afraid I must ask you to work in a far more primitive place. I want you to transfer your activities to the New World."

She raised an eyebrow. "I didn't know that there was anything in either the British or French colonies of the New World worthy of Your Eminence's attention," she said.

The cardinal pressed his fingertips together and stared thoughtfully at the blackened ceiling beams. "My dear Lady Celeste," he replied, "the New World is vital to England's future, and even more important to the future of France. Neither nation yet realizes it, but I tell you with certainty that he who grasps control of the New World will also control Europe. America is the very key to the domination of Europe."

"Go on. I'm not certain I understand," she said.

"For the present," the cardinal explained, "there are vast fortunes to be made in timber and furs. But that's only the beginning. There's untold mineral wealth in the New World, and there's an immense land waiting to be colonized. The nation that has the biggest and strongest empire in the New World will emerge as the first power of Europe."

Lady Celeste fingered the low-cut neckline of her gown of violet velvet that matched her eyes. "Obviously," she said, "you intend France to be that power."

"I do indeed," he replied. "But we haven't had much success through the conventional avenues. Our colonies have had to contend with epidemics, frigid winters, even earthquakes. We must now pursue . . . extraordinary methods. I want you to go to New Amsterdam, the capital of the Dutch colony of New Netherland, to perform several functions there. You are to keep an eye on my principal agent, Laroche. Make certain his primary concern is in France's best interests."

She realized that Mazarin had something more in mind, but knew better than to ask any questions yet and waited for him to continue.

Mazarin leaned forward in his chair and paused momentarily, lending his next words even greater import. He appreciated her delicacy. "Are you familiar with the name Peter Stuyvesant?"

She shook her head. "I've never heard of him."

"You shall, and so shall the world," Mazarin assured her. "He has been serving his government as the Dutch governor of the island of Curaçao, and he lost a leg while conducting a brilliant military campaign. He's quite full of himself just now. He's meeting me because he seeks my support for a position that he wants very badly. He's anxious to win appointment as director-general, or governor, of New Netherland, and he's disturbed because there's a rumor to the effect that someone else is in line for the post."

"Is the governorship of New Netherland such a plum?" she asked.

"Currently, no," the cardinal replied. "The colony has a natural harbor, and its trade is expanding, but it isn't all that prominent yet. It's a confused, filthy town with very few of the comforts of civilization. And there are more Englishmen there than Dutchmen. It needs a strong hand. However, whoever controls New Netherland can control the New World. It lies in the midst of the British colonies, so its strategic position is invaluable. I see no reason why either Holland or England should benefit, and I won't be satisfied until New Netherland becomes French. In time and with proper encouragement, our settlements in New France—Canada, they call it—will become stronger. Then we will take the necessary steps so the English

10

stronghold of New England will, in time, be ours also."

Lady Celeste marveled at the man's boundless ambition.

"For now, the Dutch are our allies; furthermore, Stuyvesant hates the English. I've heard it said that he despises them as much as he enjoys the company of beautiful woman. And his fondness for the female sex, I happen to know, is very considerable."

Lady Celeste nodded almost imperceptibly as she began to understand the nature of the new mission that Mazarin was calling upon her to perform. He wanted her to become the mistress of this man Stuyvesant, although he would never make the request of her in so many words. And she assumed that he would exert control over Stuyvesant, and thus, New Netherland, through her. "Is it Your Eminence's plan," she asked, "to see to it that he wins the director-generalship of New Netherland?"

Mazarin shrugged. "I shall be able to answer that question better when I analyze the fellow's attitude." He listened intently, then rose to his feet. "The commotion I hear causes me to assume he's making his appearance."

Lady Celeste listened to the blare of bugles and the clatter of horses' hooves. She followed the cardinal to the window and looked out in surprise at a burly, gaudily dressed man on horseback who was surrounded by armed guards. In his broad-brimmed hat he wore a large scarlet feather, and his shirt collar and cuffs, which showed past his coat, were made of exquisite lace. What called attention to him more than all else, however, was the wooden leg that he wore to replace the limb he had lost in battle. It stuck out stiffly at an angle from the horse's back, and the sight of it made Lady Celeste's violet eyes widen in amazement. Obviously he was inordinately proud of this war trophy, this sign of his valor. The carved wooden piece was studded with decorative silver nails and, at the knee, boasted a large satin rosette.

On anyone else it would have looked ridiculous, but the heavy-set Peter Stuyvesant managed his unusual appearance with a dramatic flair. His dark, close-set eyes were forceful and direct; his mouth and chin were firm, challenging in a humorless way; and he rode his steed with the air of one who was aware of his importance and recognized his own worth.

Minutes later, when Peter Stuyvesant strode into the cardinal's presence, Lady Celeste was nowhere to be seen, having concealed herself in deep shadow behind a medieval tapestry at a far corner of the hall. From her vantage point she could see and hear everything that took place at the meeting without revealing her presence.

"I've been informed by my intermediaries, Your Eminence, that you and I share similar concerns." Stuyvesant was wasting no time.

Cardinal Mazarin seemed amused by the man's gall. "So I've been told," he said, and deliberately allowed the Dutchman to take the lead.

"You know my background, and I believe my record speaks for itself," Stuyvesant said forcefully. "I took a floundering colony in Curaçao and turned it into a flourishing community that brings large revenues in trade to Holland. I have great plans for New Netherland, and I'm told that Your Eminence has sufficient influence to insure that I'll be appointed director-general of the colony."

"I am not without influence," Mazarin said.

Stuyvesant laughed aloud and slapped the refectory table, obviously vastly amused by the cardinal's circumspection. "Your Eminence is the most powerful and influential man in all of Europe," he said, "and may the Almighty help any fool who fails to recognize it. The rulers of every nation value your friendship and fear your enmity. I've been informed often and on the best authority that Holland's legislature will gladly jump through hoops at your bidding."

"That's something of an exaggeration," Mazarin said modestly. "However, I do have some friends in Amsterdam and The Hague who flatter me by listening to my advice."

"Let me get to the point," Stuyvesant said, and emphasized his words by again bringing his heavy, open hand down sharply on the wooden refectory table. "If you'll support me, I'll support you. It's that simple, Your Eminence, and it would be extremely helpful to both of us to strike a bargain."

The cardinal's manner changed abruptly. A gleam appeared in his eyes, and his gentle voice became harsh and firm, conforming to the needs of the situation. "I'll be completely honest with you, Peter Stuyvesant," he declared. "I have enough friends in your country to win you the post of director-general of New Netherland; there's no doubt of that. What interests me is this—what are you prepared to do for me?"

Peter Stuyvesant rose to the challenge, and Lady Celeste, watching him from behind the tapestry, was impressed by the way he handled himself.

"You and I," he explained, "have an enemy in common—England. I hate England for the same reason you hate her, Your Eminence. She has dreams of glory that interfere with French glory, just as they interfere with Dutch glory. Paris and Amsterdam understand each other and have reached an accommodation. We Dutch recognize you French as being bigger and stronger. All we ask is that we be allowed to share in the power and wealth that you are accumulating. But no such compromise is possible with the British. They demand all or nothing, and they insist on taking all every chance they get, either on the land with their colonies or on the water with shipping and fishing. It's all or nothing."

"Precisely so," the cardinal spoke very softly.

Stuyvesant nodded vigorously and responded in a booming voice that echoed in the ancient hall. "As director-general of New Netherland, I will thwart the aims of the English at every turn," he said. "French ships, like Dutch ships, will be welcomed in the harbor. English ships will be encouraged to leave. I shall apply this principle to every phase of living in the colony."

Cardinal Mazarin smiled slightly and spoke in a barely audible voice. "I believe," he said, "that you can count on my support for your candidacy, Peter Stuyvesant. In fact, I think you may consider yourself as good as appointed. Shall we confirm our understanding by dining together and discussing specifics in two hours?"

Grinning broadly, Peter Stuyvesant bowed, turned, and strode out of the refectory, slamming shut the large oak door.

Lady Celeste, watching from her vantage point behind the tapestry, was surprised at the ease with which he used his artificial limb. She looked at the ceiling and blew out a deep breath. Stuyvesant was as graceful as he was vigorous.

Her face revealed none of her thoughts as she emerged.

"I suggest," Mazarin said as he rose and escorted her to the door, "that you tidy yourself up a bit so you can make the acquaintance of Peter Stuyvesant at dinner tonight."

Lady Celeste smiled maliciously at the cardinal, who chuckled and took her by the elbow.

"I will formally introduce you as one of my

agents. If I judge him correctly, it won't take you very long to establish a, shall we say, more than friendly relationship with him. Besides, it won't hurt for him to know that he will be watched closely."

Her ordeal apparently over for now, Lady Celeste grew more confident. She was long accustomed to winning the hearts of men who were less susceptible to the charms of beautiful women and to whom she was less attracted. She wasn't exactly eager to face the hardships of life in the New World, but the pay was more than generous.

And actually, she had no choice.

She had no choice. The words echoed in Celeste's mind as a knock on the door downstairs disturbed her reverie and returned her attention to the present. She realized she had been daydreaming and quickly rose from her chair by the window. No doubt it was Stuyvesant and Laroche, and she would be forced to endure another long, exasperating evening. She probably would be left with the gin-soaked director-general to contend with and entertain as best she could. Stuyvesant had certainly grown to be a disappointment as a lover, she thought.

But when she opened the door, Stuyvesant was nowhere in sight. It was Laroche, and he whisked in as if he owned the place and stationed himself before the fire, removing his gloves. He motioned Celeste to sit down, and held out a square of paper for her. She unfolded it and began to read.

Laroche had already read the letter, which had arrived that very morning from Cardinal Mazarin himself. It was very brief: Lady Celeste was ordered to determine the whereabouts and status of Lady Dawn Shepherd.

Lady Dawn, like Richard Dunstable, was one of

the many Cavaliers who had fled England after King Charles was beheaded by Oliver Cromwell and the Roundheads. Some had fled to the court-in-exile in Paris, where Charles's young son had been given sanctuary by the ever-scheming Mazarin. Others had fled to the New World, among them the beautiful, red-haired Lady Dawn.

"I feel obliged to warn you," Laroche said as Lady Celeste lowered the letter to her lap, "that Lady Dawn may be dangerous. In fact, she seems to have been closely connected with the death of one of our agents in Virginia, Horace Laing."

Lady Celeste looked up at Laroche, her eyes wide. She had been only slightly acquainted with Lady Dawn at court, but she certainly never considered the woman capable of murder.

"In any case, she knows more about our operations than is good for her. I don't know how close you were to her," he continued in a nasal monotone, "but apparently Cardinal Mazarin thinks you are the best agent for this job." Laroche's upper lip twitched almost imperceptibly. The French spymaster had his own ideas as to Lady Dawn's whereabouts and was eager to interrogate two other persons on the subject, but he refrained from mentioning this to Lady Celeste. Richard Dunstable and his bride, Eliza, knew more than they were saying, Laroche suspected, but Mazarin apparently trusted them and had his own plans for them. In fact, Laroche had already sent for the young couple on the cardinal's orders, and they were probably on their way to New Amsterdam at this very moment.

Lady Celeste herself was secretly quite pleased with her assignment, although she certainly wasn't about to disclose that fact to Laroche. Normally she could manipulate any man with ease, but Laroche seemed more like an insect than a man. She quickly reread the letter, memorizing its contents, and handed it back to Laroche, who promptly laid it on the fire.

"You realize, of course," he said, "that if your inquiries in New Netherland lead nowhere, you will have to travel to the other colonies to seek out Lady Dawn. I myself would suggest that you start with New Haven."

Not waiting for a response, Laroche pulled his gloves back on, strode to the door, and bowed slightly. "Now, if you'll excuse me," he said, "I'll return in a moment with our mutual Dutch friend. I certainly hope you can keep him sober tonight." With that he stepped outside and closed the door behind him.

"Ugh!" was all Lady Celeste could say to the closed door. But despite her dislike for Laroche, a smile appeared on her face for the first time that day. A new period in her life was about to begin, and she felt almost lightheaded. She had a lot of planning to do, but that could wait; tonight, she said to herself, still smiling, she would drink right along with Peter Stuyvesant—and Laroche be damned!

Five hours out of New Haven harbor en route to New Amsterdam, the Burrows and Clayton brig rolled and creaked and pitched its way through the still-icy waters of the Great Bay. It was past nightfall, and the two most important passengers on board had just gone below deck.

Pacing the length of the small cabin he shared with his wife, Richard Dunstable ran his fingers through his crisp brown hair. He was unsuccessfully trying to convince her that she was wrong, and he grew exasperated because her beautiful blond hair and sparkling blue eyes kept distracting him.

"It's fair enough that I take risks," Richard said

vehemently. "For one thing, I'm a major in the New Haven militia, so I'm taking chances in the line of duty. For another thing, I still feel committed to the cause of the restoration of young Charles the Second to the throne of England, even though the state of affairs in London seems far removed from our life here. But I'm damned if I can see why you should be placed in this dangerous predicament."

Eliza Dunstable remained unruffled by her husband's anger. He was still upset at the loss of Prince Henry, she decided. "We've been over and over this situation," she said. "I'm entitled to take as many chances as you are."

"But, damnation, you're a woman," the irritated Richard declared.

She smiled sweetly. "All the more reason for me to take risks," she said. "I'm better equipped than you to handle them."

He gritted his teeth. "I disagree. You are the most stubborn woman in New Haven Colony. Don't you understand? This business of being double agents is extremely dangerous. If Mazarin becomes convinced that our loyalty to the English colony of New Haven prevents us from carrying out our duties, he'll drop us like hot coals. And we know too much already."

There was only one way to end the argument, and Eliza knew it. She approached him slowly and ran her hands up his doublet, then caressed his face. "If I thought I was in any real danger, my darling," she said, "I wouldn't be here now. But we have so much to gain and so little to lose that I'd be selfish if I didn't stand beside you in this time of trouble."

As she well knew, she had disarmed Richard, and he smiled feebly. "Your protection is my first consideration," he told her. "I don't give a hang about what the French may or may not be scheming, any more than I really care about the continuing struggles between the Roundheads and the Cavaliers in England. I intend to spend the rest of my days here in America, here with you, working for your father's and Tom Clayton's shipping line. To the devil with the Old World and its never-ending struggles for power."

Eliza realized that there was much he still had to learn about life in the New World. "But don't you see, Richard," she said, "we're touched by the disputes between France and England. If New Haven Colony were to become French and we were robbed of our liberties, you'd know it fast enough."

"If the colony were actively threatened, I'd march at once with the battalion," he said flatly.

"All the more reason to know what the French have in mind and what they're planning," she said. "Papa is right when he says we've been given a wonderful opportunity, and we'd be stupid if we didn't take advantage of it."

Richard sighed. He had already learned in the short time that they had been married that he was no match for his bride in an argument, and he bowed to her will. But he promised himself privately that if she should be in real danger, he would call an immediate halt to her participation in supposed espionage work for France. He would permit nothing to jeopardize Eliza's welfare.

Eliza was aware of his attitude, and although she appreciated his motives, she couldn't help resenting his feelings. She had been independent since early childhood; after her mother had died, her father had raised her according to the code of a frontier community, which meant that she had been very much on her own and had been responsible for her own safety and welfare for as long as she could remember. She was well aware of the fact that her startling beauty made her desirable to almost any man who saw her, but she was confident of her physical prowess, just as she had faith in her mental agility. She could ride and shoot as well as most men, she was exceptionally quick-witted, and as a result, she was not easily susceptible to unfounded fear. Consequently she felt certain she could look after herself, no matter what might happen. She understood that her bridegroom wanted to take care of her, and she was even grateful for his protective attitude, but at the same time she became irritated when anyone tried to interfere with what she regarded as her freedom.

Richard half understood the way she felt. What annoyed him was the certain knowledge that she was far less self-sufficient than she believed. He knew men, and he knew that she would be no match for someone who was unscrupulous, strong, and clever.

So, when they retired for the night on board ship, the atmosphere was somewhat strained. Then occurred the miracle to which neither was yet quite accustomed.

They crowded into the same cramped bunk, the one bed that the cabin afforded, and as soon as they touched, their antagonism promptly faded away. It was astonishing, but they were overwhelmed by tenderness which, little by little, gave way to an overpowering physical desire. Ultimately they made love—even wilder and less disciplined in their reactions than when they had first gone to bed together—and after their passion was sated, they relaxed in a bottomless pool of tenderness and affection. Neither Richard nor Eliza quite knew whether their mutual physical attraction was responsible for their closeness or was symbolic of it. They had learned, however, that they were incapable of analyzing their feelings for each other, and they had the good sense not to probe. It was enough for both Richard and Eliza that the other was the only person needed and that neither had ever been so much in love before. They were content, realizing they were happier than anyone they knew. They slept soundly, and the next morning, after settling down to breakfast, they were able to discuss the specifics of the problem awaiting them.

"Our first task, it seems to me, is to find out the nature and the extent of the ties that exist between the French and the Dutch," Richard said.

Eliza shook her head and smiled. "Now you're doing what you told me we must never do in our dealings with the French," she said. "You're assuming. You've jumped to the conclusion that there are ties of some sort that bind the French and the Dutch."

Richard peered at her over the rim of his teacup as he took another swallow. "You're wrong, Eliza," he said flatly. "I'm basing my judgment on fact, not guesswork. Let me illustrate. We know that Laroche is a French agent—probably the chief agent for Mazarin in the New World now that Horace Laing made the unfortunate mistake of stepping in front of one of Roaring Wolf's arrows."

"I think it's fair to say that Laroche is prominent among those employed by France on this side of the Atlantic, yes," she conceded.

"Very well," he said crisply. "The rest follows logically. He must be able to acquire and transmit a great deal of valuable information to Paris in order to satisfy Mazarin. Agreed?"

She nodded. "Of course. I met the cardinal only once, but he's obviously a hard taskmaster."

"Very well," he said. "Laroche is sufficiently active to satisfy Cardinal Mazarin. That means he probably knows what the Dutch government here is doing, and he probably keeps abreast of commercial and other activities in the town as well."

She nodded, not seeing the point he was trying to make.

"I haven't had the honor of meeting Governor Peter Stuyvesant as yet," Richard said, "but we must either call him an utter fool or a man of considerable intelligence. He's reputed to be of unusual intelligence as well as being a soldier of considerable merit. From what I hear, he rules New Netherland with a very firm hand and brooks no interference from anyone, which only emphasizes the point I am trying to make. I find it inconceivable that Laroche could function successfully for month after month as a French agent in New Amsterdam without coming to the attention of the Dutch authorities—specifically, without the knowledge of Governor Stuyvesant. There must be an understanding of some sort that enables Laroche to operate in New Amsterdam with impunity."

"Call it what you will," Eliza said, "I still think that you're assuming. But I do catch a glimpse of what you're trying to prove. What I don't understand is, how do we prove that Stuyvesant is somehow the puppet of Cardinal Mazarin? Farfetched as the idea may be."

"I wish you hadn't raised the point," Richard said ruefully. "I have no idea how we go about proving the impossible. That's one of the fascinations of spy work. If we were able to establish a definite tie between the French and the Dutch, the English colonies would have a far clearer picture of their enemies and would be far more amenable to acting in concert. I may be overly ambitious when I say our first goal is to explore the extent of a French-Dutch understanding. But I do know that if we're to be worth our salt to New Haven and to the trust your father has placed in us, we need to come up with that definite information."

"You have a real genius for complicating our existence," Eliza said with a grin. "It's just my luck to have fallen hopelessly and permanently in love with a perfectionist."

"Be glad I'm a perfectionist," he replied with a chuckle, leaning forward and kissing her on the nose. "That's why I happen to love you. As for the work that's awaiting us, it won't be easy. That's why, whether you like it or not, I reserve the right for you to resign whenever the assignment becomes too rough or too complicated for you."

Eliza smiled sweetly, but made no reply. She vowed privately, however, that nothing would persuade her to give up the task she had undertaken. She had involved herself in Richard's affairs, and Mazarin had chosen her as well as him, appreciating her potential value. If she proved valuable to France, she would be even more essential to the English colonies; she was also determined to prove her worth to her husband. It was important to Eliza to establish early in their marriage that she could be trusted as an equal.

As the daughter of a prominent New Haven military man who confided in her freely, Eliza knew that the British colonies would be seriously threatened if the French and the Dutch made a pact against them. France had land claims to the north and to the far west. The Dutch held valuable ground directly southwest of New England and claimed vast tracts of territory on both sides of Hudson's River—some of it land that New Haven Colony also claimed. The mission in which she and Richard were engaged was crucial to the future of New Haven and the other English colonies.

The young couple went on deck and watched in silent approval as the master of the brig, sailing with consummate skill, brought the craft down the East River toward the busy harbor of New Amsterdam. The sails slapped in the spring breeze as he brought the vessel about near the fortress at the southern tip of the island. After a few deft maneuvers, the vessel tied up at a dock that Adam Burrows had purchased many years earlier. The adjoining docks were the property of other English settlers in North America. Richard and Eliza went ashore, and Eliza, who was acquainted with the many shipowners and masters whose vessels came to New Haven, exchanged greetings with the captains of three ships.

"It's very strange," Richard said as he and his wife, walking arm in arm, struck out for their immediate destination, the Thorn and Thistle Inn, "but New Amsterdam seems far more like an English colony than it does the property of the Netherlands."

Eliza nodded. "Why should that be?"

"For the simple reason that the English so overwhelmingly outnumber the Dutch here. Official documents are written and printed in Dutch, but it's no accident that they must be translated into English when they're posted in order to become effective. Why, Stuyvesant himself speaks English fluently. I would estimate that two-thirds of the population of this colony is English rather than Dutch. We'll never find out precisely because the Dutch are aware that they're outnumbered, and they keep very quiet on the subject. But that doesn't alter the facts of the case."

"Are you saying that you think New Netherland will become an English colony someday?"

"I suspect that it may be inevitable," Richard replied thoughtfully. "At one point, several years ago, a war between the English and the Dutch would have been necessary to achieve that end. Now I'm more inclined to believe that it will be worked out amicably, perhaps in a sale of some kind. As the English colonists acquire more property here, naturally they're more reluctant to see their land placed in jeopardy in a war."

"It's true that the holdings of the Dutch in North America are limited, particularly when compared to those of the English and the French. But I don't see them relinquishing their grasp as a result."

"Indeed not," Richard declared. "They'll hang on for the highest price. New Netherland becomes more valuable as the rivalry between the English and the French intensifies and the stakes become much higher. Judging from the lack of effort in Holland to promote New World colonization, I suspect they're planning to relinquish this colony to either London or Paris, depending on which bids the most."

"We have far more immediately at stake here than the French," Eliza said.

"Be that as it may," Richard replied, "you and I will have our work cut out for us."

They were silent as they made their way up the cobbled streets past the neat houses of clapboard and stone that lined every thoroughfare. The majority of residents indeed may have been English, but the Dutch influence still dominated the community. The steps of each home were spotless—it was the local custom to scrub them and the pavement in front of each house daily. Street vendors sold vegetables, wild turkey, shellfish, and other foods without fanfare. This calm order was a direct result of Stuyvesant's efforts; he ruled the once rowdy town with an iron hand. In Boston and other English colonial centers, the sellers shouted the prices and the quality of their wares. Here, however, all was quiet; the merchandise spoke for itself, and buyers had to be alert for the best bargains.

Otherwise the atmosphere was almost identical to that of New Haven and other English towns. Indians, some in colorful paint, all in their native costumes, wandered the streets freely, many of them having come to sell furs, and they were accepted as a natural part of the scenery. Sailors, too, were everywhere. Ships of every size from many nations put into harbor here, and it was obvious that not even Boston or New Haven currently enjoyed a larger trade. New Amsterdam was destined to become the most important commercial seaport in North America.

Arriving at the unpretentious but comfortable Thorn and Thistle Inn, Richard immediately inquired for the proprietor and his wife, Angus and Mollie Williams MacNeill. Mollie and her son, Bart Williams, had been shipmates of Richard Dunstable and Lady Dawn Shepherd when they had first come to the New World. Mollie, hurrying toward Richard through the public rooms, was overjoyed to see the man who had befriended her and who had helped her so much. MacNeill, a canny Scotsman, was equally pleased, but both he and his wife were uncomfortable in Eliza's presence. She was aware of their reaction to her, but could not understand the reason for it.

Actually their motives were simply explained. Both had expected Richard to marry Lady Dawn Shepherd. But she had married Ezekiel Clayton instead, and Richard had unexpectedly turned up with this glamorous, breathtakingly beautiful young bride. The truth of the matter was that the MacNeills needed time to adjust to Richard's ultimate choice.

After assigning the couple to the inn's best room, Angus and Mollie insisted on having tea with them in a private dining room. There, Richard took a deep breath and told Mollie about the death of her son in battle.

"He fought on the side of the French, which sur-

26

prised me, Mollie," he said. "What didn't surprise me was that Bart fought well and with great courage. He died like a man after fighting like a man."

Mollie MacNeill was made of stern stuff. She was not too surprised to hear the news, having been aware of the possibility that Bart might be dead. She bowed her head for a long moment, and her eyes were dry when she raised it again. "I thank you kindly for tellin' me, Richard," she said. "I'm much obliged to you. Is he buried in a proper grave?"

"He is, Mollie. I saw to that," Richard answered gently.

Angus MacNeill cleared his throat. "Do you know how he happened to be fighting alongside our natural enemies, the French?" he asked.

Richard explained as best he could. "The French weren't directly involved in the battle," he said. "Their Indian allies served as substitutes for them, but they were led by several white men who obviously had been recruited and trained by the French. Bart was one of those men."

Mollie MacNeill's composure broke for the first time. "Laroche recruited him for the French! May the Lord damn his soul to eternal perdition," she cried in a shaking voice. "I'll have justice for this if it's the last thing I do with me last breath on earth."

Richard reached out a hand and placed it on her arm to steady her. "Now, now, Mollie," he said. "Don't go jumping to conclusions."

She shook her head, eyeing him fiercely. "I know what I'm talkin' about," she said, her voice cold. "Bart got friendly with that Laroche, who comes so often to our taproom and conducts his filthy business from a corner table. It's no secret to me, nor to any who dwell in New Amsterdam, that Laroche is an agent of the French."

"You're sure of that?" Eliza asked, astonished at the woman's familiarity with Laroche's vocation.

Perhaps Richard was right when he said that there was some connection between the Dutch and the French.

Mollie sounded disgusted. "Even the fools who dwell in this town know the true identity of Laroche and who his masters be," she declared. "I tell you plain, he filled me Bart's head with dreams of riches and glory, and he recruited the lad for his evil purposes and sent him to his death."

Richard wanted to console her, to explain that what had happened to Bart had been the fate of many innocent men in these trying times. He glanced at Angus MacNeill, who told him silently to leave Mollie to him. Richard was glad to be relieved of the responsibility of consoling her.

Angus turned to lighter subjects, and they chatted about inconsequentials. But Richard's mind continued to function rapidly. He was convinced that he and Eliza were on the track of something—something big. His hunch about Laroche apparently had been right. Surely if Mollie MacNeill knew he was in the employ of France and claimed that his vocation was general knowledge, the Dutch authorities were well aware of his identity. Director-General Stuyvesant, who reputedly was anything but a weak, indecisive man, could have ordered Laroche sent off to New France or to France itself on the first available sailing ship. Instead he tolerated the man's continued presence in New Amsterdam, and Richard regarded this as strange. His fears for his wife's safety temporarily forgotten as he contemplated the situation, he knew that he was looking forward to that night's meeting with Laroche with far greater interest than he had believed possible.

28

II

RICHARD spent the day visiting clients and prospective clients of Burrows and Clayton. He was not allowing himself to forget that he was a business agent for his father-in-law, and he was determined to make his mark in the shipping industry.

In the meantime, Eliza, who had not previously been acquainted with Mollie MacNeill, accompanied her on errands to the butcher, the greengrocer, the baker, and other local tradespeople. She marveled silently at the extensive preparations necessary to operate the public room at the MacNeill's inn. Mollie, perhaps because of her shyness, was far less outgoing when alone with Eliza and kept most of her thoughts to herself.

But there was no question that she meant well. That night she herself supervised the preparation and serving of supper to the young couple and took delight in the praise that Eliza lavished on her for the superb quality of the various dishes.

Not until the end of the meal did Richard indicate the reason that he and his bride had come to New Amsterdam. "We're meeting Laroche tonight, Mollie," he said.

Mollie stood ramrod straight and spoke through clenched teeth. "May his soul rot," she said. "If you decide to put a knife in him, I'll be the last to object."

"I don't think we'll become quite that violent," Richard said, but took care not to mention the precise nature of their business with the French agent.

He and Eliza left the dining room. When they made their way into the adjoining taproom, they saw that Laroche was already seated at his customary table in the far corner. Lean and saturnine, with glowing eyes that noted everything of significance, he instantly became aware of their presence. The French spymaster, dressed in black as was his custom, was of indeterminate age, falling somewhere between thirty and fifty. There was nothing remarkable about his face or his manner, and his ability to blend into the surroundings had been a studied art.

Eliza would have joined him at his table, but Richard placed a hand on her arm and held her back. That was not the way meetings with Laroche were arranged. Instead he led his bride to a vacant table a short distance from where Laroche sat, and when Mollie came to take their order, he asked for two mugs of tea, each with a dollop of rum.

Almost immediately after Mollie had served them, they were joined by Laroche, who casually drew up a chair. "You're precisely on time," he told them. "I like that—very much."

Richard smiled, but made no reply. It was preferable to hear what Laroche had to say and to keep his own opinions to himself. The spymaster quickly adjusted to the pair's lack of verbosity.

"You've been highly recommended," he said, "for a very special assignment."

Both knew instantly what he meant: Their orders had come from Mazarin himself.

"The subject," Laroche said, "requires conversa-

tion far freer than we can engage in here. Be good
enough to join me tomorrow at a house on Broad
Street. Its yard is bordered by a yellow picket fence,
and the windows have yellow shutters as well. You
won't miss it. I shall expect you precisely at noon."
Not waiting for a reply, Laroche rose and returned
to his own table. Richard and Eliza exchanged surprised glances, but did not speak until they returned
to their bedchamber for the night.

"What did you make of that?" she asked.

He shrugged. "I don't know. We'll find out soon
enough."

Nevertheless, not trusting Laroche, Richard preferred to take no unnecessary risks. Therefore, after
breakfast the next morning, he armed himself with
his pistols and throwing knives, which he concealed
under his long coat. At his instigation, Eliza hid a
small, double-bladed poniard beneath one voluminous sleeve of her gown. It was unlikely that Laroche
intended to trick them, but if he did, they were prepared.

As they suspected, they had been personally
selected by Cardinal Mazarin to perform a series of
tasks for which he considered them the perfect
agents. Nowhere did British and Dutch claims clash
more bitterly than in the areas north and east of
New Amsterdam. The Dutch had discovered the territory and had laid the first claim to it. But they had
been negligent in pursuing and developing these
holdings, and as a result, the English, who had settled just up the coast in Fairfield, Stratford, and
New Haven, had been quick to seize the initiative,
not only laying claim to the territory, but actually
developing it. As Mazarin had stated in his missive
to Laroche, he had no agents better suited than the
daughter and son-in-law of Adam Burrows, the
English colonies' most prominent shipowner, who
also commanded the New Haven militia.

The gathering of information, Mazarin had decreed, was to be supervised by Peter Stuyvesant himself, since he would be required to counter any moves that the English settlers who encroached on Dutch land might make.

Consequently, when Richard and Eliza appeared promptly at noon at the house on Broad Street, they were surprised to be greeted by Director-General Stuyvesant as well as by Laroche.

Stuyvesant's presence was explained away to the young couple as strictly coincidental. He was an old friend, Laroche said, who had dropped in to pay a social visit just a few moments before the Dunstables arrived.

Richard and Eliza accepted the story with a grain of salt. The tie between the director-general of New Netherland and the French spymaster seemed to point more firmly than ever to the probability that the two Continental powers were working together for their mutual benefit and to the detriment of the English colonies. The evidence, to be sure, was circumstantial, but Richard felt they were making good progress.

Sipping a glass of wine, Peter Stuyvesant enjoyed himself thoroughly and loudly. Gesticulating broadly, he regaled the young couple with stories of his exploits in Curaçao and in his native Holland. It was not accidental that he was the hero of every tale he told, in all of which he either outwitted or outfought his many enemies.

But he did far more than talk about himself. He asked shrewd, penetrating questions, listened with great concentration to the answers, and quietly made his own judgments of both Richard and Eliza.

It became evident to Richard that whatever Laroche's motive had been in inviting them to this house, nothing of real consequence would be accomplished at this meeting. He had a difficult time concealing the resentment he felt toward Director-General Stuyvesant, who flirted baldly with Eliza, treating her as though she were an unmarried woman.

It annoyed him, too, to discover that Eliza responded to the preening, posturing governor. She listened to him attentively, laughed far more than was necessary at his little jokes, and seemed to be enjoying his attention. Consequently, Richard was relieved when he was able to call a halt to the session after a reasonable period of time, claiming that he and Eliza had another engagement elsewhere.

As the Dunstables took their leave, Laroche said quietly, "You shall hear from me before the day ends."

Richard contained his anger until he and Eliza were alone. "You needn't have encouraged Governor Stuyvesant, you know," he said as they made their way up Broad Street. "He went rather far in his flirtation with you."

Eliza laughed smugly. "He's an interesting man," she said, "and he's extraordinarily colorful. I admit that I didn't discourage him, but surely you know I was playing a part. You must realize how important it is to form a friendship with him."

"I realize," Richard replied tartly, "that he was devouring you the entire time that we were sitting there. I assure you that he'd like nothing better in this world than to bed you."

Her grip tightened on her husband's arm. "Why, Richard!" she said, her voice rising with wonder. "I actually believe you're jealous!"

He started to protest that he was not, but quickly changed his mind and admitted the truth. "All right," he said, "I was jealous. It bothered me to see you being so open to the old fool."

"Peter Stuyvesant is neither old nor is he a fool," Eliza replied. "I admit freely that I was flattered by his obvious interest in me. However, any woman would have reacted as I did." She inched closer to him. "But I hope you realize one thing, Richard Dunstable, and I trust you'll never forget it. I love you, and you alone. I save my favors for you and for you alone. I belong to you completely and without reservation."

He immediately felt sorry for his outburst. "Forgive me," he muttered. "My problem, I guess, is that we've been married such a short time. I'm not yet accustomed to seeing every man who meets you being drawn to you. I suppose in time I'll get used to it. Please be patient with me."

Her smile assured him of her patience, and they continued on to the Thorn and Thistle in perfect amity.

In the meantime, at the house they had just left, Peter Stuyvesant's wooden leg beat a tattoo on the pine floor of the parlor as he stamped up and down. "When you next write to Cardinal Mazarin, Laroche," he said, "extend to him my felicitations. I have no idea how he succeeded in recruiting a couple as perfect for our purposes as the Dunstables, but I marvel at his talents."

Laroche nodded, but said nothing. He would write what he saw fit to Mazarin regarding Stuyvesant's initial meeting with the Dunstables. Laroche was well aware that Stuyvesant was hedging on his deal with Mazarin. The Dutchman was reluctant to close the port entirely to English shipping, insisting instead that with the lure of greater profits —and now with the help of the Dunstable woman —he could induce English captains to defect to the flag of the Dutch West Indies Company.

"The man seems earnest, and I daresay he's both brave and competent," Stuyvesant continued. "He's not like most Cavaliers I've encountered."

"Dunstable is a courageous and clever man, in my

opinion," Laroche replied. Perhaps too clever for his own good, the French spymaster thought to himself.

"And the young lady," Stuyvesant said, "is extraordinary. You neglected to mention that she's such a striking beauty."

Laroche shrugged. "It didn't occur to me, Your Excellency."

"In my time," Peter Stuyvesant said, "I have known many attractive women. I've yet to encounter one as lovely as Eliza Dunstable." He was lost in thought for a moment, his pale eyes clouded; suddenly he smiled and moistened his thick lips. "I shall enjoy having her assigned to work for me," he said. "I must say I appreciate Mazarin's inadvertent kindness. First having Lady Celeste, and now Mistress Dunstable. Of course, there are some obstacles in the way of the type of relationship that I prefer."

"The obstacles are rather serious, I believe," Laroche said, his voice ironic. "For one thing, I don't believe that Sir Richard Dunstable will look with any great favor on Your Excellency's plans."

Stuyvesant chuckled. "You underestimate me, Laroche," he said, "and I'm surprised. I would think that after four years you'd know me well enough to realize that I always get what I want."

"Perhaps you're right," the French agent added quietly. "Anyway, I don't think Lady Celeste will stand in your way."

For a second Peter Stuyvesant looked uneasy. Then he smiled broadly. "Getting rid of her will be no problem," he declared. "I'm sure that she's as bored with me as I am with her, and she's undoubtedly looking forward to greener fields in which to carry out the good cardinal's directives. As for Sir Richard Dunstable, I don't regard him as an insurmountable obstacle, either. He will soon be returning to New Haven Colony. Thereafter, I'll keep him busy—very busy—traveling to the other English colonies to acquire information. Naturally, I intend to keep his delectable wife close at hand in New Amsterdam. I firmly believe that he who creates his own opportunities best reaps the benefits that those opportunities offer. I trust that I make myself clear to you, Laroche." Stuyvesant chuckled silently, his broad shoulders heaving.

Never one to waste time, Peter Stuyvesant told Lady Celeste all about his meeting with the Dunstables, and broached the subject of relocating her headquarters. He found her more cooperative than he had expected. She said she would gladly consider moving to another colony, but that she was curious why he was suddenly so eager to get rid of her. Stuyvesant merely smiled innocently, then excused himself, claiming a pressing business appointment.

Knowing Stuyvesant far better than he himself realized, Lady Celeste went off to the Thorn and Thistle for her dinner. When she saw the couple that she quickly identified as Richard and Eliza Dunstable, the governor's motives were very clear to her. He intended to replace her with Eliza not only as an agent, but also as his mistress.

Lady Celeste was willing to grant that Stuyvesant was a hard-driving soldier who administered the affairs of the Dutch colony with efficiency and dispatch. As a lover, however, she found him inconsiderate and unimaginative, and she had been bored with him for some time. Undoubtedly he planned to separate the Dunstables in order to give himself a freer hand with the blond Eliza. So far so good—that would fit right in with her own plans.

Lady Celeste scrutinized Richard with care, and she liked what she saw. He was tall and handsome and gave off an aura of clean masculine strength. She had no doubt of her own ability to entice him once he was no longer encumbered by his wife's proximity. Furthermore, she might be able to kill another bird with the same stone. She had found out in a subsequent meeting with Laroche that Lady Dawn Shepherd had probably come to America on board the same ship as Sir Richard Dunstable, so there was a good chance that he knew what had become of her after she had disappeared from Horace Laing's Virginia estate. Certainly the matter was worth exploring. So she returned from the inn to the director-general's house, and there she spoke bluntly to Peter Stuyvesant.

"So you've found another mistress, have you?" she asked with a broad smile.

He tried to protest.

She held up a hand. "Please, Peter, let's not dissemble. We know each other far too well for that. If I have guessed your motives, I, at least, continue to respect you enough that I won't mention them, much less question them, and I ask the same consideration from you. I can operate far better for our mutual friend from a community other than New Amsterdam, so I believe I shall take myself elsewhere. That makes my house here available, but I have little doubt that you'll find another tenant for it." She smiled innocently.

Stuyvesant realized that she had guessed his plans, and thinking swiftly, he decided not to dispute the matter with her. "You're free to do what you please," he told her. "You've always worked directly with Mazarin, and have been in my employ at your own pleasure, so you don't need my approval to go. Naturally, I'll be grateful if you'll keep me informed of any developments that you think I should be aware of. Where are you thinking of going?"

"To New Haven," she replied promptly.

He raised a bushy eyebrow. "Aha! Anything done

in that colony interests me, as you well know. You can perform a function of great benefit to Holland as well as to France."

Lady Celeste regarded him coolly. "As you know, I don't dispense favors lightly. I would expect to be paid—handsomely paid—for any information of value that I might pass on to you."

Stuyvesant hid his annoyance. She had long had the privilege of being his mistress, and he certainly had expected her to be more cooperative and less selfish. Nevertheless, he was in no position to argue with her. "Very well," he replied curtly, bringing the interview to an abrupt close. "Rest assured that you shall be recompensed fully for any and all information you can relay to me."

Richard and Eliza were surprised late that same afternoon at receiving a message at the Thorn and Thistle summoning them without delay to the official residence of the director-general of New Netherland. Uncertain of what to expect, they went at once to the modest two-story home of white clapboard that stood near the fortress at the bottom tip of Manhattan Island. Peter Stuyvesant demonstrably had a high opinion of himself, but he certainly put on no airs in his living style. His dwelling was no more imposing than the homes of a number of prominent Dutch and English merchants, and certainly it was much smaller than the home of Eliza's father in New Haven. The Dutch flag and the personal ensign of the director-general flew from twin flagpoles planted in the front yard. A Dutch soldier in a drab, dark gray uniform and a cumbersome cuirass stood sentry duty at the front gate outside a shelter to which he retreated in inclement weather.

A sour-faced Dutch serving woman of middle years admitted the couple past four pikemen standing guard in the front hall of the house. Peter Stuyvesant greeted his guests cordially in a small parlor, where a cheerful fire was burning in the grate. Neither Richard nor Eliza was surprised to find that Laroche also was a guest. The French spymaster held a large glass of wine in his hand and obviously felt at home here.

Stuyvesant came to the point at once. "Master Laroche and I have an understanding," he said, pacing the room. "It is based on the fact that the interests of Holland and the interests of France often coincide. Indeed, all of us here in the New World owe a great deal to the nations of our origin. I'm sure you feel the same way toward England, Sir Richard." The observation was anything but accurate, but Richard, who had been deprived of his baronetcy by the Roundheads and, as a member of the New World's citizenry, had dropped his title anyway, merely nodded. It was none of Stuyvesant's business that he felt little loyalty to England, but had developed instead a fierce and abiding sense of patriotic duty to New Haven Colony.

"We sometimes exchange favors," Laroche added. "For example, when France has no pressing duties for those of us who are in her employ here, I loan our better agents to Governor Stuyvesant."

The explanation was as lame as it was absurd. Richard knew enough of the ways of the Old World to know that the agents of one nation weren't "loaned" to another country. His guess that France and the Netherlands were working together under the terms of a secret alliance seemed to be confirmed, but he indicated nothing of what he was thinking as he nodded, seemingly accepting the outrageous statements that his host and the French spymaster were making.

"I have work—important work for both of you," Stuyvesant said forcefully. "Master Laroche has kindly consented to release you from your obligations to him and has given me assurances that you'll gladly work for me instead."

Richard decided to make the task no easier for either Stuyvesant or Laroche. "Actually," he said, "we're in the employ of Cardinal Mazarin, and we take our orders from him."

Laroche seemed somewhat flustered. "Naturally," he said, "I shall keep the cardinal fully informed of your activities."

Richard felt increasingly certain that he and Eliza were onto something significant. They had been summoned to New Amsterdam ostensibly on Mazarin's direct order, but now Laroche wanted them to believe that the cardinal knew nothing of their activities as they were being handed over to the principal administrator of the Dutch colony. Richard did not for a moment believe that to be the case. Cardinal Mazarin, he felt certain, already knew that he and Eliza were being requested to transfer their allegiance, temporarily, to the Dutch, and he had no doubt that the move was being made with the full approval of France's first minister.

"You've not only risen high in the councils of New Haven Colony, Sir Richard," Peter Stuyvesant said, "but you've traveled extensively in the other New England colonies. I shall be grateful to you if you will visit key communities, as your time permits, and keep me informed of anything that may be of interest to me in my capacity as director-general here for the Dutch."

Richard was moved to protest. "Certainly you don't expect me to do or say anything, Your Excellency, that would be harmful to England. I am loyal to her, if not to Cromwell, and I have worked for Cardinal Mazarin with the hope and intention that he would be able to restore young Charles to the throne. I would not intentionally hurt England or the cause of her colonies."

Stuyvesant feigned horror. "I would be the last in the world to ask you to commit an act of treason," he declared fervently. "I seek only a better understanding and a closer rapport with the English colonies. Anything that will lead to that result is all to the good. I hope and expect that you'll keep that in mind as you work for me, and at no time would I expect you to betray the interests of any English colony."

Richard had to admire the man. Stuyvesant gave the impression of being a bumbling bull, but he was actually very clever, very adroit.

The governor turned to Eliza and bowed a trifle stiffly. "As for you, Lady Dunstable," he said, "I have work in mind for you that only you in all the world can perform. Your father is a renowned shipowner, and there's no one in New England or in the Caribbean who is his equal. I assume, since you've always been close to your father, that you must be acquainted with most English shipowners and the captains of individual vessels."

Eliza was somewhat surprised, but felt compelled to speak the truth. "I wouldn't say that I've ever done business with any of these gentlemen, but I'm certainly well acquainted with them," she said.

Peter Stuyvesant smiled persuasively. "That's exactly what I've hoped. I offer you a special position, madam, as an ambassadress who will cultivate good relations between the British and this Dutch colony, particularly British shipowners and sea captains who visit New Amsterdam. I offer you a house, a servant, and your living expenses, as well as wages to be mutually determined." He neglected to add that the house had been vacated only an hour earlier by Lady Celeste.

The offer was so unexpected that Eliza was overwhelmed. "I—I don't quite know what to say," she replied.

Richard clenched his fists. Certainly she had the wits to understand that Stuyvesant would not be making her such a generous offer if all she had to do was cultivate the goodwill of English shipowners and ship captains. It was far more likely that she would be expected to persuade them to give up their loyalties to England and to sail thereafter under the Dutch flag. The Dutch, as Richard well knew, had been conducting a campaign in Europe to convince English shipping interests that it was to their advantage to join forces with Holland. The offer to Eliza appeared to be no more and no less than a continuation of this policy.

"I repeat," Peter Stuyvesant said solemnly, "that of all people in the entire New World, only you are capable of bringing about this closer relationship between the shipping interests of our great mother nations."

Eliza appeared impressed. She nodded.

Stuyvesant struck hard and fast. "Shall we consider that we've reached an agreement?" he asked.

Richard's own duty was plain. "Speaking for myself," he said, "I'm amenable to the ideas that you advance, Your Excellency, and I'm willing to enter your employ." His father-in-law would approve, he knew, and he stood a far better chance of proving—from the inside—that a tie existed that bound France and Holland together. He disapproved heartily of Eliza's participation in the venture, as he knew her father would, and was on the verge of saying as much when she interrupted.

"I'm flattered by the chance to serve the causes of both our countries, Your Excellency," she said. "My father has always believed that the more commerce there is between nations, the more peaceful their relations will be. It will be good for him to know that I'm making a positive contribution to the cause of peace between the English and the Dutch here in the New World."

She had undercut Richard, making it impossible for him to reject the offer of a position on her behalf.

Stuyvesant insisted that they cement their new "partnership" with glasses of brandy. Then he escorted them across an open area to a smaller dwelling. "Here is your new house, Lady Dunstable," he said. "Use it as if it were your own property."

Richard became moody as he followed his wife from room to room through the house that had just been vacated by Lady Celeste. When they were alone, he shook his head and said morosely, "You went too far. I tried to signal you, but you paid no attention."

"I saw your signals," Eliza replied firmly, "but I chose to ignore them. I know all the arguments you're going to present, and all your reasons for insisting that I reject the offer of Governor Stuyvesant and return to New Haven. But I won't do it. We're in this together, Richie. Both of us were recruited by Cardinal Mazarin, and I'm convinced— as I'm sure you are—that Mazarin is behind this new move. I also take Stuyvesant's remarks about the good I'll be doing for England with a grain of salt. I know very well that his real object is to maneuver me into a position where I would have to betray England for Holland. And I know that every shipowner or ship master I persuade to enter the service of Holland would be a loss not only to England but to the colonies as well. I have no intention of cutting off my father's nose or injuring his shipping business." Richard stared at her, scarcely able to control his temper.

"Then would you mind explaining to me," he demanded, "why in heaven's name you insist on going through with this farce and entering Governor Stuyvesant's employ?"

"It's a very simple matter, really," Eliza said. "We're searching for something very big and very important. If we can establish a definite tie between France and Holland, even the Roundheads who now control Parliament will be forced to listen to us. Oliver Cromwell will be forced to listen. They've been so busy rounding up Cavalier sympathizers and the Stuarts that they've neglected foreign affairs. That neglect is reflected in their indifference to England's New World colonies. The future of the colonies is at stake, as I'm sure you will agree."

"Of course it is," he said, "but I don't—"

"You'll have chances, I'm sure, to establish the relationship between France and Holland," she said, giving him no chance to speak. "But if I'm here in New Amsterdam, ostensibly in the employ of the director-general, think how many more opportunities I'll have to ferret out the truth."

"You'll have ample opportunities to get into very hot water," Richard said flatly. "You're an exceptionally attractive woman, Eliza, and if you're living here by yourself—in this house that's only a stone's throw from Peter Stuyvesant's house—you're virtually asking the governor to make advances to you."

Eliza was hurt. "Honestly, Richard," she said, "I thought you knew me better than that."

"I'm not worried about you," he said. "What concerns me is the target you'll present to men who are less scrupulous and less honest than I am."

Eliza hated to admit that in spite of her great beauty, her experience with men was limited. She had been closely protected by her father and subsequently had been sheltered by Ezekiel Clayton, whom she had admired, but had not loved. She knew in theory that many men were lacking in scruples, but she had been spared unpleasant experiences.

Richard had to admit that her argument was sound. She, far more than he, would be in a position to expose the alliance of France and Holland that struck at the heart of English interests in the New World and the security of the English colonies. On the other hand, he could not in good conscience leave his wife unattended. "I'll agree to your staying on in New Amsterdam," he said, "on one condition. You must allow me to send Roaring Wolf down here from New Haven immediately and let him keep watch over you. If you get into trouble of any sort, you can let him know, and he'll be on hand to protect you."

Eliza was relieved and readily accepted her husband's offer, but she did not explain her reasons for her complete acquiescence. Actually, Roaring Wolf's presence would be of great value to her for reasons that she knew better than to outline to Richard.

Her feminine instinct told her that Peter Stuyvesant was interested in her as a woman and that she could pick up information that would expose the Dutch alliance with France only if she drew closer to him. Therefore, she knew she would be playing a hazardous cat-and-mouse game that Richard would certainly disapprove of. She would be compelled to lead Stuyvesant on, allowing him to believe—or at least to hope—that she would become intimate with him. She knew that she could play this game for a limited period of time only, and that ultimately he would expect her to yield to him. If that time came before she gained the information she sought, it might be necessary to call on Roaring Wolf for assistance. The brave was both resourceful and courageous, and if she should be backed into a corner by Stuyvesant, the Pequot would be useful in extricating her from her predicament. She dared not mention any of this to Richard, however, for fear that his jealousy would flare up again and that he would refuse to allow her to remain alone in New Amsterdam.

Eliza knew that she had the opportunity to be involved only because she was Richard's wife and Adam Burrows's daughter. All the more reason, then, to prove her worth and demonstrate her competence. She was determined to live up to the expectations of her father and her husband, and she intended not to allow their male prejudices to stand in the way of her success.

Richard did not stop to wonder why Eliza unconditionally accepted his suggestion that Roaring Wolf come to New Amsterdam to keep watch over her. It was enough for him that she agreed; therefore, he consented to let her remain in the town. He had lived in dread of what might develop ever since they had first been recruited by Cardinal Mazarin. Now, as nearly as he could judge, Eliza was being given a simple task to perform, and it would be possible for Roaring Wolf to offer protection even though Richard himself would be elsewhere.

So their lives entered new phases, with results that would have shocked both of them if they'd had the foresight to envision what would happen.

Eliza found several dark hairpins in a tray on her dressing room table, and this evidence, combined with the strong scent of perfume in the clothes cupboards, told her that her predecessor in the house had been a woman, probably a brunette. But neither Governor Stuyvesant nor Laroche made any mention of the woman, and she felt it was best not to make inquiries.

She fell into a routine very quickly. Although she had a servant to attend to her needs, every morning Eliza chose to walk the short distance to the shops, where she stopped at the greengrocer, the butcher, the fishmonger, and the baker. There she bought enough food to last her for a few meals, and she was amply supplied with funds for the purpose by Stuyvesant. Richard had promised to send the better part of her wardrobe after her on the next Burrows and Clayton ship to New Amsterdam. In the meantime, Peter Stuyvesant urged her to have some new dresses made, saying that he would give her whatever funds she needed for the purpose. She hesitated and finally rejected the offer because it would have felt wrong to have accepted money for clothes from a strange man.

Apparently the mere fact that Eliza lived in the house adjacent to that of the director-general identified her to any number of the residents of New Amsterdam. She noticed the butcher and his assistant exchange swift, knowing glances when they found out where she was living, and their reaction was typical of what she encountered from many tradespeople. Her curiosity was aroused; she wondered what these people thought of her, but she was content to bide her time until she had the opportunity to become better acquainted with them. She was settling in for a long siege, she reminded herself, and needed to act accordingly.

A scant forty-eight hours after she moved into the little house, Governor Stuyvesant called on her, accompanied by Laroche.

"We'll get right to work," Stuyvesant said. "I'll see to it that you're kept informed of all ship arrivals. In that way, you can be sure that you're aware of the identity of the individual vessels and their masters."

"I'll supply you with the information myself, Mistress Dunstable," Laroche told her.

Her duties did not seem particularly formidable, Eliza thought.

"I want to stress to you," Stuyvesant said, "that I know of nothing more important than the mission you've just been given. Cromwell will soon be making a strong bid to control the seas in this part of the world. English ships are already flooding every port on the Atlantic and may be found conducting business on virtually every island in the Caribbean Sea. The Dutch have been trying to keep up a steady trade, but our resources are no match for those of the English. To put it bluntly, it's important that the English ship masters be urged to switch their allegiance to the Dutch West Indies Company and similar organizations based in Amsterdam."

Well, so much for the ambassadress-of-good-relations story, Eliza thought. Stuyvesant certainly didn't waste time. She quickly pondered the problem, but had already decided that her conscience would not permit her to try too hard to woo the allegiance of shipowners away from companies like her father's. "Most ship captains," she said, "are practical men—hardheaded realists. What inducements can I offer them to join forces with the Dutch?"

Stuyvesant thought she was joking, and laughed loudly.

But Laroche realized that she was serious. "I urge you," he said, "to study your reflection in a pier glass, Mistress Dunstable, and to make a list of your many assets. I find it impossible to believe that many men would reject them, particularly those who have been at sea for extended periods of time and have lacked the companionship of ladies."

His bluntness startled Eliza. So she was expected to offer herself in payment to the shipowners and sea captains! She could tell by the attitudes of both Stuyvesant and Laroche that this was the behavior that they expected of her, and she gleaned, too, that Stuyvesant, at least, thought she was sufficiently worldly to handle such relationships in her stride.

Richard would be furious if he knew what her duties comprised. Eliza herself was stunned, and she knew that under no circumstances—not even for the sake of obtaining information vital to the existence of the English colonies—would she become a trollop. The very idea was unthinkable.

If she expressed her thoughts freely, if she revealed what she really thought of her assignment, she would be dismissed at once and packed off to New Haven without delay. Or knowing too much, she might "mysteriously disappear" by Stuyvesant's orders. Her pride would not permit her to suffer such a humiliating, open defeat—and she surely did not want to be murdered. So she said nothing and confined her reaction to a slow, taut smile.

She didn't realize that her expression was enigmatic, and that consequently Peter Stuyvesant would jump to his own conclusions. He leaned forward in his chair and, with a large beefy hand, stroked her arm. "I knew we could count on you, my dear," he said heartily. "I sensed it the instant I set eyes on you."

He could not have been more mistaken in his impression of her character. Eliza continued to smile steadily at the Dutch governor, and did not withdraw her hand, instead allowing him to paw it and to form his own conclusions.

The weeks that stretched ahead promised to be the most complex, hazardous period she had ever known.

When Richard returned to New Haven, he immediately sought Roaring Wolf, who was at work in the Burrows and Clayton shipyard. Taking the Pequot to his office, Richard explained the circumstances that had forced him to leave his bride behind in New Amsterdam. "I will appreciate it," he said, "if my brother, Roaring Wolf, will go to the town of the Dutch and seek the company of my wife, Eliza. She will give you shelter and food. In return you will protect her from all who are evil, especially those who would make love to her or harm her in other ways."

The squat, compactly built Roaring Wolf, who looked and acted far younger than would be expected of a brave of forty summers, nodded soberly. "Roaring Wolf will do as Richard, my brother, has directed," he said. "Roaring Wolf will protect the life of Eliza with his life. Roaring Wolf shall tell Richard all that he sees and hears."

The Indian departed for New Amsterdam at once, and Richard, breathing more easily, arranged to dine with his father-in-law. The husky gray-haired Colonel Adam Burrows sat in the Dunstables' small dining room and sipped his glass of sack as he listened to Richard's account of what had happened in the Dutch city.

"I tried my best to persuade Eliza to come home with me and to give up any thought of acting as a double agent," Richard said. "But she wouldn't listen. You know how she can dig in her heels when she sets her mind to it."

"Indeed I do," her father replied with a weary smile. "But this is one time when I'm forced to confess that I'm glad she's being stubborn. We stand to gain a great deal, especially if she finds solid evidence that links the Dutch and the French."

Richard reluctantly agreed with him and then went on to explain that he had sent Roaring Wolf to watch over Eliza.

Colonel Burrows grinned. "That's good to know," he said. "I sometimes wonder if I was wrong to bring her up as I did. She doesn't know the meaning of fear, and that can be very dangerous."

"I've decided," Richard said, "to let her play this

game one move at a time. If Eliza appears to be in any real jeopardy, I'll bring her home regardless of how angry it makes her or how much it sets back our cause. I'm her husband first and foremost; then I'm a patriot."

Adam raised his goblet to his son-in-law. "With you looking after Eliza, I have no need to worry. I know that. Now, then—what are your own plans?"

"Governor Stuyvesant," Richard replied, "has asked me to make a survey of the other colonies of New England and to report their moods and activities to him. I figure I can kill two birds with one stone in most towns because they lie along the seacoast, and I can promote Burrows and Clayton business there. So I don't too much mind going through the motions for Stuyvesant."

Adam Burrows nodded slightly, his eyes gleaming. "I find that I approve more and more of our scheme to have you play the role of a double agent," he said. "Not only might you be picking up information of great value to us that we could obtain in no other way, but you'll also be in a position to feed our rivals and potential enemies with false tales that we want them to believe." He chuckled aloud and winked at Richard. "I won't be in the least surprised if every New England colony is in a superb state of preparedness for any trouble that might arise."

Richard kept his father-in-law's words in mind when he set out on his journey in a small Burrows and Clayton vessel headed for Boston. No matter what state the British colonies were in, he would report to Stuyvesant that they were thriving and well able to defend themselves.

Actually, as he made his way east along the shores of the Great Bay and subsequently north along the Atlantic coast, he found colony after colony doing exceptionally well. Trade was increasing rapidly in Pequot, a town some of the newer colonists were now calling New London. Providence Plantations was growing so rapidly that it had doubled its original population many times. And Boston was becoming a major city. Of all the towns in the New World, Boston was most under the influence of the Puritans who had dethroned and beheaded Charles I. But even in Boston, Richard was pleased to note, the influences of the New World were at work. The proximity of the limitless wilderness, the availability of free land for homesteads, the judging of each man by his deeds rather than by his family pedigree—all these were responsible for the creation of a new breed of men and women in America. Although British subjects, these people were far different from the Old World inhabitants Richard had known. And, just as they had changed, so he himself had changed, for together they loved liberty above all else on earth; their sense of justice was sharper, and no matter what the individual's station in life, he was willing to fight for the beliefs he held precious.

Encouraged by the similar attitudes he encountered everywhere, Richard began to realize that these people were the true inheritors of the British traditions, and liberty was safe in their keeping. Let France and Holland and other powers of the European continent combine their efforts to subvert, overthrow, and destroy the English colonies; they would fail. The colonies were imbued with a spirit that would enable them to survive. Of that much he felt certain.

Leaving the seacoast in Boston, Richard struck out through the forests of Massachusetts Bay Colony for the interior, and after several days of traveling alone in the thick, silent woods he loved, he came at last to the little farming community of Taunton, on a river that emptied into Narragansett

Bay. There he headed for the house of sharp-tongued "Aunt" Hester Browne, a widow who owned a thriving farm in partnership with a young couple. Richard was greeted happily by a towheaded young man at work behind a plow in the broad fields. Dempster Chaney and his equally attractive wife, Robbin, were Cavalier refugees whom Richard had befriended and brought with him to the New World, and they still regarded him as their mentor. Dempster promptly led his workhorses back toward his barn. "A visit from you is the only excuse I'd accept to stop working, Richard," he declared. "I'm doing no more work today!"

"If I'd known that I was going to have that effect on you," Richard said with a laugh, "I'd have delayed my arrival until evening."

"Well, I'm awful glad that you're here now," Dempster told him. "I need to bring you up to date on what's been happening."

A short time later, after greeting Robbin and Aunt Hester, Richard sat with Dempster and the two women in the spacious kitchen in the farmhouse. There, over mugs of herb tea, which Robbin served with some freshly baked fruit bread, Dempster brought the visitor up to date.

"I'm a captain in the Massachusetts Bay militia now," Dempster said modestly. "Matter of fact, I'm commanding a company of infantry."

Richard was proud of the way his protégé was establishing deep, firm roots in the soil of the New World. "I'm delighted to hear it," he said.

"You wouldn't have been so happy if you had been in Robbin's shoes and mine," Aunt Hester informed him. "He was suddenly called away to active duty, and we were left with all the chores to do hereabouts ourselves."

She spoke with such earnest ferocity that Richard couldn't help laughing.

"My company was sent to the frontier settlements about eighty miles west," Dempster said. "Agawam and Springfield. The Indians of the district were kicking up their heels."

Richard was interested but not surprised. "That isn't the first time I've heard of Indian troubles there," he said. "The Pocomtuc are the principal tribe out yonder, aren't they?"

Dempster nodded. "We got there in time to prevent serious problems," he said. "Their warriors had made several raids, but they lost their appetite for attacking defenseless people when we met them with our full strength."

"Did you suffer any casualties?" Richard asked.

"None to speak of," the young militia officer replied. "A couple of the lads were wounded by arrows, but they'll soon mend. But only a few Indians were using bows and arrows. The others had muskets."

"Muskets?" Richard asked, his mind racing.

"We're still trying to figure out the reason for the uprising. As I see it, the braves were feeling giddy because they'd been supplied with new firearms."

Richard was thunderstruck. "And?" he encouraged Dempster to continue.

"We took identical muskets from every warrior we killed. Here, let me show you." He rose from the table, walked to a shelf, and produced a cumbersome musket with a heavy steel barrel and a short, flared wooden butt.

Richard picked up the musket and examined it with care.

"If you're looking for a clue as to where it was made, don't waste your time," Dempster told him. "I've searched every inch of every weapon, and there's no indication as to where they're from."

Richard made no reply, but continued to examine the musket. It looked suspiciously like a Dutch weapon he had seen produced near The Hague, but he was not prepared to swear to it. He had familiarized himself with most of the firearms made in Europe during the years of his service as the hereditary king's forester in England. His father-in-law was even more of an expert, particularly where Dutch weapons were concerned, and Richard wanted to show him a captured musket before making a serious accusation. If the Dutch truly were supplying New England Indian tribes with weapons, the situation was far graver than he had assumed.

"Can you spare this weapon, Dempster?" he asked.

The young militia officer nodded. "Sure, I've got plenty of them," he said. "As you'll see for yourself when you look at them, they're all alike."

"I want to take this musket back to New Haven with me," Richard said. "In due time I can return it to you. Meanwhile I want to examine it. If it originated where I think it did, we're in for real trouble." He refrained from explaining.

Dempster knew better than to question him, realizing anew that Richard was engaged in enterprises that it was best to know nothing about.

Richard decided he would have to cut his tour short. He had all the harmless information he needed about the various English settlements—information he could willingly pass along to Peter Stuyvesant. And now he also had evidence of a different kind—information that could prove to be of grave consequence for all the English colonies.

The European powers were engaged in a grim struggle for supremacy in the New World, and there were few rules of fair play in their fight. But there was one unspoken rule for survival that was obeyed by every nation trying to develop colonies in America. The English and French, the Spanish and Dutch, the Swedes and Portuguese all understood and scrupulously obeyed a strict injunction: Under no circumstances were firearms to be supplied to the Indians by any European power. No matter how great the enmity between nations, this rule was universally observed and its precepts upheld vigorously by governments and individuals alike.

If the Indians of the Massachusetts Bay western frontier indeed had been supplied with Dutch muskets, this could mean only that Peter Stuyvesant, for whatever his reasons, had violated the agreement. In that event, Stuyvesant had to offer some valid explanation for conduct that placed him beyond the pale of civilized men.

Richard wasted no time. Returning by ship and arriving in New Haven late the next day, he went directly to his father-in-law's office and placed the captured musket on his desk. "Tell me the origin of this piece," he said, challenging the older man.

Adam was always meticulous and precise. He picked up the musket and examined it at length before he spoke. "You've probably noted," he said, "that the name of the maker, which was burned onto the stock, has been eliminated. Apparently it was whittled away with a knife."

"I noticed," Richard said.

The colonel continued to turn the musket over in his hands. "I'm not prepared to swear to this," he said, "but I strongly suspect that this weapon is of Dutch make."

"Exactly what I thought," Richard declared. "It looks to me like the muskets made by van Geyran near The Hague."

Adam nodded slowly. "We're thinking along the same lines," he said, and sat very still.

Richard repeated the information he had gleaned from Dempster Chaney to the effect that similar muskets had been found beside the bodies of a number of warriors killed when the militiamen had halted the Indian raids on the frontier settlements of the Massachusetts Bay Colony.

"We'll borrow this musket indefinitely," the colonel said. "I want to make very certain we're correct before we make any accusations. But I must say this is very unsettling and frightening news. It well could be that our neighbor to the west, instead of being a harmless Dutchman interested in commerce for mutual profit, is a dangerous lunatic who will set the entire continent of North America on fire by giving arms to the native warriors."

Richard was forced to agree with his father-in-law's assessment, and his blood ran cold when he thought that Peter Stuyvesant might indeed be guilty of inciting Indians to murder English settlers. Eliza was near the governor and supposedly under his protection. She might be in grave danger indeed.

In New Amsterdam, Eliza Dunstable was learning little by little that her new position was complicating her existence and causing problems where there originally had been none. She began her new duties by agreeing to dine with Captain Hiram Pritchett, a shipowner who served as his own master. She had long been acquainted with him because he invariably put into New Haven on his return from voyages to the Caribbean. He had been delighted to find her in New Amsterdam, and when he invited her to dine with him, she had promptly proved agreeable.

Thus it happened that Eliza, wearing a provocatively low-cut gown that enhanced her dazzling beauty, sat at a table in the dining room of the Thorn and Thistle Inn, and to the astonishment and disgust of Mollie MacNeill, she flirted boldly with the bronzed clean-cut Captain Pritchett. It was impossible for her to explain to Mollie that she meant nothing personal by her attitude, and that if she could persuade the shipowner to transfer his commercial allegiance to Holland, the price would be small and the return great because she would succeed in winning the confidence of Peter Stuyvesant.

It was simple enough, she discovered, to use every trick in her repertoire. Her eyes never left Hiram Pritchett's jolly face as he spoke, and she seemed completely fascinated by everything he said. From time to time, she leaned across the table toward him, allowing her long blond hair to fall across his hands. Occasionally, when responding to him, she reached out and touched his arm, seemingly without being aware of the gesture. She gave the appearance of being totally absorbed by the seafaring man.

Her beauty was so great that Pritchett could not help responding to her, and the prospect of making a conquest of this most delectable of young women dazed him.

Eliza saw to it that they were plentifully supplied with wine, and she matched Pritchett drink for drink. She laughed quietly at his jokes, pretending to enjoy his lively sense of humor. Most of all, she appeared to wrap them in an air of intimacy from which all others were excluded. A stranger glancing at them for the first time would have sworn that here was a couple very much in love.

As the meal drew to a close, Eliza guided the conversation into channels convenient to her purpose, and finally she said boldly, "I don't understand why you don't take advantage of your independence and join the Dutch West Indies Company. They'll finance your cargoes, you know, and you'll increase your profits by at least fifty percent."

"That much?" Hiram Pritchett was not forgetting that she was the daughter of Adam Burrows and, consequently, could be highly knowledgeable in such matters.

"I've seen the results of such associations with my own eyes," Eliza declared, "and if I were a man who owned my own ship, I'd lose no time making a contract with the Dutch."

Pritchett grinned, his dark eyes shining. "I'm much obliged to you for the advice," he said. "I'll do something about it first thing tomorrow morning."

"I'm sure you won't regret it," Eliza told him, secretly pleased because she could now solidify her position with Stuyvesant and Laroche. "The Dutch West Indies Company offices are located not far from your dock."

"Never fear," he said emphatically, "I'll be there first thing in the morning."

They had sat down at the table in broad daylight, but had lingered so long that they finished their meal by candlelight. Not until they left the Thorn and Thistle, closely watched by a frowning Mollie, who shook her head, did Eliza give thought to her own immediate predicament. She held firmly to Hiram Pritchett's arm as he walked her to her own little house, and she was vaguely conscious of Roaring Wolf hovering behind them in the shadows. The brave's proximity, however, did her no immediate good in her present situation. She had flirted so consistently with Pritchett that she had succeeded in turning his head, and she knew that he was looking forward to making love to her once they reached the house. Somehow she had to find a way to cool his ardor. Under no circumstances would she contemplate being unfaithful to Richard, and the mere thought of becoming intimate with Pritchett—or any other man—actually made her feel queasy.

They reached Eliza's house before any clear plan to evade Hiram Pritchett had formed in her mind, and suddenly it was too late. He stood silently, expectantly poised, while she searched for her key.

She found it at last and unlocked the door. Pritchett acted suddenly and decisively, taking her in his arms and kissing her at length.

Eliza knew that she would reveal her feelings completely if she withdrew too soon, so she pressed close to him and, keeping her eyes tightly closed, pretended that she was being kissed by Richard. Only in this way was the intimacy possible.

Then, quickly, she moved away from him, breaking off all physical contact. Pritchett stared at her for a moment in stunned disbelief, and then smiled at her coyness and instinctively reached for her again.

Eliza avoided his grasp. "We've got to be careful," she whispered. "I have neighbors and my reputation to consider." She was well aware that Roaring Wolf was lurking in the shadows nearby.

It was as obvious to Captain Pritchett as it was to the woman herself that no neighbors were aware of what was taking place. Doors remained closed, the street was as deserted as it had been when they arrived, and as far as he could tell, no one was peering at them from behind closed curtains.

"That's easily remedied," he said with a broad smile. "I suggest we go inside and simply close the door behind us."

Eliza almost panicked. The situation was rapidly moving beyond her control—if she were alone with this man in the house, it would be impossible to fend off his advances.

"No!" she cried, unconsciously raising her voice to a shout.

Pritchett blinked at her, unable to comprehend the vehemence of her negative response.

Eliza realized that she had gone too far in her rejection of him and that she had to make amends. At the very least, she had to find some way to make her refusal sound logical. Her mind worked furiously. "It would be so cold-blooded," she said, "to become intimate that way. There would be no spontaneity and no warmth; without them, what we would do together would prove intolerable."

At best her explanation made only partial sense to Hiram Pritchett. He didn't pretend to understand what she had in mind, but she was obviously so sincere, so earnest in her protestation that he had to believe that she meant what she said. Beautiful women were sometimes silly and nervous, he knew. He could insist on taking her into the house, of course, but he knew that if he did, the mood that had enveloped them would be spoiled. She was so pretty and so charming that he felt compelled to give in to her nonsense even though it frustrated him. "Very well," he said reluctantly, "I'll abide by your wishes."

A sense of infinite relief flooded Eliza, and her smile was radiant. Her sense of cunning returned, and she knew that she had to dangle a promise in front of the sea captain, even if she had no intention of keeping her word. It was unfortunate that she was forced to lead him on in this way, but she had no real choice. She lifted her face to his and took the initiative in another long, lingering kiss.

"You won't regret this," she murmured as they parted, and before he could reply, she closed the door swiftly, leaving him on the stoop outside. Only then did she feel safe, and she bolted the door and leaned against it weakly. Slowly she raised a trembling hand to her mouth and wiped her lips as though trying to erase the memory of his kiss.

Pritchett stood for a few moments, unable to decide what to do next. Finally he straightened his cap and stalked off down the street, making his way back to his inn. He had no idea when he would see the lovely creature again, but he was determined to have her.

A puzzled Roaring Wolf remained in the shadows. The ways of white people were beyond his understanding. He had seen Eliza submit to the stranger's initial embrace and, subsequently, take the initiative in kissing him again. It seemed to the warrior that Eliza, as Richard's wife, had behaved dishonorably. He was upset and angry on his friend's behalf and wondered whether he should go to New Haven at once to tell Richard what had happened.

Inside the house, Eliza gradually regained her strength and calm. She had succeeded, she knew, in enticing the sea captain to the side of the Dutch West Indies Company. She had convinced him that the prospect of associating with the Dutch was sufficiently attractive, and he would almost certainly go ahead with the bargain. She had succeeded in her original plan, but the cost had been almost greater than she had been willing to bear.

Now she knew she would be obliged to avoid Hiram Pritchett at all costs. As good-natured as he was, he still would expect her to engage in an affair with him when he next saw her, and in all justice, he had every right to his expectations. She knew she was cheapening herself by playing such a game, but she had no choice. When she had accepted the offer of employment from Peter Stuyvesant out of her innocence, she hadn't realized what the position entailed. Now that she knew, she had to avoid paying the price at all costs. At the same time, however, she was determined to continue in Stuyvesant's employ until such time as she obtained proof positive that he was working in concert with Cardinal Mazarin to destroy the English colonies.

III

THE arrival of Lady Celeste Murette in New Haven created an immediate stir. Her glamorous appearance, combined with her apparent wealth, attracted the attention of the entire community when she rented a house and hired a cook and a serving maid. She had hardly been settled two weeks when she sent formal invitations to all citizens of substance to attend a partly at her house, and curiosity impelled a large number of citizens to appear.

Lady Celeste greeted Richard Dunstable demurely, and after the other guests had arrived, she contrived to spend most of her time in his company. She flirted with him subtly, with the result that he saw her as a young woman of great charm. At no time did he even remotely suspect that she was in the employ of France.

Lady Celeste enjoyed an unexpected bonus from her reception. Among her guests were the Ezekiel Claytons, and she felt a surge of elation when the beautiful red-haired Mimi Clayton arrived on her husband's arm. Celeste recognized her instantly as Lady Dawn Shepherd.

So she had found the elusive young woman Cardinal Mazarin was so anxious to locate! Apparently Laroche had known what he was talking about when he suggested she start her search in New Haven. By finding Lady Dawn she had fulfilled her own obligation, and she knew her value would rise accordingly with Mazarin. It did not occur to her— not that it would matter if it had—that when she reported that Lady Dawn was now living in New Haven as Mimi Clayton, she would be placing the young woman's life in serious jeopardy.

Her first reaction was to send the news to Mazarin in a message that she would dispatch via Laroche in New Amsterdam. But she hesitated to write to him openly. The delivery of mail between New Haven and New Amsterdam was uncertain at best, and letters often disappeared. Under no circumstances did Lady Celeste want to reveal her own connection with Cardinal Mazarin. So, reluctantly, she decided to wait until she next visited New Amsterdam. Then she would write out her report and give it in person to Laroche to be forwarded to the cardinal. Her experience as an agent had taught her always to reduce risks to an absolute minimum.

As for Mimi, she had accepted an introduction from Lady Celeste calmly, giving no indication that they had been distantly acquainted at the court of the executed Stuart monarch. She kept her opinions to herself throughout the reception, and not until she and Ezekiel returned home with Richard, whom they had invited to dine with them, did she unburden herself.

"I hope you won't take it amiss if I speak candidly with you, Richard," she said, "but with Eliza in New Amsterdam, you need someone to take care of you. I think you'd be wise to watch your step with Lady Celeste Murette."

Richard was surprised, as was Ezekiel Clayton.

They exchanged quick glances, and Ezekiel paused in his carving of the roast long enough to shrug. It was unlike his wife to express her disapproval so openly.

"She finds you attractive," Mimi said, "and she intends to add your scalp to her collection."

Richard laughed uncomfortably. "I think you're going a bit far," he said. "I made a point of telling her that I'm a married man, and that my wife, whom I miss very much, is only temporarily out of town."

Mimi sighed. "I know Celeste," she said, "and I'm warning you. She can be unscrupulous."

"Where did you know her?" her husband asked.

"She was part of what was called the outer circle at the Whitehall court of the late King Charles," she said. "I don't pretend that I knew her well; I wasn't at the court that often. I recognize her when I see her; that's about all. I doubt if we ever conversed privately, either at Whitehall or at any of the king's summer palaces."

"Then you don't really know her," Ezekiel said pointedly.

Richard nodded in agreement.

"There are many people at court with questionable reputations," Mimi said firmly, "and none was worse than that of Lady Celeste Murette. She was said to have the morals of an alley cat. It was common knowledge that she would go to bed with any man, provided he helped to raise her social standing."

Again the two young men looked at each other.

"Do you actually know of any affairs in which she engaged?" Richard asked quietly.

Mimi was annoyed. "If I searched my mind, I daresay I would be able to recall any number of them," she said. "What are you trying to say?"

"Only this," Richard replied. "I know that many reputations at court were unjustified."

"You ought to know that without being told," Ezekiel added. "You yourself suffered ostracism because it was rumored at Whitehall that you were the mistress of King Charles, when in fact he was no more than a close friend of your late father. So you should realize how groundless these stories can be."

"I'm well aware of the flimsy nature of gossip," Mimi replied. "But in the case of Celeste Murette, I feel certain the talk was justified."

"I don't know how you can say that," her husband declared tartly. "I'd think that you, of all people, would be tolerant and forbearing."

"I've no desire to get into an argument about Celeste Murette, of all people," she replied. "I like Richard and Eliza, and I feel very close to both of them. I spoke out because I wanted him to avoid complications in his life. That was my only motive."

"I appreciate your candor," Richard said, deciding that the best way to smooth ruffled feathers was to agree with her. "I'll exercise great caution in my dealings with the lady."

"Good," Mimi said with a sniff. "Then I didn't waste my breath."

Richard wanted to tell her that they were no longer in England, but in the New World, where an individual was accepted for what he or she was, rather than for what had once been. The American way was to wipe the slate clean and give each individual a chance to start anew. As far as he was concerned, Lady Celeste Murette certainly deserved such a chance. In deference to Mimi's sensitivity, he would drop the subject, but he had already made up his mind that he would not allow her to prejudice him against Lady Celeste.

* * *

The peace of New England was destroyed, suddenly and inexplicably, when community after community was struck by Indian raiders. The plague was nearly universal, and each town, village, and hamlet had its share of misery.

New Haven alone was spared. The Indian nation that lived closest to the colony, the Mohegan, had made a pact the previous year, and they were true to their word and kept the peace.

As far as Colonel Burrows could determine from the sketchy reports he pieced together, the attacks were not closely coordinated. But one ominous rumor persisted and grew each time a ship from another colony docked in New Haven harbor—a rumor that the Indians were being supplied with muskets.

Puzzling over this strange development, the colonel discussed the problem one night when he and Richard were dining together. "If this is Stuyvesant's work, it's got me baffled. What could he possibly gain by it? I have to admit I don't understand it," Adam said, shaking his head.

"It is strange," Richard replied. "Providence Plantations has always been at peace with its Indian neighbors, and the towns on Cape Cod haven't been molested in many years." Richard was lost in thought for a few moments and then cleared his throat. "If you wish, sir, I'll gladly volunteer to make another tour of our colonies in order to see if I can confirm what we both fear—that it is indeed Stuyvesant's work."

"You just came home a short time ago," his father-in-law replied. "I don't want to take advantage of your good nature."

Richard refrained from mentioning that, with Eliza away from home, he had no real incentive to stay in New Haven. In fact, he preferred traveling because it kept him busy and he had less time to brood about missing his wife. "I appreciate your concern, but I don't mind. I'll leave in the next day or so," he said, "as soon as I can clean the papers off my desk at the shipyard."

Thirty-six hours later Richard returned to the wilderness trail. He had some idea of what to expect, but he tried to keep an open mind as he questioned the local militia commanders about recent disturbances. Yet everywhere he heard the same story: The Indian warriors who had attacked the communities had not used their customary bows and arrows, but had been armed with muskets, which they had fired with far greater abandon than skill. In almost every instance, the raiders had been repelled after doing little or no damage.

At Hartford, in Connecticut, a militia captain showed Richard a musket abandoned by the Indian attackers. At Providence Plantations, he was shown a similar weapon, and at New London, he saw yet another musket taken from the body of a warrior who had been slain.

All three weapons were identical, and all closely resembled the rifle that Richard had brought back to New Haven from Taunton in Massachusetts Bay. In every case, the name of the manufacturer had been removed from the stock of the musket. With great reluctance, he reached an inescapable conclusion: The Indians, regardless of tribe or locale, were being supplied with firearms by the Dutch.

Richard knew he could not yet prove his conclusion, any more than he had been able to prove beyond doubt that the musket captured by Dempster Chaney's men near Springfield had been supplied to the braves there by the Dutch.

Nevertheless, he knew far more than he had before setting out on his journey, and he had enough to satisfy himself and his father-in-law, and maybe even other leaders of the English colonies. And he hoped that somehow Eliza would be able to provide more solid evidence.

When he reached New Haven he went directly to Adam Burrows's office and was surprised to find that neither the colonel nor his partner, Tom Clayton, was there. Instead, Ezekiel, Tom's son, hurried down the corridor to greet his friend.

"I hate to welcome you with bad news, Richard," Ezekiel said, "but I know only one way to do this, and that's to speak the truth straight out. I'm afraid that Mimi was right, and you and I were wrong—dead wrong—about Lady Celeste Murette. Now she has her hooks out for Colonel Burrows, and I'm sorry to say he's fallen for her. My father and mother have tried talking to him, and so have Mimi and I, but he won't be swayed. Maybe he'll listen to you."

Richard absorbed the surprising information in silence. "Where is he right now?"

"I reckon he's where he is every day at this hour," Ezekiel replied. "He's at Lady Celeste's house eating dinner. He seems to have all his meals there."

Richard remained unperturbed. "Then I guess my news will have to await his return to the office," he said.

Ezekiel looked at him sharply. "You don't seem in the least upset."

"I see no reason why I should be," Richard replied flatly. "Adam Burrows is old enough to know what he wants and to keep himself out of trouble. He's been a widower for a good many years, and with Eliza married to me, he lost his companion. If he's interested in an attractive, charming lady, more power to him, I say. I hope he wins her hand, if that's what he wants."

"You don't understand," Ezekiel replied. "Even

my father is convinced that Lady Celeste has ulterior motives in this romance."

"What could they be?" Richard demanded.

Ezekiel Clayton shrugged. "I'm damned if I know, but if you could see her working on him, ladling out charm and flattery, you'd know she isn't sincere."

Richard shrugged, convinced that Ezekiel had been influenced by his wife's strong antipathy to her fellow English noblewoman. Certainly he himself was not concerned, and he knew that Eliza would not be upset when she heard the news, either. It was far more important that he report his own findings to Colonel Burrows. The future of the New England colonies depended upon whether Adam Burrows decided to wage war or reach a peaceful accommodation with the Dutch.

When Adam Burrows returned to his office, he listened in attentive silence to his son-in-law's report, and then he shook his head. "I assume you're quite sure of your facts, Richard," he said at last.

"I'm very sure, sir," Richard replied. "I realize that peace between England and Holland is at stake at the very least, and I make no loose accusations."

"But you can't prove that the captured muskets are being supplied by the Dutch."

"No, sir," Richard replied. "But isn't it enough that you and I know it?"

"It's enough to convince me that the situation we face is very grave," Colonel Burrows replied, "but I don't think our word would persuade the Roundhead Parliament in England to take a firm stand against the Dutch, do you? They stand rather close to the Dutch on religious grounds, and they're going to need hard evidence to cause them to take any real action."

Richard shrugged. "The kind of proof that you want, sir, is yet to be obtained."

"Let's think about the problem for a while," Adam Burrows said, "and perhaps we'll come up with a sound solution. Or it may be that Eliza will provide us with the evidence we seek. In any event, this is an exceptionally serious situation, and we can't afford to move until we've considered every aspect of the problem. So, as I say, let's ponder it for a spell." He patted Richard on the shoulder, and that ended the subject for the time being.

That evening Richard was invited to his father-in-law's home for supper. When he arrived there, he found Tom and Mary Clayton on hand, as well as Ezekiel and his wife, Mimi. The gray-haired, distinguished-looking Tom Clayton, Adam Burrows's partner, appeared to be in a foul mood. The reason quickly became apparent when one more guest arrived. He glowered when Lady Celeste Murette came into the room, making no secret of his distaste for her.

Lady Celeste proved herself equal to the occasion, and Richard had to admire her. She was in uncommonly high spirits and seemed to be enjoying herself thoroughly, undeterred by the attitude of Tom Clayton and the better-disguised hostility of Mimi. In fact, although neither Richard nor his father-in-law realized it, Lady Celeste was giving one of her best performances. She flirted first with one, then with the other, and was so subtle in her approach that neither realized her intent. Only Mimi saw and recognized precisely what she was doing, but she was powerless to halt the other woman, and she knew that neither Adam nor Richard would listen if she subsequently warned them.

During dinner Adam spoke so freely about the movements of his merchant fleet that Richard was surprised by his candor. The movements of the vessels that sailed under the Burrows and Clayton flag were closely guarded secrets, never publicly revealed. The purpose behind this secrecy, as Richard understood it, was to prevent attacks on the vessels by pirates who preyed on English colonial shipping.

Apparently Adam did not believe he had anything to fear from Lady Celeste, for he spoke with complete freedom in her presence. Richard, looking at her, had to admit that she did not seem to be the least interested in the movements of the vessels, but she nevertheless gave the appearance of listening intently, as though fascinated by the speaker more so than the topic.

What Richard failed to suspect was that Lady Celeste was indeed interested in the movements of the Burrows and Clayton fleet. She kept a running memorandum of these moves at home, knowing how valuable this information would be to the Dutch and French, who were the principal competitors of the English colonies for the trade of New England and the islands of the Caribbean.

Before the meal ended, Adam surprised his son-in-law by revealing to the guests what Richard had uncovered on his recent travels through the New England colonies. "Here's a pretty kettle of fish," Adam said. "If we accuse the Dutch of providing firearms to the Indians, Governor Stuyvesant could be so outraged that he'd declare war on us. On the other hand, if Richard's surmises are accurate, as I assume they are, we're duty-bound to make war on Stuyvesant."

Tom Clayton's face grew red. Still upset because his partner had revealed so much information on ship movements, he was aghast that anyone should speak so loosely in front of a newcomer to New Haven Colony.

But Richard noted that Lady Celeste showed only

polite interest as she listened to the colonel and that her attitude seemed much like that of Mary Clayton. He could see no cause for alarm over the colonel's indiscretion.

"I'm telling you what Richard found because I want your advice," Adam said. "What would you do if you wore my boots and commanded the New Haven militia? Tom, I'll be obliged if you'll speak first."

Tom Clayton composed himself with some effort, glanced uneasily at Lady Celeste, then straightened his shoulders. "In a matter of this importance," he huffed, "I think I'd arrange a meeting with Governor Stuyvesant of New Netherland and I'd speak to him with all frankness about what Richard found. Whether we go to war against the Dutch or not would depend on Stuyvesant's reaction to what you tell him." He was not willing to elaborate further in the presence of Lady Celeste.

"Those are precisely my sentiments," Ezekiel said. "I'm in favor of showing our cards."

Adam looked at his partner's wife. "What about you, Mary?" he asked. "What would you do?"

Mary Clayton's shrug was self-deprecatory. "I'm the wrong person to ask," she said. "I've never concerned myself with matters of state."

"Neither have I," Mimi said, "but in a matter this serious, I'm afraid I'd be obliged to speak up. I'd tell Governor Stuyvesant what we think, then I'd leave it up to him to admit or deny the charge."

"What about you?" Adam demanded of his son-in-law.

"I'm not certain," Richard replied. "I can see the value of candor, yet I can also see the equally great value of silence."

"It strikes me," Lady Celeste said, "that in this instance silence is all-important. Assume for a moment, if you will, that Governor Stuyvesant is guilty, as you seem to suspect him of being. If you go to him with your suspicions, you'll put him on his guard. Presumably, he isn't arming the Indians unless he's also taking steps to protect himself and his colony in the event that trouble develops with the English. I see no reason to put him on guard."

Adam was deeply impressed by her perception. "Hear! Hear!" he said, reaching out and patting her hand. "You show great wisdom in matters of statecraft, my dear. You surprise me."

Richard was equally surprised and impressed by the insight Lady Celeste demonstrated. He couldn't refrain from saying, "I'm glad that no decision is required tonight. I wouldn't know what to do."

Lady Celeste smiled blandly and presented a calm facade. It was becoming increasingly important with each passing day that she find some reason to journey to New Amsterdam. The information that she was accumulating for Peter Stuyvesant would be of vital interest to him, and she could not delay much longer in calling to his attention what he needed to know so badly.

After supper, when the modest little party drew to a close, Adam Burrows asked his son-in-law if he would escort Lady Celeste to her home. Her rented house was only a short distance from his own dwelling, and he affably agreed. The Claytons, senior and junior, lived in the opposite direction, so Richard and Lady Celeste started out alone.

The night was clear. The elm trees of New Haven were laden with full heavy buds ready to unfold at last after a long winter. There was the sweet scent of pine in the cool air, enhanced by the pleasant sea breeze that blew in from the harbor. Lady Celeste took leisurely steps which prolonged the walk, but Richard was in no hurry to go off to his own lonely house.

Perhaps the woman sensed his willingness to

tarry. In any event, when they reached her house, she said, "The evening is still young. Won't you come in and join me for a glass of brandy?"

Richard thanked her and accepted with alacrity. He built up a fire in the parlor hearth for her, and then they seated themselves on mounds of cushions piled on the floor in front of the fireplace.

Lady Celeste raised her glass in a silent toast. He made a similar gesture and was surprised by the mellow potency of the brandy. "This is good brandy," he said.

She nodded approvingly.

"Unless I'm very much mistaken," he declared, "this comes from France. The French product is infinitely superior to any other."

"Yes," she replied blithely. "I was fortunate enough to be able to bring several bottles with me when I migrated to the New World."

"What led you to come to New Haven?" he asked curiously.

"I made as thorough a study as I could of the towns in New England," she replied glibly. "Boston is by far the largest, of course, but I don't care for the attitudes of the Roundheads who are in charge of the government there." She shrugged, seemingly unmindful of the fact that her dress slipped off one smoothly rounded, white shoulder.

Richard had to tear his gaze from her nude shoulder and look again at her face.

"Providence Plantations seemed interesting, but again, the people there appear to be too fanatically independent and serious. I'm not. I'm convinced that we all live but once, and I'm determined to enjoy every moment of my stay on earth to the best of my ability."

She was so frank that Richard laughed aloud.

Picking up the decanter, Lady Celeste splashed more brandy into their glasses. "I don't envy you your long journey through the colonies," she said, leaning on one elbow so her gown artfully slipped a bit lower yet. "The hardships of travel in the New World appall me."

"Wilderness living is a matter of taste," Richard said. "I enjoy it very much."

"Does your wife like it too?" she asked.

He shook his head and grinned. "She claims she likes it well enough," he said, "but whenever I've suggested an extended outing in the wilderness, I've noticed that she finds an excuse to avoid it."

"I don't blame her," Lady Celeste replied. "I prefer comforts like this." She slid a trifle lower on her cushions, exposing still more of her shoulder and a portion of one well-developed breast.

Richard stirred uneasily. The scene was becoming too intimate for him. He had been alone for too long, and had to fight his sudden craving for this attractive and desirable young woman.

Lady Celeste was expert in gauging his reactions. One moment she looked up at him, her gaze as provocative as the way she held her body. Then suddenly she became demure, reaching for her dress, repositioning the shoulder fabric, and sitting upright.

Richard was nonplussed and did not quite know how to react.

She saved him the trouble. She was in her element, and knowing that she was in complete command of the situation, she acted accordingly. "Do you mind if I speak to you very frankly?" she asked softly.

"Of course not," he muttered, and surreptitiously wiped the moist palms of his hands on the sides of his breeches.

"I don't know your wife," she said, "so I don't intend this as a criticism of her. All I know is that if I were married to a man as devastatingly attractive to women as you are, I wouldn't go off to New Amsterdam—or anywhere else—and leave him alone for weeks at a time. I'd be afraid I might lose him to someone unscrupulous."

"Eliza knows me well enough," he replied, "to realize that I'll be waiting for her when she comes home."

"Are you so confident of your self-control?" she demanded.

He nodded, even though he felt a trifle foolish.

Lady Celeste half-slid, half-inched closer to him. "You find me attractive, don't you?" she oozed.

It was senseless to pretend. "Indeed I do," he replied. "Any man would."

"And you want me." She made a flat statement rather than a question.

Richard wanted to deny the charge, but with her eyes fastened on his, he could not lie. The truth of the matter was that he wanted this exceptionally attractive brunette so badly he was nearly in pain, and he could not hide his feelings for her.

Before he could move or speak, Lady Celeste reached up, curled a hand around his head, and kissed him lightly, but soundly, full on the mouth. Then she withdrew swiftly, even as he instinctively reached for her.

She laughed softly.

In confusion, Richard felt for his glass, then drained it.

She replenished his glass before she spoke. "I think I've just proved to you," she said, "that you're not quite as invulnerable as you'd like to believe. Or perhaps as your wife would like to believe, either. I just thought I'd give you a little food for thought."

She had proved her point, conveying finality in her tone. But he still wanted her.

She retreated beyond his reach, then drew herself gracefully to her feet. "The hour is growing late," she said. "Perhaps you'd be wise to go."

He realized that her advice was sound. He had to withdraw now before his yearning for her overwhelmed him and caused untold complications. He scrambled to his feet.

"By all means, finish your brandy," Lady Celeste said with a light laugh. "I don't mean to drive you out all that rapidly."

He raised his glass and again drained the contents in a single gulp.

She remained beyond his reach as she escorted him to the door, and stayed at arm's length from him as she bade him good night.

As he made his way home, Richard repeatedly inhaled the cool, damp air of the sea, and gradually his thoughts became more orderly. What shocked him most about his encounter with Lady Celeste had been his willingness—even his eagerness—to commit adultery. She, not he, had drawn back and had called a halt. Had she proved willing, he undoubtedly would have become intimate with her.

He knew he loved Eliza, and was ashamed of himself for the weakness he had displayed. Similarly, he had been disloyal to his father-in-law, who, as he well knew, had developed a keen interest in the young woman. But Richard, although attractive and married, was limited in his experience with women of Celeste's ilk. He had grown up in the country and had been betrothed to a young and modest country girl. Never had he been at the mercy of a practiced seductress who orchestrated every encounter.

In fact, he completely failed to recognize the role that Lady Celeste had played in the incident. It did not cross his mind that she had been deliberately seductive, that she had led him on with the experienced skill of a woman who had long used her body to gain whatever stature, wealth, and power she had in the world. He was blaming only himself, and he did not know that this was what Lady Celeste had wanted. She knew precisely what she was doing, and he was reacting exactly as she wished.

Cardinal Mazarin leafed through the brief messages he had received from Governor Stuyvesant of New Netherland. Little more than notes, these communications were terse and factual, exactly what he would have expected from someone of Stuyvesant's character.

Then, warming his feet before a blazing wood fire, the first minister of France took his time as he absorbed the much longer and more detailed reports that Laroche and Lady Celeste Murette had sent. From them, he gleaned all he needed to know about the situation in New Amsterdam, and he disliked the conclusions that he inevitably drew. It was obvious to him, painfully obvious, that France and the Netherlands were losing their undeclared war with England in the Dutch colony of New Netherland, and that the efforts of his agents were not impeding the steady progress made by the British settlers in New Amsterdam. Their numbers were multiplying rapidly under the policy of the Dutch government to admit settlers of any nationality. That policy could not now be reversed without gravely offending Oliver Cromwell and the British Parliament, who were glad to clear England's soil of Royalist sympathizers, and the Dutch did not want to risk a war with their neighbor across the English Channel.

Just as the English population was expanding, that of the Dutch settlers was at a standstill. There was virtually no immigration from Holland to the New World these days, and the Dutch families who had carved huge estates for themselves in New Netherland were content to earn their profits and live quietly. The British settlers controlled the shipping industry and hence the trading power of New Amsterdam. They were building small workshops for the manufacture of merchandise hard to obtain from Europe. They were even showing a lively interest in politics and had almost gained a majority of seats on the colonial council that acted as an advisory committee to the governor.

There was nothing Laroche could do to reverse this situation. He was no politician. And certainly the developments were beyond the control of Lady Celeste. Only Peter Stuyvesant could bring about the reemergence of the primacy of the Dutch settlers. This he could do with relative ease because his acts could be ascribed to patriotic motives.

Mazarin had dealt gently with the director-general of New Netherland, treating him as an equal rather than a subordinate. But now the time had come when he would require Peter Stuyvesant to pay his just debts. Stuyvesant well knew that he owed his very position as director-general to the cardinal's intervention on his behalf. He had become wealthy in the New World because Mazarin had seen to it that French merchantmen that put into port had paid their tariffs directly to the director-general. Sighing gently, Mazarin sipped wine from a crystal goblet sparkling in the firelight; then he picked up a quill and dipped it into a bottle of ink. There was no sound in the room but the hissing and crackling of the logs on the fire and the scratching of his pen on the paper.

A curious half-smile appeared on Mazarin's lips, and his eyes looked remote, almost dreamy. The recipient of the letter he was writing would never forget the communication, for Mazarin had a rare knack for dealing in words, and he did not hesitate to speak his mind freely. By the time he finished the letter and attached his seal to it, he knew he had done all that he could possibly do.

The rest was up to Peter Stuyvesant.

Director-General Stuyvesant was pleased with Eliza Dunstable when he learned that Captain Hiram Pritchett had voluntarily placed his ship under the flag of the Dutch West Indies Company. The director-general neither knew nor cared about the complications that Eliza suffered as a result.

For three days and nights she virtually went into hiding, unable to leave her house. Pritchett called on her a number of times—always when her maid was gone—and stood for long periods knocking patiently on the door while she remained inside, carefully concealing herself in the hope that he would think she was not at home.

She had won a victory that boosted her standing enormously with the Dutch, it was true, but the cost to her pride and conscience was great. She had cheated Captain Pritchett and well knew it, leading him to believe that she would become intimate with him and then avoiding him like the plague. She had chosen the lesser evil—hiding instead of relenting —but she felt no happier because of it.

Stuyvesant's high spirits were dampened somewhat when he received the stern communication from Cardinal Mazarin. As usual, the letter was delivered by Laroche, who sat opposite Stuyvesant while the director-general read and absorbed the contents. Then Stuyvesant handed the paper to the French spymaster, who shredded it and cast the pieces into the fire. This was a required procedure, Laroche had told him, and it guaranteed that no communications from the first minister of France would fall into the wrong hands.

Stuyvesant smarted under Mazarin's criticism.

He could hardly be held responsible for the increase of British immigration into New Amsterdam and for the drop in Dutch immigration. Nevertheless, he was being ordered by Mazarin to equalize the odds, so he moved quickly, decisively, and ruthlessly.

At times such as this, he missed Lady Celeste Murette, whom he had used as a sounding board for his various acts and plots. With her no longer in the colony, he was deprived of her brilliant, scheming mind, and he had not yet become sufficiently intimate with Eliza Dunstable to speak freely with her. Therefore, he called in his secretary, an earnest fellow named van Dooren, and glowered at the young man.

"I want to write an official proclamation," Stuyvesant said.

Van Dooren excused himself and returned in a few moments with a quill, ink, and paper.

The initial paragraph of the proclamation was startling: By order of the director-general of New Netherland, all non-Dutch residents were required to relinquish their firearms to the government of the colony without delay.

"This is unprecedented, Your Excellency," van Dooren sputtered. "I don't think it's going to be well received."

Stuyvesant was annoyed. "Why not?" he demanded.

The young man took a deep breath. "Because you'll be depriving the people of the colony of their primary means of defending themselves. Most of them are independent-minded Englishmen, and if I know them, they'll simply tell you to go to the devil."

Stuyvesant chuckled. "You have a fair understanding of the English colonists, van Dooren," he said, "but I think I know them a bit better. I'm not yet finished with the proclamation."

He went on to dictate a second paragraph, in which he offered to pay eight guilders for each pistol and twelve for each musket the colonists turned in. What made the offer truly astonishing was that a pistol could be purchased for two or three guilders, and a musket cost no more than four guilders; therefore, he was offering several times their worth in the open market. And of course he would halt the sale of firearms in the colony so the weapons could not be easily replaced.

Leaning back in his chair, Stuyvesant grinned confidently. "The greed of the English will overcome their fears for their safety," he said. "I don't necessarily believe that we'll collect every last weapon in the colony, but I assure you most of them will turn up at our warehouse."

Van Dooren shook his head in wonder. The scheme was, as he knew, virtually foolproof and guaranteed that the English colonists would lose their weapons.

The proclamation was posted that same day. Within a week, the number of weapons turned in exceeded all expectations. Even Laroche was impressed.

Having effectively rendered the English colonists incapable of rebelling, Stuyvesant was now free to move against them as he wished. He immediately took steps to make their lives as unpleasant as possible.

First he browbeat the town surveyors—inoffensive Dutchmen who had lived in peace with their neighbors for years—and persuaded them to condemn a number of English-owned properties, including homes and businesses. This meant that the proprietors would be obliged to move elsewhere, as the condemned buildings would be torn down by Dutch troops.

It did not seem to occur to anyone in New Amsterdam that only English residents were harmed by the unfair condemnation proceedings. Those who were affected by the edict were unhappy, but there was nothing they could do to have this injustice rectified. Governor Stuyvesant simply ignored their appeals.

His next act was more subtle—he doubled the tax to be paid by the owners of all public establishments selling wine, ale, and hard liquor. Of the many taverns in New Amsterdam, only two or three were owned by Dutchmen; the vast majority of proprietors were English, and therefore they would be the principal sufferers. In effect, all but the most popular establishments would be forced to close their doors because of the new tax.

Finally, Stuyvesant, no longer able to procrastinate in his deal with Mazarin, levied a prohibitive tax on all non-Dutch ships that came to the colony. The French, the Swedes, and other foreigners were affected by this tax, but the British—especially the colonials—again were hardest hit. Stuyvesant, however, figured that if he played his cards right, the Dutch West Indies Company would be the beneficiary.

The angry seafaring men were both vocal and fearless. The captain's mates and crews of nine British-owned ships that were docked in the slips on the East River marched to the governor's house to urge him to repeal the unfair tax, which was unprecedented in the New World.

Stuyvesant appeared on the steps and listened to the impassioned speeches of three members of the group. Then he shrugged and spread out his hands.

"I sympathize with you, gentlemen, but there's nothing I can do," Stuyvesant said. "I'm under orders from my own government, and I'm required to do as I am bidden."

The protesters were bitterly angry and disappointed as they retreated to the waterfront.

It would be many months, if ever, Peter Stuyvesant knew, before they learned the truth—that he, rather than Holland's legislature, was responsible for the discriminatory tax. By that time, he hoped, many of the British and colonial-owned ships would be flying the flag of the Dutch West Indies Company, and equally important, Englishmen who had contemplated settling in New Amsterdam would have changed their minds about moving to a colony so inhospitable to them.

Stuyvesant could show almost unlimited patience in affairs of state, but in his personal life, he was far less placid. It annoyed him when he realized that the very attractive Eliza Dunstable seemed to be avoiding him. She rarely called on him—and only at midday—and then she stated her business and rapidly departed. He had been led to believe, or at least to hope, that they would develop a far more gratifying relationship, and he finally determined to do something about it.

When Eliza received a short note inviting her to dine at the governor's house the following evening, she knew that there was no way she could avoid the summons. She realized, too, that the evening would present many difficulties. She felt uncomfortable whenever Stuyvestant eyed her, and she was convinced that he intended to force himself on her.

The following evening, when Eliza walked the short distance from her house to the governor's dwelling, she was dismayed, but not surprised, to discover that she was his only guest. She knew that her mettle and her courage would soon be tested.

Stuyvestant was in a boisterous, jovial mood and chatted volubly as he poured quantities of aromatic

Dutch gin into a mug, and he downed the liquor with relish.

Eliza had refused to drink, but he had insisted on pouring a large quantity of sack for her, and she thought it expedient to go through the motions of sipping it as she struggled to keep up her end of the conversation.

"I wonder," the governor said, "whether you've noticed anything out of the ordinary in New Amsterdam in the past couple of weeks?"

Eliza could think of nothing. "Should I have been aware of something unusual?" she asked.

He chuckled. "The English residents, I am told, never tire of cursing me. I understand they've invented a great many unflattering names for me."

"I pay no attention to gossip," she replied diplomatically. It was true, to be sure, that she had become aware of unrest among the English-speaking citizenry, and she had heard that Angus and Mollie MacNeill were very bitter about the increase they had to pay on spirits served in the Thorn and Thistle taproom.

"My one aim," Peter Stuyvesant declared, "is to serve my own country well. If I do that, I'm satisfied."

"A laudable ambition, Your Excellency," Eliza replied cautiously.

He stared hard at her. "You, of course," he said, "are working in the service of France, for which I can't blame you. The Roundheads who control England are a despicable and pathetic lot."

She nodded in seeming agreement.

"What I don't think you quite understand," he said, "is that you can best serve France by serving the interests of Holland."

Eliza contrived to look innocent. "That's interesting," she murmured. "I didn't know there was a tie that binds Holland and France together."

He sidestepped neatly. "Whether there's a tie or not is totally irrelevant to you at this time," he declared. "What is important is that the interests of France and the interests of the Netherlands in the New World are identical. By aiding one, you aid the other."

"I see," she said, as unconvincingly as possible, and wondered how she could get him to elaborate on the relationship between the two Continental powers.

She succeeded in appearing bewildered, and Peter Stuyvesant assumed that she was thickheaded. "I suggest," he said, reaching out and stroking the woman's hand, "that you put yourself entirely under my protection."

She had to fight hard to prevent herself from snatching her hand away. "Your protection, Your Excellency?" She managed to look wide-eyed.

Peter Stuyvesant hitched his chair closer to hers and took another fortifying swallow of gin. "I can do you a great deal of good," he said. "I can improve your standing with the French, and at the same time, I can make your existence far more pleasant for you. It can't be very enjoyable for a young and attractive woman to be spending virtually all of her evenings alone."

"I—I don't mind," Eliza said, realizing that a crisis was fast approaching.

He leered at her, reached out, and caught hold of her arm, his hamlike fingers compressing her flesh. "You and I," he announced, "have been destined to share in the future of New Amsterdam."

"I'm flattered," she murmured, hoping desperately that an unpleasant scene could be avoided. Certainly she had no intention of granting him any favors.

Mistaking the woman's natural reticence for shyness, Governor Stuyvesant acted accordingly, deciding to overwhelm her. He rose and his wooden leg clattered on the pine floor as he faced Eliza, pulling her up from her chair. He smiled broadly, his eyes glittering as he held on to her, one huge hand sliding around her slender, supple waist, pulling her against him.

He had the strength of a bear, Eliza discovered, and she was unable to escape from his grasp. Rather than become engaged in a physical contest that she knew she couldn't win, she gave in for the moment and yielded to him. While he kissed her far too passionately for the brevity of the encounter, Eliza looked over his shoulder, and suddenly she realized they were standing in front of a large window and were plainly visible from the outside of the house. She realized, too, that Roaring Wolf had followed her and undoubtedly was witnessing the entire scene.

That couldn't be helped. There was no way she could explain her predicament to the Pequot, and she was too concerned about her safety to care what Roaring Wolf might think.

Peter Stuyvesant rubbed his body against hers and, bending his head, kissed the hollow of her throat above the low neckline of her gown. Eliza was so startled that she gasped. Stuyvesant misunderstood her reaction and interpreted it as a sign of pleasure. His grip tightened.

Eliza knew now that she could no longer avoid making a scene in order to save herself. She had not wanted a confrontation, but he was making it impossible. She stood very still, allowing him to kiss, fondle, and hug her as he pleased, while she frantically took stock of her precarious situation.

The door to the library was carelessly left ajar, and through the opening, she could see four armed Dutch pikemen stationed at the front door. There was no way she could make her way past those guards, so she quickly abandoned that route of escape.

Peter Stuyvesant began to paw her in earnest. Eliza knew she had no time to lose. Within moments he would begin tearing off her clothes. She had to resort to a stratagem, that much was clear. So she allowed her entire body to go limp, feigning a swoon. Stuyvesant picked up her seemingly lifeless form and deposited her on a divan on the far side of the room.

This was precisely the respite she needed. Before he could recover from his surprise, Eliza leaped to her feet and, gathering her skirts around her, raced out of the library.

Stuyvesant was so stunned that he simply stood and stared after her for a few moments. Then he followed her, muttering furiously under his breath, but because of his wooden leg he fell far behind her.

Scarcely knowing where she was heading, Eliza followed the line of least resistance and raced up a narrow staircase, realizing too late that she could possibly be running in the direction of Stuyvesant's bedchamber. She threw open a door and breathlessly ran inside a room, bolting the door behind her. Gasping for air, she leaned against the door, her heart pounding in her ears. To her vast relief, she saw that she apparently was in a guest bedroom, not in Stuyvesant's own chambers.

She was safe, at least for the moment, but her situation was even worse than it had been a few moments earlier. She had revealed to the governor that she wanted nothing to do with him, and at the same time had locked herself into an upstairs bedchamber and was consequently at his mercy. Making certain that the door could not be opened, she groped in the dark until she found a tinderbox and flint and lighted a small oil lamp. To orient herself with regard to the street, Eliza carried the lamp to the window, where she placed the light on the sill.

Roaring Wolf saw her appear in the window, and from his vantage point across the street he could only regard it as significant that she had gone upstairs in the governor's house. Already suspicious of her behavior, he became even more firmly convinced that she was being unfaithful to his good friend, Richard Dunstable.

Peter Stuyvesant stomped slowly up the stairs to the second floor, saw the closed bedchamber door, and optimistically tried to open it. Realizing that his prey had locked herself in, he limped on to his own quarters to review the situation.

He was livid, but that, as he well knew, was irrelevant. He had his staff and reputation to think about, including a majordomo, housemaids, and a squad of soldiers. He would be a laughingstock if they discovered that the beautiful young lady he was entertaining had fled from him and locked him out of a guest room in his own house. He decided that he would be obliged to make the best of a bad situation by outwaiting Eliza. It was far from a perfect solution, but it was the best he could devise.

In the bedchamber, Eliza gradually became calmer, and ultimately it dawned on her that Governor Stuyvesant did not intend to force open the door. That much, at least, was to the good. Uncertain how to proceed, she sank into a chair and decided to wait.

Time passed slowly, marked by a clock on the mantle, the hands crawling forward almost imperceptibly. Then, to Eliza's dismay, the lamp flickered, and she realized that she had burned the last of the oil. Unable to find another light in spite of a frantic search in the dark, she had to resign herself to the inevitable—she would see clearly again only when the sun came up the next morning.

Roaring Wolf, continuing to stare up at the second floor of the governor's house, saw the light go out in the room that he knew Eliza was occupying, and he formed his own conclusions, assuming that she was in bed with Stuyvesant and that they were making love in the dark.

The woman, he reflected, was no more reliable than were the squaws of the Pequot who engaged in affairs with braves who were available when their husbands went on the warpath or were absent on hunting expeditions. He told himself that he shouldn't be surprised; he had assumed that white women were different, particularly the one whom his mentor had married, but obviously that was not the case.

He would be obliged to tell Richard the truth at their next meeting; their friendship demanded as much. Certainly there was nothing to be gained by staying hidden in the shrubbery opposite the governor's house any longer, so Roaring Wolf returned to Eliza's nearby dwelling, where he had cleared a sleeping place for himself in the shed. There he would be comfortable for the rest of the night.

Meanwhile time dragged for Eliza, and in spite of her predicament, she became drowsy. The chair in which she had seated herself was comfortable, and finally sleep overcame her.

She had no idea what awakened her or how long she had been asleep, but when she opened her eyes and sat upright in her chair, she was horrified to see the first streaks of dawn appearing in the sky outside the window. She had slept for hours! Escape was paramount in her mind, and somewhat befuddled by sleep, she rose, quietly unlocked the door, and started to make her way stealthily down the corridor.

All at once the bulk of Peter Stuyvesant loomed in front of her. "I trust you've enjoyed your rest,

Lady Dunstable," he said, his voice thick with sarcasm.

Eliza was so upset, so frightened, that she could not reply. Her hand flew to her mouth, and she was speechless as she stared at him.

"You have nothing to fear from me, my dear Lady Dunstable," he told her. "I do not molest women or force myself on them against their will."

Gaping at him in the dim light provided by candles in a wall-holder, she hoped he meant what he said.

"I have a position to maintain here," he declared, bowing.

Eliza began to breathe more easily.

"I'll escort you only as far as the front door," the governor told her. "I'm sure you can make your way home without incident."

She finally found her voice. "You're very kind," she murmured.

"Not at all," Peter Stuyvesant replied. "I have many good qualities, but kindness is not one of them. I may have maintained my reputation, but I remain sorely disappointed. I urge you to reconsider. I urge it wholeheartedly, Lady Dunstable, for your own good. I am in a position to be of great help to you and can advance your career. On the other hand, I can impede your progress and cause you great harm. I am not one to threaten, but I am not one to speak lightly, either. Other ladies have not found me objectionable, so I am hoping that you will change your mind after due reflection." He turned and headed toward the stairway.

Eliza was astonished by this latest development in the strangest evening she had ever spent. Peter Stuyvesant, for all his faults, was releasing her without further ado. She understood that by protecting his own reputation, he meant simply to allow his household staff to conclude that she had become his mistress. That was a small price to pay for her freedom.

"Rest assured, Your Excellency," she said softly, following him, "I will never do anything to cause you embarrassment."

"I'm pleased to hear it," he replied. "When you change your views toward me, my happiness will be complete."

Stuyvesant amazed her by offering her his arm. Eliza took it, and as they reached the bottom of the stairs, he escorted her to the door, where four pikemen were on duty. She had no idea whether these were the sentries she had seen the night before or whether they had replaced their comrades. In any event, she had a role to play now.

Stuyvesant bowed over her hand and kissed it. "I bid you farewell, my dear," he said.

Eliza saw the Dutch sentries exchange glances. Let them think what they would; her honor was intact and that was what really mattered. "Good night, Peter," she replied, and was sufficiently accomplished an actress to sound as though she regretted her departure after spending the night with him. A moment later the door opened and closed behind her. She was free at last.

Settling her light cloak over her shoulders, Eliza walked to the back of the governor's house and crossed to her own dwelling. Her heels sank in the soft turf, but she was unaware of any discomfort. She had survived the night, and for that much she was grateful.

Whether she had harmed her ability to act as a successful double agent remained to be seen. For the present, all she knew and cared about was that she had avoided entanglements. But it was going to be a long, difficult summer, she told herself with a sigh.

IV

No one realized when the *Wayfarer,* a brig of seventy tons, put in to the New Amsterdam harbor and tied up at a berth on the East River, that an international incident was in the making. Captain Silas Sharp, the brig's master, had sailed directly to the Dutch colony from Plymouth, England. As he explained to the two Dutch customs officers who came aboard and examined his manifest, he carried a cargo that had been ordered specifically by a New Amsterdam-based merchant.

"I have a cousin, also named Sharp, who owns a shop here," he said, "and he's ordered every last ounce of the cargo that I carry. I've got iron pots and pans, bolts of wool, and a quantity of high-grade gunpowder."

"Your cargo will be very welcome here," the senior customs official replied. "There's a need for these articles in New Amsterdam, and Master Sharp, whom I have the honor to know, is a wise Englishman to have requested this merchandise. He will sell all of it rapidly at a good profit."

"I'm glad to hear it," Silas Sharp replied.

The customs officer made some quick calculations. "You are obliged now to pay the sum of seven hundred and fifty guilders, Mijnheer," he said.

Captain Sharp stared at him in amazement. "That's more than two hundred sovereigns!"

The Dutchman continued. "If you'll be patient for a moment, I'll let you know the precise amount."

"My God!" Silas Sharp exclaimed. "You're talking about a fortune! Why do I owe that much to your government? I have never had to pay that much before."

The junior customs agent realized the problem. "It appears," he said, "that you are unaware of our new law. We demand a tariff before foreigners are permitted to do business here."

"My cousin has lived in New Amsterdam for many years," the ship captain protested. "Surely he's not considered a foreigner."

The customs official smiled and shook his head. "He is English, is he not?"

"Of course he's English! But what has that—"

"Then he is a foreigner," the Dutchman said flatly. "You have a simple choice, Mijnheer. Either you pay the seven hundred and fifty guilders, or I am obliged under the edict of Governor Stuyvesant to confiscate your cargo."

Silas Sharp was outraged. "You would actually confiscate a cargo worth hundreds of pounds?" he demanded incredulously.

The Dutchman shrugged. "That is the law of New Amsterdam, Mijnheer, and I am obliged to enforce it."

"Well, sir," Silas Sharp threatened hotly, "I'll be damned if I am going to pay the outrageous tribute you demand, and I'll be hanged if I'll stand by while you confiscate my cargo. I'd rather put out to sea again!"

The senior Dutch customs official shrugged. "As you wish, Mijnheer. That is your choice."

Silas Sharp struggled to control his temper. "I suppose there's a charge for taking on a few barrels of potable water as well?"

"Indeed there is," the younger customs official said. "The price per barrel is—"

"To hell with you and to hell with your prices," Sharp exploded. "I wouldn't pay a ha'penny for drinking water here if my crew and I had our tongues hanging out for want of it. Get off my ship, because if you don't, you'll be sailing with us!"

The two Dutch officials scampered ashore, their dignity shattered, and the *Wayfarer*'s master stood on the quarterdeck, bellowing orders to his surprised crew. They obeyed him without question, however, and the brig slid out of her berth, her sails filled, and she made her way to midriver. Then she came about and tacked slowly up the East River toward the Great Bay.

The Dutch officials wrote a report of the incident and put it out of their minds. They'd grown accustomed to the indignation of British sea captains since Director-General Stuyvesant's new law had gone into effect.

Arriving in New Haven late the next day, Captain Sharp was guided by a pilot boat to a dock owned by Burrows and Clayton. Adam Burrows came on board, and the ship's indignant captain immediately told him what had happened in New Amsterdam.

"I'm not surprised," a sympathetic Adam Burrows said. "I've heard the same story told a dozen times by various masters. Maybe we can help you. Let me see your manifest, if you will."

Silas Sharp handed him the sheet of paper.

Adam studied it. "We'll take your woolen goods off your hands," he said, "and we'll pay you as much as you would have received in New Amsterdam. We'll also pay a good price for your gunpowder. Your cooking utensils are another matter. There's little market for them here; we just received two large shipments of ironware last month. Let me think for a minute or two." He paced up and down the length of the master's cabin.

Silas Sharp watched him in silence, frowning over the prospect of having a large cargo of kitchen utensils on his hands and disappointing his cousin who had ordered the goods.

Suddenly Adam halted and smiled. "Where there's a will there's usually a way," he said. "You sure don't want to upset your cousin in New Amsterdam, who's no doubt counting on a juicy profit for himself."

Sharp nodded cautiously.

"We'll sail down the coast. I'll take you myself," Adam declared. "Then I'll show you where the border lies that divides New Haven from New Amsterdam. You can put your cargo ashore there. We'll hire a messenger to take word to your cousin in New Amsterdam. He can send some packhorses overland for your cargo. It can be snug and safe in New Amsterdam by the end of the week, without a tariff cutting into your profits."

The captain of the *Wayfarer* was confused. "How is that possible, sir?" he asked. "If customs officers come on board my ship, there will surely be other customs officers at the border."

Adam shook his head. "We don't have much organization here in the New World," he said. "We lack the manpower for it. The border is an imaginary line drawn through the wilderness, and ninety percent of the time there isn't a living soul within miles of it. You could move a good many tons of merchandise from New Haven into New Amsterdam, and the Dutch customs officials would never know the difference."

Silas Sharp understood now, and all at once started to laugh loud and long. "I don't in the least bit mind cheating the Dutch out of the tariff money," he hooted. "Their greed got my dander up. If I can smuggle those kitchen utensils into the colony without paying a farthing of duty, so much the better."

"You shall do exactly that," Adam Burrows told him with a twinkle in his eye. "It does my heart good, too, to hoodwink that Stuyvesant!"

A messenger was dispatched to New Amsterdam bearing a letter to Silas Sharp's cousin. Then the members of the *Wayfarer's* crew took their leisure for seventy-two hours and were entertained by the citizens of New Haven. The whole town, it seemed, was privy to the scheme, and everyone was hoping that the Dutch authorities would be fooled.

When enough time had passed for the New Amsterdam merchant to send an appropriate number of pack animals to the rendezvous point, the brig set sail again with Adam Burrows and several of his employees on board. The voyage down the coast of the Great Bay was uneventful. As Adam had indicated, the border between New Haven and New Amsterdam was unpatrolled. On both sides, the forest of maple and oak, cedar and pine was as unlimited as the blue-green waters of the sea.

Nevertheless, no risks were taken, and the cargo was not unloaded until dusk, when it was transferred to the ship's longboat and rowed ashore. The boat had to make several trips back and forth between the brig and the shore, but by late in the evening the task was accomplished. Silas Sharp shook hands with his cousin, who gave the order for his overland caravan to return to New Amsterdam. Barring trouble, they would reach Manhattan Island by early morning, and soon thereafter the goods would be safe in Master Sharp's shop. The customs officers would be none the wiser, and the merchandise would be admitted to the Dutch colony without the payment of as much as a single guilder of tribute. The *Wayfarer* returned to New Haven, and when she tied up at the dock, the whole town seemed to explode with joy over her accomplishment. Captain Sharp and the members of his crew were inundated with dinner invitations, far more than they could accept. Everyone was in a festive mood, celebrating the victory over the unpopular Stuyvesant and his equally unpopular tariff.

So many people in both New Haven and New Amsterdam became aware of the "secret" that news of the exploit inevitably leaked out, and just as inevitably, Peter Stuyvesant learned of it.

His temper ungovernable under the best of circumstances, Stuyvesant was enraged. He had not only been outsmarted, but his foes had made a laughingstock of him, and that was one thing he could not tolerate.

He immediately plotted a countermove. Taking care that no outsider learned what he had in mind, he secretly recruited a small but effective force. Then, on Saturday night, when the taverns of New Amsterdam were filled with citizens relaxing after a week of hard labor, Stuyvesant and his band quietly set sail on board a small but fast armed merchantman.

Its destination revealed to no one, the ship sailed up the coast and timed its arrival in New Haven perfectly. It nosed into the harbor shortly after ten on Sunday morning, an hour when virtually the entire population of the town was attending services at one or another of the community's churches.

Stuyvesant moved swiftly and efficiently, demonstrating to those who did not know him that he was a man to be taken seriously. He and a number of his hand-picked seamen boarded their ship's longboat and crossed the harbor to the *Wayfarer*. Hurrying on board, they quickly subdued the two crew members who had been left to guard the vessel. Within moments, the brig was untied from her dock, her sails were spread, and she gathered speed as she glided out of the harbor under her own power, manned by Stuyvesant's crewmen.

By the time the people of New Haven emerged from church services at noon, Stuyvesant had completed his task. He had succeeded in spiriting the *Wayfarer* out of town under the noses of the inhabitants.

Captain Sharp was the first to realize what was amiss. He recognized his brig's familiar silhouette as it followed the Dutch merchantman into the open waters of the Great Bay. Unable to believe the evidence of his own eyes, he raced to the waterfront and there confirmed his worst fears: The *Wayfarer* had vanished from her berth.

It was far too late to give chase to the vessels. By the time crews could be assembled to board ships in the harbor for a chase, the *Wayfarer* and her escort would be out of sight. The last laugh in the controversy, it appeared, belonged to Peter Stuyvesant.

Adding insult to injury, Stuyvesant's first act when he reached New Amsterdam was to sign a decree that officially confiscated the *Wayfarer*. New Haven's sovereignty had been violated, and her pride had been dealt a severe blow. The entire colony demanded vengeance at once. A special town assembly responded to the fiery oratory of speaker after speaker, and by an overwhelming vote, Colonel Adam Burrows was authorized to take whatever steps he deemed necessary to restore the good name and stature of New Haven.

Adam conferred with his son-in-law. "This is one of those incidents that's likely to get completely out of hand," he said. "I can see a full-fledged war between New Haven and New Amsterdam developing over this, a war that would involve both mother countries as well."

"I don't think there's much doubt about it," Richard said. "The attitudes of both sides can be argued endlessly, and both are right, just as both are wrong."

"How would you like to undertake another very delicate mission?" his father-in-law asked.

Richard shrugged. "I'll do whatever is necessary, of course," he replied.

"You are already acquainted with Peter Stuyvesant, which is a help. I therefore propose to send you to him as an official representative of New Haven. Needless to say, your trip to New Amsterdam will give you an opportunity to be reunited, at least temporarily, with Eliza."

Richard smiled broadly. "I would gladly undertake any mission for the sake of seeing my wife again."

It soon became public knowledge in New Haven that Richard was going to travel to New Amsterdam to beard the Dutch lion in his den.

No one was more interested in this news than Lady Celeste Murette. She was well aware of a strong physical magnetism that passed between them whenever they were together, and she knew that Richard was aware of it, too; but he somehow managed to keep his distance from her, much to her annoyance. Now, however, she saw an opportunity to gain ground in her quiet campaign to seduce him, while at the same time serving her own political interests. She was eager to pass along to Laroche the letter she had written to Cardinal Mazarin telling him that Lady Dawn Shepherd had married and was living quietly in New Haven as Mistress Ezekiel Clayton.

She went to Richard without delay. "I'll be grateful," she told him, "more grateful than I can ever tell you, if you'll escort me to New Amsterdam. I have private business there, and I'll be very much in your debt."

He knew of no way that he could turn down the simple request without being rude. "I don't plan to tarry on the trail," he said. "By all means, you're welcome to come with me if you can make your way through the wilderness rapidly without too much difficulty."

She had no intention of revealing to him that she had never set foot in the wilderness. "I'll manage," she promised him brightly.

He had to be satisfied and was forced to agree to allow her to accompany him. So they set out together on horseback, with Richard carrying what passed for a full-dress uniform of the New Haven militia in his saddlebag. Lady Celeste's open-throated dress was undeniably attractive, although it was far from practical for the trip.

Richard soon discovered her deception about her wilderness experience, but by that time it was too late. He could not abandon her to her own devices on the trail, and consequently he was forced to reduce his own pace of travel.

There were compensations, however. Lady Celeste went out of her way to be pleasant and charming, and she turned out to be a splendid traveling companion. She made no complaint over the hardships of travel, and she insisted on helping with their meals in spite of her unfamiliarity with outdoor cooking fires. He was forced to admire her spirit, and was secretly relieved that in spite of the natural chemistry that seemed to draw them together, she avoided embarrassing him by placing him in compromising situations.

The first night they stopped at the small English settlement at Stratford. The second night, however, they were forced to camp on the trail, and Richard fashioned a small tent for his companion while he himself slept in the open, wrapped in his blanket. Lady Celeste contemplated asking Richard to share her tent—which would have meant sharing her bed—but she decided such a move might be premature and would succeed only in frightening him. She was making excellent progress in gaining his confidence, so she was content to leave well enough alone. In due time he would become ripe for an affair; until then, she would proceed with great caution.

After another day on the trail, and another uneventful night, they crossed to Manhattan by ferry, and in the forest on the upper reaches of the island, Richard donned his New Haven militia uniform, which consisted of little more than a distinctive bandolier worn over his usual clothing. Now he was ready to confront the governor.

Lady Celeste made no mention of the fact that she, too, intended to go to Stuyvesant's house and that she would stay there as his guest during her sojourn in the city. They parted company amicably, and Richard proceeded at once to the small house that his wife occupied.

As it happened, Roaring Wolf was absent from his post at the time that Richard arrived, but Eliza was at home and was as elated as she was surprised to see her husband. She clung to him for a long time, returning his fervent kisses wordlessly, so overcome by emotion that she was incapable of speaking.

Richard explained his mission to her and said that he intended to visit the director-general without delay. "Do you know when he's in his office?" he asked.

"He's always in residence before dinner, in the early evening," she replied.

That gave them two or three hours alone, and both realized it. There was no need for words, and their actions spoke for themselves.

The miracle of their lovemaking, although it occurred frequently, was ever new. Somehow, in a way that neither understood, they communed their every thought and feeling without the need to express themselves in words. Each had a sixth sense for the other's desires and needs. From the moment they first embraced and kissed, and their passion began to rise, they each knew instinctively what would give the greatest pleasure to the other.

The secret of their communion, if it was a secret, was that both completely cast aside their inhibitions. As Richard had once expressed it, he was no gentleman when he made love to Eliza, and she, fortunately, forgot that she was a lady. Instinct told them how far to go in order to bring the marital partner to a peak of desire, and they did exactly as their instincts prompted. Still, their lovemaking was never the same twice in succession. They were guided by their imaginations and by their unselfish urge to please each other.

Only after their long-contained desires had been sated were they able to speak freely and to bring each other up to date on their activities.

As they lay beside each other, Richard discussed his travels throughout New England and talked at some length about the finding of Dutch firearms in the hands of Indians.

Eliza faced a more complex situation. So far she had not accomplished her mission in New Amsterdam, and she knew that if she admitted to Richard that she had to be on guard constantly to protect her honor, he would insist on her returning to New Haven with him, which would mean abandoning her task of acting as a double agent.

So her description of her life in New Amsterdam was vague. She told him about her activities persuading ship captains to enlist under the banner of the Dutch West Indies Company, but refrained from mentioning that the masters of these vessels often pursued her to her extreme discomfort. She made no mention, either, of the incident at Governor Stuyvesant's house when she had locked herself into a bedchamber at night. Certainly she avoided telling him that she was regarded by the residents of New Amsterdam as the governor's mistress, or that she did nothing to dispel this falsehood.

One piece of news Eliza could relate, however, was that she was learning the language of the local Indian tribe from a brave Stuyvesant had recently hired as a groundskeeper and factotum. Richard prided himself on his ability to speak Indian tongues, and she kept him laughing for fifteen minutes just trying to get him to pronounce the tribe's name—the Reckagawawanc.

Their hours together passed swiftly. Before they knew it, time had come for Richard to pay his visit to Peter Stuyvesant. He dressed and started out across the yard that separated the small dwelling from the governor's house. As he passed the shed, Roaring Wolf, who had returned to his post, saw Richard and raced out to greet him, and they had a boisterous reunion. But Roaring Wolf was troubled as he walked with Richard to the entrance of the governor's residence. He wondered if he should tell Richard that he had twice seen Eliza embracing other men and that she had spent an entire night in a bedchamber in Stuyvesant's house.

However, the Pequot warrior was intelligent and possessed a native shrewdness. He realized the weakness of his position. He could not prove his charges against Eliza, and he knew that in the event of a showdown Richard would accept his wife's avowal of innocence as opposed to the word of his friend. Consequently, although it left him sorely troubled, Roaring Wolf decided he would say nothing. Later, perhaps, he would have a chance to enlighten Richard.

Richard was admitted to the house by the pikemen, and an aide to the governor hurried out to an anteroom to greet the officer who wore what he said was the uniform of an English colony.

"May I inquire your business with the governor, Major?" he asked politely.

"You may," Richard replied politely, "but my business is exclusively with Governor Stuyvesant." His manner was austere.

The aide excused himself and returned in a few moments to lead the visitor to the office of the director-general of New Netherland. Peter Stuyvesant stood to greet his guest, and he raised an eyebrow when he recognized Richard. "Ah, it's you, Dunstable," he said. "I was concerned when I was told that an English major was here to see me."

Richard did not smile. "I have come, Your Excellency, as the official representative of New Haven Colony, not as a representative of France." He spoke firmly and with great self-confidence.

Stuyvesant concealed his surprise. He had assumed that anyone who worked for Cardinal Mazarin would be malleable, but Dunstable's attitude was harsh and rigid.

"The matter that has brought me here, Your Excellency, is the theft of the brig *Wayfarer*."

Stuyvesant stalled for time while he organized his thoughts. "Theft?" he asked.

"That is the most polite term I can find for it, Your Excellency," he said. "It was safe at a private dock in New Haven when it was stolen by persons unknown, and subsequently—almost immediately —it turned up here in New Amsterdam. Your confiscation order deprives the vessel's owners of their ship, contrary to the customs and laws of all nations."

Stuyvesant held his ground. "Smuggling is also a violation of the laws of all nations. Had the *Wayfarer* stayed in port here, she would have been required to pay a customs fee. Instead she chose to flee to New Haven, and subsequently, with the full knowledge and cooperation of officials in New Haven, her cargo was smuggled across our border. I am not in a position to identify the exact culprits, unfortunately, but if I could, I would hang them as an example to all who break our laws in the future." Stuyvesant paused long enough to let his implied threat sink in. "Be that as it may, Dunstable, I consider the seizure of the *Wayfarer* a just act in retaliation for her avoidance of the payment of fees that were due my government."

The subject was touchy, but there was a principle at stake, and Richard held firm. "I know nothing about the imposing of duties by your customs office on the master of the *Wayfarer*. That is a commercial matter and none of my concern. But I shall be blunt with you, Your Excellency. It is said on the best of good authority that you personally took part in the raid that resulted in the capture of the brig. You are not an ordinary citizen; you are the director-general of a Dutch colony, and anything you do, therefore, assumes significance. I regret to inform you that the people and government of the British colony of New Haven regard your participation in this incident as an unprovoked, unfriendly act."

"I don't deny my participation!" Peter Stuyvesant exploded. "In fact, I'm quite proud of what I've done, and I'm prepared to pay the consequences."

"I regret to inform Your Excellency," Richard said stiffly, "that the consequences in this instance are going to be expensive. So expensive, in fact, that Your Excellency may wish to reconsider. I am authorized to request that the brig be handed over to me without further ado, and that I be permitted to sail in her, with a crew of compatriots whom I will recruit here. I'm to be allowed to depart in the *Wayfarer* at my earliest convenience. This is Wednesday. If I have not appeared with the ship, unharmed, in New Haven harbor by noon on Saturday, the colony of New Haven is prepared to declare war on the colony of New Netherland."

Stuyvesant glared at him and saw that he was not joking. "Do you suppose for a single minute," he demanded, "that Cromwell will countenance a war that is going to involve both England and the Netherlands?"

"I can't speak for Cromwell or for his Parliament," Richard replied. "But as for common sense, I know it will be virtually impossible for England to avoid participation in a colony's war with a foreign power. What's more," he added, "you can be assured that every other English colony in the New World will come to the immediate assistance of New Haven and will join with us in our declaration of war against New Netherland."

Peter Stuyvesant realized that he was not exaggerating. Certainly the other English colonies would join forces in a war with the Dutch colony. If Amsterdam and The Hague took steps to lend their support to their overseas possession, it was virtually inevitable that England would be forced to enter the conflict on the other side.

Stuyvesant was a courageous man, but he was too accomplished a military strategist not to recognize that the odds were overwhelmingly against him. The English colonies outweighed New Netherland in area, population, and resources. Furthermore, he was crippled by the presence in his own community of more English subjects than Dutch citizens. He faced almost certain defeat.

"I shall need time to consider your demand," he said.

Richard's instructions were firm. "I'm under orders, Your Excellency, to permit no delays. In the event that you cannot provide an affirmative answer to my demands at once, I am to act as though you have rejected my requests. In that case, I am to notify all English subjects in New Amsterdam of the situation at once in order to give them an opportunity to pack their belongings and evacuate the community before hostilities break out."

Richard's uncompromising stance was sufficient to convince Peter Stuyvesant that New Haven meant business. He was being threatened, to be sure, and given full blame for a situation in which justice demanded that both sides share the responsibility. But he was hemmed in, and his alternatives were stark: Either he could swallow his pride and capitulate, or he would meet certain defeat. It was not an easy matter for a ferociously proud man like Stuyvesant to swallow his pride. "Very well," he said. "You win this round, Major Dunstable. I capitulate to the government of New Haven, and I accept your terms. You may feel free to seek recruits for a crew, and you may leave the harbor in the *Wayfarer* whenever it suits your convenience."

The victory gave Richard no satisfaction. His

wife was still living in New Amsterdam, only a stone's throw from the governor's house, and her safety depended on Peter Stuyvesant's goodwill. Therefore, he thought it politic to make amends as best he could. "I hope you understand, Your Excellency, that there's been nothing personal in the stand I've taken. I simply obey orders as a good militia officer should."

If Stuyvesant was mollified, he did not show it; his only reply was a stiff nod of his massive head.

"With the incident of the *Wayfarer* behind us," Richard said, "I trust it will be possible for the settlers of English and Dutch descent to live in friendship side by side."

Stuyvesant showed extreme annoyance. "The Dutch know who their friends are and who their enemies are," he said. "And I trust that you and your wife are not ignorant of your own obligations."

The threat was veiled, but was still obvious. "Indeed, Your Excellency, we are ever mindful of them," Richard assured him.

That was more like it! The young Englishman's tone was respectful, cautious, and placatory. That calmed Stuyvesant somewhat, and his mood improved as he dismissed the visitor.

Later in the afternoon, in the comforting arms of Lady Celeste Murette, Stuyvesant was persuaded, bit by bit, to reveal the humiliation he had been forced to endure.

Lady Celeste, having known him well over the course of several years, realized that the loss of the *Wayfarer* undoubtedly made him furious. She couldn't help feeling sorry for the young woman whom she regarded as her successor. "I gather," she said, "that Mistress Dunstable played no role in the incident."

"None," Stuyvesant said curtly.

"In that case, she's still of use to you."

"Assuredly." He was relieved that Celeste didn't know that Eliza merely posed as his mistress.

Meanwhile Richard returned to his wife's small house, and with her accompanying him, he went directly to the Thorn and Thistle, where he explained the situation to Angus and Mollie Mac-Neill and requested that they help.

"Any sailors you can recruit for me will be very welcome," he said. "I need a crew of about fifteen men to sail the *Wayfarer*. As I understand it, there are enough seafaring English colonials in this town to fill dozens of such crews."

The MacNeills assured him that they would encounter no difficulties in obtaining the services of reliable men for him.

Richard turned to Eliza with a smile. "It may be," he said, "that you know of some lads, too, who could be useful."

His wife shook her head.

Mollie stiffened perceptibly. "I should think," she said, "that Lady Dunstable has been too busy to keep track of the comings and goings of *ordinary* English sailors."

There was no mistaking the malice in her tone or the contempt in her attitude. Eliza understood the reason at once. Mollie had seen Eliza in the company of shipowners and sea captains when she was fulfilling her obligations to Laroche.

Fortunately, Richard was preoccupied with the *Wayfarer* problem and therefore not attuned to subtleties. Hence he did not become aware of Mollie's attitude. It was just as well, Eliza thought, that he remained in the dark. When her assignment ended—when she obtained hard evidence linking Stuyvesant and the French—there would be ample time to tell Richard of the great deception she had succeeded in perpetrating.

*　*　*

It proved far easier than Richard had anticipated to recruit a temporary crew to sail the captured brig from New Amsterdam to New Haven. Word of Peter Stuyvesant's capitulation had traveled swiftly through the English community in New Amsterdam, and as a consequence, Richard was besieged by requests from men who wanted to share in the glory of the incident's aftermath. He spent most of his time with Eliza. His duties were light: He had only to take on enough food and water for the short voyage and to pick a seasoned crew from the host of volunteers.

He spent the better part of an hour with Roaring Wolf and assured himself of the Pequot's well-being. He did not know that the warrior continued his severe inner struggle over Eliza's infidelity.

Eliza accompanied her husband to the ship when he took his departure, and he finally broached a subject that had been very much on his mind. "Are you ready to come back to New Haven with me?" he wanted to know.

She gripped his arm more firmly and walked with him several paces before she replied. "If it were up to me and the way I feel," she said, "we wouldn't have been separated in the first place. But I'm obligated to continue until I ferret out the truth, or until you learn it. Only then will I be able to come home and resume a normal life there with a clear mind and conscience."

"I still feel as I always have," Richard said. "It's enough that I expose myself to danger and take risks. I see no reason why you should have to be involved."

"You knew before you married me," Eliza told him, "that I'm not the type of woman who can be content to spend my life keeping house for a man and rearing a family. Just because I'm a woman doesn't mean that I must hide under a bed, taking no risks. We've been given a very important assignment. The future of the English colonies depends on what we learn. I'll think of retirement to a safe place once we've accomplished our mission." Her jaw was set and her tone was firm.

Richard sighed quietly, then grinned at her. In spite of his constant concern for her, he was proud of her and the determination and courage she displayed. Somehow, he thought, when he was with her his worries diminished. She seemed well able to take care of herself.

They had already said good-bye in private, so their leave-taking on the dock was far more impersonal, almost perfunctory.

"I hope," Eliza said, "that the worst of our separation is over and that we'll soon be reunited for all time."

"Amen to that," Richard replied, and he kissed her hard and briefly. Then he went aboard the brig, and Eliza, after a farewell wave, quickly returned home.

Acting for the rightful owner of the ship, Richard went to the quarterdeck and remained there while the vessel cast off and made her way slowly up the East River. Once he assured himself that they were safely under way and that Peter Stuyvesant had no intention of halting the vessel, Richard made his way below to the owner's cabin, which he had reserved for his own use. He opened the door, then stopped short. There, sitting in a chair facing him, was a calm Lady Celeste Murette, her long, dark hair tumbling about her shoulders.

Before Richard could open his mouth to protest, Lady Celeste held up her hand to silence him. "Don't worry, I assure you everything is quite proper. I've booked the first mate's cabin right next door. The captain was ever so kind as to let me have it for a small fee." She smiled at him sweetly. Richard, still speechless, couldn't help smiling.

"Anyway," she continued, "I had finished my business in New Amsterdam, and I prefer infinitely to return to New Haven by ship rather than suffer that long overland march."

At last Richard remembered his manners. "Well, you're welcome on board, I'm sure."

"I would have contacted you earlier in the day to let you know my intentions," Lady Celeste said, "but I knew you were busy and preoccupied with your wife, so I didn't want to interrupt. I thought it would be time enough for you to find out my intentions once we were on board." She refrained from adding that, by waiting until now, she had made certain that he could not refuse permission for her to go back to New Haven on board the *Wayfarer*.

Richard found that he was quickly becoming unsettled by the proximity of Lady Celeste in the small cabin. Perhaps it reminded him too much of his recent voyage across the Atlantic, when he had shared a cabin with Lady Dawn Shepherd. He was vastly relieved when Lady Celeste rose from her chair and suggested they go on deck. Once they left the cabin, however, Richard soon realized from the looks on the faces of the crew that he was going to have to explain her presence on board. Apparently the captain had not informed the crew that Lady Celeste would be joining them on the voyage to New Haven.

Lady Celeste herself seemed amused, and having been long accustomed to the admiration of men from all walks of life, she handled the ship's crew with deft self-assurance.

Later, at dinner, Richard couldn't help noting that she persuaded the officers to talk about themselves but said very little about her own activities or her presence on board. She allowed them to assume what they would. They were all in high spirits, and aided by a bottle of brandy Lady Celeste had earlier donated to the captain, they soon became even more convivial. The assembly finally broke up reluctantly when two of their company had to return to their duties on deck.

Celeste blithely bade the small group good night, and throwing a lacy black shawl over her shoulders, she stood by her cabin door and waited for Richard to open it for her. Richard quickly said good night and repaired to his own cabin, still uncomfortably aware of the presence of Celeste next door. But the gentle rolling of the ship and the brandy he had consumed at dinner soon took their effect, and he fell hard asleep.

A little while later a hand on his shoulder brought him quickly awake. Lady Celeste stood in the center of the cabin, wearing a thin peignoir and a gown of rose-colored satin that clung to her. A small oil lamp glowed on the table behind her, and her silhouetted form loomed only a few feet away. Richard sat up halfway and swallowed hard.

"I've never been in such a foul-smelling bed in my life," she whispered, "and I simply can't sleep. I'm sorry to wake you, but I just had to talk to someone." At this she sat down in the chair she had occupied earlier in the day and began to recite a long and detailed account of her experiences at sea.

Chatting amiably, without apparent self-consciousness, Celeste seemed unaware of Richard's extreme discomfort. Actually the opposite was true. She was conscious not only of the way he felt, but also of the reasons for it. She was wise enough to know that he could relax only if she kept their relationship on an impersonal basis. She would tease him with her nearness and her unconcealed beauty, but under no circumstances, she knew, could she initiate any move that suggested intimacy. He would be reminded of his wife, with whom he undoubtedly had shared lovemaking only hours before, and his guilt would become so overwhelming that he would flee from her.

So, demonstrating consummate skill, Celeste succeeded in avoiding the embarrassment that Richard dreaded. He gradually relaxed, and they talked at considerable length, and he soon found himself confiding to her the story of his encounter earlier in the day with Governor Stuyvesant.

Celeste was secretly amused. She had long despised Governor Stuyvesant and had continued to sleep with him only because it had been expected of her. His humiliation delighted her. It also amused her to hear about the confrontation from the points of view of both men. But she thought it only fair to warn this young man for whom she was developing a genuine liking of the difficulties that might lie ahead for him.

"Your wife, I take it, is staying on in New Amsterdam," she said.

Richard nodded. "Yes, she has business there." He realized the explanation was lame, but there was no way he could go into further detail.

"I spent considerable time in the colony," she said, "and I came to know Peter Stuyvesant fairly well. I hope that you and your wife are maintaining a careful guard."

He felt a tightening in the pit of his stomach. "Would you mind being less cryptic?" he asked.

She shrugged, allowing the lace-edged neckline of her peignoir to fall open. "Stuyvesant," she said, "is engaged in a serious, lifelong love affair—with Peter Stuyvesant. His opinion of himself is very inflated, and he despises those who succeed in exposing him as a mere mortal. You did precisely that today."

"I explained to him that I was just doing my

116

duty, and that there was nothing personal in the ultimatum I gave to him," Richard explained.

Celeste laughed, and her long black hair swayed when she shook her head. "As if that mattered," she said. "Regardless of whether your remarks were intended to be personal or not, it was *you* who exposed him. It was *you* who humiliated him, it was *you* who forced him to back down. This ship had become the symbol of a great victory in his mind, and all at once you transformed it into a symbol of a crushing defeat. Believe me, he won't forget. If I know him at all, he will always remember Richard Dunstable as the cause of great humiliation."

"I see," he said.

"I don't mean to worry you," Celeste said, "but your wife is a natural target for Stuyvesant's fury. He's vindictive, and she's living alone in New Amsterdam. I would urge you to make other arrangements."

"Such as?"

"Arrange for her to leave New Amsterdam at once and to absent herself from the colony for a long period of time until the humiliating incident is forgotten. Or, if your wife must remain, provide her with adequate protection. Just how she can be protected from the wrath of a vindictive Dutchman, I don't know."

"You're very kind," Richard told her.

She smiled and shook her head. "I'm anything but kind. If you knew me better, you'd realize that every word I've spoken was for my own benefit."

Her reply was so startling that he could only stare at her.

"I'm going to be quite blunt now. I can only hope that you won't take offense." She smiled and leaned toward him. "It's been obvious to me for a long time, ever since we first met, that you and I have an attraction for each other. I've felt it, and I'm sure that if you'll be honest, you'll admit that you've felt it, too."

He failed to recognize the connection with what she had said previously, but decided it would do no harm to be honest. "Yes," he said, "it's true, I do feel very much drawn to you."

"There you have it," she said triumphantly, and then added quietly, "If something untoward should happen to your wife, I am going to come after you. I'm ready to overcome any obstacles in order to become your second wife."

He was so taken aback by her candor that he didn't know what to say. He felt ridiculously mute, like an immature boy overwhelmed by an older woman. But as much as he wanted to respond, nothing came into his befuddled mind.

"I want it very clearly understood," she said, "that I warned you that your wife is in danger living so near to Peter Stuyvesant. If something unfortunate happens to her, I hope you'll remember that I warned you. I wouldn't want her memory to come between us."

Richard was so shocked that he felt numb.

"But enough of this," she cried quietly. "I don't believe in preaching gloom! It may be that I'm overly sensitive and that your wife will be perfectly safe in New Amsterdam. Pay no attention to what I've said, Richard. I'm just a silly woman, and our proximity has made me giddy." She rose and crossed the cabin, her hips swaying seductively, and when she reached the table on which the oil lamp was affixed, she lighted a small candle from the flame and extinguished the lamp. Then she walked slowly to the bed, very much aware that he was following her every move with his eyes.

Lady Celeste seemed to read his mind. "Don't you dare move, Richard Dunstable! There's ample space right here for both of us," she said, patting the tiny featherbed that occupied a good part of the cabin.

Richard was embarrassed and cleared his throat.

Lady Celeste seemed to understand precisely what was troubling him. "I know what you think of your wife," she said, "and I don't for a moment suggest that you become unfaithful to her. As it happens, I see no reason we can't share these quarters without becoming intimate."

She had placed him on the defensive, and Richard would have felt foolish not to agree with her. "I suppose that is possible," he muttered.

So their arrangements were settled, much to Richard's discomfort.

Resting the candle on a shallow dish on a small bedside table, Celeste turned and took her time removing her peignoir, slowly over one shoulder, then the other, until it fell to the floor behind her.

Ultimately, in spite of his tension, Richard knew that he had to try to go back to sleep. His sense of uneasiness increasing, he wondered if he dared trust himself to remain in the same bed with Lady Celeste Murette.

She snuggled under the covers, turned her back to him, and soon her even breathing indicated that she had fallen asleep. In actuality, however, she was very much awake, very much aware of every move that he made and of what he was feeling. She smiled in the dark.

She would be surprised if he made love to her tonight—so much the better if he did—and was willing to wait and see what developed. She was softening him, she reflected, and after tonight's intimacy it would be impossible for him truly to keep his distance from her.

She was in no rush; she wanted this man and fully intended to possess him. This was a game that she had played under varying circumstances, and she had always emerged the winner. She did not intend to lose now.

Far more than her vanity was at stake. When she had met with Laroche earlier in the day and had told him that Lady Dawn Shepherd, whom Cardinal Mazarin had sought so eagerly, was alive and living in New Haven, the French spymaster had become specific in his demands.

"I shall send your letter to His Eminence in Paris without delay," Laroche said. "But I want to know one thing myself. Did you include any information to the effect that Lady Dawn's escape from our people in Virginia was in any way due to the efforts of Sir Richard Dunstable?"

"That thought simply hadn't occurred to me," she said honestly.

"By all means, then, find out. I assume that you're returning to New Haven, and that he also is going back there."

She nodded.

"Then devote every effort to learning the truth about Lady Dawn's escape. Cardinal Mazarin will need to know. It's the only way he can judge whether he can really trust Dunstable, or whether the rascal is two-faced, which I wouldn't put past him."

Reflecting now on that conversation, Lady Celeste felt reasonably certain that Richard, so without guile in his dealings, had been innocent and in no way connected with Lady Dawn's escape. Richard was too direct, too honest for his own good.

Amusing herself, Celeste rolled over, ostensibly in her sleep, and stretched out an arm, which landed across Richard's body. She almost laughed aloud when she felt his entire body grow taut. He was revealing far more than he knew about his desire for her.

She could wait, Celeste thought. At an appropriate time, she would give herself to him, would take him for herself, and simultaneously would learn about his involvement, if any, in the escape of Lady Dawn. Rarely had she enjoyed an assignment so much.

V

PETER Stuyvesant was restless and dissatisfied after he gave in to the demand of New Haven Colony to release the brig *Wayfarer* without delay. His sense of triumph had turned to ashes, his victory had become an ignoble defeat, and he was afraid he would be the laughingstock of the New World. Certainly the English colonies, which had no reason to love him and were opposed to him in most things, would not hesitate to ridicule him.

What irritated Stuyvesant even more was the realization that the ultimatum had been presented to him by an officer who was in actuality a secret French agent and presumably his own subordinate. Richard had hoped his roles—militia major and French agent—would be kept separate in Stuyvesant's mind, but the Dutch governor's wrath and humiliation rendered him incapable of making such fine distinctions.

Richard's wife, moreover, was very much present in New Amsterdam, a constant reminder to the director-general of the ignominy he had suffered at her husband's hand. Stuyvesant had not spoken with Eliza since the night she had eluded him by locking herself into a second-floor bedchamber. Now the unpleasant memory of that incident rose again in his mind. Perhaps, in some way he had not yet defined even to himself, he could use her as an instrument to even the score with the English colonies. To that end, he sent her a demand that she present herself in his office that very evening.

Eliza knew the moment she received the governor's note that serious trouble loomed ahead for her. She didn't necessarily connect the summons with Richard's confrontation with him; on the other hand, it was certainly a coincidence that he should send for her as soon as he had lost the battle of wits and courage with New Haven.

Uncertain as to his precise motive, Eliza felt it necessary to do what she could for her own benefit. She realized that her appearance was perhaps her greatest asset in dealing with Peter Stuyvesant, so she chose a low-cut royal blue gown that set off her wheat-colored hair to good advantage and gave her a wickedly sophisticated look.

After applying cosmetics and primping before her bedchamber mirror, she was satisfied with her appearance, but one more step was needed. She took her tiny double-edged poniard and concealed it under a band above her wrist beneath the left sleeve of her gown. Now she was ready for any contingency.

Roaring Wolf was in the kitchen eating a supper of cold meat and bread when Eliza was ready to depart. Rather than have him interrupt his meal, she went to him and said, "I'm just going to see Governor Stuyvesant, so don't disturb yourself."

The Pequot's eyes widened, but he made no comment. It was significant, he thought, that Eliza should return to the governor's house the very first evening that her husband had left New Amsterdam.

Eliza was admitted to the governor's home without delay. She had to wait only a few moments before Peter Stuyvesant received her in a small, comfortably furnished parlor where a fire was burning cheerfully. He had intended to deal coldly with her, but her lovely appearance changed his mind, and his faint scowl quickly changed to a broad smile. He bowed and waved her to a chair near the fire. Then he moved to a chair opposite her.

"I suppose you know the reason your husband came to New Amsterdam," he said, "and I daresay you're familiar with the outcome of his visit."

Eliza saw nothing to be gained by dissembling. "Yes," she said. "He told me the story, and," she added hastily, strictly for Stuyvesant's benefit, "I think Richard was wrong, and so was the whole colony of New Haven. They were responsible for the incident that involved the *Wayfarer*. They had no right to make such a critical issue out of your natural attempt to protect the interests of New Amsterdam."

He was surprised by her sympathetic approach, and his attitude toward her softened considerably. "I would have thought," he said, "that you would have approved of the strong-arm tactics that your compatriots used."

She knew she was making a favorable impression on him and reacted accordingly. "In my opinion," she said, "they handled the whole affair badly. They were crude and uncivilized. As I told Richard, they'll win little sympathy anywhere in the Old World by their conduct."

Peter Stuyvesant hadn't yet bothered to wonder about Europe's reaction to the recent drama. "You really think so?" he asked.

He seemed pathetically eager to be consoled, and Eliza actually felt a little sorry for this big, brash man who was so accustomed to having his own way that he became bewildered when he lost control of any situation. "I can only tell you what I told Richard," she said. "The Dutch will be furious, the French will be contemptuous of New Haven, and I'm certain that the people of England will be ashamed at the spectacle that a leading colony made of itself."

She spoke so earnestly and with such seeming sincerity that Stuyvesant was convinced that she meant what she said. The situation was being presented to him in a new light, a light he had not considered, and his gloom lifted somewhat. He rose to his feet, then stomped to a sideboard and poured himself a portion of Dutch gin. "Could I get you a glass?" he asked.

"I'm afraid your gin has a taste that I haven't yet acquired," Eliza said diplomatically. "If you have something else . . . "

"Indeed I have." Without further ado, he poured a quantity of fiery West Indian rum into a glass, handing it to the woman with a flourish.

Eliza almost choked on the strong liquor and immediately was on her guard. It could not have been accidental that she had been served so potent an alcoholic beverage. Stuyvesant downed his drink in a single gulp, refilled his glass, and then resumed his seat. "I've missed you since the night of our, ah, little misunderstanding," he said.

Eliza smiled and nodded warily.

"In any event," he said, "I'd like to make amends to you." He rose and suddenly lunged toward her.

His move was so unexpected that Eliza was caught completely off guard. By the time she was alert to the danger, he had hauled her out of her chair and was clasping her arms down firmly at each side. *Not again,* she said to herself with a sinking feeling. Still, her instincts told her that under no circumstances should she create a scene or call for assistance. His need to save face was too great. If she humiliated him now, he was likely to lash out at her for her rejection and for Richard's confrontation.

So she submitted to his embrace, and having no choice, allowed him to kiss her. Reacting to her passivity, Stuyvesant released her arms and embraced her.

Winding her arms around his neck, she managed to free the poniard. Gripping it, she freed her mouth from his and took a sudden step backward. "I dislike being mauled," she said coldly.

Stuyvesant stared in astonishment at the small glittering steel blade. "There's no need for violence," he said with an uneasy laugh.

She took no chances and continued to hold the small dagger ready for instant use. "I mean Your Excellency no harm," she declared, "but I expect the same consideration from you that I give to you."

"You're simply making it clear that you want nothing personal to do with me," he stated.

She shook her head, hoping to soften her stand and perhaps blur the edges of her rejection. "Not at all," she said. "I simply need time to accustom myself to something new. The idea of taking you as my lover is very new and very unexpected."

He found her candor remarkable. "Are you telling me," he demanded, "that in time you might——"

"Indeed I am," Eliza cut in, lying badly.

He was mollified and took a single backward step with his wooden leg, muttering under his breath. He shook his head and sipped his gin again. Then he ordered brusquely, "Sit down!"

The woman had no idea what might be coming next, but at least he wasn't forcing himself on her, and she was thankful for that much. She sat and concealed the poniard from view, although she continued to hold it in her hand.

"You've been honest with me," Stuyvesant said. "Now I shall be equally frank with you. It's obvious to you that I want you, but I'm in no rush. At my age I've learned patience, and I'm content to wait."

Relief flooded Eliza, and she rewarded him with a dazzling smile. He was going to be far easier to handle than she had anticipated.

"In the meantime," he said, "I still have my reputation to consider. You are already aware of this, I believe, because you reacted correctly with my pikemen at dawn recently. I'm a somewhat vain man, if I do say so, and I have a certain standard that I try to maintain."

For a man who had professed candor, he was being very abstruse, and she had no idea what he meant.

"I would—for a time—be quite satisfied with an accommodation of a sort," he said.

Eliza stared at him and discovered he was peering at her, awaiting her decision. What it was precisely that she was supposed to decide was beyond her. "Are you telling me," she said slowly, "that you'd be content to wait until I can give myself to you freely, provided that in the meantime I pose as your mistress? That I allow the world to believe that you and I—"

"Exactly!" he cut in eagerly, his voice booming. "That's precisely the agreement that I have in mind."

Eliza knew her good name was already compromised and that to engage more openly in deception would not do all that much additional harm. The sacrifice of her reputation was a small price to pay for the sake of the future welfare of the English colonies in the New World. Ultimately, to be sure, she would need to explain the situation to Richard, and she hoped that he would agree with her decision. In the meantime, she felt compelled to take the risk.

Slowly she smiled, and even more slowly she extended her right hand. "We have an agreement, Your Excellency."

Peter Stuyvesant seized her hand and kissed it. "You won't regret this!" he told her enthusiastically.

The tension was cleared, and they worked out details of the arrangement. They were not to Eliza's liking, but she had no choice; still, she reminded herself that henceforth she would be close to Governor Stuyvesant and therefore in a far better position to prove the nature and extent of his relationship with France.

It was agreed that she would continue to live in her own small house nearby, but that she would spend a far greater portion of her time under the roof of the governor's house. She would be expected to spend at least every other night there, and Stuyvesant offered her the use of the guest bedchamber adjacent to his own suite. She would accompany the governor to unofficial dinners and would, on occasion, entertain as his hostess at his own house.

Some of the requirements caused Eliza to cringe, but there was no escape, as she well knew. She was deliberately becoming a party to a far greater deception than she had anticipated, but the end results might be well worth the effort, and the loss of her good name could well result in an enormous gain for the English colonies of North America.

The brig *Wayfarer* pitched and rolled gently in the waters of the Great Bay as it beat its way up the coast toward New Haven Colony. Richard Dunstable slept soundly and was utterly enjoying a very pleasant dream in which he was making love to Eliza. Then suddenly it occurred to him that the body he was fondling passionately was more petite than his wife's. When he opened his eyes, he caught a glimpse of a mass of Lady Celeste Murette's dark hair. Only then did he realize that he was not dreaming, and that Celeste not only was the object of his lovemaking, but was returning his fervor with a vehemence that matched his own.

He had no idea how the lovemaking had started. The last he had known, he and Celeste had fallen asleep lying back to back. Which of them had made the advances that had resulted in the present situation was beyond him, and in a sense, the question no longer mattered.

The truth was that Richard and Celeste had gone too far to call a halt now. Both divested themselves of their nightwear, and their responses to each other were explosively violent.

Richard was no longer capable of coherent thought. It did not even occur to him that he was being unfaithful to Eliza. All he knew was that the woman sharing his bed was lovely and desirable, and that he wanted her desperately. He also realized that she wanted him just as badly.

Embracing, kissing, and fondling each other, they abandoned all inhibitions, and their mutual desire soared until it became uncontrollable. They were in the grip of emotions too strong to be curbed. They became one and rapidly found release simultaneously. Then, gradually, their desire ebbed, and they became more calm.

To Richard, the most remarkable aspect of this strange, unexpected union was that it seemed to have started so naturally. Actually, Celeste knew better and had furtively initiated the encounter, slowly, gently, while Richard slept, but she did not reveal the truth in any way.

Still entwined in a tight embrace with the luscious creature who had just become his mistress, Richard was horrified. He could not in all honesty tell her that his lovemaking had been inadvertent and apologize, explaining that he hadn't meant it. At the same time, he felt compelled to make her understand that he'd given his heart to Eliza, and that it belonged to no one else. He not only didn't know what to say, but he had no idea how to even begin.

Clinging to him and wriggling ecstatically, Lady Celeste Murette knew her hunch had been right. She had obtained greater gratification from this man than from anyone else. Now her future was far clearer than it had been. If the opportunity presented itself, she would become Lady Dunstable in the wink of an eye. As a realist, however, she knew she might not get that chance, so she had another string to her bow—if she failed with Richard, she would simply switch her affections and welcome a marriage to his father-in-law, the wealthy Adam Burrows.

One thing was certain—she was never again going to live as precariously as she had done for so many years. She had discovered, to her astonishment, that she actually enjoyed the open life that people lived in the New World. Never again would she become embroiled in the machinations that had been her lot in Europe.

She knew she still had something important to learn about Richard, however. She had to find out whether he had been instrumental in winning freedom for Lady Dawn Shepherd from her captors in Virginia. But she no longer worried about that. Now that they had become intimate, Richard would begin to confide in her—she would see to that. It was just a matter of time before she learned the full extent of the role that he had played, if any, in the affair involving Lady Dawn.

Richard forced himself to speak. "If I apologize to you," he said hoarsely, "I'll be a cad. But if I don't, I'll be even worse."

Celeste's husky laugh filled the cabin as she pressed closer to him.

She was making his task no easier; perhaps she didn't understand what he was trying to tell her.

"I'm a married man," Richard said, "though I'll grant you I haven't acted like it."

She rested her head on his shoulder and caressed him gently. "I'm aware of your marriage," she replied. "I knew it last night when we went to bed, and I didn't forget it this morning. But it hasn't seemed to make much difference to either of us, has it? I don't know when I've obtained such complete satisfaction, and if you're honest, you'll admit the same."

She was forcing him to face the issue squarely. "My relations with my wife are no more intense than those we have just enjoyed," he admitted, "but they're different."

Celeste wisely chose not to press the matter. "I'm content, and I know you must be, too. That's quite good enough for me." She refrained from saying that he played a major role in her long-range plans.

At the risk of becoming a boor, Richard knew he had to make his feelings perfectly clear to Celeste. "You and I," he said, "have a mysterious power over each other. I don't pretend to understand it, but I know it exists. After the way that we've reacted, I'd be stupid to deny it." He took a deep breath and swallowed hard. "All the same," he said, "I love Eliza."

Celeste had to admire his courage. It was a rare man who could make such an admission under the circumstances in which he found himself. "Of course you do," she murmured, "but you and I are here on this ship now, and she's far away in New Amsterdam. Perhaps," she added with a touch of light malice, "she's enjoying herself in the same way with Peter Stuyvesant."

"I think not," Richard said flatly.

Celeste again refrained from pursuing the issue. In due time, after she confided some of Stuyvesant's habits to him, he would be less certain of his wife's fidelity—but there would be ample time for that. She had learned that in all matters dealing with the relations of a man and his wife, it was wise never to rush.

Richard released the young woman, disentangled himself, and sat up in bed. "I won't pretend that I regret what we've done," he said. "I'd be lying if I claimed that I did. But I do know one thing for sure —it's an experience we're not going to repeat."

Again Celeste's husky laugh echoed against the stout bulkhead of the cabin.

In spite of himself he was faintly annoyed. "Perhaps you'll share the joke with me," he said.

"Gladly," she replied, and deliberately nestled close to him again, hauling him down beside her.

Richard tried to edge away.

"Hold still," Celeste commanded. "I'm proving something to you."

He did as he was bid. She caressed him and kissed him. Then, a mocking smile appearing on her face in the half-light of the cabin, she looked up at him. "I dare you in all candor to tell me that you don't enjoy that."

"But you know I do," he replied.

"Of course," she murmured. "That's the whole point I'm trying to make. You and I can swear that we shall never make love again and that both of us are going to honor your marriage, but we won't keep our word. We aren't strong enough to keep it. We want each other far too much for that."

With slow, calculated movements, she pressed against him again and deliberately aroused him.

In spite of himself, Richard responded and soon even took the initiative. The pace of their lovemaking became frenzied, and following the pattern they had established previously, they found release together once again.

Both were forced to rest for a time. Celeste was the first to regain her voice. "You see what I mean, don't you, my dear?"

Richard had no idea that she was using every trick at her command to bind him to her, that she was utilizing her vastly greater knowledge and experience to confuse him.

As much as he hated himself for being weak, he had to admit that Celeste was extremely desirable. He loved Eliza and would have been willing to swear that he wanted her exclusively, but he was powerless to avert his craving for this beautiful, crafty, and knowledgeable woman.

Celeste was well satisfied with her efforts. She had no doubt that she would in time gain complete control over Richard, as she had over so many other men in the past. She was ready to use him to achieve the happiness she craved, even if she had to be ruthless in her treatment of his wife.

Nearly every citizen of New Haven was at the docks when the *Wayfarer* entered the town's harbor under reduced sail. Richard Dunstable stood on the quarterdeck and waved his hat.

That gesture was all the townspeople needed. Paying scant attention to the extremely attractive brunette who stood beside him, they cheered so loudly that seagulls landing on the brig's rigging abruptly took to the air again, their wings flapping wildly.

A fife and drum corps, on hand for the occasion, struck up a lively tune. The citizens of New Haven were steadily working themselves into a frenzy of excitement. Screaming, shouting, and waving, they surged onto the wharf, and Adam Burrows was required to call on his warehouse and dock workers to push the crowd back so the *Wayfarer* could tie up without anyone being injured.

Mimi and Ezekiel Clayton were present, of course, and Mimi, more than anyone else in the throng, was aware of Lady Celeste Murette's presence. Mimi was almost certain that Celeste and Richard had become lovers. She read it in the reposed expression of satisfaction on the other woman's face, and she sensed it in the proprietary way that Celeste reached out to touch Richard's arm.

Never one to underestimate a dangerous woman, Mimi wondered whether she should write a letter to Eliza and urge her to come home. Certainly her marriage was severely threatened. She took hold of Ezekiel's arm and stretched herself up to get a better look at Lady Celeste.

Richard caught sight of the couple and waved, but as he came ashore, the crowd surged forward again and demanded a speech.

"You'd better give them what they want, lad," Adam Burrows shouted. "It's the only way they'll be satisfied and let you go."

Richard nodded and mounted a tea box on the dock. Speaking succinctly, he related how he had presented an ultimatum to Governor Stuyvesant. "Obviously," he concluded, smiling broadly, "the director-general of New Netherland capitulated and the *Wayfarer* is here to prove it. I take great pleasure in turning the ship over to her rightful master." He leaned over and shook hands with Captain Sharp, who stood directly below him.

The crowd went wild, and Richard was hoisted onto brawny shoulders. The fife and drum corps struck up another tune, and an impromptu parade got under way. With a pack of children and dogs in the lead, the entire assemblage moved toward the green in the center of town. Lady Celeste took

Adam Burrows's arm, making the gesture seem natural and easy as they fell in with the throng.

"Why is everyone so excited?" Celeste wanted to know. "Why the wild celebration?"

Adam grinned at her. "Because we've beaten Peter Stuyvesant at his own game," he said. "You need to have lived in New Haven for a spell to understand how folks hereabouts feel about Stuyvesant. The festivities pretty much tell you the whole story."

Celeste's first reaction was that she would write to Stuyvesant and tell him in detail about the depths of unpopularity to which he had sunk in New Haven. On second thought, however, she decided to refrain from mentioning the matter to him. Relations between New Haven and New Netherland were tenuous at best, and she knew that Cardinal Mazarin didn't want them to become so bad that a war might break out between the British and the Dutch colonies. The mood of New Haven was definitely belligerent. She knew Stuyvesant well enough to realize that he would feel challenged if he heard the story of the *Wayfarer*'s reception. She sensed that the two colonies were drifting toward hostilities, and she didn't want to play an active part in the outbreak of war.

On reaching the green, Richard's bearers returned him to the ground, and seeing Adam Burrows beckoning to him urgently, Richard made his way to his side. He was conscious of the fact that Lady Celeste Murette stood beside his father-in-law and was smiling up at him, but he tried to block her from his vision and his mind.

"I think you should try to get away from this mob," Adam said. "You're wanted—badly wanted—at my house."

Richard looked at him in surprise.

"An hour or so ago," Adam Burrows explained, "just before I left for the dock, a most important visitor arrived at my house looking for you. No doubt you remember Sa-ro-an-wen, the sachem of the Mohegan."

"Of course," Richard replied. "I'd hardly be likely to forget him." The sachem, or chief, of the Mohegan had signed a treaty of friendship with Richard the previous year after Richard had saved Ilia-awi, the daughter of Sa-ro-an-wen, from an attacking bear and, most certainly, an untimely death. The treaty was responsible for the peace that the English colony still enjoyed. Richard was mindful of the fact that it was the only English colony in all of New England not having trouble with Indian attacks.

"I told the servants to feed him well," Adam said, "and I asked him to be patient until you could come to him, but I don't think you want to keep him waiting too much longer."

"I'll go to him right now," Richard replied.

Lady Celeste was curious. "I've never seen a sachem from an Indian tribe," she said. "May I come, too?"

"By all means," Adam replied fondly, and with her still holding his arm, he led the way to his house. There, seated cross-legged on the dining room floor, in front of the fire, Sa-ro-an-wen was enjoying the last morsels of a mammoth repast. Beef and chicken bones were scattered around him on the hearth, as were the remains of dishes that he had not found to his liking. He promptly wiped his mouth with the back of one hand, which he then raised in stiff salute as he climbed to his feet.

Richard returned the salutation solemnly.

Lady Celeste was fascinated by the sight of the Mohegan sachem. Naked to the waist and clad only in a breechcloth and moccasins, his face and torso brown and leathery, the chief cut a fearsome figure. On his head was a bonnet that contained a number of wild turkey feathers, the symbol of his rank. He spoke at length in his own tongue, and Richard replied in the same language.

"They're exchanging greetings," Adam explained to Lady Celeste. "They go through a formal rigmarole that lasts for some time."

His prediction proved accurate. The sachem and Richard seemed to vie with each other in their exchange of long-winded expressions.

Then, to the woman's amazement, the Indian and Richard lowered themselves to the floor in front of the hearth and, sitting cross-legged, fell into an earnest discussion. Adam and the young woman were ignored, so he motioned to Lady Celeste to accompany him as he tiptoed out of the room.

"Whatever the Mohegan's reason for coming here," he said, "he's explaining it now, and we have no proper place there."

"I had no idea that Richard spoke the language of the native barbarians," she said.

"He has a natural ability to speak languages," Adam replied, "and I'm grateful that he does. So far it has stood us in very good stead."

Richard and Sa-ro-an-wen conversed in low tones at length, and when they rose to their feet at last, Richard led the Indian to the kitchen. There, to the astonishment and indignation of Mistress Miller, Adam Burrows's gray-haired housekeeper-cook, he plied the sachem with gifts of food, slicing off a choice hunk of roast and giving him half of a freshly baked apple-and-raisin pie. Then, adding insult to injury, he presented the Indian with the sharp knife he had used to cut the pie.

Mistress Miller started to protest heatedly, but Adam Burrows silenced her. Richard and the sachem now exchanged prolonged farewells. They spoke interminably, and Lady Celeste became restless. Adam, however, smiled imperturbably, as though enjoying the experience. At last the Mohegan departed.

"Land sakes alive," Mistress Miller fumed. "You're too much, Master Richard. Not only did you give that benighted savage half of the dinner that I cooked for you and the colonel, but you gave him one of my good knives, cool as you please."

Richard laughed. "Sorry, Mistress Miller, but that's Indian hospitality, and he'd have been insulted if I hadn't done what was expected of me. I promise you I'll bring you another knife exactly like the one I gave to Sa-ro-an-wen. We have a number of them in our warehouse."

The housekeeper sniffed, but was mollified. "Dinner is ready," she said. "I advise you to eat it at once before someone else wanders in off the road and you give the rest away."

Richard chuckled as he accompanied Adam and Lady Celeste to the dining room table. There, as they began to eat, he grew somber as he related what he had learned in his talk with the Mohegan chief.

"Sa-ro-an-wen is very badly disturbed," he said. "He's afraid that the days of his treaty with us are numbered, and he will be forced to break what he and his people have regarded as a sacred agreement."

The roast was delicious, but Adam Burrows had no appetite for it. "Why should that happen?" he demanded.

"The sachems of the Niantic and Narragansett tribes recently paid a visit to the land of the Mohegan," Richard said. "There they explained that all of the Indian nations of New England are banding together to drive us—the English colonists—into the sea."

Adam Burrows shook his head. Lady Celeste was incredulous. Certainly she recognized the source of the anti-English drive, but she was astonished by its daring and depth.

"The Mohegan were offered considerable inducements to join in the confederation," Richard said. "To be specific, they were promised several hundred blankets and all the metal cooking containers that they're able to use. They were promised the usual gewgaws—mirrors, beads, and the like." He paused and added significantly, "They were also promised firearms. Enough so that every brave in the tribe would have his own musket and ample supplies of ammunition for it."

Adam Burrows was thunderstruck. "How can that be?" he demanded.

"It's apparent," Richard said, "that the offer is being made by a European power. The Indians aren't banding together of their own volition. Some nation is sufficiently eager to be rid of us and our like that they're being extremely generous in their offers to the Indians."

"It has to be Stuyvesant, then. I can't believe that the French would be stupid enough to offer firearms to Indian braves," Adam muttered.

"I quite agree with you," Richard said. "I quizzed Sa-ro-an-wen on that very point. He assured me that the Ottawa, the Huron, and the Micmac are receiving no supplies and no arms of any kind. Inasmuch as they are the principal allies of New France, it's reasonably certain that the French are not responsible for this plot." Richard shrugged. "In view of the fact that we found muskets of Dutch manufacture in the hands of tribe after tribe, I'd say the evidence points overwhelmingly toward the Dutch as the culprits."

Adam cut a slice of meat and ate it in silence as he assimilated the information. "I can't possibly see officials of the Dutch West Indies Company in Holland being responsible for all of this," he said.

"They're too remote from the scene, and they wouldn't know one Indian nation from another. That leads to the inescapable conclusion that the culprit must be Peter Stuyvesant himself."

"You're quite right," Richard said grimly. "It has to be Stuyvesant."

He made up his mind to send off a letter to Eliza at once, apprising her of the situation and urging her to redouble her efforts to pin down the hidden activities of the director-general of New Netherland.

"He deserves," Adam said bitterly, "to be horsewhipped or shot. He's been in the New World long enough to be aware of the dangers of supplying Indians with firearms. I know of no excuse for this behavior."

"There *is* no excuse," Richard replied firmly.

Listening to the two men as they discussed the problem freely, Lady Celeste Murette was privately horrified. In his eagerness to be rid of the English settlements and to make Holland the supreme power south of New France, Peter Stuyvesant had gone too far. Obviously he was incurring the undying enmity of the most influential men of New Haven. She knew what would be decided next.

Adam Burrows did not disappoint her. "I shall send a personal letter to each and every militia commander in each and every colony," he said. "We have our differences, but we've got to put them aside now for the common good."

Richard nodded soberly. "There's no question about it," he said. "We've got to band together and prepare for any eventuality."

Lady Celeste couldn't help asking, "Does that mean you'll go to war against the Dutch in New Netherland?"

"I hope our relationship doesn't deteriorate that far," Adam replied, "but unless the Dutch stop sending firearms to the Indian nations—and stop at once—I don't see how a war can be avoided."

"We much prefer not to fight them," Richard explained to the woman. "There are more English than Dutch in New Netherland, and even though the flag of Holland flies from the governor's house, we really think of the New Netherland colony as being English. However, we don't have too much choice. The entire frontier will catch fire unless we take vigorous steps to prevent the outbreak of this blaze that can consume all of us."

He turned back to his father-in-law. "With your permission, sir, I'll go at once to the land of the Mohegan, and I'll address their council. I know that Sa-ro-an-wen half expects us to match the Dutch offer."

"Under no circumstances," his father-in-law replied firmly, "will we provide the Mohegan braves with firearms! No matter what may happen! Even if they break the treaty and we find ourselves at war with them!"

"All I can do," Richard said, "is to try to reason with them, which won't be easy; but once they understand that we're not going to take part in a competition for their favors, I believe—at least I hope—that they'll be sensible."

Colonel Burrows was so eager to begin planning his grand strategy and to get in touch with the militia commanders of the various colonies that immediately after supper he asked Richard to escort Lady Celeste to her home. "I'm sorry," Adam apologized to her, "but we face a critical situation, and I must deal with it accordingly."

Celeste took Richard's arm as they made their way down the elm-lined street. "Do you really think that Peter Stuyvesant is providing the natives with arms?" she wanted to know.

Richard tried to put the effect of her physical

proximity out of his mind. "There's no doubt of it," he said. "As you told me, he's cursed with a tremendous ego. His vanity is so great that he somehow convinces himself that he can do no wrong. Well, in this case, he's not only hurting the English colonies, but he's also doing irreparable damage to his own Dutch compatriots."

She was forced to agree with his assessment. When they reached her house, she paused on the threshold and smiled up at him. "Won't you come in for a glass of brandy?" she asked with a sly look.

He shook his head firmly. "I'm not going to give in to the temptation of a drink," he told her, "because I lack the strength to resist an even greater temptation once you and I are alone behind the closed door of your house."

She was tempted to test her power over him, but decided it was better not to push. Knowing men, she realized that Richard was virile and vigorous, and that in time his memories of the intimacy they had enjoyed would grow in his mind until they became irresistible. It was far better that she wait and let him come to her voluntarily. So she made no issue of the matter and allowed him to go on his way. But before he departed, she reached up and gave him a lingering, passionate kiss that she felt certain would jar him.

Alone behind the closed, barred door of her house, she went to her writing desk, where she took out a bottle of ink, a quill pen, and a large sheet of paper. Then, breaking her self-imposed rule that forbade her to interfere with matters of state that were not her direct assignment or concern, she wrote a long, earnest, and blunt letter to Peter Stuyvesant. He was wrong, she declared, to be giving arms to the Indians, and the policy was certain to have an effect far different from that which he intended. He would drive the English colonies into banding together and presenting a united front against their foes. *You are completely misguided,* she wrote to him. *Reverse your policies before it's too late.*

Once again she faced the difficulty of arranging to have a letter sent to New Amsterdam without anyone in New Haven knowing she had written it. This constituted a problem that she was incapable of solving immediately, so she was obliged to put the finished, sealed letter aside and await an opportunity to have it safely sent on to Peter Stuyvesant.

In the meantime, she was well satisfied with the progress being made in her private plans. The impending departure of Richard Dunstable for the land of the Mohegan would be followed by a quick, urgent tour of the other New England colonies, so he would be absent from New Haven for quite some time. That meant she would be able to concentrate completely on Adam Burrows, and she was confident that she could have him proposing marriage at any time she wished. So her own future seemed secure and comfortable, and that was, as always, her principal consideration.

Peter Stuyvesant prided himself on ruling New Amsterdam with an iron hand, and he seldom missed an opportunity to flaunt his power or to remind the populace of his beneficence. Consequently, the annual harvest fair in New Amsterdam was an occasion of great pomp, and everyone was expected to lay down his work for the day.

The festivities traditionally began with a full-scale military review that the entire town attended. Wild turkeys and sides of oxen and venison were to be roasted, and there would be free food for all and an unlimited supply of ale. The highlight of the day, of course, was the speech by the director-general of the colony, and after dark, fireworks would end the celebration.

Two days before the event, Peter Stuyvesant surprised Eliza Dunstable when he said, "You'll make your first public appearance with me during the coming festival."

She looked at him, but made no comment.

"It's an informal occasion, and the entire colony will attend the festivities," he said. "So I'll expect you to accompany me, share the outdoor meal with me, and, of course, listen to my address."

"Is there any particular reason I'm to be on display?" Eliza wanted to know.

Stuyvesant grinned at her. "A great many people in town are whispering about us," he said. "It's high time we gave the entire population something to talk about openly."

What small fragment that was left of her reputation would be shredded, but Eliza was in no position to object. She reminded herself of the confidential, hastily written letter she had received from Richard, explaining the military situation and urging her to devote every effort to proving that Stuyvesant was responsible for arming the Indian nations. Therefore, she felt she had to placate the governor, and that meant pandering to his wishes and exhibiting herself in public as his mistress.

She decided, after some hesitation, to play the role to the hilt. She wore a figure-hugging gown of pale silk, and allowing her wheat-colored hair to fall freely below her shoulders, she used far more cosmetics than was her custom. Looking at herself in the mirror of the room she used in the governor's home, she told herself wryly that any stranger who happened to see her would be convinced she was a fallen woman.

The feast day dawned bright and clear, and the residents of New Amsterdam were awakened by the booming of cannon on a Dutch warship anchored in the East River. By the time Eliza descended the stairs and joined Peter Stuyvesant in the parlor, the streets were crowded and the atmosphere was already festive.

Stuyvesant looked Eliza up and down appreciatively. "You look stunning," he told her. "Anyone who sees you will certainly remember you."

As she smiled and bowed her head in thanks for the compliment, she couldn't help wondering anew if there were some hidden motive causing him to put her on display. She promised herself to keep her eyes and ears open.

Eliza rode in an open carriage beside Stuyvesant as they traveled the short distance to the fortress, where the festivities were being held. She wanted to shrink from view when scores of people, Dutch and English residents alike, gaped at her. She remained in the carriage while Stuyvesant mounted a horse for the military review, and then he subjected her to further embarrassment by presenting her with a large bouquet of tulips that the children of New Amsterdam gave to him.

Eliza left the carriage to nibble turkey and to sip a glass of pungent claret. This experience proved the most trying of all for her, because she no longer felt the protection of the carriage and was thrust into direct contact with the crowd.

The people of New Amsterdam mingled freely, and there were no restraints on anyone who wished to approach the governor and his companion. As a result, dozens of people came up to Eliza and spoke to her. She soon realized that some were motivated by curiosity, while others were interested in ingratiating themselves with her. What she had not anticipated was the reaction of New Amsterdam's English-born citizens. Many of them glared at her with unconcealed contempt, and it was obvious that they thought of her as an opportunistic harlot who had become Stuyvesant's mistress for purposes of self-aggrandizement.

A shock awaited her when she caught sight of Mollie and Angus MacNeill in the throng. She was about to call a friendy greeting to them, but something cold and removed in their manner warned her off, so she remained silent.

Mollie looked at her and then through her, not deigning to recognize her.

Angus, not as closely connected to Richard as was Mollie, was less capable of snubbing Eliza directly, so he did the next best thing and avoided looking at her. He simply pretended she did not exist. Eliza wanted to shout that she was true to her husband, that she had not become Peter Stuyvesant's mistress, but it was impossible. Her lips were sealed, and she had to bear the consequences of her association with Stuyvesant.

The final blow was an open snub that she received from Roaring Wolf when the Pequot passed within arm's length of her in the throng. He held his head high with his gaze averted. His attitude made it clear that he had little use for this woman who he believed was dishonoring his friend and mentor.

Eliza knew that she had done nothing wrong, that on the contrary, her behavior was actually admirable; but the reactions of people such as the MacNeills and Roaring Wolf were so strong that she couldn't help feeling cheap and ashamed of herself.

It was almost as bad, she reflected, as it would be if she really were Peter Stuyvesant's mistress. Well, she had been branded now for the whole community to see, and henceforth she would be universally recognized as the governor's woman, so there was no escape.

She was seated with a small group of officials for Stuyvesant's mercifully brief address. While he spoke, her mind wandered, and then suddenly she stiffened. Standing directly behind the seated officials were a cluster of Indians. Having spent her entire life on the frontier, Eliza learned all she needed to know about them at a glance: They were representatives of a half-dozen or more New England tribes that lived between New Amsterdam and Massachusetts Bay, including the Wappinger, the Niantic from Connecticut, and the Narragansett from Rhode Island. No explanation was offered for their presence.

After Stuyvesant delivered his speech, he escorted Eliza to the open carriage, and they rode back to the governor's house, where their public appearance ended.

But her duties for the day were not yet over. A buffet had been set up in the dining room. Among the guests were representatives of the Indian tribes. All of them, Eliza noted, were either sachems or principal-medicine men. They tended to treat her with the same casual disregard they showed all women, although they demonstrated a surface politeness because of her supposed relationship with the governor. She decided to use this outstanding opportunity to probe for information, and addressed the braves in their own tongues. They were so astonished to find this attractive and fashionable white woman speaking their language that their attitude toward her changed abruptly and they became much friendlier.

Eliza knew that she had to take her time in approaching them. She followed the ancient custom of inquiring at length after the health of their relatives, even their distant kinsmen. At last she felt that sufficient preliminaries had been observed for her to get to the point. "How does it happen that you have come to New Amsterdam for this white man's feast?" she inquired.

The sachems and medicine men exchanged quiet,

almost surreptitious glances, and there was a long silence.

Finally the chief of the Niantic replied. "The sachems," he declared solemnly, "are the brothers of the leader of the Dutch."

Eliza knew how the minds of Indians worked, and felt that perhaps this was a promising lead. She pretended to look surprised.

"Why are you brothers of the Dutch?" she asked innocently.

Again there was a long silence, and the sachem of the Narragansett, a middle-aged man whose expression indicated that he was both cunning and crafty, called a sudden halt. "Why is the sky filled with birds one day when the next day there is none?" he demanded. "Why is game plentiful in the forests, and then it disappears, bringing a time of famine? Why is it that a warrior who is known for his courage sometimes crumbles in fear before he goes into battle against his nation's enemies?"

His questions succeeded, as Eliza well knew, in digressing markedly from the information that she was trying to unearth. She recognized the futility of pressing the subject, however. No one could be more evasive than an Indian who was reluctant to reveal information. A door had been slammed in her face, and her investigation necessarily came to an abrupt end.

Eliza had felt certain that in return for the loss of her good name, she would acquire solid information that would be of help in solving the mystery to which she had been assigned, but she realized now that her expectations had been naive, almost childish. Her reputation was ruined, and all she had learned was that several prominent New England tribes had become friends with the Dutch. Well, that was better than nothing, she supposed.

Later that evening she wrote to Richard, relating

the few facts she had garnered. When she had finished, she reread the letter and sighed. It was no use. Her word alone simply wasn't good enough. She needed hard evidence, but where could she get it?

Weary after her long day, she was about to retire when a quiet tap sounded at her door. She opened it, and was surprised to see Peter Stuyvesant standing on the threshold.

"I wanted to thank you," he said, "for all of your help today. You were very gracious, and I'm more appreciative than you realize."

"I'm glad Your Excellency is pleased," she replied, again wondering why it had been so important for her to dissemble in public.

He smiled at her roguishly. "I know what's going through your mind," he said. "You're wondering why I chose to make our alleged affair public on this particular occasion."

He was so shrewd that his thinking was sometimes uncanny. "I was wondering something of the sort," Eliza admitted.

Stuyvesant chuckled aloud and pointed to his silver-studded wooden leg. "The Indians who were here today," he said, "are more impressed by my peg leg than by anything else. The mere sight of it convinces them that I am an invincible warrior. By the same token, they look at someone as lovely as you, who is supposedly my mistress, and my reputation rises still higher in their esteem. I realize that what I am telling you sounds crude, but they are primitive barbarians, and we must deal with them accordingly."

At last Eliza understood, and she said, "Thank you for confiding in me, Peter. I've actually wondered all day why I was being required to put on such an elaborate masquerade."

His smile vanished and his gaze was steady as he said, "I wish it weren't a masquerade."

She knew that serious trouble was imminent.

"I am being very patient," he told her, "far more than is my custom. I trust you intend to reward me soon."

She seized the slight loophole that he offered her.

"It will be soon, Peter," she said a trifle breathlessly. "Very soon. Just give me enough time to get my bearings."

He reached for her hand and held it firmly in his grasp. "I'm giving you ample time," he said.

"Indeed you are, and I'm grateful to you." She reached up and kissed him lightly on the cheek.

The gesture seemed to satisfy him, and he released his grip on her hand. A moment later she was alone.

Breathing a sigh of relief, Eliza closed the door behind him and took the precaution of bolting it. She preferred to take no chances in case he changed his mind and returned.

It occurred to the woman, forcefully, that she was walking on the thinnest of ice. All at once Governor Stuyvesant's patience would wear out, and then she would be expected to live up to the promise that her public stance so loudly and blatantly proclaimed.

Well, she had obtained scraps of information today and had learned the identity of some of the Indian nations that had become the allies of Holland. This was inadequate, but at least it was a beginning.

Perhaps, if her luck held, she would be able to complete her mission and return unscathed to her husband waiting in New Haven. That, at least, was her devout wish, and she vowed to redouble her efforts to unearth the secrets that New Haven and the other English colonies so badly needed in order to protect themselves from the Dutch and Indian threat.

Richard headed north through the trackless wilderness that lay between New Haven and the land of the Mohegan. As he traveled, a sense of tranquility gradually crept over him. This experience, he knew, was his reason for settling in the New World rather than carrying on the struggle abroad for the restoration of Charles II to the throne of England. The wilderness was all-encompassing. For those who knew and understood it, it provided all things—food and shelter, warm clothing, and above all, a sense of security.

Richard well knew that few people agreed with him. The wilderness was dangerous to them, and they felt insecure, unsafe in it. But he had grown to manhood preparing for his future role as a hereditary king's forester and felt completely at ease in these surroundings. The silence was welcome, and the truth of the matter was that he did not feel alone. He saw signs of animal life everywhere. Here were the tracks of a bear, there the distinctive deep hoofprints that told him a deer had passed by only hours earlier. He was conscious of the chattering of birds in the thick foliage overhead. When he stopped to take water from an icy brook, he knew that no water anywhere else tasted as pure and cold.

His mind cleared in the wilderness, and his tensions and concerns ebbed away. When peace came to the English colonies—real and lasting peace—this is where he truly wanted to live. He would build a spacious cabin for Eliza and himself with his own hands, and they would dwell here, far from the complications of a civilization that he secretly despised.

In the deep forest, he had the courage to face himself without subterfuge. He knew that under no circumstances could he surrender again to his sexual desire for Celeste Murette. What had happened between them had been natural and had arisen because of circumstances that were beyond control— at least he had assumed that they were beyond control, and it did not occur to him that Celeste had contrived them. Well, he was a man and had a man's natural physical yearnings, so he was able to excuse himself for what had happened and to feel relatively guiltless.

Now, however, he knew better. If he gave in again and resumed his affair with Celeste, he would be truly unfaithful to Eliza and would deserve to have his marriage to her terminated.

So many other phases of his life became clearer to him in the wilderness, too. He had a natural talent for military leadership, he knew, but he disliked making war. He was doing well in his father-in-law's shipping company, but he also realized he would never be satisfied as a man of business. He sought only the peace and solitude of the forest, the knowledge that he lived close to the earth and that he flourished as a consequence.

His feelings were so sharp, so intense that he felt slightly frightened. What was bothering him? Analyzing his reactions, it occurred to him that he did not know whether Eliza felt as he did. Oh, he had learned that she enjoyed herself well enough in the wilderness, that she liked hunting for game and loved eating and sleeping in the open. But when he suggested staying in the forest for extended periods, she refused, armed with excuses. Whether she cared to give up the so-called benefits of town living for wilderness life was not certain. Eliza was young and beautiful. He certainly couldn't blame her if she felt that she would be wasting her substance in the wilderness.

Fortunately, there was no immediate reason to

make that decision. He had a job to do, and Eliza also had vitally important work to finish before they could look forward to a peaceful existence together. He ruthlessly put his mental meanderings aside.

Richard was aware of the proximity of a Mohegan sentry as he drew nearer to the main village of the tribe, but he caught no glimpse of the sentinel. He heard an owl calling mournfully to its mate and knew that the sentry was sending a signal heralding his arrival. Then drums throbbed, their echoes reverberating through the wilderness and causing the leaves of maples and oaks to tremble slightly.

Suddenly several figures appeared seemingly out of nowhere. Richard was surprised when he recognized Sa-ro-an-wen, who was accompanied by an escort of warriors. The sachem of the Mohegan had done him the unprecedented honor of coming out in person to greet him. They exchanged stiff-armed salutes, clasped each other's forearms in the Indian manner, and then went on, side by side, to the village. All of the tribe was on hand to welcome the visitor. Proud warriors raised their brawny arms in salute, as did the elders and the medicine men of the tribe. The squaws, ordinarily shy and retiring, appeared in great numbers and grinned at him, welcoming him as an old friend. Even the small children, accompanied by numerous dogs, surrounded him as he came through the gates of the village, and Sa-ro-an-wen had difficulty leading him to the hut where he would lodge overnight.

Ilia-awi, the sachem's daughter, was nowhere to be seen, but Richard knew it would be bad manners to inquire as to her whereabouts. At sundown, the Mohegan gathered around a huge cooking pit outside the palisade, and a dozen or more squaws hastened with the final preparations of the meal that would be served in honor of Richard's arrival.

The first course consisted of a stewlike soup.

Squash, beans, and corn—the three principal vegetables of the Indian diet—had been cut up and placed in a cauldron, together with chunks of venison and bear meat and a number of animal bones, and the broth had then simmered for many hours. A number of wild herbs had been added to the mixture, and the aroma that floated over the area was delicious.

Richard was given a place of honor, and sat cross-legged on the ground directly opposite Sa-ro-an-wen.

To his surprise, a special servant had been assigned to him, and he could not help gaping when he recognized Ilia-awi. She was far more attractive, infinitely more mature than she had been when he had saved her life in the wilderness and had won her eternal gratitude. Her blue-black hair hung to her waist and was held in place by a strip of beaded leather that she wore around her forehead. Her young, nubile body was encased in a single garment, a dress of supple animal skin decorated with dyed porcupine quills that had been arranged to form geometric patterns. Her dark, limpid eyes shone when she looked at Richard, and her full lips parted in a silent smile of warm greeting. Her dark skin glowed, and she seemed to come to life in the presence of this white man.

She handed him a bowl of the thick soup, taking care that her hands did not touch his; then she lowered herself to the ground, prostrating herself in obeisance. Richard was embarrassed and wanted to urge her to rise again rapidly, but he was unfamiliar with rituals of the tribe, so he remained silent. To his infinite relief, Ilia-awi soon rose effortlessly and glided away on bare feet.

Before the meal ended she had brought him course after course. She served him a steamed fish with pure, firm white meat that was more delicious than any fish he had ever tasted. Another dish consisted of large dripping chunks of still-smoking venison, served on trenchers of flat bread that had been fashioned from cornmeal and baked on flat rocks.

The final offering consisted of fresh berries, over which maple syrup had been poured. Although Richard had already eaten far more than was his custom, he sensed that Ilia-awi would be insulted if he refused the dessert. After he had eaten, he was relieved to discover that he had been correct; she had picked the berries herself and had prepared the dish with her own hands. When the meal was ended, the women, including Ilia-awi, vanished into the shadows, and the warriors moved forward toward the fires where they could see and be seen.

Sa-ro-an-wen rose and welcomed the visitor with an interminable speech that was so long-winded that Richard had a hard time to keep from smiling. The sachem declared that the visitor was the brother of the Mohegan and would be welcome in their midst for as long as he lived. Their foes were his foes, and they would share their food and lodging with him always.

Richard knew what was expected of him, and he replied in kind, making a very long address in which he extolled the virtues, real and imagined, of the Mohegan. Only when he was afraid that his voice was becoming hoarse did he finally cut short his remarks. The ceremonials having been observed, all warriors departed except the elders, medicine men, and war chiefs who made up the Mohegan council. They moved closer to the visitor, and other warriors took up sentinel duty nearby, guarding the council members with bows and drawn, nocked arrows.

Here was Richard's opportunity to counter the machinations of Peter Stuyvesant, so he promptly did his utmost. The English colonists, he declared, were the natural allies of the Mohegan, and they would be faithful to their alliance for all time. They could not make gifts to the Mohegan of worldly goods like blankets and cooking utensils—and above all, firearms—because they suffered from a lack of these goods themselves. When they acquired enough, he said, they would gladly share their wealth with the Mohegan. In the meantime, they offered their allies something far more precious than worldly goods: unswerving loyalty.

He spoke forcefully, with great vigor, and although he did not consider himself much of an orator, he made a deep impression on his audience, largely because of his utter candor and sincerity. When he was through speaking, the members of the council replied one by one. It soon became evident from the tenor of their remarks that Richard had indeed succeeded in swaying them. They, too, would remain faithful to their alliance with the people of New Haven and would reject the blandishments of the wicked Dutchman who would make them his slaves if he could.

Richard felt infinite relief and told himself that he had succeeded in his first mission—he had persuaded the Mohegan not to abandon their alliance with New Haven. He had accomplished a good night's work, he reflected, and was looking forward to sleeping on the bed of soft pine boughs that had been gathered for him in the lodge he would occupy. The council members escorted him to the lodge, and there he bade them good night and went inside. Without removing his clothes, he wrapped himself in a blanket and stretched out on the bed of pine boughs.

He was just dropping off to sleep when he heard someone creeping into the lodge. The hut had only one opening, and the night was so dark that no light entered, so Richard took no chances and grasped the long-handled bone knife that he had brought with him. Then something soft and silky brushed against his cheek and hand, and he realized it was the long blue-black hair of Ilia-awi. Although surprised that the girl had appeared, he was relieved and slid the knife back into his belt.

Ilia-awi made herself at home, sitting cross-legged on the ground close beside him. "It has been many moons since the daughter of Sa-ro-an-wen has seen him who saved her from death," she whispered. "But she has thought of him many times."

He tried to reply diplomatically. "I have been very busy and have traveled to many places," he said, "but I have thought often of the people of this land, and my thoughts have returned most often to Ilia-awi."

A tremulous sigh escaped the girl's lips.

Richard silently cursed himself for his shortsightedness. The daughter of the sachem was romantically inclined, and that created a terrible, immediate dilemma for him. Under no circumstances could he engage in an affair with her now, any more than he could have when they first met. His relationship with Celeste Murette was disgraceful enough; nothing would excuse an affair with Ilia-awi.

On the other hand, if he rejected her again, she well might feel doubly insulted. If her father and other leaders of the nation shared her disgrace, that could mean the end of the treaty he had so fortunately been able to preserve tonight.

As he groped for something appropriate to say, Ilia-awi addressed him again. "The gods who protect the Mohegan," she said, "brought Ri-chard to this place and made it possible for him to save the life of Ilia-awi from a wild beast." She pronounced his name as though it were two words. "Now they have sent Ri-chard to me again. I heed their wishes, and I give myself to him freely." She leaned toward him, and in the half-light he felt the heat of her breath on his face and saw the glow of her eyes.

His honor demanded that he reject the lovesick girl, regardless of the consequences. "The gods who watch over the Mohegan also protect me," he said, "and if I were to take Ilia-awi now, they would be very angry. Surely they would demand that I forfeit my life."

She was stunned and bewildered and could only stare at him.

"It was the gods who led me to Ilia-awi when her life was threatened," he declared, "and it was they who gave me the skill and the presence of mind to slay the beast who threatened her. If I were to claim her body as my reward, I would be cheapening the gesture that the gods permitted me to perform on their behalf. The will of the gods does not change: It is the same this night as it was many moons ago."

He was speaking gibberish, he knew, but he hoped desperately to make some sort of impression on the girl. He had used the same excuse months ago when the sachem first offered Ilia-awi to Richard as a reward for his bravery.

He succeeded far better than he realized. The Mohegan were superstitious to an extent beyond compare, and the mere suggestion that the gods might become angry filled Ilia-awi with terror. "Would they also be angry with the daughter of Sa-ro-an-wen?" she wanted to know.

Richard shrugged. "It is not my place to speak for the gods or to pretend that I know what is in their minds," he said. "I know only that what was right is still right."

In spite of herself, she listened to him, and his words impressed her.

"Ilia-awi and Richard come from different

worlds," he said. "Their ways are not similar, their thoughts are not similar. If Ilia-awi and Richard become closest friends, lovers, would they follow the ways of the Mohegan, or would they leave the wilderness and follow the ways of the white man?" He paused, then added forcefully, but gently, "No, only unhappiness would come of such a union. That is why the gods would be angry. They would feel that Richard and Ilia-awi were mocking them."

The girl could only blink at him. "Ilia-awi and Richard," he went on, meaning every word he said, "will be friends always, for all time, but they will not become lovers. It is right for Ilia-awi to marry a warrior of her own people and to bring sons into the world who will be courageous braves, braves who will carry on the traditions of the Mohegan. Then the gods will be satisfied."

"What will become of Ri-chard?" she asked meekly.

He thought it wise not to tell her that he was already married. "The gods," he replied with as much feigned regret as he could muster, "will find a wife for Richard among his own people." There, that was as close as he could come to the absolute truth. She would have to accept it or reject it, and what would happen to the treaty was anybody's guess.

For a long, tense moment, Ilia-awi stared into space. Then she lowered her head and crossed her hands over her breasts. "Ri-chard," she said, "speaks words of wisdom. It is right that he and Ilia-awi do the will of the gods. There are warriors who call for Ilia-awi to become their squaw. She will ask the gods to join her in making her choice." She rose silently, effortlessly, and vanished from the lodge as quickly as she had come.

Richard discovered that he was perspiring heavily and felt weak. At least his honesty had preserved the treaty that meant so much to the people of New

Haven, and he had not been forced to cheat on Eliza. He was thankful that the sachem's daughter was willing to believe his excuse.

The next morning he departed from the village of the Mohegan with all the inhabitants seeing him off. A dozen young, husky warriors provided him with an escort to the border of their land. The treaty was safe, and now he could concentrate on the equally important task of persuading the colonies of New England to unite in the face of common danger.

The gilt double doors of Cardinal Mazarin's office were closed. Customarily they were open all day, and the great and near-great of France and the rest of Europe poured in and out, receiving instructions, taking orders, and working indefatigably for the greater glory of France.

This morning, however, it was rumored that the cardinal had received a communication from the New World and had promptly locked himself in. He was not to be disturbed.

No one quite knew the torment that Mazarin was suffering. He had, indeed, received a letter from the New World, from Lady Celeste Murette, to be precise. The news she had sent him was deeply disturbing. She had confirmed that Lady Dawn was alive and well, married and comfortably settled in New Haven. How she had arrived there after escaping from Mazarin's agents in Virginia was left totally unexplained.

In a sense details were irrelevant. They were important only if Richard Dunstable had participated in her rescue and had brought her to New Haven, where he was working for Lady Dawn's father-in-law, Thomas Clayton. The coincidence struck the cardinal as being too close for comfort. He strongly suspected that Richard had had a hand in the rescue of the young noblewoman.

If so, he was totally untrustworthy, and both he and his wife would have to be eliminated immediately.

But their fate was secondary to the fate of Lady Dawn herself. She undoubtedly knew of Mazarin's schemes and network of agents in the English colonies. She could not help but know of them, yet she had survived and had escaped from the net that he had cast for her.

As a man of God, Mazarin was opposed to wanton violence and shrank from ordering Lady Dawn killed. As the first minister of France, however, he knew it was essential that the elaborate organization he had built in the English colonies be kept secret so it could continue to function.

Consequently he had no choice. He pondered the problem at great length behind the closed office door, and decided finally to give the task of getting rid of the woman to her fellow English noblewoman, Lady Celeste Murette.

Celeste had never before been ordered to act as an executioner, but Mazarin knew her well enough to feel that she would not shrink from the task. She was remarkably resourceful and courageous, and he had full confidence in her abilities as well as in her willingness to follow orders, no matter how distasteful they might be. And she was the natural choice. She, too, was living in New Haven, and undoubtedly would find some way to murder Lady Dawn without bringing suspicion on her own head.

Once he had made up his mind, Cardinal Mazarin acted swiftly. He wrote a brief communication in which he gave his instructions in no uncertain terms to Celeste. Then he sealed the letter and sent it on its way to Laroche in the Dutch colony of

New Netherland, instructing him to forward it at once to Celeste in New Haven.

His immediate problem solved, Mazarin opened his door, and the visitors who crowded the anteroom were admitted, one at a time. The state business of France was resumed, and all was normal.

In the New World, no one yet realized that Mimi Clayton's death warrant had been signed. In New Amsterdam, Eliza Dunstable was still searching for evidence to connect Governor Peter Stuyvesant directly with the sale of firearms to the Indian tribes of New England. Her repeated failures would have discouraged someone less stubborn, but Eliza refused to admit defeat.

One warm afternoon shortly after the harvest festival, however, she decided to relax and do nothing. She was tired of the strain of her work, tired of posing as Stuyvesant's mistress. She had acted as his hostess at a dinner for several officials of the Dutch West Indies Company, and now, later in the afternoon, she hoped that her day's work was ended.

The Dutch officials had returned to their local office, and to the best of her knowledge, Stuyvesant was in his study. Certainly she had no intention of finding out.

She wandered out to the garden, where a soft seat breeze blew in from the harbor, and she relished the warmth of the sun on her bare arms. How she missed New Haven! She couldn't allow herself to think of such things, however. She meandered up a gravel path in the garden, admiring the last few flowers of the season. She disliked Stuyvesant immensely, but had to admit that his attempts to beautify New Amsterdam with thousands of tulips and rose bushes were paying handsome dividends. The town was infinitely more attractive than before.

Absorbed in the beauty of the flowers, she paid

scant attention to her surroundings and suddenly stopped short when she heard voices directly ahead. Stuyvesant was speaking with a visitor in his study. Afraid she might be accused of eavesdropping, which had not been her intention, Eliza stood very quietly.

"Hear the words that I speak, O Ni-ni-gret." Stuyvesant was speaking the language of the Mohegan brokenly. Most tribes in New England communicated in that tongue, and Stuyvesant apparently had learned just enough to be able to make himself understood.

Eliza was interested in spite of herself. Ni-ni-gret, she knew, was the sachem of the Niantic tribe, and she wondered why an Indian nation that lived so far to the east, beyond New Haven Colony, should have business with the governor of the Dutch colony.

"We have been friends for a long time," Stuyvesant went on.

"It is true," the leader of the small, normally peaceful nation declared, "that the Dutch have been the friends of my people in the past. But that friendship is now being tested."

"Put us to the test," Stuyvesant said emphatically, "and then judge for yourself whether we are your friends or enemies."

"It is not hard for our warriors to judge," Ni-ni-gret replied. "The English colonists take more and more land. They take our hunting grounds. We need two hundred firesticks in order to drive them off our lands and into the sea. Will our brother, the leader of the Dutch, give us these firesticks and the small arrows made of lead that they shoot?"

Eliza held her breath.

Stuyvesant did not hesitate. "I have made gifts of one hundred firesticks to you in the past as a token of our friendship," he said. "Now I will obtain two hundred more."

Eliza's blood ran cold. Here was the information she had been seeking.

"The Niantic," Ni-ni-gret said, "are a poor people. They cannot pay with furs for these firesticks."

Peter Stuyvesant's chuckle floated out into the yard. "That," he said grandly, "is of no consequence. You will repay us amply—many times over —when you drive the English settlers into the sea."

Eliza had heard enough—more than enough. Now she had to leave in a hurry before Stuyvesant discovered her presence. Wishing she were wearing soft-soled moccasins instead of fashionable high-heeled slippers, she tiptoed back across the lawn in the direction from which she had come.

She almost screamed when she nearly collided with Stuyvesant's Indian groundskeeper. But he just smiled at her, and with a sigh of relief she returned his greeting politely and continued back to her house.

She kept watch on the governor's house. At last her vigil was rewarded when she saw the Indian depart and Peter Stuyvesant head off down the street escorted by his usual company of men-at-arms. No one was in sight. Now was her chance to gain concrete evidence of Stuyvesant's perfidy, even though she would be taking a very great risk.

Steeling herself, she returned to his house and forced herself to go into his study. There, as waves of panic assailed her, she shuffled through the papers on his desk, and after what seemed like minutes, she found an order written in his own hand. It was in Dutch, but Eliza could make out that it was addressed to the master-at-arms, that it mentioned *"75 musketen,"* and that it repeatedly mentioned the name Ni-ni-gret. That was all the evidence she needed. Folding the document and thrusting it into the neckline of her dress, she picked up her skirts and raced out of the house. Then she deliberately slowed herself in case anyone saw her and walked sedately back to her own house. There, her heart still pounding, she immediately sat down and wrote a letter to Richard, in which she enclosed the damning document she had stolen. Her mission was a success, and she had found out exactly what it had been so necessary for her to know, but still she felt no sense of elation. On the contrary, what she had learned made her queasy.

It was inconceivable to her that Peter Stuyvesant could have been so shortsighted. She found it almost impossible to believe that he had violated the unspoken agreement about firearms that was the first rule among all the European powers with colonies in America. As she thought about the situation, a resolve gradually formed within her. It was not enough that she furnish this vital information to Richard and her father. It was urgently necessary that she halt the flow of firearms to the Indians if she possibly could. She pondered the problem briefly and came to the only possible conclusion.

She herself would have to write to Cardinal Mazarin and acquaint him with the facts. She could not believe that he knew Stuyvesant approved of a plan with so violent and devastating an outcome— the entire wilderness of North America thrown into flames, death, and unending warfare.

Her mind made up, Eliza hastily wrote a communication to Mazarin, the first letter that she had addressed directly to him since he had tricked her into working for France. It was dark by the time she sealed the letter. She went in search of Roaring Wolf and found him, as she had anticipated, in the shed behind her small house. He was sitting cross-legged, sharpening his knife.

She told him only as much as she deemed it safe

for him to know. "Roaring Wolf," she said, "I have written a letter of great importance to my husband. The peace of all the colonies depends on his receipt of it. Can I trust you to deliver it to him?"

The Pequot warrior grunted his assent.

"Good," she said, and handed him the letter.

He saw that she held still another letter in her hand, and he looked at her questioningly.

"This," she told him, "I must deliver myself."

The Indian nodded and inspected the blade on his knife. Eliza returned to the house for her cloak.

Ordinarily, Roaring Wolf would have left at once for New Haven, but he was confused by the second letter that Eliza claimed needed to be delivered. Not trusting her, and convinced that she was unfaithful to her husband, he decided to follow her. He could leave for New Haven later in the evening.

As Eliza made her way to the Thorn and Thistle in order to meet the French agent at his usual headquarters, she had no idea that the Pequot Warrior was trailing after her in the shadows.

The taproom of the inn was almost filled, and Mollie MacNeill was busy attending to the orders of a large number of customers. She looked up at the woman who wore heavy cosmetics and who was, at least by Mollie's standards, far too frivolously dressed. The proprietress of the Thorn and Thistle sniffed aloud, showing her contempt, but said nothing.

It was impossible to explain her deception to Mollie, so Eliza bore the brunt of her ostracism and came to the point quickly. "Mollie," she said, "I'll be obliged to you if you'll seat me at a table near the place that Master Laroche occupies every evening.

Mollie MacNeill glowered at her. "You know where he sits," she said. "Go place yourself where you please." She turned away curtly, terminating the conversation and giving the younger woman no opportunity to continue their talk.

Eliza was rebuffed, and a wave of discomfort swept over her as she made her way past chatting patrons to an empty table adjacent to the one that Laroche soon would occupy. She couldn't help feeling cheap, even though she had done nothing wrong.

Eliza ordered a glass of watered wine, then relaxed and sipped her drink. At last her patience was rewarded when Laroche entered and sat down with his back to her.

Eliza had to admire his professionalism. He gave no indication whatsoever that he was even remotely acquainted with her and did not so much as glance in her direction as he took his seat. She waited until he had ordered a drink; then, under cover of her voluminous cape, she slipped him the letter she had written to Cardinal Mazarin. Laroche gave no sign that he had received the communication, but after a time he grunted, indicating that he had accepted the letter for transfer.

Her business at the inn was completed, and Eliza left money on the table for her bill and a tip. Conscious of the fact that people were staring at her and aware of the buzz of conversation that marked her exit, she departed. There was no question in her mind that the patrons were commenting on the fact that Peter Stuyvesant's mistress had stopped in at the Thorn and Thistle for a drink. Eliza went home quickly, unaware that Roaring Wolf was still lingering in the shadows outside.

Laroche had no other business to keep him occupied that evening, so his own stay at the tavern was brief. He finished his drink and left. Because the hour was early, he took the long way home, going out of his way by several city blocks.

An agent of long experience, he immediately realized that he was being followed. Laroche slowed his pace and managed to catch an occasional glimpse of the form of his pursuer, but he had no idea that the man was an Indian warrior.

Roaring Wolf was none too sure in his own mind why he was following the French agent. He had a vague idea about retrieving the letter that he had seen Eliza surreptitiously transfer to the man in black, but knew he was exceeding his authority. Richard had not given him permission to interfere directly in Eliza's business, and he was afraid that he might be taking too much upon himself. On the other hand, the letter was the only proof he could offer to Richard that his wife was dishonoring him. In the brave's mind, it was probable that she had written a love letter to Laroche—or to someone— and he thought that if he could retrieve it and deliver it to Richard along with the letter that Eliza had given to him, he would be performing a great service to his friend and benefactor. Therefore, he stayed on Laroche's trail, neither advancing closer nor falling behind.

Had Roaring Wolf been conducting his surveillance in the wilderness, Laroche would have had no idea that he was being followed. But a cobbled city street lined with houses and shops was a far cry from the silent domain of oak and maple and pine.

Laroche kept track of his pursuer's every move. The agent made up his mind quickly. In his business one did not hesitate. He drew a slender, double-bladed knife from one sleeve and, gripping it expertly, prepared to do battle with the man who was trailing him. Why he was being followed was not important; the mere fact that someone found him sufficiently interesting to follow was enough to seal the death warrant of the pursuer.

Changing direction, Laroche started toward the worst part of town. The streets narrowed and were lined with brothels and taverns filled with noisy sailors.

The French agent at last found what he was seeking, a narrow alley between two waterfront warehouses. He walked a short distance past some stacked empty crates, then flattened himself against the wall and waited.

Roaring Wolf advanced cautiously, making no sound. He was almost within Laroche's reach when his sixth sense told him that the man he was following had set a trap. Suddenly Roaring Wolf threw himself to one side, smashing into the wall of the warehouse.

A split second later Laroche's upraised arm swept in a downward arc, the thin knife flashing in the moonlight. The blade grazed the Pequot's sleeve, cutting into his leather shirt.

Now, for the first time, Laroche realized that his pursuer was an Indian. But he also sensed that the man was no ordinary vagrant or sneak thief, as were many of the braves who had traded life in the wilderness for a marginal existence in the Dutch colony. He had been too persistent, too polished in his pursuit, and the French agent automatically assumed the worst—he was convinced that the man had been hired by persons unknown to kill him. The creed that had enabled Laroche to survive for so long told him to kill quickly or be killed. Whirling on his foe, he lunged again with his knife.

Roaring Wolf was prepared this time. He caught hold of the Frenchman's wrist, then hung on tenaciously. Laroche was bigger, brawnier, and at least five years younger than the Pequot, but he lacked the quickness and native stamina of the warrior.

They struggled for possession of the knife, and ultimately, somewhat to Laroche's surprise, he was able to wrench his wrist free. Scarcely pausing for breath, he slashed repeatedly at his assailant.

Backing quickly away, Roaring Wolf reached into his belt for his own bone-handled knife. The steel point was fine and penetrating, and the blade itself was razor-sharp. He advanced, apparently indifferent to his own fate.

It occurred to Laroche that only an Indian could be so nonchalant about his own safety. Either this man was stupid or he was reckless beyond the boundaries of courage. Retreating slowly, Laroche searched for an opportunity to reverse himself and catch the Indian off-balance.

Roaring Wolf circled his opponent and even began to enjoy himself. His eyes had become accustomed to the gloom, and he could see his foe as clearly as if it were midday. The Pequot had taken his opponent's measure. He knew now beyond all doubt that this man was not instinctively a fighter: He was far too cautious and wanted to be sure of victory before he committed himself to combat.

That was all Roaring Wolf needed to know, for he himself was perfectly amenable to taking risks, provided the odds against him were not too great.

The French agent took a fresh grip on his knife as he turned, always facing his foe, waiting for a chance to strike. Suddenly he twisted sideways; at the same moment his arm shot forward as he tried to bring his steel in contact with the warrior's flesh.

This was the moment Roaring Wolf had awaited. The wilderness had taught him to be patient yet alert from the time he had been a small boy, and his reaction now came as second nature. He shifted his stance slightly to the right so that the French agent's arm missed him and the blade cut harmlessly through the air. At the same moment, the Pequot balanced himself on the balls of his feet and drove forward, holding his knife low and directly in front of him and sweeping it upward in an underhand motion. His sharp steel cut through Laroche's clothes and into his stomach as though it were slicing through butter. The French agent gasped and doubled over.

By that time Roaring Wolf had withdrawn the blade and struck again, this time making a curiously semicircular motion with his arm. His knife caught Laroche just below the jaw and almost severed his head from his neck. Bleeding profusely, the French agent dropped to the cobblestones and died without making another sound.

Roaring Wolf wiped the blood from his knife on his victim's coat, but wisely refrained from doing that which he most wanted to do—scalping the dead man. He had spent enough time in New Amsterdam to realize that if he scalped his foe, it would be a sure indication to the constabulary that the murder had been committed by an Indian. It was best not to leave such an obvious clue.

Roaring Wolf searched the inner pockets of Laroche's jacket and soon found the large, square envelope that he sought. He peered at it in the dark, recognized Eliza's handwriting, and was satisfied. He had no idea what else Laroche might have been carrying and did not care.

Creeping to the end of the alleyway, he looked out and saw that the street to the right and to the left was nearly deserted. Far off in the direction from which he had come, a harlot stood in the entrance to a brothel, haggling over her price with a sailor. Roaring Wolf darted into the street and headed the opposite way. Staying close to the buildings, he moved rapidly, his pace increasing to a fast walk as he hastened to put as much distance as he could between himself and the site of the stabbing.

He left the waterfront area, and when he reached the more heavily populated portion of town, he slowed his pace to a sedate walk. Then, seeming not to hurry, but maintaining a steady gait, he left New

Amsterdam and followed the path through the woods that would take him to the end of Manhattan Island. In the pouch at his belt he carried the letter that Eliza had given him to deliver to Richard and the letter that she had intended Laroche to send to Cardinal Mazarin. He would turn both over to Richard Dunstable in New Haven as fast as he could get there.

He had no idea that in killing Laroche he had inadvertently saved the life of Lady Dawn Shepherd, now Mimi Clayton. For among the documents that still remained in Laroche's pocket, soaked with blood, was a letter he had received that very day from Cardinal Mazarin with instructions that he forward it to Celeste. The cardinal's order to dispose of the young English noblewoman who now resided in New Haven and who knew too much of French activities in the New World would never find its way to its recipient. Mimi would never know she had been given a reprieve.

In fact, when the body was discovered the following day by a member of the constabulary, the letter was illegible, having been immersed in Laroche's blood. The constabulary officer who examined it was incapable of reading a word through the caked blood, and disposed of it by throwing it into a fire.

VI

PETER Stuyvesant believed he had misplaced the order to his master-at-arms. At least that was what Eliza assumed when the furor she had anticipated did not materialize. Indeed, she reacted without really thinking when, the very next day, she received word from Stuyvesant requiring her presence as hostess at a noon dinner for the representatives of the Dutch West Indies Company. She applied cosmetics with a heavy hand, donned one of her flimsy gowns of silk and, hating herself, went off to the Governor's clapboard house. The worst part of these occasions, she reflected, was their incredible dullness. She was tired of pretending she was Stuyvesant's mistress, just as she was tired of entertaining his guests.

The two men from Holland were stolid, serious businessmen whose principal interest in life was how much money their various enterprises brought into the company. Eliza's attempts to joke with them throughout the protracted dinner fell flat, and her efforts to discuss what they had seen in the New World evoked no response. She realized, however, that both men were definitely interested in her as a woman. Between the mouthfuls of food on which they gorged themselves, they looked at her with gleaming eyes, but when she took notice of their interest, they immediately averted their gazes and became strictly impersonal.

Peter Stuyvesant also was quick to note the interest of his company's directors in Eliza, and he could not resist teasing them in his own fashion. As they adjourned from the dining room to his sitting room for glasses of schnapps, he deliberately slid an arm around Eliza's slender waist and hauled her close to him. She was obliged to suffer his familiarity in silence; supposedly she was long accustomed to being mauled by him. The expressions on the faces of the two Dutchmen reflected their envy.

Stuyvesant was unable to resist the temptation to go a step further. Cupping one of Eliza's breasts in his hand, he began to fondle it with seeming absentmindedness as they made their way to the sitting room.

She squirmed beneath his heavy-handed touch, but there was no escape from his grasp. When she tried to free herself, he playfully pulled her still closer and forcibly seated her on his lap. Then, twisting her around to face him, he kissed her resoundingly and resumed fondling her breast.

Eliza was infuriated, but she knew better than to make a scene in the presence of the two Dutch visitors. She had made an agreement and was abiding by it, even though Stuyvesant was taking unfair advantage of her.

He downed glass after glass of the potent schnapps, urging her to join him and in the meantime insisting that she remain seated on his lap. The enforced proximity had its effect on him, and Eliza realized that his desire for her had come to life. He wanted her badly now, and she knew that when his visitors left he intended to have her. She had stalled long enough, and his patience had come to an end.

She realized she was in for a grim scene, the outcome of which she did not care to predict. Fortunately, however, she won a temporary respite. The representatives of the Dutch West Indies Company had business to discuss with him, and so when one of them presented Stuyvesant with a contract that required his undivided attention, he allowed the woman to slip off his lap. Straightening her attire and regaining what she could of her dignity, Eliza escaped to an adjoining chamber. Presumably, she was expected to wait there and rejoin the governor at his convenience.

Instead, however, she fled to her own small house. The thought occurred to her forcefully for the first time that there was no need for her to subject herself to Stuyvesant's boorish conduct ever again. She had sent evidence to Richard that conclusively proved Stuyvesant was responsible for arming the Indian tribes, so she had completed her mission successfully. By this time, she guessed, Roaring Wolf would be halfway to New Haven, and she had every reason to believe that he would safely deliver the letter to Richard. Similarly, knowing nothing about the death of Laroche, she assumed that her letter to Cardinal Mazarin would soon cross the Atlantic to its destination. She had no real reason to stay in New Amsterdam a moment longer.

Knowing she had no time to spare, she did not bother to pack the contents of the wardrobe closets. That would have to be forfeited, or wait until some other time when Richard would accompany her to New Amsterdam and she would be safe. She snatched up her cloak and fled from the house.

She left none too soon, she saw as she made her way up the street. A detachment of Dutch pikemen was crossing the lawn between her house and the governor's, and she had no doubt that they had been dispatched to deliver her to his presence. She increased her pace to a near run.

She had raced over several cobbled streets when it occurred to her that she had no destination in mind. Knowing that Stuyvesant would be furious about her escape and would be sure to humiliate her accordingly if she were returned to him, she thought frantically. She had no real friends in New Amsterdam, and she knew that it would be futile to appeal to any of the ship captains in the harbor, for English ships were scarce lately; and besides, that would be the first place Stuyvesant would look. Eliza could think of nowhere to go except the Thorn and Thistle, so she hurried there without giving the matter further thought.

The taproom was deserted, but Mollie MacNeill was seated at a table at the far end of the bar, laboriously poring over bills from the butcher and the greengrocer. Eliza hurried toward the older woman.

Mollie became aware of Eliza's presence, looked up and eyed her coldly.

Reacting to Mollie's contemptuous gaze as though she had been struck a physical blow, Eliza was conscious of her too-liberal use of cosmetics and her scant clothing. Breathless and fearful that the governor's pikemen might at any moment find her, Eliza began to babble semicoherently, thinking that she was pouring out a story that was making sense.

Mollie was unmoved. Aware of the phlegmatic reaction, Eliza became even more frantic.

"You make no sense, wench," Mollie said.

Her remark was so unexpected that Eliza reacted to it as she would to a slap. Oddly, the curt contempt in the older woman's face steadied her and enabled her to gain control of herself. She knew now that she had to tell her story with great caution. Richard had warned her that under no circumstances was she to reveal that she was a double agent. Such knowledge would deny her the protection that ordinarily would be afforded to someone of her sex and nationality. If it became known that she was spying for the French, but was actually acting as an agent for the English colonies, her foes would feel justified in summarily doing away with her.

So Eliza steadied herself and said quietly, "I am not what I appear to be, Mollie."

The woman was struck by her manner, but merely raised an eyebrow.

Eliza was gaining a toehold of credibility. "Appearances," she said, "can be misleading. In my case they are."

Mollie looked her up and down slowly, studying her intently. "You mean," she said, "that you ain't the doxy of the governor?"

Eliza was encouraged. She appeared to be breaking the wall of the woman's stubborn resistance. "I am not Peter Stuyvesant's mistress," she said flatly. "I have never been his mistress nor any other man's."

Mollie remained unyielding. "You look like a doxy," she insisted.

Eliza flushed, and her cheeks felt as though they were on fire. It was true that her clothes and her cosmetics branded her as a high-class harlot. Suddenly, probably because of her tension, she giggled. "It is not accidental that I look as I do," she replied slowly.

For the first time, Mollie MacNeill looked a trifle unsure of herself. The younger woman was being so positive in her declarations that Mollie's preconceived notions were shaken.

Eliza had to run a degree of risk, or she would face almost certain capture by the pikemen, the constabulary, or the Dutch troops, all of which were under Peter Stuyvesant's control. "I believe you know something about certain activities in which my husband has engaged from time to time," she said slowly. "Is that correct?"

A great light dawned, and Mollie nodded slowly. It was true, she knew, that Richard Dunstable had been involved in some sort of activity about which he remained very silent. He had been engaged in this work on board ship when he had first come to the New World, and it had occupied him from that time forward. In fact, it was through his secret activities that he had known how her son, Bart, had died, and she had never questioned his credibility or his sources. "I—I think I begin to understand," she murmured.

"I'm telling you nothing of interest or of value," Eliza declared. "I cannot help it if you jump to certain conclusions, but you do this of your own volition, having learned nothing from me."

Mollie knew nothing whatsoever about spy work, but she definitely understood what Eliza was implying. She, like her husband, appeared to be a patriot whose activities could be discussed with no one. Mollie felt secretly relieved, having grieved over the infidelity of the lovely young woman who had become Richard Dunstable's bride.

"I need your help now," Eliza said. "Because Governor Stuyvesant is insistent that I become his, ah, doxy in fact as well as in appearance. He's sent his pikemen to search for me. I'm sure they'll be joined, if they haven't been already, by the New Amsterdam constabulary and by the entire garrison of Dutch troops."

Mollie seemed stunned by the revelation. "Do you mean," she demanded, "that he would actually use soldiers and constables to make you his woman against your wishes?"

She was so naive that Eliza smiled wearily as she nodded assent. "He's the sort of man," she said, "that will stop at nothing to gain his ends, whatever they might be."

That statement, it appeared, struck a familiar chord. "Angus keeps tellin' me that the governor is unscrupulous," she said. "I reckon he must be."

"He is." Eliza was wasting valuable time and could procrastinate no longer. "Will you give me refuge?"

Mollie MacNeill was torn. Richard Dunstable had befriended her and her son before she had fled from the Roundheads and had come without a penny to the New World. She was not sure if the young woman was telling the truth, but she had to accept her word or risk letting down Richard when his wife desperately needed help.

She tucked a wisp of gray hair into place. All at once she made up her mind. "I'll help you all I can," she declared.

Relief flooded Eliza, but she knew they could not tarry in the taproom of the Thorn and Thistle. "At any time, the men will arrive here searching for me," she said. "You'll have to hide me quickly."

Mollie jumped to her feet, reached for a large ring from which numerous keys dangled, then started toward the stairs of the inn, beckoning peremptorily. Here was action at last, and Eliza followed her eagerly.

Mollie led her up a narrow stairway above the second floor to a chamber beneath the eaves. "Nobody knows this room even exists," she said. "You'll be safe enough here. I'll bring your meals and water meself, and you can stay here as long as need be."

"I'll stay only until I find some way to leave

New Amsterdam," Eliza told her. "In the meantime, I'm beholden to you, more than I can ever tell you."

The woman waved aside her thanks. "You've brought no other dresses with you?" she demanded.

"I left my house too quickly for that," the woman confessed. "I was lucky to escape at all." She knew what Mollie had in mind. Her flimsy gown made her very conspicuous, and it would be extremely difficult for her to leave New Amsterdam in her present attire. But she had no choice; when the time came, she would have to rely on her cloak for concealment.

Mollie looked at her somberly. "How do you plan to get away?" she asked.

Eliza knew that her best hope of escape rested in Roaring Wolf, but he would still be on his way to New Haven on the errand she had given him.

"There's an Indian warrior whom Richard assigned to watch over me," she said. "You might keep watch for him. When you see him, tell him that I'm in hiding here. His name is Roaring Wolf."

Mollie considered the request and nodded somewhat reluctantly. "Would it be amiss," she wanted to know, "if Angus and I send word to Richard that you face serious trouble?"

"I'd much prefer that you not get in touch with Richard at present," Eliza said carefully, "simply because it will be more difficult than ever to get a private message delivered to him without arousing the suspicions of the Dutch authorities. To be on the safe side, I'd rather wait and rely on Roaring Wolf for help."

Having committed herself to aid Eliza, Mollie had to accept the younger woman's judgment.

"We'll proceed as you see fit," she said. "I'll tell Angus all you've told me. You can be sure that he'll stand beside you in your time of travail, too."

"You're wonderful friends, both of you," Eliza said, and meant it. The couple could lose their inn-keepers' license and be forced by Governor Stuy-vesant to leave the colony if their role in her escape became known. Yet they willingly risked their entire futures, if not for her sake, certainly out of friendship for her husband.

Mollie MacNeill patted her soothingly on the shoulder, then withdrew. Alone and safe at last, at least temporarily, Eliza walked to the room's small cot and slumped wearily, leaning against the wall as she closed her eyes. She could hear a disturb-ance in the inn below. It sounded like official voices, probably those of the governor's pikemen. She shuddered and wrapped herself tightly in the cloak. Only by exercising the greatest willpower was she able to refrain from weeping. Her status had changed; her whole life had changed. Suddenly she had become a fugitive in the domain of Peter Stuyvesant. She had done her duty and had suc-ceeded brilliantly in her mission. Now she needed to be rescued, or surely she would be killed.

The atmosphere at the supper table was strained, so stiff that Lady Celeste Murette, the hostess, had to concede that perhaps she had outsmarted her-self. She had invited Adam Burrows's partner, Tom Clayton, and his wife, Mary, to supper, along with the younger Ezekiel Clayton and his wife, Mimi. It had been her intention to solidify her relations with the Claytons for the sake of her association with Adam. The elder Claytons apparently accepted Ad-am's interest in her for the sake of their old friend, but Mimi proved to be a serious problem.

Her manner innocent, her eyes wide, Mimi asked at the dinner table, "Tell me, my dear, what do you hear from the duke of Somerset and the earl of Rockland?"

The names meant nothing to the English colonials who were present, but Celeste Murette was instantly aware of the affront. As anyone who had spent time at the court of the late King Charles well realized, she had achieved notoriety as the mistress first of Somerset, then of Rockland. But she refused to let the other woman see that she had scored, and her manner was bland as she shrugged her shoulders.

"I'm afraid I hear nothing from either of them," Celeste said, sounding a trifle regretful. "The last I heard of Somerset, he had joined the court-in-exile of young King Charles in France. As for Rockland, he proved to be a turncoat, you know, and joined forces with the Roundheads after poor Charles was executed."

Mimi had actually known what had become of both nobles, but she pretended to be absorbing fascinating information. "Do you find you miss the court?" she asked.

Celeste shook her head. "No, I can't say I really do," she replied. "But I can understand what a wrench the civil war must be for you. After all, you were much closer to King Charles than I was." There! Celeste thought maliciously, she had evened the score. Lady Dawn had long been rumored to have been a mistress of King Charles, and even though the stories had been untrue, she would have something to explain to her husband and perhaps to his parents.

Mimi seemed to be enjoying the verbal duel. "I've settled down here in the New World," she said, "and I'm so content with my lot that the glamour of court life seems very far away. I don't miss it in the least. But you were so immersed in it that I should think you'd feel very strange and alien here."

Now it was Celeste's turn again. "No," she said

as she looked fondly at Adam. "The people here have such common sense and are *so* straightforward—" she paused and smiled at Mimi, "that their way of life more than compensates for the glitter and excitement of the court. I shall be very happy to spend the rest of my days here."

That ended the conflict. Ezekiel could not understand why tensions continued to run so high between his wife and the other young woman. Not until later, after he and Mimi returned home, did he have a chance to discuss the subject with her.

"That was quite an undercurrent between you and Lady Celeste," he said. "We all felt it."

"That can't be helped," his wife replied. "She's winding poor Adam around her little finger, and with Eliza not here to help him open his eyes to what she really is, I felt I had to intervene."

Her husband looked surprised. "She seems very pleasant and charming to me," he said.

Mimi sniffed. "She's an adventuress! She's an opportunist. It's no accident, you know, that she's set her trap for Adam Burrows—the wealthiest man in New Haven Colony."

"I think you're being unfair," Ezekiel said. "She lives quietly, and she's fitted rather well into the community. I know Richard thinks very highly of her."

"That's something else that worries me!" she retorted. "I don't know if Celeste's friendship with Richard is as innocent as it should be, considering the fact that Richard is married."

Ezekiel shrugged. "Richard Dunstable," he said, "can look after himself. Never you fear."

"Indeed he can," she replied, "but there's a man-eating monster that's circling around him, and he's none too safe, nor for that matter is Adam."

"Why are you so opposed to Celeste Murette?" Ezekiel demanded.

Mimi continued to bristle. "I should think that's fairly obvious," she replied. "She had as bad a reputation as any woman at Whitehall, and that includes some worthy competition. She was recognized by everyone who had any decency as being an obvious trollop. I hate to see a man as vulnerable as Adam Burrows getting involved with her, just as I dislike seeing Richard jeopardizing his marriage in the name of his so-called friendship with her."

He shook his head. "I well remember your telling me before we were married that you had a reputation as the mistress of King Charles, and I recall, too, that the story was untrue. Isn't it possible that Lady Celeste is also the innocent victim of vicious rumors?"

"It is not!" Mimi said firmly. "I can't offer you proof positive that she's a harlot, but I hope you'll take my word for it."

"I'll take your word for anything and everything," Ezekiel said, "but I'm afraid you'll need concrete proof to offer to Colonel Burrows. He's smitten, and there's no getting around it. In fact, my mother and father expect him to propose marriage to Lady Celeste at any time."

"That's precisely what must be avoided," she said. "If Eliza were here, I'm sure she would intervene. As her friend I must do all I can on her behalf."

Her husband shrugged. "Good luck," he said, "but I've known Adam Burrows all of my life, and he'll need more than a few vague rumors to discourage him. Besides, I don't see that it would be so terrible if he and Lady Celeste were to marry."

Mimi was aghast. "You're joking!" She stared at him incredulously.

He shrugged. "She's attractive, intelligent, and she appears to be independently well-to-do. Since she has no ties or affiliations with anyone, she'd make a good wife for the colonel. He's been alone for years, and he deserves all the happiness that he can find."

Mimi recognized the futility of the argument and dropped the subject. There was no way that she could persuade Ezekiel to adopt her point of view, but her mind was certainly made up. She would do everything in her power to break up the romance between Adam Burrows and Celeste Murette.

Covering the same ground he had visited previously, Richard traveled from colony to colony throughout New England, and everywhere he preached the same gospel. It was essential, he argued, that all the people of New England, for their common welfare, unite to form an army to repel the imminent Indian invasion and to force a showdown with their Dutch foes.

However, his information about the timing of an invasion of the English colonies was vague and conjectural, so he failed to accomplish his goal. Local pride and jealousy interfered constantly. Newport and Providence Plantations pointed out that although they could supply fewer infantrymen to a combined force than could other colonies, they would provide the ships to transfer these troops; therefore, they demanded a dominant voice in the war councils. Massachusetts Bay insisted that it should have the final word in all decision-making, and insisted that as the most populous colony, with by far the largest number of militiamen, it should also supply the commander in chief. The threat was unspoken but clear: If the commander were not a Boston officer, the militia from that town would refrain from participating in joint ventures.

And so it went, town by town. No two communities thought alike, and each demanded that its own special interests be preserved. Richard tried hard to counter these arguments, but he could not persuade any colony to set aside its individual demands for the common good.

By the time he reached Taunton, he was thoroughly discouraged. At the insistence of Dempster Chaney, he was an overnight guest at the farmhouse that Dempster and Robbin shared with Aunt Hester Browne. The next day at noon dinner—a hearty meal of stewed beef and dumplings—Richard unburdened himself.

Robbin was sympathetic, but nevertheless remained reserved. "I can see both sides of the argument," she said. "Here we are living on the edge of Indian country. Our militia has a difficult time in maintaining the peace. Only because Dempster is such an able commander can our men prevent the Indians of our district from burning settlement after settlement. If I were a leader of our militia, I'd be inclined to think long and hard before I'd give up any portion of our sovereignty to some outsider."

"That's precisely the problem I face everywhere," Richard said wearily.

To his surprise, Aunt Hester struck her pewter water goblet with her fork. "You need to be more firm, young man," she declared. "At the present rate, you'll never form a command that's unified, and you'll win no real battles against anyone until you do."

Richard looked at her with a tired grin. "You're quite right, ma'am," he said, running his fingers back through his hair in a familiar gesture of fatigue, "but I've been unable to persuade the leaders of any colony to agree. I think New Haven is unique."

"You have the intelligence to realize that the Dutch threat is real," she said. "The other colonies are too literal-minded. As a result, they're short-sighted. They're so concerned over their immediate safety that they can't look down the road and see what's staring them in the face."

Richard turned to Dempster. "Would you place yourself and your militia company under the orders of an outside commander?"

Dempster considered the question judiciously. "If you were that commander, Richard," he said, "I'd agree in a minute. As to someone else—well, I'd have to know first who he is, and second, I'd have to study his qualifications. I certainly wouldn't leap blindfolded into a unified command."

"There you have it, ma'am," Richard said to Aunt Hester. "There's our problem in a nutshell."

The white-haired woman looked at her young partner, her eyes blazing. "Ordinarily you show good sense, Dempster," she said. "You know how fondly I regard you, but if you persist in this attitude, my opinion of you will decline rather drastically. I can't see for the life of me, frankly, why the needs of Taunton should be greater than those of New Haven. Or why Providence Plantations should take precedence over Springfield. We're all English. We speak the same language, we share a common heritage—a heritage of personal freedom. We're a trifle confused in our loyalties these days since we're paying lip service to Cromwell instead of to young King Charlie, but that's irrelevant. What matters is that we all stand together; if not, we will all face extermination. Our choice is very clear."

"That's well put, ma'am," Richard said admiringly. "I wish I had your knack for clarifying the issues. Perhaps it would be easier for me to persuade the colonies to join forces."

"I've lived a great many years," Aunt Hester said, "and I've seen much in this lifetime. I shouldn't worry if I were you, young man. The colonies will either heed your call, or they'll perish and become satraps of Paris or Amsterdam. They have no real choice. I think they'll demonstrate their good sense in due time. But if what you say is true, that time is at hand. Well, the way I see it, freedom belongs to those who are willing to die in order that their children may be free. That's the old English tradition, you know. We've inherited it, and surrounded as we are by hostile enemies in a hostile wilderness, we have ample opportunity to demonstrate that we're worthy of enjoying the freedom that we claim is our heritage."

Richard looked at her in wonder. "How does it happen that you grasp so firmly the principles of what's at stake?"

Aunt Hester got up and pointed out of the window.

He looked in the indicated direction and saw the end of the clearing that marked her property. Beyond it was the beginning of the limitless forest, the vast unexplored ocean of trees that extended thousands of miles across the continent of North America.

"My opinions," Aunt Hester said softly, "have been shaped by this wilderness which my late husband and I tamed and where I've made my home for so many years. I've tried to pass on the lessons I've learned to Dempster. Either he will learn them as well and will flourish, or he will fail to grasp them and will perish. The New World belongs to those who are strong and courageous and who love freedom. It's the love of freedom that is paramount. That's why I'm convinced that this land will be populated by people of English descent rather than continental Europeans. We, of all people in the world, understand freedom and appreciate it. We have our chance to perpetuate our beliefs and keep the torches of truth richly burning in the New World. If we succeed in that, we shall have achieved our purpose on earth."

Richard was discouraged when he hastened back to New Haven from his tour of the colonies, but he was also grimly determined to continue in his efforts to unite the colonies in a joint stand against their common foes. He arrived late one evening, too late to go to the docks or to disturb Adam Burrows at home, so he went straight to his own house. There he found Roaring Wolf waiting for him. The Pequot handed him two communications from Eliza —the one she had written to him, and the one he had taken from the body of Laroche. Richard listened patiently to Roaring Wolf's long-winded and obscure explanation of how he had come by the letter addressed to Mazarin. Then he opened and read both letters.

Richard's first reaction was one of utter elation. Here, at last, was the evidence that had been lacking, the proof positive that Stuyvesant was conspiring against the English colonies!

Richard could not wait to break the news to his father-in-law. He set off for the Burrows house, his mind racing. With Laroche dead—the French spy, no doubt, was the man Roaring Wolf had killed— he knew of no way to forward Eliza's letter to Cardinal Mazarin, and he himself had no way of getting in touch with the first minister of France. No French ships called at English ports, and English colonials were hesitant to set foot on French soil. There were rumors of fishermen from the Maine district who had inadvertently found themselves in the waters claimed by New France and who had been imprisoned by the French as a consequence.

It was possible, perhaps, to find some means of forwarding the communication to Paris from one of the Dutch colonies in the West Indies, but Richard knew of no one trustworthy enough in the Caribbean, and he realized that the complications that stood in the way of such a move were too great for him to solve, so he hastily abandoned the idea. Not until he had almost reached the house of Colonel Burrows did it cross his mind that Eliza had now completed her mission and should be evacuated from New Amsterdam at the first opportunity. She had made no mention of her immediate plans in her letter to him, and apparently had written it so soon after learning of Peter Stuyvesant's plans that she had had no opportunity to make decisions regarding her own plight. He knew he would have to arrange for her return to New Haven immediately.

A dim light was burning in the master bedroom on the second floor of Adam Burrows's house, and the colonel looked a trifle startled and more than a little sheepish when he answered his son-in-law's summons. Not until they reached the study and closed the door behind them did it dawn on Richard that his father-in-law, who was wearing a dressing gown, had been entertaining a lady and that he had interrupted them. He tried to apologize for his intrusion.

Adam silenced him with a wave. "Never mind that. Sit down. How did you fare on your trip? I assume that's why you're here."

"That's only one reason," Richard replied, and told him succinctly about his failure to win the cooperation of the various colonies in a military alliance.

The colonel's face clouded.

"The day is saved, however," Richard went on in triumph, and handed him Eliza's letter.

His father-in-law scanned the communication hurriedly, then carefully studied Stuyvesant's order, and laughed aloud. "I'll be damned," he said, "if you two haven't done it. I've doubted—more than I can ever tell you—that Eliza could ever succeed in this harebrained mission that you two youngsters undertook, but she's proved me wrong. Now I'll eat my words."

"When the other colonies learn what Eliza has uncovered," Richard said, "I don't think there will be much doubt that they'll cooperate with us and with each other. I think we'll get our unified force."

"Yes," Adam said softly. "It won't surprise me in the least if we go to war with Stuyvesant. I've been aching to teach that insolent Dutchman a lesson that he will remember."

"The first task that awaits us," Richard said, "is to rescue Eliza from New Amsterdam."

"You'll go there to fetch her?" his father-in-law was eager to know.

The young Englishman shook his head. "I think I'd be adding to her dangers rather than helping her," he said. "Stuyvesant knows that I've been in the employ of France, as Eliza has been. I don't want him halting me in any way. The simplest way of getting her out, I think, is to send Roaring Wolf to fetch her. He can lead her out by any one of a dozen wilderness routes without arousing Stuyvesant's suspicion. It's important, I think, that we don't give away our hand to Peter Stuyvesant."

Colonel Burrows pondered for a time, then nodded. "Quite right," he said. "He must not know that we're aware of his perfidy until we've had a chance to confront him as united colonies. What worries me is that we can so ill afford a major war with the Dutch."

"I know," Richard frowned as he gazed into the small fire burning in the grate.

The colonel rose, tugged at the belt of his dressing gown, and unconsciously removed a long black hair from the sleeve. "It's unfortunate," he said, "that we must deal with reality as it exists. By all means, send Roaring Wolf for Eliza. If he encounters any difficulty, we'll think of some better plan."

Richard rose, and after shaking the colonel's hand, returned to his own house. He had not seen the woman who he assumed had been sharing Adam Burrows's bedchamber, and it was just as well that he remained in ignorance. His father-in-law's private life was none of his business—he had enough matters of pressing interest to occupy his mind.

Roaring Wolf was waiting for his friend, and Richard promptly charged him with his new mission. "Go back to New Amsterdam at once," he said, "and find my wife. Bring her safely back to New Haven. I don't know whether she's in danger, but take no chances. Remember that her safety comes first."

The Pequot nodded, grasping his friend's forearm, and departed at once for New Amsterdam. The so-called civilization of whites was beyond his understanding, he decided, and he was glad he had not confided his suspicions about Eliza to her husband. Richard's concern for her was genuine, and the Pequot was flattered because he had been given a mission of great trust. He intended to fulfill it to the very best of his ability.

He made his way through the wilderness swiftly, taking only a few hours to rest and eat each day. Late the third night he reached the bank of the Harlem River opposite the northern end of Manhattan Island. He cut down several young pines, made a raft for himself, and crossed the river quietly. When he landed on the island, however, a sixth sense told him to beware, so he promptly hid his raft and concealed himself in the woods.

To his surprise, a small detachment of soldiers carrying torches passed within a few feet of his place of concealment. Obviously they were on patrol duty, and it was equally evident that they were specifically searching for someone or something. Thereafter Roaring Wolf exercised great caution. He managed to avoid two other patrols as he worked his way southward through the wilderness of the upper part of the island, and he avoided Dutch sentries when he reached the town of New Amsterdam shortly after sunrise. To be on the safe side, he gave members of the constabulary a wide berth, too, as he went by a circuitous route to the small house where Eliza lived.

To his consternation, he found several Dutch pikemen on duty there. The first thought that occurred to the Indian was that Eliza was being held prisoner inside. He concealed himself in a small wooded area a good distance away, where he knew he could keep both houses in sight. For most of the day he searched these compound and the windows of the houses for sight of the woman, but she was nowhere to be seen. Exhausted from his long journey, he eventually fell asleep.

When Roaring Wolf awoke, it was near dawn and there was still no sign of Eliza. Keeping Richard's injunction well in mind, he wandered through town, searching from street to street without avail. Finally, even his great stamina gave way, and he knew that he needed food.

Richard had provided him with some English money, so Roaring Wolf dragged himself to the Thorn and Thistle for a meal.

He went directly to the kitchen, where the MacNeills were beginning their day's work. Angus had just made a fire and was kneading dough for the loaves of bread he would bake for the customers' breakfasts. Meanwhile Mollie was busy scaling and filleting fish prior to frying them. Both stopped work and stared at the Pequot. Roaring Wolf, not knowing the reason for their intense scrutiny, was somewhat unnerved.

"You give Roaring Wolf food to eat," he said, "and he give you English money."

They reacted as though he were a long-lost son. "Roaring Wolf!" Mollie said. "We've searched everywhere for you."

He thought it strange that the innkeeper should show an interest in him, and he shrugged. "Roaring Wolf go to New Haven to see Richard," he said. "Now he come back."

Angus took over. "You'll get all the food you can eat. It won't cost you a penny," he said. "But first come with me." Explaining nothing, he led the warrior up to the entrance to the attic room, where he tapped on the door and then disappeared.

Eliza Dunstable struggled off the cot, slipped into the dressing gown she had been lent by Mollie, then went to the door. She had been alternately bored, frightened, and depressed for what seemed like months. She opened the door, saw Roaring Wolf, and caught her breath.

The warrior was uncertain whether she was laughing or crying when she dragged him into the chamber and shut the door behind him. Both of them began to speak simultaneously until Eliza restored order, wanting first to hear what the Pequot had to report, then bringing him up to date on her own situation.

"The soldiers who were searching the end of the island undoubtedly were looking for me," she said. "I understand from Angus and Mollie MacNeill that Governor Stuyvesant has actually offered a substantial reward for my capture. He's determined to get me into his possession."

Roaring Wolf listened intently, his arms folded across his chest, his eyes narrowed to slits. He made no comment until she had finished speaking.

Certainly his friend Richard had no idea of the precariousness of her position.

"Soldiers and constables all look for Eliza?" he asked.

"All of them," she replied.

"Dutch soldiers with spears hunt, too?" he asked, referring to the corps of pikemen.

She nodded and grimaced. "Just about everyone in New Amsterdam is looking for me," she said. "I've spent so much time in this room that I could scream, but I'm so grateful to the MacNeills. If it weren't for them I'd have been captured and been made a prisoner of the governor a long time ago." She saw no point in adding that Stuyvesant would have forced her to become his mistress.

Roaring Wolf was lost in thought. "Governor bad man," he said at last.

Her laugh was prolonged. "That's the nicest thing you could have said about him," she declared.

He did not smile, and his eyes remained serious. "Richard want Roaring Wolf to make Eliza safe and bring Eliza home," he said. "This Roaring Wolf do."

"How?" she demanded breathlessly.

The Pequot shrugged. "Roaring Wolf not know yet," he replied, "but soon find way." Without further ado he left the chamber and returned to the kitchen.

There the MacNeills respected his silence as he sat at a small table and consumed an enormous breakfast that included several fried fish, a small beefsteak with fried eggs on it, a slab of cake, and a pint of cider. When he was finished, to the astonishment of his host and hostess, he insisted on paying them two shillings. They accepted the money rather than injure his pride.

A serving maid busied herself, throwing the previous week's soiled linen into a large wicker basket, which she dragged from one end of the kitchen to the other. The MacNeills paid no attention to her activity, but Roaring Wolf was fascinated.

"Where girl take blankets?" he demanded of Mollie.

The question seemed irrelevant to the problem at hand, and Mollie could not conceal her irritation. "She's goin' down to the river to wash the linen because we don't have enough water here. Then she'll bring it back and spread it in our yard to dry. Why do you ask?"

Roaring Wolf looked solemn, but made no reply. His expression was inscrutable, but Angus thought he read something in the Pequot's eyes, and he took the warrior off to the small office at the rear of the kitchen.

"Now then," Angus said, "You have something on your mind. What is it?"

Roaring Wolf chuckled aloud, obviously enjoying himself thoroughly. Then, taking no chances, he rose and closed the door before resuming his seat and explaining in full the idea that had occurred to him. Angus listened carefully and nodded in approval.

"You will work with Roaring Wolf?" the Indian asked. "You will help?"

Angus MacNeill hauled his vast bulk to his feet and extended a hamlike hand. "I'm with you all the way, Indian," he said. "You can count on me!"

Two days later, shortly before sundown, a large cart pulled by the Thorn and Thistle workhorse headed toward the river. In the cart was piled all the laundry from the inn. Mollie MacNeill herself was taking the washing down to the waterfront, and because the load was so bulky, she was accompanied by an Indian. A constable passing nearby waved a greeting at Mollie, and didn't notice that Roaring Wolf's hand was only a matter of inches from two pistols partly concealed in the wagon beside him. Mollie smiled and waved back at the constable, cursing him beneath her breath.

When they reached the waterfront, she was relieved to find that no one else was washing nearby. She had relied on the fact that most laundry was washed early in the morning so it could be dried outside during the day. Residents of New Amsterdam rarely took advantage of the evening for washing.

The wagon was rolled onto the makeshift wharf where the laundry was customarily done. They searched the area and assured each other with nods that no passerby was paying any attention to them. Then, while Mollie slowly proceeded to remove the laundry piled in the cart, Roaring Wolf trotted off and busied himself uncovering a birchbark canoe he had purchased the previous day from a local Indian and hidden in the tall weeds just upriver.

As Roaring Wolf glided silently up to the wharf in the canoe, Mollie spoke sharply and distinctly. "Now, Eliza," she said. "Now!"

Eliza Dunstable's head emerged from beneath the tumbled linen, and then her body followed. She was not properly clad for the adventure on which she was embarked, as she was wearing only her flimsy silk dress with her cloak thrown over it.

She stepped into the canoe, and Roaring Wolf held the frail craft steady while the fugitive positioned herself in the prow. She was surprisingly quick and graceful, and it was obvious that she was no stranger to an Indian craft as a means of transportation.

Mollie passed the pistols to the Indian brave, then grabbed a sheet and plunged it into the water, seemingly intent on doing her laundry.

At Roaring Wolf's direction, Eliza sank low, sliding down so that she was out of view. Roaring Wolf wasted no time. Snatching up a paddle as he knelt in the stern, he dug the blade into the water, and the canoe shot away from the wharf.

Watching intently, Mollie MacNeill did not breathe easier until the canoe was far away from shore and she was sure that no one was paying any attention to the craft. To the best of her knowledge, Eliza was now safe.

As the shore gradually faded from view, Eliza breathed more easily, and eventually sat upright, convinced now that no constable or soldier would be able to see her.

Roaring Wolf silently concentrated on his task of paddling. The current was swift and unpredictable. He was moving quickly downriver, so he had to use considerable skill and effort as he guided the slender craft through the swirling waters.

Eliza huddled in her cloak against the chill from the water. "Where are you taking me?"

"Eliza go," the Pequot replied, "to where Dutch call Staten Island." He again lapsed into silence, obviously feeling he had given her enough information.

Staten Island was only a name to Eliza, who knew nothing about the place. "Why there?" she asked uneasily.

He continued to paddle steadily, his stroke rhythmic. "On island," he said, "lives Raritan nation. Raritan have long been enemy of Dutch. He who is now governor has tried four times to kill all Raritan, but warriors are too fierce and fight with too much strength. Indians turn back invaders, and Indians remain free. Raritan will give Eliza shelter. Eliza will be safe there until Richard comes."

Eliza still looked apprehensive, and the normally unflappable Roaring Wolf, his patience apparently wearing thin, stopped paddling, as if to emphasize what he was about to say.

"Brave who sell Roaring Wolf canoe friend of Raritan. Brave tell Roaring Wolf where to go. Roaring Wolf not blind like lovesick moose. Do not worry."

Eliza nodded, struck by the thoroughness that had gone into the planning of her escape. Regardless of the outcome, and whether or not the Raritan would agree to accept her, she was deeply indebted to the MacNeills and Roaring Wolf.

The warrior resumed paddling with undiminished vigor for more than one hour, then for a second hour. At no time did he tire, at no time did he slacken his pace or speak a word. The sky above was filled with stars, but no moon shone and the night was dark. Eliza could only hope that Roaring Wolf knew where he was going.

Suddenly land loomed directly ahead. She could just make out low-lying, heavily wooded hills. Roaring Wolf slowed his paddling. As they approached the shore, he made a sound remarkably like the prolonged trilling of a bird.

Herself a product of the frontier, Eliza knew instantly what he was doing: His whistle was a way of notifying the local Indians that he was a friend. Certainly no white man could have known the correct bird call for this message.

Eliza stared ahead, her eyes piercing the gloom. All at once she made out several figures of dark warriors, clad only in loincloths, their heads shaved on both sides of a central scalp lock. All were armed with tomahawks, and all carried large bows and arrows.

Again the undaunted Roaring Wolf trilled. One of the warriors replied in kind, indicating that the newcomers would be treated with friendship, at least until they were identified. Dark hands reached out, and the canoe was hauled up onto the beach.

As Eliza climbed out onto the sand, she felt the

braves staring at her. They took in every aspect of her appearance, and she felt naked. She could only hope they were indeed friendly. It would be catastrophic if they decided to use her sexually, because her chances of escape from Staten Island were even worse than the opportunities to get away from Peter Stuyvesant had been.

Roaring Wolf was both serious and self-assured. "Where is your sachem?" he asked, speaking the language of the Mohegan.

The warriors knew he was addressing them in an Indian tongue, but they failed to understand it and stared at him blankly. Eliza felt compelled to intervene and decided to take a chance on speaking the tongue of the Reckagawawanc, which she had been trying to learn from Stuyvesant's groundskeeper in her spare time. She reasoned that the Reckagawawanc lived close to the Raritan, and it was possible that their languages would be similar. She repeated the Pequot's request, speaking haltingly.

The faces of the warriors brightened, and it was obvious that they understood her perfectly. They surrounded the couple and indicated with gestures that they would act as escorts. Roaring Wolf relinquished neither his knife nor his pistols, making it evident that he was being cautious. The braves did not insist on disarming him.

They came at last to a collection of huts made of wood and clay, with animal skins covering the entrances and windows of the various buildings. The dwellings were far cruder than those of the Pequot or the Mohegan, and Roaring Wolf tried to hide his contempt. The Raritan, in his opinion, were an inferior people.

Certainly they were an agricultural people, subsisting principally on the grains and vegetables they grew in the rolling fields beyond their village. There were occasional deer to be found on Staten Island, along with other game, but the tribe lived almost exclusively on its crops, which were supplemented by an abundant supply of seafood of all varieties.

Eliza proved to be of immediate interest to both squaws and braves, elders and youngsters alike. They stared at her critically as she walked past with her head held high. Their faces reflected neither friendship nor animosity. The only whites they had known were the Dutch, whom they regarded as mortal enemies, and this foreign woman who had been escorted here by an alien Indian appeared to be other than Dutch. The sachem of the tribe, who introduced himself as Pah-goom, invited the newcomers into his hut for a parley. They were asked to sit, and Eliza quickly proved equal to the occasion, sitting cross-legged with ease and spreading her skirts gracefully over her knees.

Pah-goom offered his visitors a rank-smelling paste made from chopped, slightly fermented fish. The odor was nauseating, but Eliza forced herself to take several bites of the noisome mixture. It would have been the worst of bad manners to refuse what was intended as a delicacy.

Eliza was secretly amused because the usual roles were reversed. The Pequot spoke in his own tongue and she acted as translator, changing his words into the tongue of the Reckagawawanc so the leader of the Raritan would understand. Roaring Wolf introduced her first and foremost as the implacable enemy of the Dutch. This in itself assured her of welcome and refuge in the land of the Raritan. Although Eliza hadn't conferred with Roaring Wolf, she approved wholeheartedly of his strategy. Next, he said, she was the daughter of the great sachem of the English who lived in New Haven, and she was the squaw of a mighty warrior.

Pah-goom looked at her with respect, as did the braves who had escorted her to his dwelling and who crowded into the hut behind her.

The Dutch, Roaring Wolf declared, had taken her captive and had intended to hold her as a hostage to insure the surrender of her people. But she had outsmarted them—with his aid, he added modestly—and had escaped.

Now, he told them, she threw herself on the mercy of the Raritan and begged for the right to stay here and live in peace in their midst until her husband could come for her and take her home safely.

Pah-goom listened carefully to the recital, his face revealing none of his reactions. When Roaring Wolf was finished and had folded his hands, Eliza did the same and allowed her head to droop. There was a long silence, and then Pah-goom inquired whether the Pequot also sought refuge for himself.

Roaring Wolf declared he had a duty to perform: He had to hurry to New Haven and inform the great warrior, who was Eliza's husband, of her whereabouts.

It occurred to Eliza that if this tribe wanted to enslave her, it would be a simple enough matter to kill Roaring Wolf and to do as they pleased with her. Presumably no one, including her husband, would ever find out what had become of her.

But Pah-goom quickly indicated that his intentions were honorable. Feeling no need to confer with any of his subordinates, he unconditionally accepted the presence of the woman. The mere fact that she was a foe of the Dutch made her welcome, precisely as Roaring Wolf had anticipated. She could stay here indefinitely, Pah-goom said, and she would be safely housed in the lodge of the married women whose husbands were absent on sentry duty or fishing trips.

That settled the matter, and Roaring Wolf made ready to depart. He would paddle his canoe up the opposite shore of Hudson's River from New Amsterdam, avoiding the colony on Manhattan Island, and would then cross the river and proceed with all due haste to New Haven to apprise Richard of his wife's whereabouts.

As a token of their friendship, the Raritan presented him with a bag of cornmeal and some sundried fish to eat on his journey.

His farewell to Eliza was brief. "Roaring Wolf go now," he told Eliza. "May Great Spirit be with you."

Anxious to reach New Haven as soon as possible, he left Staten Island without further ado. The grateful Eliza walked to the shore with him and watched until she could no longer see his canoe in the dark night. She was comforted by the sound of his paddle, but it, too, gradually faded, and she felt very much alone.

Taking stock of her situation, she found little cause for rejoicing. It was true she had escaped from the net that Peter Stuyvesant had set for her, but the cost might be higher than she was willing to pay. She found herself alone and unprotected, thrust into the midst of a tribe of savages whose way of life was strange to her and about whom she knew virtually nothing. She was as isolated on Staten Island as she would have been in the remote wilds of New France, and she knew she was at the mercy of her hosts.

Their intentions seemed questionable, at best. A half-dozen braves clustered near her as she listened to the slowly fading sound of Roaring Wolf's paddles. When she turned away from the water, one of the warriors startled her by approaching her and clutching at her with both hands.

Eliza was alarmed and hastily took a backward step. This manhandling certainly was not in line with what Pah-goom had indicated would be the treatment she would receive here. The brave grinned at her, then said something in a strange tongue that caused his comrades to laugh.

Eliza didn't care for the sound of that laughter. She couldn't understand a word of what had been said, but she knew that the boastful, preening young males of all nations were alike, and she formed her own conclusions. She had to look out for herself, apparently, so she produced her small poniard from beneath her cloak, and gesturing broadly, indicated her willingness to use it. This startled the warriors, who conferred with one another at length in low, worried undertones.

Eliza would have had to push past them to return to the hut of Pah-goom, so she chose instead simply to hold her ground firmly.

She felt relief when she saw a woman about her own age, clad in a dress of animal skins, with a band of deep green paint smeared on her forehead. The Indian woman obviously had become aware of her distress and had come to determine its cause. She, too, spoke in the language of the Raritan, and Eliza failed to understand her.

Again relying on the tongue of the Reckagawa-wanc, Eliza explained hastily that Pah-goom had promised her sanctuary from her enemies, the Dutch, but the warrior who had tried to assault her apparently had other ideas. The squaw understood and nodded sympathetically as she listened to the white woman's recital. Then, speaking the tongue of the Reckagawawanc with great difficulty, the woman explained the problem.

"The warriors were not to blame," she said.

"They regarded the newcomer as fair game because she was not identified as a squaw."

Eliza listened intently, piecing together the other woman's words, and then said indignantly, "But I am married! I do have a husband!"

The eyes of the woman of the Raritan grew wider and larger. Meanwhile Eliza noted uneasily that the half-dozen warriors were crowding uncomfortably close to her.

The Raritan woman spoke authoritatively and quickly and somehow managed to find the right words in the language of the Reckagawawanc. "Give me your hand at once," she directed.

The mystified Eliza did as she was bidden. The woman drew the other's hand across the green smear on her own forehead.

When Eliza looked down at her fingers, she saw they were thick with dark green paint, and all at once she knew what was expected of her. Needing no further instructions, she daubed the paint on her own forehead. She had identified herself now as a married woman, and that was sufficient to hold off the amorous braves. They stopped their advances at once and stood aside to let her pass.

Escorted by her new ally, Eliza was taken to a long, low building. Animal skins covered the window openings, and the only fresh air entered through a hole in the ceiling above a fire pit in the center of the one-room structure. The fire provided illumination, but the rising heat and smoke cut off most of the outside air.

The squaw explained the situation of the white woman to the seven or eight other women in the building. Eliza had no idea what was being said, but she knew that these women, apparently the wives of absent warriors, understood and supported her. All began to talk at once, and she could make no sense out of the bedlam.

Gradually one fact emerged, however: The squaws were urging her to change from her flimsy silk gown into a crude dress of limp but stout animal skin. Inasmuch as her appearance had been at least partly responsible for the behavior of the braves, Eliza did as she was requested and, removing her own attire, donned the native dress. The squaws studied her at length, giggling. They demanded that she also remove her shoes. She complied, and, like them, stood barefoot.

Then, to her surprise, two of them came forward and plaited her long blond hair, winding the two braids around her head. As a final touch, someone produced a gourd of the smelly green paint that adorned all of their foreheads, and a considerable quantity was smeared on Eliza's face.

Now she realized she looked respectable because she resembled the young squaws of the Raritan. Her hostesses studied their efforts, and their fresh giggles indicated their satisfaction. Then one of the squaws pointed to a shelflike ledge that stood several inches from the ground and was covered with pine boughs. From the gestures of the Indian women, it dawned on her that this was a bed and she was being invited to use it. She stretched out on it obediently.

The burning wood from the fire was reduced to glowing coals. As the large hut grew dark and silent, Eliza became conscious again of the overpowering odors that had assailed her nostrils when she first entered the married women's hut. The air was so thick and close that it was difficult for her to breathe, and her nose told her in no uncertain terms that the squaws of the Raritan bathed and washed their garments infrequently.

She consoled herself with the thought that at least she was safe. Now it appeared that the braves would no longer molest her, and Pah-goom would be able to keep his pledge. The other married women would look after her, and she would be safe in their midst as she awaited Richard's arrival.

She had made good her escape from Peter Stuyvesant, and for that she would be eternally grateful.

VII

THE leaders of New Haven Colony gathered in Colonel Adam Burrows's library, and their conference dragged on hour after hour as they tried to come to grips with a problem that appeared insoluble.

"Unfortunately, gentlemen," the colonel said, "we know the answer, but we have no way of persuading others to find it, too."

Richard Dunstable, present in his capacity as major and field commander of the colony's militia, nodded in agreement. "There's no argument among us," he said. "All of us are of one mind. We and the other English colonies must unite in order to eliminate the danger that threatens to annihilate us."

"We clearly see the threat that Peter Stuyvesant and his Dutch pose to us," Adam declared. "Our sister colonies are so busy feuding and are so immersed in their own petty concerns that they seem incapable of grasping what to us are obvious facts."

"Our real problem," Richard continued, "is that we can't afford to procrastinate. If we waste time, the Dutch will nibble our colonies to death one by one, beginning with New Haven and working their way north through all of New England."

Tom Clayton, impulsive by nature, could not control his anger. "The shortsightedness of the other colonies makes me sick," he said angrily.

Adam Burrows showed greater patience than did his partner. "A show of temper will avail us nothing," he said. "It strikes me that we have but one choice. We must invite the military and civil leaders of the neighboring colonies to a parley here. At that meeting, we must muster our best rhetorical skills and persuade them to unite at once for the common good. We now have hard evidence that Stuyvesant is supplying muskets to the Indians." He held up the document Eliza had stolen from Stuyvesant's desk. The leaders had all agreed it was damning evidence. "All we have to do now is convince the other colonies that the Indians mean to turn those muskets on them. Perhaps we'll be inspired in some way; I don't really know. I do know that we have to try to make them see the danger we all face."

The others nodded wearily. They had been discussing the one subject for hours and were ready to agree to anything that seemed to have a fair chance of succeeding. Therefore it was voted unanimously to invite the other colonies to a conference in the immediate future. Letters would be written first thing in the morning and dispatched by special messengers.

One by one those who had attended the meeting went off to their own homes. Richard was one of the last to leave his father-in-law's dwelling, and as he walked down the tree-lined streets to his own house, he decided he would have a drink before going to bed. He was unaccustomed to such late-night meetings, and decided that a mug of ale would help him sleep.

He realized that what was really bothering him was his loneliness and his concern for Eliza. He had been emotionally crippled, he decided, ever since they had been separated, and he bitterly regretted his decision to agree to their living apart for this long a time. However, she had covered herself with glory, and there was no question but that her findings marked a turning point in the relations of the English New World colonies with Holland. He still believed that the French were involved in some way on the side of the Dutch, but that was not important at the moment. The troops of Peter Stuyvesant and their armed Indian allies represented a sufficiently great threat to the future of the English colonies that the stand taken by the French was almost irrelevant. His mind whirling, Richard let himself into his house and went at once to his study, where he lighted an oil lamp. He could hear the maid walking around upstairs, but decided not to bother her. Instead, taking a candle and lighting it from the lamp, he made his way down to the damp, cool cellar for the ale that he kept there. Returning with a mug of it to the first floor, he stiffened suddenly. He was not alone.

To his utter amazement he saw Celeste Murette leaning nonchalantly in the doorway of his study. Her dark hair had been loosened and cascaded in waves past her shoulders and down her back. Her artfully applied cosmetics made her shining lavender eyes enormous and emphasized her sensual, pouting mouth. He realized that her off-the-shoulder gown was specially chosen for its provocative style.

She laughed huskily and crossed the floor toward him, her hips swaying gently. Taking his mug of ale, she sipped from it. "This is not bad," she whispered, "but I prefer a drink of West Indian rum. I've grown very fond of that libation since I've been in New England."

The confused Richard found a mug for her and poured her a drink of rum, to which he added water from a pitcher.

Celeste raised her drink to salute him, then peered at him coyly over the top of her mug. "You seem astonished to see me," she said.

Richard could only nod.

"I decided I had to see you and get something settled with you tonight," she said. "The maid let me in. I had no idea you would be out so late."

"Neither did I," he muttered. "The leaders' conference at Adam's house went on and on."

"Oh?" she asked. "What was decided?"

"We're going to invite the civil and military leaders of the other English colonies to a meeting here, and we're going to do our best to persuade them to band together so that we can be united in our opposition to Governor Stuyvesant of New Netherland."

Celeste was hardly surprised; the decision was exactly what she had anticipated. Stuyvesant was a vain and overly ambitious fool who had gone too far when he had supplied firearms to the Indians.

It was that judgment that had led Celeste Murette to assess her own position. She had to admit that she had grown tired of her role as an agent for France; she longed for the day when she could settle down in comfort. Somewhat to her surprise, she actually enjoyed the New World, where she was far freer than she had ever been in England or in Europe. She had decided, furthermore, that her first choice of the right man for her was Sir Richard Dunstable.

Eliza was still an obstacle, of course. But Celeste had learned from Adam Burrows how Richard's wife had outsmarted Stuyvesant, and she had a hunch that Eliza's future welfare was none too certain now. Consequently, Celeste had come to Richard's house intending to try for the last time to soften his resistance. She was fully prepared, if necessary, to seduce him. Like Adam Burrows, he could well afford to support her in the style that she enjoyed, and she freely admitted to herself that his rugged masculinity held an irresistible appeal to her.

She had no intention of sending in her resignation to Cardinal Mazarin just yet, however. Long a believer in the theory that it was unwise to throw out stale water until she obtained fresh, she wanted to establish herself securely in New Haven before she terminated her employment with the first minister of France. But she revealed none of her thinking now as she smiled steadily up at Richard.

Richard had no wish, however, to prolong this confrontation. Not only was the hour late, but he was aware—uncomfortably so—of the woman's femininity and his vulnerability. Her appeal to him was almost too strong for him to resist, and therefore he was eager to bring this discussion to a close.

"What's on your mind?" he demanded brusquely.

Celeste decided to use shock tactics. "I can think only of you and me," she replied softly.

He was so startled he sucked in his breath.

"I haven't forgotten our lovemaking," she said, putting a hand on his arm, "and I know from your expression that you haven't, either. We had an extraordinary experience, and it couldn't have been accidental. I felt compelled to talk to you about our mutual future."

Richard knew of only one way to handle the embarrassing situation, and decided to be blunt. "You forget," he declared, "that I'm married. I regret to say that you temporarily overwhelmed me, but I have no intention of allowing that to happen again."

212

Celeste was only slightly deterred. She didn't want to arouse his fears for Eliza's safety—that would accomplish nothing now—but she could appeal to his masculine pride. "For your sake," she said, "I hope you aren't putting too much faith in a woman who absents herself from her own home for weeks at a time."

Some explanation was necessary, but he could only reply awakwardly, "She has duties that keep her in New Amsterdam."

"I've heard rumors about those duties," Celeste said archly, "and I'm astonished that you haven't heard them, also. It's said to be common knowledge in New Amsterdam that Eliza Dunstable is the mistress of Governor Stuyvesant."

Richard drew a deep breath and hoped his voice was steady as he replied. "I hadn't heard the rumors. A husband is always said to be the last to become aware of them, of course. But I have sufficient faith in Eliza to place no credence whatsoever in rumors. I know she's faithful to me."

Celeste raised an eyebrow and then asked gently, "As faithful, perhaps, as you've been to her?"

He winced, but he couldn't blame her for the sarcasm. He had treated this woman shabbily, and couldn't blame her if she resented it. "Celeste," he said, "I lost my head over you, and I admit it freely. You—you overwhelmed me, and all I knew was that I had to have you. I've done you an injustice, and I sincerely regret it."

She knew he meant what he said, and became all the more determined to have him. He was honest almost to a fault, and with her previous experience with so many dishonest men, he became all the more honorable, all the more desirable.

"I hear what you're saying," she said, "but I don't accept your rejection. I've waited too long for you to come into my life. I'm not going to give you up now without a real battle."

He took a long, fortifying swallow of his ale and wondered how he could convince her that they had no future together. "I've never known anyone quite like you. Whenever I'm in your presence I feel as though a powerful magnet is drawing me toward you. But that is an unfortunate feeling I must learn to control. I am a married man—may the Lord have mercy on my soul—and I dare not forget it. I took advantage of you, and I wish I could make amends in some way, but I'm afraid I don't know how to proceed."

Celeste was glad he was naive enough to think that he had taken advantage of her when the opposite had been true. Well, she was prepared to do her utmost again. Sighing gently, she rose, went to him, and winding her arms around his neck, she pressed her body against his. "I want you," she breathed. "I want you more than anything on earth."

Richard knew that this was a moment of supreme crisis in his domestic life. He had given into temptation once and, to his own surprise, had been unfaithful to Eliza. Now, however, he knew what to expect, and if he failed in his fidelity again, his conduct would be inexcusable. If he gave in to his own yearnings now, he did not deserve to stay married to Eliza. He stood up straight and, bracing himself rigidly, caught hold of Celeste's wrists and forced them to her sides.

Never had she been subjected to such treatment. She had been able to overwhelm any man at will, yet here was one, already familiar with her charms, who dared to turn her down.

"I'm sorry," Richard told her, his tone conveying the finality of his decision.

All at once she gave up. She knew she had lost the struggle, and she had no intention of humiliating or debasing herself. One alternative was still open to her, and she intended to pursue it vigorously.

She took a half-step backwards, and her regret was genuine as she said, "I'm sorry, too. You and I could have been wonderful together, but I hope you'll find the happiness you deserve with Eliza."

"I hope so, too," he replied.

She thought quickly and made an immediate decision. "It's far too late now for me to go home," she said, "but I know better than to suggest that we share the same bed innocently. Perhaps you'll allow me to spend what's left of the night in a spare bedroom."

"Of course," he replied gallantly, relieved that the incident had ended without rancor. "I will have the maid ready the room for you."

They retired separately, with Celeste adjourning to a guest room, and as the weary Richard dragged himself off to bed, he put her out of his mind. He was relieved that she appeared to have accepted his marriage, and he looked back on their relationship as a mistake.

In the morning he went into the dining room for breakfast, which had been prepared by the maid. There his father-in-law found him and joined him at the table as they went over the text of the communication that Colonel Burrows had written to the leaders of the other colonies, inviting them to New Haven.

Neither man realized that Celeste Murette stood on the far side of the door, eavesdropping and making up her mind how to proceed. She had never lacked resourcefulness, and she knew what had to be done. She would act with great boldness now and salvage much for her future. If she couldn't have Richard Dunstable, Adam Burrows was an excellent second choice. His wealth was far greater than that of his son-in-law, his standing in the community was impeccable, and any woman he married would automatically become the first lady of New Haven Colony. There were far worse lives to live.

Celeste had refreshed her makeup carefully. After glancing at her reflection in a pier glass for reassurance, she opened the door and swept into the dining room. "Good morning, gentlemen," she said blandly.

Adam stared at her, frozen in his seat.

Richard was mortified; his first thought was that Celeste was tricking him.

That, however, was not the case, as she rapidly made clear. "I'm so glad you're here, Adam," she said. "I wanted to come to you last night, but you had too many men meeting at your house. That's why I came here instead. It was so late by the time I'd explained my mission that Richard was kind enough to allow me to use his guest room."

"I see," the Colonel muttered, but it was obvious that he was still confused. However, a look at the seemingly unperturbed maid assured him that nothing improper had occurred the previous evening.

Richard breathed a trifle more easily, but he had no idea what Lady Celeste had in mind.

"As I explained to Richard," she said, turning to him for an instant and allowing one eyelid to droop in a quick suggestion of a wink, "I believe I can be of considerable assistance to you and to New Haven Colony in the problem that faces you."

Colonel Burrows turned, looking at her doubtfully. Richard was too astonished to react.

"I have lived in New Amsterdam, you know," she said. "I spent more than three years there, and I came to know Peter Stuyvesant rather well." She refrained from saying that she had been his mistress. "I am convinced that Stuyvesant has supplied firearms to one Indian tribe after another. I have told Richard that I am prepared to go before a meeting of New England leaders and address them myself. Perhaps I can convince them of their need to band together."

"What a marvelous idea!" Colonel Burrows exclaimed.

Richard nodded slowly. He had to hand it to Celeste Murette. She was ingenious almost beyond belief, the most clever young woman he had ever encountered. There was no question in his mind that her beauty would sway the leaders of the other colonies far more persuasively than anything that he or Colonel Burrows could say to them.

She continued to smile blandly. "I'm so glad you approve, my dear," she said. "Richard thought the idea was quite sound, too." With seeming impulsiveness she reached out a hand toward Adam.

Impervious to the presence of his son-in-law, he took hold of her hand and grasped it firmly.

Celeste's look would have melted steel, Richard thought, and he wondered for an instant whether she was capable of simulating a passionate interest in a man. No, he decided, that was unfair of him and did not do her justice. She had accepted his own withdrawal with good grace, and he owed her his full support as a result.

"I told Lady Celeste," he said, lying almost as glibly as she had done, "that I thought that she might be able to turn the tide in our favor. New Haven—in fact, all of New England—is going to be indebted to her."

Colonel Burrows beamed, and his grip on her hand tightened. He had hesitated to ask her to marry him because of his awareness of the gulf of years that separated them—after all, she was only a year or two older than his daughter. But her interest in him seemed so genuine that he faltered in his resolve.

"I'm new to the English colonies and to your ways," she murmured, "but I felt that this was something I had to do strictly for you, dear Adam."

That settled it! Adam Burrows decided he would propose to her as soon as he could. He thanked her for her generosity, and then fell silent while she ate a small portion of fish and drank a cup of tea.

"I'll take Celeste home before I join you at the office, Richie," he said. "So if you don't mind taking this letter, the staff can make fair copies of it immediately."

Richard took the letter and rose to his feet. He was aware that he was in the way and sensed the growing intimacy between the couple, but he was too jarred by the unexpected denouement of the events of the previous day to think clearly. It was enough for him, certainly, that Lady Celeste had provided a possible solution to the seemingly insurmountable problem of allied unity.

Eliza quickly fitted into the lives of the Raritan Indians, and as weeks passed, she grew accustomed to the daily routine. She awakened early and joined the other young women with whom she shared quarters at a breakfast of cornmeal and fish, which was cooked right in front of the lodge. Then they all trooped out to the fields beyond the confines of the village. There they worked all day—now harvesting the last ears of maize, which was their principal food.

The squaws used either their bare hands or the most primitive of tools, and Eliza necessarily did the same. Her hands grew rough, and she acquired a glowing, tanned skin. She was secretly amused by her transition from the glamorous, supposed mistress of Peter Stuyvesant to an Indian squaw. In fact, had it not been for her pale blond hair, she would have been indistinguishable from the other women of the Raritan tribe.

The workers returned to the village shortly before sundown, and all of the women then joined in the preparations for their supper. This also consisted of fish, along with large quantities of beans, squash, and corn, the staples of the diet of all the tribes on the eastern seaboard of North America. After supper, the women sat outside their lodge, sewing with large bone needles, repairing items of apparel, and watching the other members of the tribe passing to and fro. This was a time devoted to gossip and storytelling. By listening carefully, Eliza was able to pick up at least a working knowledge of the Raritan language, building on her knowledge of the similar Reckagawawanc tongue.

She instituted one innovation of her own when she completed her day's work and returned to the town: She took time before beginning preparations for supper to go down to the beach, where she enjoyed a refreshing swim. The other women thought it strange at first, but one by one they joined her, and seemed to enjoy the outing. At least, as Eliza told herself, they became clean in the salt water and the odors in the lodge became bearable.

They swam in the nude without self-consciousness, and warriors of the tribe wandered down toward the beach and watched from a safe distance. The Raritan had strict moral standards, and the women were so indignant that they complained to Pah-goom and his principal medicine men. Eliza had no idea what steps they took, but the following day the warriors were nowhere in sight when the young women went to the sea to swim.

The women of the tribe accepted Eliza from the outset, although they maintained a natural reserve. This attitude gradually vanished because she did her fair share of labor.

Others in the tribe were curious about the white woman, but as they became familiar with her as she fitted smoothly into their daily lives, they, too, began to take her presence for granted.

Although she wore the green paint of a married woman, the warriors continued to study her surreptitiously. Her beauty was so striking and her hair so pale that she fascinated them. None was more interested in her than a tall senior warrior named Jono-ta, one of the braves who had watched her when she swam. At night after supper, as the other squaws pointed out to her, he seemed to make it his business to wander back and forth near their lodge, smiling, nodding, and ogling. One of the women found occasion to discuss him one day when she and Eliza were husking corn near each other. "Jono-ta," the woman said, "admires the new squaw who has come to live with the people of the Raritan."

The revelation was not surprising, and Eliza nodded. "He has seen the paint on my forehead," she replied, "and knows that I am married. I hope he will keep his distance."

The squaw giggled at length, then shrugged. "Of all the warriors of the Raritan," she said, "there is no other so fierce as Jo-no-ta. Only the gods know what he will do."

Eliza was far from reassured, but told herself that the man appeared to be sensible, and that in all probability he would not molest her.

One evening shortly thereafter, Jo-no-ta paused as he walked past Eliza, who was sitting outside her lodge learning how to dye porcupine quills. He appeared to be on the verge of speaking to her. She did not see how direct contact could be avoided, so she raised her head and greeted him with a half-smile. The warrior, presumably the most ferocious of the Raritan, promptly fled.

Eliza saw no sign of him for almost forty-eight hours. She next encountered him one afternoon after she emerged from the sea, letting the sun and air dry her before she donned her leather dress. With her hair duly braided, she started back toward the village with two companions. Suddenly a tall, square-shouldered figure appeared before her, emerging from behind the crest of a sand dune. Jo-no-ta awaited her.

The only way Eliza could have avoided him would have meant making a wide detour, but that would have been an obvious slight, and she didn't want to hurt his feelings. So she continued to move toward him in a direct line, regretting that she had not brought any green forehead paint to the beach with her as the other women often did. She noted, too, that the brave was exceptionally rugged and well built, and wondered why she had never noted this about him previously. He raised his right hand, arm outstretched and palm forward in the customary Indian greeting.

She slowed her pace and raised her own arm briefly in return. A direct confrontation, she realized, could no longer be avoided.

It suddenly occurred to her that her companions had disappeared from sight. Whether they had vanished because of prearrangement with Jo-no-ta, or whether discretion impelled them to make themselves scarce, she could not determine. In any event, she knew she would be seeing him alone on a vast expanse of unoccupied beach, and she became justifiably concerned and nervous.

The warrior's dark eyes studied her intently. Eliza felt naked beneath his prolonged gaze.

"Jo-no-ta, greatest warrior of the Raritan," he said gravely, "greets the sun-haired maiden who has come from another land."

She was quick to become aware of the major inaccuracy in his statement. "She who comes from another land," she replied, "is no maiden. Jo-no-ta has seen the paint that tells all that she is a squaw. He has seen with his own eyes that she wears this paint on her forehead." She regretted deeply that she had thought it unnecessary to borrow such paint from one of the other women at the beach.

The brave was in no way disconcerted. "She is married to a warrior?" he demanded, folding his arms across his chest.

Eliza nodded and said with slow emphasis, "He is a very great warrior. He has killed many enemies with his firestick," she announced. "He has thrown his knives and sent many others fleeing in terror." She hoped her words were making an appropriate impression.

Jo-no-ta's expression remained inscrutable, and he promptly demonstrated that he had a practical turn of mind. "This warrior," he said, "lives far from the land of the Raritan."

She could not argue the point, and nodded in agreement.

"He is not here," Jo-no-ta said, "but his squaw is here."

His logic, unfortunately, was unassailable. "He who is married to the squaw called Eliza," she said emphatically, "will soon come to the land of the Raritan. He comes to rejoin his squaw, and she awaits him here. Soon he will be here." She folded her arms across her breast and looked up defiantly at the warrior.

Jo-no-ta, to Eliza's surprise, laughed aloud. His laughter broke the tension between them, and Eliza smiled broadly. It was a genuine, spontaneous smile. In spite of the vast gap that separated her from this Indian, each had understood perfectly what the other was trying to say.

The warrior promptly showed that he bore no

grudges. "Jo-no-ta of the Raritan," he declared, "will be the brother of the warrior who is married to Eliza. Until that day comes, he will be the friend of Eliza."

Her instinct told her that she could trust this savage. He was not lying in order to catch her off guard or seduce her. She felt certain he meant what he said, and she was grateful to him for his fundamental decency. "Eliza," she said firmly, "would like to be the friend of Jo-no-ta." She wanted to extend her hand to him, but was afraid that he might misunderstand the gesture, so she refrained.

Her words satisfied him. He fell in beside her, walking back to the village of the Raritan with her and escorting her back to her lodge. She wished she had some token she could give him to seal the bond of their new and unexpected friendship, but she had brought nothing with her from New Amsterdam other than a dress and cloak plus the jewelry she had been wearing at the time. Tokens were important to Indians, and she thought quickly of all her belongings, but knew of nothing appropriate that she could give him.

Obviously, he felt as she did. He reached into the belt at the top of his loincloth, drew out a bone-handled knife, and presented it to her with a flourish.

All at once, Eliza knew what was required of her in return. She asked him to wait, dashed into the lodge, and returned with her double-bladed poniard, which she handed to him with a flourish. The warrior took it, his eyes bright, and examined the sharp steel, unlike any that he had ever seen. Here was an extraordinary instrument, and the squaw had presented it to him of her own free will. He was almost overwhelmed by the gift and, reaching out, caught hold of her forearm. His grip was so strong that Eliza found it difficult to refrain from wincing.

Assuring her again of his friendship, he abruptly took his leave. The other women who resided in the lodge were deeply impressed. Jo-no-ta was no ordinary brave, at least in their opinion, and his friendship was to be prized.

All Eliza knew was that she had avoided an embarrassing and potentially dangerous situation by turning a primitive, would-be seducer into an ally and friend. That was good enough for her, and she was relieved that the incident had ended without trouble.

Adam Burrows's letter from New Haven to the other New England colonies stressed the urgency of the meeting he proposed. He made it plain that a crisis had arisen in the lives of all who had come to live in the New World, and that the decisions reached at the meeting would determine the prospects for survival for many years to come.

Even those colonies that thought he might be exaggerating the perils from the Dutch acceded to his wishes and sent their militia chiefs and at least one of their highest civil officials to New Haven. The quickness of the response to his plea was heartening.

Everyone who had room to spare provided housing for the visitors. Richard Dunstable offered two bedrooms in his house, Ezekiel and Mimi Clayton volunteered one, and the colonel made the better part of his house available to guests. Celeste Murette further ingratiated herself with Adam by insisting on housing several of the colonial leaders under her own roof.

At the initial meetings of the group, Richard repeated much of what he had said previously on his visits to the individual colonies. He pointed out that muskets had been captured from Indians in several uprisings in different colonies, and that he was virtually certain that the weapons were of Dutch manufacture. Now he also had written proof that Peter Stuyvesant was providing the Indians with arms, thus breaking the unspoken agreement upheld by all the European powers claiming territory in the New World. He passed around the order Eliza had stolen from Stuyvesant's desk, and the various delegates perused it closely, murmuring to one another. They seemed reluctant to believe that Stuyvesant's order was genuine.

Adam Burrows followed his son-in-law's address by making a speech of his own. He stressed the ambitious nature of Stuyvesant and his subordinates as seen by New Haven Colony, the closest neighbor of the Dutch. He urged immediate action.

Riddled with jealousies and burdened with their own problems, the colonial leaders shortsightedly remained reluctant to act. The time had come, Adam decided, to call on Celeste.

She responded instantly and rose to the challenge. Dressing simply and using cosmetics with a far lighter touch than was her custom, she joined the conferees at Colonel Burrows's house and launched into a recital that left them stunned.

Stressing that she had lived in New Amsterdam for more than three years, she related that she had become well acquainted with Governor Stuyvesant. Speaking earnestly, she stressed that he was stubborn and often ruthless in his determination to have his own way. He wanted the Netherlands to become the predominant power in the New World, she explained, because he saw himself in the role of the governor-general of a vast territory. At no time even intimating that she had been Stuyvesant's mistress, she nevertheless painted a full word picture of him that left little to the imagination of her listeners. When she finished speaking, her audience sat spellbound.

Dempster Chaney broke the tense silence. Did she know for a fact, he demanded, that Peter Stuyvesant sought to enlarge the boundaries of New Netherland and that he saw himself as the presiding authority in the New World?

"There's no question about it," Celeste answered flatly, aware that she was burning her bridges behind her, and that as long as Stuyvesant remained in New Netherland, she could not return to the Dutch colony. "He spoke very frankly to me and indicated his ambitions on numerous occasions—in so many words."

There was little that anyone present could say to denigrate the importance of what the leaders had learned.

The meeting was recessed for the noon meal. Celeste remained at the Burrows house and was the center of attention throughout dinner. The leaders of the other colonies, as the truth of the Dutch menace dawned on them, questioned her closely about the military preparations that Stuyvesant had made and about his overall plans for extending Dutch influence.

Celeste replied candidly and at length. Having committed herself, she held nothing back, and felt that she had everything to gain and nothing to lose by being honest.

It was true, to be sure, that she was being disloyal not only to the Dutch, but also to Cardinal Mazarin of France, with whom she held a special place as a secret agent. She had deliberately cast aside that role and was embarking now on a totally new career, a new life.

The meeting reconvened immediately after dinner. Dempster Chaney, one of the youngest of the participants, summed up the feelings of all when he said, "We've been blind, I reckon. Major Dunstable and Colonel Burrows have tried to open our eyes to the truth, but we've been too stubborn to see the situation that really exists. All I can say now is that the town of Taunton in Massachusetts Bay Colony pledges full support to New Haven in the crisis with the Dutch."

One by one the other colonies also promised their full support. Colonel Burrows was delighted; he beamed at Celeste Murette, who sat inconspicuously in the back of the room while awaiting the outcome of the deliberations. He held her responsible for changing the atmosphere and making so pronounced a shift in the opinion of the colonial leaders.

Practical matters were arranged swiftly. Colonel Burrows explained that neither he nor anyone else knew whether the British Parliament and Oliver Cromwell would support a full-scale colonial war against the Netherlands that well might spill over into Europe and involve the mother countries. "For that reason," he said, "a direct confrontation with the Dutch, which might make such a war inevitable, has to be avoided. However, there's more than one way to skin a polecat."

His son-in-law took up the theme. Richard explained that a number of the Indian allies of the Dutch were gathering in New Amsterdam, presumably for the purpose of acquiring still more firearms. He proposed that the English colonies send a joint expedition across the New Amsterdam border to meet these Indians in battle and defeat them. He made it clear that the expedition should not directly threaten the Dutch and that word should be sent to Governor Stuyvesant that his people would not be attacked unless they deliberately provoked a confrontation or engaged in the battle.

"There are many more English than Dutch residents of the city of New Amsterdam," Richard said, "so I feel reasonably confident that Governor Stuyvesant will not actively seek to join in combat against us, and instead will be glad to avoid such combat."

The key to the success of an English expedition, Colonel Burrows declared, lay in the ability of the troops to defeat the Indian tribes that were allies of Stuyvesant. If this could be done, the plans of the Dutch would collapse. If the Indians won, however, there would be nothing to halt Stuyvesant's expansion of his powers.

"I want to clarify one thing above all," Richard declared. "The longer we take to march, the more our chances of victory are diminished. The reasons are obvious. Indians who have never in their lives handled firearms are being given muskets. As yet they have, at best, a limited knowledge of how to use these weapons. They are almost certain to be inferior marksmen. If we give them time to become practiced in the use of firearms, however, they are certain to improve. I shudder to think of what will happen to us and our colonies if armed savages who outnumber us many times over become expert in the use of firearms. I say that we must strike hard now, while we still have the advantage."

His point made such obvious good sense that there was little discussion, and the vote in favor of a campaign in the very near future was unanimous.

Richard had one additional point to stress. "Make no secret of your mobilizations, gentlemen," he said. "Don't gather your troops in silence or dispatch them in secrecy. The Indians in your various districts should know what you're planning. The more decisive and more encompassing the victory, the safer we'll be for many years to come from any plotting that the Dutch might do."

A voice vote was taken, and his ideas were approved. All that remained to be decided was the number of men to be dispatched from each of the colonies and the election of a joint field commander. The mood of those participating in the meeting had changed so drastically that colony after colony pledged itself to send the maximum force available. Richard Dunstable was elected by acclamation as field commander of the expedition.

Celeste Murette, sitting at the rear of the room, realized that history was being made in New Haven that day. Of primary significance to her was the indisputable fact that the first minister of France had gambled and had lost. Cardinal Mazarin had supported the Dutch in the hope that they would carry the burden of France and would triumph over the English in the New World. Now, it appeared, an expeditionary force was being gathered that would crush the allies of the Dutch and would make it impossible for Peter Stuyvesant to realize his ambitions. Even more important, France would be stripped of her secret ally, and her private plans to gain possession of the more populous and lucrative English colonies would be dealt a severe blow.

She was right, she reasoned, to be deserting the French cause. She had to look out for herself, and it was obvious to her that the united English colonials would dominate the New World for at least a generation to come.

Their primary business concluded, the colonial leaders adjourned, with the heads of militia going off to Richard's house to discuss details of the coming campaign.

At Adam Burrows's request, Celeste remained behind after all of the guests had departed. Adam smiled at her and shook his head in admiration as he said, "When the annals of the New England colonies are written, I hope you'll be given your just due as their savior. You have no idea what a great service you've rendered to all of us today.

"You exaggerate, Adam," she replied modestly. "But if I've made a contribution to the cause of freedom, I'm more than satisfied."

"You've done a marvelous thing for the English colonies, and you're much too modest," he said emphatically. "I'm overwhelmed by your contribution."

"What I've done," Celeste replied, "was the least I could do for the land that has adopted me and been so kind to me. I've faced the hostility of an alien government in New Amsterdam, and the atmosphere here is as different as night from day." She was telling the truth, at least to an extent, and she felt she was on solid ground. She had no means of communication now with Cardinal Mazarin, and her past would be revealed only if Peter Stuyvesant talked out of turn.

Adam steeled himself, rose to his feet, and bowed. "I can best express my own feelings by becoming more personal," he said. "I—I hope you will do me the honor of becoming Mistress Burrows." He hesitated and swallowed hard. "If you do not, of course, I can't blame you. I'm many years older than you, and the things you seek in life may not be what I have to offer."

She looked up at him, a hint of mischief in her lavender eyes as she said, "You present cogent reasons, sir, for my rejecting your offer. Do you have any reasons that might cause me to accept?"

Adam grimaced. "I can only say that I offer you my whole heart, my dear."

Celeste was deeply touched. She had initiated a relationship with Adam Burrows as a means of assuring her own safety in the event that her romance with Richard Dunstable turned sour. Well, Richard had rejected her advances, and she had turned to the

colonel as a sure means of achieving the security
and comfort that his position and wealth could offer. He was so sincere in his protestations, however,
that she could not help but respond to him. Rising
to her feet, she approached him slowly. "I shall be
honored," she said, "to become Mistress Burrows,
and I shall devote myself wholeheartedly to your
welfare." She slid her arms around his neck and
kissed him soundly.

Adam was overcome; he trembled slightly as he
returned the embrace and kiss of the woman who
was so many years his junior. Then, as he recovered his equilibrium, his natural dignity asserted itself. He knew that his family might object. He
was secretly relieved that Eliza was absent from
New Haven and hence could not oppose his marriage.

But he was convinced he knew what he was doing, and felt certain that the woman who had just
accepted him was as fine and noble as she appeared. The critics would be confounded and
forced to retreat in disgrace when they came to
know her as well as he did.

Virtually the entire New Haven regiment volunteered for action in the coming campaign. Richard,
however, did not want to deprive the colony of all
its defenders. Consequently he decided, with Colonel Burrows's approval, to leave a small force in
New Haven and take the rest with him into New
Netherland. He selected his men carefully for the
campaign, choosing those who had the greatest endurance, those who best knew the wilderness, and
those who were superior marksmen.

He was engaged in this task on the green when a
familiar travel-stained figure approached him. Roaring Wolf's moccasins were covered with dust, there
were bramble scratches on his arms and legs, and

it was obvious that he had come a considerable distance in a hurry. He looked weary, too, but nevertheless he smiled broadly when he saw his good friend.

Richard instantly thought of his wife. After he greeted the Pequot, he drew him aside and asked, "What news do you bring of Eliza?"

Roaring Wolf related in great detail how Governor Stuyvesant had put his troops and constabulary to searching for her, and how he had been outsmarted by Eliza's escape to the land of the Raritan on Staten Island.

Richard listened carefully to the recital, his mind seething, but he did not interrupt. He waited until the warrior had finished speaking, then demanded, "Are you certain she's safe?"

The Pequot nodded. "Roaring Wolf is sure," he declared.

Knowing almost nothing about the Raritan Indians, Richard was less certain, but his friend hastened to reassure him that the sachem of the tribe was an honorable man and that the Raritan were opposed to the Dutch in all things at all times. The fact that the governor of New Netherland sought to capture Eliza had automatically made her a heroine in the eyes of the natives, who would do their utmost to protect her.

Richard hastened to his father-in-law with the news, and they pondered it for a time. "I wonder," Colonel Burrows said, "if Stuyvesant got wind of the fact that Eliza was actually a double agent and was spying on his actions for us?"

"It seems logical," Richard replied cautiously.

"Well," his father-in-law said, "I can imagine no other reason why he would be so anxious to capture her."

"I can," Richard replied grimly.

A light dawned, and Adam Burrows decided it

was best to drop the subject. He was treading on sensitive ground and thought it best to leave well enough alone.

Richard was eager to set out at once to escort his wife back to New Haven. However, with the campaign in New Amsterdam impending, this was the worst of all possible times for him to absent himself from the colony. As the commander of the New Haven contingent and leader of the entire expedition, he was needed here and could not be spared to travel on personal business—not even for a week —even though his wife was involved.

Adam suggested that they send others to retrieve Eliza and bring her back safely, but Richard demurred. He alone would be responsible for her return to New Haven. The only possible solution, he decided, was to wait until the campaign was well under way. Then, since he would be much closer to Staten Island than he was at present, he would hurry there as soon as he could. In the meantime, Richard thought, the least he could do would be to advise Eliza of his plans. He wrote her a carefully cryptic letter, ever mindful of the fact that it might fall into the hands of the Dutch, whom he had no desire to inform of the military plans of the English colonies. He urged her to continue to be patient and promised that he would come to Staten Island for her at the first possible moment.

Roaring Wolf was eager to participate in the coming campaign with his friend, but it was far more important, Richard decided, for the brave to return to the land of the Raritan with the communication to Eliza. Only the Indian was sufficiently familiar with the territory to undertake this mission. Therefore, after resting for a full day, the Pequot again set out alone through the wilderness, retracing his steps to the place he had left his canoe less than a week earlier.

His return journey to the land of the Raritan required far more time than he had anticipated, however. To his surprise, scores of Indian tribes who were allied with the Dutch were gathering north of Manhattan on Dutch soil. There even were Abnaki warriors from the Maine district far to the north of Massachusetts Bay, together with nearly every nation that lived between them and the Wappinger on the shore of the Great Bay. The Indians obviously had heard about Stuyvesant's gifts of muskets and saw this as their best opportunity to benefit from the governor's generosity.

It was necessary for Roaring Wolf to proceed with great caution. He gave these parties of warriors as wide a berth as he could and did not pause to rest or eat while in their vicinity. At last he was able to launch his canoe, and after paddling for hours, he reached the Staten Island shore. There he was taken into custody by the young braves who acted as sentries, and they conducted him to Pahgoom.

Soon he was alone with Eliza and delivered her husband's letter to her. She read it eagerly, and although she had borne her vicissitudes with courage and good humor, her eyes suddenly filled with tears.

Roaring Wolf, observing her, revised the low opinion he had held of her for so long. To his astonishment, she looked like an Indian squaw now; only her pale hair and eyes revealed her true race. As nearly as he could judge, he had been mistaken in his assumption that she had been unfaithful to her husband with Stuyvesant and other men as well. He knew now where his duty lay, and he made up his mind instantly.

"Roaring Wolf," he said, "will stay with Eliza until Richard comes for her."

"That won't be necessary," she protested.

"Roaring Wolf will stay," the Pequot replied firmly, and refusing to discuss the subject further with her, he went off to notify the sachem of the Raritan of his decision.

The braves of the tribe accepted this interloper's presence with good grace. Only Jo-no-ta was hostile to him, seeming to resent Roaring Wolf's closeness to Eliza, with whom the Raritan warrior prided himself on his special friendship.

The Pequot's presence in no way altered Eliza's routine. She continued to work alongside the young squaws and to share their lot. Then, one warm afternoon, while she and the others were mending fishing nets, they heard a piercing cry raised in the direction of the beach. The cry was repeated, and apparently it was a signal. All of the woman stopped their work and ran as rapidly as they could in the direction of the sound.

The whole tribe was gathering on the beach, and everyone appeared to be talking at once; the babble was so intense that Eliza could make no sense of what was being said.

Eventually, however, a few basic facts made themselves clear to her. Two of the young warriors of the Raritan had gone fishing, and through sheer coincidence, they had sighted a large flotilla of canoes headed in the direction of Staten Island. In the craft were heavily armed warriors, all of them wearing the war paint of the Wappinger. It appeared certain that a surprise attack was about to be launched by these close friends and allies of the Dutch.

Eliza immediately understood the reason behind the assault: The Dutch had inspired their allies to attack because they wanted their rear position protected in the coming showdown with the New England colonies. It was obvious that the Indians, aware of military preparations in the colonies, had notified Peter Stuyvesant of the mobilization.

The Raritan warriors hastened to get their bows and arrows. The squaws rushed about, organizing the defenses of the village's lodges. At last the tribe's strategy began to manifest itself and became clear to Eliza. The braves were gathering on the beach, where they were preparing to repel the canoes of the invaders, while the women remained behind, prepared to defend the village.

The strategy was a mistake, she thought, and she inadvertently declared, "No! This must not be."

Several of the Raritan stared at her as she hurried to the hut of Pah-goom.

"You will lose many braves," Eliza told him, "if those who fight for the honor of the Raritan wait for their foes on the sand. It would be far better to surprise the enemy rather than make the move that he expects."

The elderly sachem was intrigued, even slightly amused by her effrontery. Never before had a mere squaw dared to offer a battle plan. "What do you suggest?" he asked in a challenging tone.

Eliza replied without hesitation. "Let the squaws and children remain in the village, where they are now. But let all of the warriors draw back to the far side of the tops of the hills of sand that face the beach. There they will conceal themselves. They will see the enemy, but they will not be seen in return. Then as the foes land, let the arrows of the Raritan be directed at those who have dared to invade their soil."

Her advice was sound, and Pah-goom recognized it for its worth. So did a number of senior warriors, among them Jo-no-ta, who immediately began to put her scheme into action. Orders were given quietly, and the Raritan demonstrated that they were a disciplined people, even in times of emergency.

Within a few minutes the women and children had vanished, and the braves had retreated beyond the crests of the sand dunes that faced the sea. The beach was deserted and looked as though the Raritan nation had no idea that an attack was impending.

Staring out to sea, Eliza saw several dots on the horizon that grew steadily larger, and she realized that these were the war canoes of the Wappinger. It also occurred to her that she was alone, standing unprotected on the beach. She withdrew slowly, climbing the tallest of the sand dunes, and suddenly someone reached out and hauled her out of sight.

She found herself facing Jo-no-ta, who looked at her reproachfully. "The place of Eliza," he said, "is with the other squaws."

She shook her head. "The place of Eliza is here," she declared. "You are going into battle on my terms, and I deserve to witness the fight."

She realized that Roaring Wolf had materialized quietly behind her. He, like Jo-no-ta and the warriors of the Raritan, carried a bow and a quiver of arrows. He was not required to fight on the side of the tribe he was visiting, but he had chosen to throw in his lot with them.

So had Eliza. She made her position clear by drawing one of the two pistols Roaring Wolf proudly carried in his belt. Although she made no comment, she well knew she was a superior marksman to the Indian, and she intended to demonstrate her skill and assist her Indian hosts. The weapon was loaded, she was grateful to note, and as she waited for the flotilla of canoes to draw near, she cocked it.

The Wappinger were noted for their discipline and lack of emotion, and the braves lived up to their reputation. The lead canoe swept up onto the beach, and the occupants promptly climbed out and formed in a single line as they faced the dunes.

Eliza noted at once that they were armed with muskets; no doubt they had been supplied the fire-arms by Peter Stuyvesant. It appeared to her critical eye that they handled the weapons rather clumsily, and she hoped she was right in her assumption that they were unfamiliar with them. That would make the task that awaited the Raritan that much easier to perform.

Several of the defenders nocked their arrows in their bows and were on the verge of firing, but Eliza shook her head fiercely. Jo-no-ta had no idea what she had in mind, but raised a hand authorita-tively, and the other warriors obeyed him and held their fire. It was difficult for Eliza to explain what she had in mind. The language barrier that separated her from the Raritan was considerable, and the need to whisper in order that the enemy not hear added yet another handicap. She reflected that the Raritan would have to take her counsel on good faith. If the defenders fired their arrows prema-turely, the other boatloads of attacking warriors would be warned and therefore able to adjust their assault accordingly. It was far preferable, she knew, to catch as many of the invaders unawares as pos-sible.

Eliza hoped her manner conveyed confidence as she shook her head, holding one cautioning hand upraised as she studied the approaching canoes. Something in her manner caused the Raritan to hold back their assault. Eliza watched in grim, expectant silence as the other canoes drew closer. A second craft was beached, and the braves came ashore. This boat was soon followed by a third and then a fourth. By this time the first braves ashore had ad-vanced about twenty or thirty feet toward the dunes.

The Raritan were obviously apprehensive, but they continued to hold their fire, awaiting a signal from Jo-no-ta. The senior warrior obviously placed great faith in the judgment of the young white woman. His gaze darted toward her, then toward the advancing Wappinger, but he made no move.

By now, Eliza estimated, at least half of the invading force had come ashore, and others were advancing rapidly. Those who led the assault were drawing ever nearer to the dunes, and she realized she could not wait much longer.

The worried expression on Roaring Wolf's face told her that, in his opinion, it was time to surprise the foe with an assault in force. She nodded, rose from a prone position to one knee, and took careful aim with the pistol. As she squeezed the trigger, the sound of the shot filled the air and echoed across the dunes. To the astonishment of the assembled Raritan braves, one of the attackers reached up, clutched his shoulder, and then pitched forward onto the ground, his blood turning the sand red. Somehow the white squaw had proved to be an accurate marksman and had found her target.

The defenders needed no further encouragement to participate in the battle. They instantly erupted into a chorus of screams, and the air was filled with a shower of arrows that descended on the Wappinger warriors. It was unusual for the Raritan to miss at such close range, and they did what was expected of them, killing as many braves as they could as quickly as possible.

In the meantime, the Raritan themselves were almost unassailable targets. Protected by the dunes and by the dense outcroppings of tall grass, they were able to hide from their foes as they continued to rain arrows on them.

Jo-na-ta set an example for his comrades, fitting an arrow into his bow, letting fly, and swiftly rocking yet another, yelping fiercely all the while. Roaring Wolf, who was enjoying himself thoroughly, entered an unspoken competition with the senior warrior of the Raritan, matching him arrow for arrow, victim for victim. Grinning to himself, the Pequot warrior chuckled loudly as he repeatedly took aim and fired.

This was the first battle Eliza had ever witnessed —and she not only was taking part in it, she suddenly realized, but had actually started it! None of the warriors who surrounded her knew it, but she was stunned by her own boldness. What astonished her more than anything was that her aim had been true.

However, she could not and would not allow herself to think about the brave she had shot. It was one thing to think of a battle in theoretical terms, but it was quite another matter to kill a man in cold blood. She grabbed the cartridge bag from Roaring Wolf and reloaded the pistol as her father had taught her so long ago. With both hands she coolly took aim and fired a second time.

Some of the younger Raritan braves unleashed spine-chilling war cries when she again struck her target, wounding a second attacker.

The Wappinger had realized immediately that they had been outsmarted. Not only were the warriors of the defending tribe ready and lying in wait for them, but it appeared that they had the assistance of a white leader.

Consequently, after their first few braves fell, the rest of the Wappinger reacted unthinkingly with an almost simultaneous barrage of musket fire as deafening as it was ineffective, and now their firesticks were as good as useless. Under the steady hail of arrows from the defenders, the Wappinger quickly became confused and disheartened.

Jo-no-ta was the first of the defenders to recognize this fundamental change in the situation. He unleashed a war cry so penetrating that Eliza felt goose pimples on her arms.

Suddenly the entire defending force responded to this signal, and the Raritan were on their feet, advancing en masse toward the beach, drawing and releasing their arrows as they moved. Roaring Wolf was in their midst and enthusiastically joined in the fray.

Eliza realized dimly that she should leave well enough alone and refrain from further participation in the combat, but her spirits were aroused, too, and when she saw her two comrades sweeping forward, she reacted without thinking and joined them.

The invaders, thrown suddenly and unexpectedly onto the defensive, braced themselves. However, the sight of the blond squaw armed with a pistol was too much for them. Never had they been defeated in battle by a woman—but this was no ordinary woman. The legends of the tribes of the area had it that the more fortunate of the warriors were under the protection of a sun goddess, so the superstitious Wappinger promptly jumped to the conclusion that the squaw with blond braids who wielded a white man's firestick had to be the personification of that goddess.

Heedless of her own safety, Eliza finished reloading, raised her pistol, and fired again. This time, because she was moving at a trot, her aim was less effective and she struck no one.

But, in a sense, this was the most effective shot she had fired. The Wappinger braves gaped as they saw smoke emerging from the muzzle of her pistol. This might be a goddess who had joined the Raritan, but her weapon was very real, and the attackers promptly lost their appetite for combat. Several of the younger braves threw down their muskets and immediately took to their heels and ran back toward the water.

Their panic was contagious, and soon the entire attacking force was racing toward the canoes that had carried them to Staten Island. They were no longer able to fight cohesively, and for all practical purposes they had admitted total defeat as they abandoned the field of combat.

Jo-no-ta was afraid that his leading warriors would soon overrun and intermingle with the fleeing Wappinger, so he shouted an order to halt. Again setting the example, he laid aside his bow and arrows, and instead reached for his tomahawk. He hurled it to good effect, and a Wappinger brave fell hard to the ground. The other Raritan immediately began to hurl their tomahawks.

Eliza had the good sense to halt before she advanced past the line of Raritan warriors who were leading the counterattack. Once again she reloaded her pistol and fired it, and once again her aim was faulty—but it no longer mattered. The golden goddess obviously was invincible, and the Wappinger were almost numb with terror. Losing all sense of organization, they piled pell-mell into their canoes and put out to sea as rapidly as they could, leaving their dead and wounded behind.

Their retreat was a total shambles. The Raritan had won a notable victory and they made the most of it. Warriors raced from the body of one fallen foe to the next, and in their haste to accumulate booty, they scalped the living as well as the dead. Only after no more battle trophies were left to be taken were the wounded put out of their misery by swift, expert knife blows. This savagery was too much for Eliza. She hastily turned back, retiring past the crest of a dune so that she would not have to witness the sickening slaughter.

There Roaring Wolf found her, and within moments, they were joined by Jo-na-ta.

"Richard will be proud," Roaring Wolf said, "when he learns Eliza sent many braves fleeing."

"I'm not so sure of that," Eliza replied candidly. "He may become very angry with me and tell me I shouldn't have interfered in matters that do not concern a woman."

Jo-no-ta nodded sagely. "She who shot firestick," he declared, "won great battle for Raritan, so she is entitled to wear victory feather in her hair."

His solemnity was too much for her, and Eliza began to laugh. "I'm happy that the invaders were repelled," she said. "That's quite enough for me."

Actually, as she later confided to Roaring Wolf, she was delighted, too, because of the backhanded slap the Raritan had delivered to the Dutch. The Indians who had been repelled were allies of Governor Stuyvesant, and a blow at them was a blow to him. His object, protection of the rear positions during the upcoming battle with the English colonials, had been foiled.

One other result of the abortive raid was the increased esteem in which the Raritan held Eliza. Warriors and squaws alike not only accepted her, but treated her with a respect that they showed only to Pah-goom and their principal medicine man. It was obvious that she had earned a special place in the affections of the tribe, and that place made her position there secure. She would be safe for as long as she cared to stay, for as long as it was necessary for her to stay until Richard came for her.

VIII

ONE by one, the New England colonies had voted to join in the forthcoming military campaign against the Indian tribes allied to the Dutch, and one by one they began their preparations accordingly. The agreement to send troops to play an active role in the campaign was not achieved easily. One of the greatest faults of the colonies to date was their tendency to act in total disregard of one another, to see themselves as separate and distinct, owing certain allegiances to England, but having little or nothing to do with their neighbors. It was here that the influence Lady Celeste Murette had exerted played a decisive role. The leaders well remembered the rousing speech she had made, and they quoted it freely as they persuaded their fellow officials to support the campaign.

It proved to be far more difficult, however, to talk the militia units into participating. Made up of volunteers who received little or no pay in return for their efforts, the militia would gladly snatch up rifles and go out into their own fields to protect homes, families, and land, as they had proved time and time again. To march the very considerable distance to New Amsterdam, however, and to cross the border of territory claimed by another European power, was a far different matter, and the majority of militiamen in most colonies were reluctant to take such a major step. Their own leaders left them unmoved, and they required persuasion.

One by one the various militia heads wrote to Adam Burrows, asking if the woman who had so inspired them would mind traveling to this or that colony and repeating her address there for the benefit of the volunteer militia. Adam Burrows decided to leave the matter up to Lady Celeste.

She quickly saw the advantages of active cooperation. By expending effort and visiting the various colonies, she would be assuring herself of a major role and a major voice in the future of England's New World possessions. Only one factor caused her to hesitate—she was still in the employ of France and had not yet resigned the confidential position she held on behalf of Cardinal Mazarin. Mazarin would be furious when he learned she had intervened so decisively in a campaign that, if successful, would vastly reduce the New World influence of the Dutch, France's secret ally. No doubt the diabolical cardinal would find a way to repay her for what he would view as treason.

After weighing the matter for a couple of days, Lady Celeste decided she would be obliged to risk Mazarin's displeasure. She was casting her lot with the leader of New Haven, and his problems had become her problems. She no longer had any real choice, and she wished she could confide in someone she could trust. There was no such person, however, so she had to proceed alone.

Once she had made up her mind, Celeste wasted no time in letting Adam know. "I've decided to do it," she said. "I'll go to every village and town that has asked for me, and I'll gladly speak to the militia there. Provided," she added hastily, "that you think I can do some positive good."

"There's no question about it," Adam replied, "but I'm not sure I want you to accept such a burden. I feel it is an imposition on you."

She shook her head. "A victory in this coming campaign is terribly important," she said. "What would happen if the Indian nations were to defeat the militia?"

"I don't like to think about it," Adam replied. "Every colony in New England would be subject to attack—I don't think there's much question of that —and the net result wouldn't be too encouraging. We'd lose a great many lives, and huge amounts of valuable property would be burned."

"Then it's obvious that my burden, as you call it, is worth bearing," she replied decisively.

"Very well," he said, "provided you allow me to escort you. I can't have you traipsing unattended all over New England."

Celeste agreed, secretly pleased because his attendance would bind him to her even more closely. They made their preparations, and letters were sent to the other colonies announcing their imminent arrival.

Everywhere the reactions were similiar. The militia leaders who had heard Celeste's impassioned address in New Haven welcomed her eagerly, but the rank and file were apathetic and attended the sessions only because their presence was obligatory.

Her beauty invariably surprised them and toned down the hostility that otherwise would have been shown toward her. That slight edge was all that Lady Celeste Murette required.

Again she spoke eloquently about the years she had lived in Dutch New Amsterdam, and she stressed the inordinate ambitions of Peter Stuyvesant. By the time she reached a climactic note, explaining that it was Stuyvesant beyond any doubt who was supplying firearms to the Indians, she had her audiences well in hand. Invariably her remarks were heavily applauded, and thereafter a majority of militiamen voted in favor of joining an expedition to New Amsterdam.

By the time that Celeste, escorted by Adam, had traveled through Connecticut and Rhode Island, the success of her journey was assured. The couple's first stop as they headed overland through Massachusetts Bay was in Taunton. There, Dempster and Robbin Chaney, knowing that Adam Burrows was Richard Dunstable's father-in-law, insisted that he and Celeste Murette stay at their farmhouse for the duration of their visit.

Both the young farmer and his wife were duly impressed by Lady Celeste and treated Adam Burrows with the respect due his position. Aunt Hester Browne, however, was far more reserved. Observing the couple but keeping her opinions to herself, she listened intently and said hardly a word, which Dempster and Robbin, who had come to know her well, regarded as atypical.

The members of Dempster's militia company were notified of Celeste's upcoming address, and a company meeting was called for the following night, with attendance mandatory.

The farmers, shopkeepers, and tradesmen who composed Captain Dempster Chaney's company of Massachusetts Bay Infantry arrived for the meeting in a surly mood. Of all the amateur soldiers who lived in the colony, they were perhaps the most self-occupied. They were busy building their own lives in a growing area far from other civilized people, and they felt that their success or failure, the safety of their very lives, depended entirely on their own efforts. Boston was an alien city located a good two to three days' march from their homes, and

Providence Plantations, though slightly nearer, seemed no less foreign.

Few Taunton soldiers had ever fought more than a short distance from home, and none expected to do so in the future. The very idea of marching to distant New Amsterdam to fight Indian tribes they had never heard of seemed silly to virtually every man in the company.

They sat in glum silence as Dempster Chaney introduced Lady Celeste, and when she rose to speak, her appearance created less of a stir than usual. The men stared at her, but being undemonstrative, they kept their admiration to themselves.

Unaccustomed to such phlegmatic reactions, Celeste faltered for the first time when she made her customary speech. Perhaps she spoke with less conviction and fire than usual, perhaps it was her audience that dampened her own enthusiasm for her subject. Whatever the reason, she left her listeners unmoved, and the applause that greeted her remarks was tepid. It appeared unlikely, Adam Burrows thought privately, that any troops from Taunton would take part in the coming campaign.

Aunt Hester Browne was sitting at the rear of the small church. She had been silent and inconspicuous, but suddenly she was on her feet and pushing past the startled Robbin Chaney. She made her way down the center aisle, her skirts rustling, her manner indignant.

When she reached the pulpit, she neither asked Dempster's permission to address his company, nor did she apologize for her unexpected interruption. She climbed to the pulpit, then stood there for some moments, glaring down at the young men who faced her.

"I've known most of you boys since you were wee tots," she said. "I helped deliver a good many of you when you came into the world, heaven help me. Now I sit here and listen to you, and I'm covered with shame. I'm ashamed of living in Taunton, ashamed that I call Massachusetts Bay Colony my home."

Her scorn was so great, her attack so sudden that the militiamen could only gape at her. Captain Chaney and Colonel Burrows were equally surprised and looked at her with their jaws hanging open. But no one was more astonished than Celeste Murette, who was feeling thoroughly dissatisfied with herself because her speech had failed to strike sparks in her audience.

"You call yourselves soldiers," Aunt Hester seethed. "Land sakes! I'd hate to tell you what I call you." She paused for breath and glared ferociously at her stunned audience. "I guess you boys need special incentives to fight," she said. "A neighbor's house has to be burned down by Indians. Maybe your neighbor's wife and children have to be killed and scalped before you get your dander up. Well, don't tell *me* that you're soldiers. I aim to write to Boston and ask for troops to be sent from the capital to give us respectable citizens the protection to which we're entitled!"

Her audience stirred uncomfortably, but no one dared to interrupt. Even Dempster could not remember a time when he had seen this feisty woman so thoroughly aroused.

"You heard what this lady said to you," Aunt Hester went on. "She's traveled all the way to Taunton from New Haven to give you fair warning of what lies in store for you if you don't join in the campaign that lies ahead for all the English colonies. Well, it isn't going to be good enough to say that you had fair warning. To be warned and to do something about it is one thing. To be warned and act as though you're deaf, dumb, and blind is something quite different."

Her scorn was so venomous that Dempster coughed and covered the lower part of his face with a hand so that his military subordinates would not see him smile.

"I guess you don't place too high a value on liberty," Aunt Hester said. "Those who prize freedom are those who are willing to fight for freedom! If the so-called militiamen of this area won't fight, I guess it's up to the rest of us to do battle for them. Colonel Burrows," she went on, looking at Adam, who was sitting in the front pew, "I don't rightly know if you're accepting lady volunteers, but if you are, be good enough to count me as one. I'm as handy with a musket as any of these lads, and I'll bring down my fair share of Indians when the fighting starts."

She had goaded the militiamen beyond endurance, which had been her intention, and a burly, bearded sergeant whose trousers and shirt of buckskin proclaimed him a wilderness dweller, leaped to his feet. "I'll be damned," he shouted, "if I'm going to let any old woman fight my battles for me. You can count on me, Captain Chaney. I'm marching to New Amsterdam with you!"

The usually sedate church erupted into total bedlam. Almost the entire company was on its feet, with men clamoring for the right to participate in the fight against the Indian allies of the Dutch. Men roared and gesticulated, but their message was the same: "I'm going to fight!"

By the time Captain Chaney had restored order, every single man present had volunteered for the forthcoming campaign. No other militia unit had responded so wholeheartedly, and Aunt Hester had succeeded where Celeste Murette had failed. Later, after the farm owner had returned to her property with her guests, Celeste tried to thank her for her intervention.

"Land sakes, I don't want any thanks," Aunt Hester said. "I felt a mite testy because the boys weren't responding to you the way they should. I didn't say a word that I didn't mean, and I reckon it's just as well that they finally volunteered, because if they hadn't, I'd be marching down to New Amsterdam myself!"

Robbin smiled as she shook her head. "You'd really do it, too, Aunt Hester," she said. "You're extraordinary."

Extraordinary was not the right word to describe the lady, Celeste Murette thought. Hester Browne was typical of the English colonials who refused to acknowledge even the possibility of defeat. It was this attitude that had caused Celeste to change her alliances and to cast her lot with the English. She felt heartened, vastly encouraged by the never-say-die attitude that Aunt Hester so ably represented.

Every colony in New England produced a contingent of troops for the campaign, and not even the smallest community went unrepresented. It had been decided that the quickest way to confront the Indians, who were now massing on the northern end of Manhattan Island, would be to march overland and rendezvous on the mainland nearby. A naval assault, Richard had decided, would take too long to coordinate.

The militiamen themselves recognized the historical significance of what they were doing, and Dempster Chaney summed up the feelings of most of his colleagues when he arrived in New Haven at the head of his company. "This will be remembered as a special year," he said. "This will be recalled as the year when the separate English colonies finally had the sense to act as one."

There was little doubt that Celeste Murette was

largely responsible for the unprecedented degree of intercolonial cooperation, and no one was more grateful to her than was Richard.

"You can say what you like about her," he told Mimi Clayton, "but she has sure produced for us in an emergency."

Mimi couldn't disagree, but she still had grave doubts about Celeste that she was forced to keep to herself. She vowed privately to keep as sharp a watch on the other woman as she could. There was little else she could do.

Richard began the march to New Amsterdam early one morning at the head of his own battalion of New Haven militia, which Ezekiel Clayton now commanded. The campaign was of primary importance to Richard, but equally significant was the imminence of his reunion with Eliza.

Colonel Burrows was on hand to take the salute from his departing troops, and to his surprise, in spite of the early hour, Celeste Murette joined him on the green, where the friends and relatives of the militiamen had gathered.

The New Haven troops, trained for combat by Richard, looked like veterans as they marched past the colonel, presenting arms with their muskets. When the brief ceremonies came to an end, Colonel Burrows shook his son-in-law's hand. "I wish you all that I would wish myself if I were in your boots," he said.

Richard thanked him gravely, then turned to Lady Celeste. "We're in your debt," he told her. "Not only here, but throughout all New England. No one connected with this campaign is going to forget the part you've played."

"May you return home victorious," she said. "That's all I ask."

He doffed his plumed hat to her, and then took his place at the head of the line. Celeste slipped her hand through Adam Burrows's arm as they watched the troops march off. As usual, her mind was functioning swiftly and smoothly as she made her own plans. She would marry Adam, she decided, during his son-in-law's absence. That she had had an affair with Richard bothered her, and although she knew he was a gentleman who would never talk out of turn, she nevertheless wanted to take no chances that he would let the truth about his relationship with her slip in the presence of his father-in-law and thereby ruin her marriage plans.

Furthermore, knowing now that Eliza was alive and well and that Richard intended to bring her home with him prompted Celeste to hurry her own plans along. As she well recognized, Eliza wielded enormous influence over her father. Therefore it would be best to secure her own position before Eliza came home.

Consequently she was determined to marry Adam Burrows right away, before either his daughter could raise objections or his son-in-law accidentally talked out of turn. It would be a simple enough matter to arrange, because Adam was extremely susceptible to her influence and would do anything to keep her happy.

Once she was Mistress Burrows, she would be truly safe from everyone and everything—except the long, vindictive arm of Cardinal Mazarin.

She had no idea that Laroche was dead, and thought that after her marriage she would find some excuse to go to New Amsterdam, where she could give the French spymaster a letter to Mazarin. If that failed, she would have to take the risk of writing to him directly and entrusting the letter to the next French merchant captain who put into New Haven—and that might be a long wait. Of one thing she was certain: She had no intention of cheating Mazarin. She knew him well enough to realize that complete honesty was essential if she hoped to escape his wrath.

Celeste Murette was not alone in thinking of Cardinal Mazarin, who was very much present in the mind of Richard Dunstable as he led his troops on the wilderness trail. Through no fault of his own he had been forced to become an agent working secretly on behalf of France. Again, without seeking the responsibility, he found himself commanding a large English expeditionary force that would soon cross into Dutch territory. With France cooperating with the Dutch, he was bound to be harming French interests in the New World in the days and weeks that lay ahead.

That, however, could not be helped, and it truly did not bother Richard. He was very certain that the safety and welfare of the English colonies was of primary importance. The frontier had to be made safe again for the generations to come. Only in this way would the English colonies survive and flourish. If they achieved this goal at the expense of not only the Dutch colonies, but also the French, so be it.

Richard had acquiesced in Mazarin's scheme because it had suited the interests of the English colonies to go along with it. Now, in the event that a conflict arose, he would abandon the French without a moment of hesitation or regret, and Mazarin be damned!

Richard was also relieved beyond measure at the prospect of extricating his wife from the grasp of the Dutch. It was good to know that she had survived whatever ordeal she had been forced to endure alone in New Amsterdam. Nonetheless, he found himself apprehensive when he thought of the forthcoming reunion with Eliza. He had no desire to hurt her, but he felt that complete candor compelled him to tell her the truth about his affair with

Celeste Murette. That would not be pleasant. He hoped that Eliza would understand that he'd been a victim of his own feelings of the moment and that his brief relationship with Celeste had had nothing to do with the great love he bore his wife.

He stayed close to the shore of the Great Bay on his march toward the southwest from New Haven, and on the fourth night he and his men approached the Dutch town of Yonkers. The community was included in a tract given by the Dutch West Indies Company several years earlier to a prominent New Netherland attorney, Adriaen Van der Donck. Although he was a loyal Dutchman, a majority of the residents of the growing community, which was rapidly becoming a trade center, were English. They made no secret of their feelings, and gathering on the edge of the town common, they cheered loudly, as did their wives and children, when the militiamen arrived.

Not wanting to wear out his welcome, and particularly anxious to give the Dutch authorities no cause for complaint, Richard gently turned down several supper invitations, choosing instead to eat a simple meal of bacon and corn bread cooked on an open fire. He was finishing his meal when a delegation of English citizens, led by a merchant named Philipse, called on him.

Mincing no words, Philipse explained his situation and that of his colleagues. "We don't know your military intentions, Major," he said, "and frankly, we have no desire to find out. In the event that you're planning to get into hostilities with Governor Stuyvesant, we'd rather not know it in advance and have our loyalties to the Dutch put to a test."

"I understand," Richard said.

"However," Philipse went on, "I think it's only fair to tell you that in the event that you should get involved in a war with the Dutch, we're to be counted as your allies. In fact, of the near one hundred adult male English citizens of this vicinity, I'd say that blame near every last one of them will cast his lot with you and will join your troops if there's a need."

"I sincerely hope that such a confrontation can be averted," Richard replied. "I know I am speaking for a number of my superiors in the English colonies when I say that they're very eager to avoid a war with the Dutch at almost any cost."

His visitors glanced at one another a trifle uncertainly. "Do I gather, then," Philipse wanted to know, "that you have no interest in the acquisition of the New Netherland colony?"

"None at all," Richard replied. "I think there's a universal recognition in the English colonies of the value of New Netherland; I'm sure that people everywhere are hoping that the English flag will fly over the harbor of New Amsterdam one day, and that English rule will be extended to the hinterlands as well. But we're not willing to go to war to acquire the colony. We leave force of arms as a solution to territorial problems to Europeans; we seek only peace. We hope that in time London and Amsterdam will address the problem and will find an amicable solution to it. In the meantime, we don't intend to attack the Dutch unless Governor Stuyvesant's behavior makes it necessary."

Several militia units were already on hand when the contingent from New Haven arrived at the rendezvous area on the bank of the Harlem River, which marked the northern boundary of New Amsterdam. Over the next twenty-four hours they were joined by others who had marched by various routes through the wilderness to the Dutch colony.

In all, there were three hundred and fifty men.

Most of them were unaccustomed to traditional military campaigns, as Richard had anticipated. This, however, was an advantage rather than a handicap, because without exception, these troops were experienced in wilderness warfare. All had fought against Indian tribes in their own neighborhoods, and as a consequence no one needed instructions on how to do battle in the deep woods, particularly against Indians. The knowledge had been painstakingly acquired at great cost and had become second nature, so Richard knew that he had a force of veterans. He could have wished for more powder and shot, but shortages were chronic, and the commanders of all the units had anticipated that their men would have to make do with what was on hand.

It was impossible to make any specific plans until they learned more about the size and disposition of the enemy forces. A number of the more experienced of the militiamen volunteered their services as scouts, and that night sneaked across the Harlem River to the upper reaches of Manhattan. There they roamed freely, and about dawn they returned, one by one, to their own encampment.

Laboriously piecing together the information each of the scouts had gleaned, Richard formed an overall picture of the enemy strength. He was surprised and slightly dismayed to discover that more than five hundred savages, representing a number of tribes, were camped on the upper part of the island, apparently awaiting an attack by the English colonists. The scouts were unanimous, too, in revealing that the warriors were armed with muskets and appeared to be plentifully supplied with powder and shot.

Richard summoned all of the officers to a council of war, and after the group had gathered under the trees, he spoke to them candidly. "It seems to me," he said, "that there's no point in our depending overmuch on a surprise attack. The Indians know we're here, just as we know they've gathered on the island. I have no doubt they've done as thorough a job of scouting us as we've done examining them."

"So you are ruling out surprise as a factor in our plans, Major?" the commander of the Providence Plantations unit asked.

"No," Richard replied. "But there's no point in totally relying on something to give us an advantage that could actually turn out to be a vulnerability."

After the group discussed the matter at length, a majority of the commanders agreed with him.

"I suggest," Richard said, "that we cross the river about a mile down from here on rafts we'll build for the purpose, and that we make the crossing after nightfall. We'll leave our campfires burning on the shore here as a means of temporarily fooling the savages into believing that we're bedding down here again. At least that will prevent us from being subjected to an assault while we're crossing the river. Once we get to the other side, I propose that we march inland about a mile to a mile and a half and take up positions opposite the main body of Indian warriors. We should be able to maneuver fairly freely, and consequently there will be ample time for the men to rest before we launch a full scale attack at dawn the next morning."

"Why dawn?" the head of the Boston group demanded. "Won't they be expecting a dawn attack?"

"Not necessarily," Richard replied. "Even if they are, however, it's still to our advantage to go into action at that hour. The troops will be relatively fresh after having rested for several hours, and at this season of the year the odds favor a fairly heavy fog in the forest early in the day. If so, we'll be in that much better a position."

Once again a majority heartily endorsed his views.

Most men carried their own food supplies, and as their pouches contained only enough dried meat and parched corn for about one week, it was obvious that any delays might prove hazardous. It was true that game was plentiful at this season of the year, but a force of three hundred and fifty men would require large quantities of meat and fish, and it would not be convenient to obtain enough for their requirements when their primary concern was success in the imminent battle.

The transfer to Manhattan Island was made late that night. They chopped down pine trees, which they then lashed together with vines, and these crude rafts provided transportation for as many as twenty men at a time.

Richard, accompanied by Ezekiel Clayton, made a point of crossing on the first raft with militiamen from New Haven. They landed undetected, and he could only assume that the cooking fires burning brightly on the north bank of the Harlem River were convincing the enemy that the militiamen were spending another night on the mainland. The entire transfer was accomplished easily and with dispatch. The troops spread out as they marched inland, and automatically maintained quiet in the wilderness, although most shared Richard's opinion that their presence would be discovered before the battle began.

They sent scouts out ahead, and when they were about a mile from a clearing where the majority of braves were encamped, they called a halt. There, without further ado, the militiamen from a number of communities wrapped themselves in their blankets and settled down for a few hours of sleep before engaging in a combat that, regardless of the outcome of the battle, was certain to alter history.

In the meantime, farther south on the island, in New Amsterdam, a lamp burned late in the private study of Governor Peter Stuyvesant. There the director-general of the Dutch colony dispassionately weighed the chances of both opponents in the coming conflict. Stuyvesant's main concern was that he not be caught red-handed and that the Netherlands be protected, no matter who won.

It was almost impossible for him to determine in advance whether the English colonists or the Indians would emerge as the victors in the struggle. The heavily armed warriors held a decided numerical advantage, to be sure, outnumbering the colonists by almost two hundred men. But as Stuyvesant well knew, they were far less familiar with the use of firearms than were their foes. Most were handling muskets for the first time. Therefore the ultimate advantage was with the colonists—provided that they persisted and did not retreat or surrender quickly.

If the English won, Stuyvesant knew, he would be obliged to make his peace with them without delay. This he was prepared to do, even to the extent of relaxing some of the New Amsterdam laws that discriminated against the English.

In addition, as he well knew, he would find it necessary to stop providing the Indian tribes with firearms. There was no way that he could persuade them to give up the muskets he had already presented to them, but by discontinuing their supplies of shot and powder, he could effectively silence their modern weapons.

If, on the other hand, the braves should be victorious, he would be in a perfect position to claim a strong share of the credit for their triumph. He was prepared to tighten his bonds with them by signing new long-term treaties with every tribe he could persuade to become Holland's ally. These pacts would not only provide that the Dutch and the Indians would come to each other's military assistance, but also would provide for increased trade, giving the Dutch a monopoly on the rights to purchase all furs acquired by the various tribes. This might anger Cardinal Mazarin by cutting into the huge revenues of the French fur traders, but the director-general was willing to wrestle with that when the time came.

Stuyvesant might have been slightly less complacent, however, had he known that a group of more than forty men left New Amsterdam during the course of the evening and, evading the Dutch sentries who guarded the town, made their way north into the wilderness by twos and threes.

They banded together after they had left the town sufficiently far behind and thereafter traveled more rapidly, although it was apparent that the majority were townsmen, unfamiliar with the wilderness.

About an hour before dawn, Richard Dunstable was awakened by a sentry who told him a delegation from New Amsterdam urgently wanted to see him. He immediately accompanied the sentinel to an outpost, where the newcomers were gathered beneath the trees, trying in vain to conceal themselves. He knew at a glance that they were anything but experienced woodsmen.

"Major," a spokesman for the group declared, "we heard your militiamen were gathered here to fight the Indian tribes, and we've come to offer our services to you. We're all English-born, and we've all kept our English citizenship, even though we now live in New Amsterdam."

Regardless of their dubious military value, Richard was delighted to have their help. "Welcome, gentlemen," he said. "You're just in time for the fireworks."

The spokesman hesitated and looked a trifle sheepish. "We have just one problem, Major," he said. "We lack firearms."

Richard was utterly flabbergasted.

"I don't know if you've heard about Governor Stuyvesant's law," the spokesman went on, "but we were required to turn in our weapons to the office of the director-general. We were paid a bonus for every musket and every pistol we turned in."

All at once Richard realized how cleverly Stuyvesant had acquired many of the weapons he had supplied to the Indians. He in effect had bought them from the English residents of his own colony!

"I regret to tell you, gentlemen, that we're lacking in spare arms ourselves," Richard said.

The newcomers looked downcast, unable to hide their bitter disappointment.

"All I can suggest, gentlemen," Richard declared, "is that you hold yourselves in reserve until we acquire some firearms from our enemies."

Several of the English residents of New Amsterdam looked at each other in amazement. "Do you mean, Major," one of them asked incredulously, "that you'll provide us with arms that you'll take on the battlefield from our foes?"

Richard shrugged. "It's one way of accomplishing our end," he said. "Until such time as we acquire them, however, I advise you to remain in the rear, out of harm's way." He hesitated and then asked delicately, "How many of you have had experience in wilderness warfare?"

Out of more than forty men in the group, only three raised their hands. Richard had no desire to discourage them from participating in the battle. The mere fact that they had sneaked out of New Amsterdam to volunteer their services to him was an indication of the complexity of the problems that

Peter Stuyvesant faced. Richard wanted nothing to dampen the spirits of these English patriots.

He decided wisely to leave well enough alone for the present. If the tide of battle should turn in favor of the militia, there would be ample opportunity for them to pick up the muskets of the warriors from the field of battle. Also, he reasoned, the introduction of amateur wilderness fighters into the combat would do no harm, provided that the militiamen were sufficiently in control of the battle to assure victory. What was important, Richard felt, was that the residents of New Amsterdam felt their efforts were being appreciated and that they were making a contribution to the cause they favored.

The camp began to stir, and the men ate a cold breakfast because Richard had banned the lighting of cooking fires until after the battle. Although it was customary in England to make speeches of exhortation to troops immediately before combat, Richard felt that it was unnecessary for him or any of the other officers to address the men. They all understood the stakes, as was demonstrated by their presence. Any man who had volunteered his services and had marched from his home, wherever he happened to live, well knew that the outcome of the battle would determine whether the English colonies would remain at peace or be constantly harassed and endangered. Besides, the sound of the speeches and the men's reactions could possibly carry through the forest to the Indian encampment. Richard did not want to take that risk.

As they formed up, every contingent insisted on leading the army into combat, and Richard knew that however he decided the issue, the majority of his men would object.

Consequently, he based his decision strictly on practical considerations. Those men with the greatest experience in fighting Indians in the wilderness would be the first to engage them now. The place of honor went to a company from Hartford, in Connecticut. Flanking them on the left was Dempster Chaney's company from Taunton, and on their right flank was a company from Springfield. Dirrectly behind these men in the front rank Richard placed his own New Haven contingent.

The only men given no assignments in the order of battle were the militiamen from Boston, who, being city dwellers, were relatively inexperienced in wilderness warfare. They brought up the rear, but their feelings were salvaged when Richard told their officers they were being held as a reserve force to be used at a strategic moment in the fight. They, in turn, were followed by the unarmed volunteers from New Amsterdam.

The scouts were in the lead, advancing slowly through the forest. As Richard had hoped, a thick morning fog enveloped the area, and this gave them a double advantage: Not only did it conceal the leather-clad militiamen, but they were able to advance almost soundlessly because the dampness permeated the leaves that littered the ground, so that footsteps striking them made little noise.

The three hundred and fifty militiamen plus the forty-odd New Amsterdam dwellers inched their way through the forest. Richard was pleased when he heard the soft clicking of muskets as the firearms were loaded and cocked. Once again his troops required no instruction and knew enough to prepare quietly for combat in their own way.

The pace continued at a crawl, then a complete halt was signaled. A sergeant of the scouts crept back to the expedition commander and murmured, "The enemy is plumb ahead of us now, Major. If we go any farther, we'll start stumbling over them." Richard nodded and passed the order to Ezekiel and the other officers to prepare to attack. He sent a messenger forward to relay the same order to the Hartford commander and to Dempster Chaney and the leader of the Springfield contingent.

There was no sound now but the quiet dripping of water from the leaves of trees. Richard checked his own special rifle, patted his coat to assure himself that his throwing knives were in place, and braced himself. He alone would give the signal to begin the attack.

He squinted up at the sky and was satisfied. Dawn was just beginning to break, and dirty streaks of gray were appearing in the inky blackness. He could not see the braves ahead, but that didn't matter, at least for the moment. He aimed his rifle in the general direction of the enemy and squeezed the trigger.

The sound of his shot echoed through the forest, electrifying the militiamen who had been anticipating it. The companies in the lead raised their own muskets to their shoulders, fired a volley, reloaded, then advanced at a brisk pace.

Richard followed closely behind them at the head of his New Haven contingent. It was impossible to see more than a few feet, but it didn't seem to matter. Apparently the enemy had been caught off guard, a turn of events Richard had hoped for but not really expected, so he had achieved an initial advantage, which he intended to exploit fully.

The companies in the lead held their fire now, waiting until they could see their targets. The men spread out instinctively, automatically, as they made their way forward through the vast sea of trees. In this way they lessened the target that they made for the enemy, protecting themselves from return fire.

But to Richard's amazement there was no return fire. He wondered if the scouts had made a mistake. He was on the verge of halting the entire column and questioning the scouts at some length when suddenly he caught a glimpse of brown-skinned braves in war paint directly ahead.

The militiamen saw the Indians, too, and needed no urging. Each man was on his own now, free to fire at will. A few sparse shots were fired, then an intense volley erupted. It was evident from the screams of the wounded that the militiamen were finding their targets. Richard maintained the advance, but slowed his men to a walk, not wanting those in the lead to penetrate too deeply behind the enemy lines and risk being cut off from the main body of troops.

The militiamen maintained an even, steady fire. When the lead companies were kneeling and reloading, the men from New Haven fired a barrage. Then, as they knelt to reload, those directly behind them in line took up the challenge, and ultimately the vanguard, having reloaded, accepted the burden once again.

So far the fight was astonishingly one-sided. The musket fire had come mainly from the militiamen, and there had been little response of any kind from the braves. This was so unusual that Richard was worried, fearing a trap.

All at once, however, the Indian warriors began to respond vigorously, and their musket fire added to the din. But it quickly became apparent to Richard as well as to the scores of others who were experienced fighters, that the Indians were wasting lead and gunpowder. Their shots were wild, most of them cutting through the upper branches of trees, high above the heads of the advancing English colonists.

Richard immediately understood. Placing his mouth close to Ezekiel Clayton's ear, he bellowed, "This is blame near miraculous!"

"I don't understand it," Ezekiel replied.

In spite of the gravity of the situation, Richard could not hold back a hearty laugh. "The savages," he said, "don't know how to use firearms. They've had no experience with them, and the muskets are practically useless in their hands."

His analysis proved accurate. The braves were proud that they had been given white men's weapons, but they had been given no instruction in their use. Under the best of circumstances, musket fire was far from precise because of the poor craftsmanship that went into the making of the crude weapons. In the hands of the painted braves, muskets were virtually useless. Thus far not one militiaman had been killed or even injured. The entire army continued to press forward.

As night turned to day and the early morning mist began to burn off, Richard was elated to see that the Indians were falling back in disarray. They were bewildered, unable to understand that the magic weapons they had been provided accomplished nothing by themselves but had to be well aimed and fired in order to be effective.

The Niantic warriors, wearing streaks of alternate black and pale blue war paint on their faces and torsos, were the first to recognize that they were accomplishing nothing with their firesticks. They did not panic, but instead threw down their muskets and withdrew in good order, falling back one hundred or more paces into the forest before they recovered sufficiently to string their bows, draw arrows from their quivers, and make a fresh stand.

The retreat of the Niantic caused the braves of a half dozen other tribes to retreat as well, and they fell back in disorder, which became more pronounced as the marksmen in the ranks of the militia picked them off at will. Only the stand taken by the Niantic, using their familiar bows and arrows, prevented the contagion of panic from becoming universal.

The bodies of dead braves littered the floor of the forest, and the English volunteers from New Amsterdam now had their pick of muskets and pouches heavy with cartridges.

The near-frenzy of the tribesmen subsided as their chiefs became aware of the stand the Niantic were making and followed the wise example of the Connecticut tribe. One by one the braves realized their foolhardiness in using unfamiliar weapons, and they fell back to rely on the primitive but far more effective bows and arrows.

By this time the rising sun had burned off what was left of the early morning fog, and Richard became uncomfortably aware of the prowess of the warriors who were using bows and arrows, and in some instances, tomahawks.

"Take cover, lads," he shouted, somehow managing to make his voice heard above the din of battle. "Take cover behind the trees."

The militiamen wasted no time in heeding his advice. Some of the more experienced had already sought cover behind the large oaks and maples and thick tangles of bramble bushes. Those who had not done so lost no opportunity now and spread out even more than they had previously.

Richard knew that he would win a victory of consequence if his men continued to hold firm. The primitive weapons of the savages were no match for the firearms of well-trained militiamen, and it was just a matter of time before his men's heavier firepower would achieve an overwhelming advantage. The colonists had already incapacitated many Indians in the first minutes of battle, equalizing the odds.

Richard ducked behind the trunk of a stout elm, took careful aim at a heavily painted war chief, and squeezed the trigger. He felt no satisfaction when he saw the leader tumble to the ground. If he had learned one thing in the New World wilderness, it was never to personalize a battle. He would not think of his foes as individuals, but would regard them collectively as enemies to be killed or dispersed.

As he reloaded his rifle, Richard was pleased to note that his militiamen were withstanding the most withering barrage of arrows that their foes could muster.

"Hold your places, lads!" he called. "Don't give up an inch. Keep up a steady fire, whatever you do!"

The captains and lieutenants of the individual units performed near-miracles, keeping their men in the most advanced forward positions while maintaining an unrelenting fire.

No one unit distinguished itself more than any of the others. The militiamen took part in a joint venture now, and they stood shoulder to shoulder, trading lethal volleys with the enemy, not flinching, not retreating, not giving up an inch of ground.

Even the English volunteers from New Amsterdam managed to fight with considerable distinction. Although unfamiliar with the techniques of forest fighting, they displayed a degree of courage that did them great credit. They learned quickly to take cover and needed no instruction. Those who could not find trees large enough to hide behind dropped to one knee in order to make themselves smaller targets for the tomahawks and arrows of their foes.

But even the city dwellers knew how to handle muskets, and the volunteers from New Amsterdam proved as effective as the rural contingents and had no cause to feel ashamed of their prowess in battle.

The Indians took a frightful beating. Richard never learned the precise extent of their casualties, but he was quite certain that they were massive. He was appalled by the stubborn determination of the warriors to fight to the end, and he gained a new respect for them. They may have demonstrated naiveté when they had tried to use firearms with which they were totally unfamiliar, but they more than made up for their mistakes by their grim determination to fight on to the end.

That end, however, was inevitable now, and every experienced militiaman sensed the imminence of victory. The troops became voluble, shouting encouragement to one another as they fired their muskets, reloaded their weapons, and then fired again. They well knew that by granting no respite to the foe, they could not be beaten.

As the sun rose still higher, Richard caught a glimpse of shining, silvery water behind the positions taken by the braves and realized that the Indians had retreated to the very edge of the island. They were fighting hard because they had no alternative. Further retreat was impossible.

The middle-aged sachem of the Niantic had had enough. Realizing his men were being killed and wounded in a confrontation that could not be won, he produced a large square of white cloth, which he tied to an arrow and waved over his head. As other Indians became aware of his capitulation, they became disconcerted.

Richard was quick to take note of the situation. "Cease fire!" he shouted repeatedly.

Gradually the musket fire died away, and the forest became silent. There was no sound now but the moans of the wounded, the gasps of the dying. The battle had ended in a victory more complete than any that Richard or any other colonial leader could have desired.

His work for the day was far from over, however. He saw an opportunity to make friends of the enemies. As the warriors threw down their arrows, bows, and tomahawks, he called out to them in the language of the Mohegan, telling them to keep their native weapons. "Your English brothers do not hate you," he informed them, speaking loudly. "Your English brothers wish you well and wish to live in peace beside you. Keep your bows and arrows. You need them for hunting. You will need them to bring food to your towns for your women, children, and old people in the winter months to come. We will take only the muskets and ammunition."

Even more significant and striking were the firm instructions that Richard issued to all unit commanders. Under no circumstances, he decreed, were militiamen to scalp any Indians. He was familiar with the fact that in a number of frontier areas the troops imitated their Indian enemies by also gathering scalps, largely because of the terror this created in the ranks of their opponents. Now, however, an opportunity existed for the introduction of a new spirit of friendship, and he wanted to ensure that the brotherhood he hoped to engender would have a chance to be nourished and grow.

The militiamen understood the reasons for the order, and in spite of their exuberance over the victory they had just won, they demonstrated self-discipline. Not one warrior, dead or alive, was molested.

This gave the tribes the opportunity to remove their wounded from the field and attend their needs, and to dispose of their dead honorably.

Perhaps the greatest miracle of all was the lack of casualties among the militiamen. Very few were wounded by arrows, and not one colonist lost his life. In no other frontier battle, several of the commanders told Richard, had such a record been achieved.

The militia units gathered in the clearing where their foes had congregated before the battle, and there Richard addressed them briefly. "I'm proud

271

of you, lads," he said. "I realize you're tired after your exertions of the morning, but there are two tasks that remain to be finished. I'm going to ask you to call on your reserves of energy and march with me—now—into the town of New Amsterdam. But first, let's gather the muskets and ammunition that were given to the Indians."

The volunteers from New Amsterdam who had joined in the final phases of the battle were alarmed, obviously thinking that the expedition's commander intended to carry the battle to the Dutch colony.

A number of the veteran troops looked bewildered, not understanding what Richard had in mind. He hastened to explain. "If we leave Manhattan Island now and return to our homes, we'll have won a signal victory against the Indian tribes who are our neighbors," he said, "but we'll have neglected the people who I believe were responsible for sparking the entire campaign against us. I don't intend to ask any of you to fire a single shot against the Dutch. I am reasonably certain they won't attack us. They have a total of one hundred to one hundred and fifty troops at their disposal, so we outnumber them heavily—so heavily that they won't fight us."

Even Ezekiel Clayton was somewhat bewildered. "May I ask what you have in mind, Major?" he asked formally.

"Of course," Richard replied cheerfully. "I'm going to confront Governor Peter Stuyvesant and let him know in no uncertain terms that what we have done today to his Indian allies we can do tomorrow to his own troops. I'll be very surprised if he doesn't take advantage of the occasion to seek a new, firm, and lasting peace treaty with the English colonies."

Some of the men hooted aloud, others merely

smiled, and the majority certainly were well satisfied, approving wholeheartedly of the plan.

The militiamen removed the grime of battle from their hands and faces in a swiftly flowing stream that emptied into the Harlem River. Then they quickly ate a meal of dried meat and parched corn, and were ready to march when the order was given. They made their way quickly through the thinning forests of Manhattan Island, and when they saw the town walls ahead, Richard ordered his standard-bearers to the front of the column. One carried a British flag, and the other had tied a white cloth to a musket. The cloth was waved vigorously, which assured the pikemen acting as sentries that the troops were on a friendly mission and were not bent on conquest. The palisade gate was opened, and Richard marched into New Amsterdam at the head of his victorious little army.

News of the battle had already been passed swiftly from person to person in the town, and hundreds of residents turned out to greet the victors.

To the pleasure and surprise of Richard and the unit commanders, the English colonists were cheered lustily by the onlookers. Apparently it did not matter whether the spectator was English or Dutch—all residents of the town seemed to share the same sentiments, and the welcome that the New Englanders received was as hearty as it was spontaneous. These residents now knew their muskets had been collected by Stuyvesant for the Indians' use, and they felt this injustice had been righted by the British colonial militia. They had also been fearful that the Indians might turn their muskets on the Dutch in New Amsterdam; now they considered this possibility as being remote with the day's stunning defeat. As the militiamen passed the Thorn and Thistle Inn, Richard saw Angus and Mollie MacNeill standing outside the entrance to their establishment. Both were cheering loudly, and he grinned as he raised his sword in salute to them.

Not pausing to rest anywhere, Richard led his column directly to the governor's house. There the troops made themselves at home on the lawn and back garden, calmly setting up their bivouac.

Richard selected three of the most senior militia officers to accompany him and went straight to the front door of the house. The pikemen on duty were apprehensive, but admitted the four English colonials without delay. A male secretary met them inside the entrance and promptly conducted them to Peter Stuyvesant's office.

Never had Stuyvesant displayed such monumental charm, such overwhelming poise, such self-control. He greeted Richard effusively, as though he were an old friend, and then shook hands vigorously with each of the other officers.

"Permit me to offer you some refreshments, gentlemen," he said, and raised an ivory-handled bell. The door opened and a middle-aged Dutch serving woman entered with a tray laden with mugs of foaming Dutch ale. The guests were quickly served. "To your victory, gentlemen," Stuyvesant said heartily. "You have made the entire Atlantic seaboard safe now for all of us."

Richard privately marveled at the man's gall. Smiling blandly, the Dutchman raised his mug to each of his visitors in turn, then drank deeply. Richard sipped his own ale and watched the governor closely over the rim of his mug.

"I was of two minds when I learned that the battle was developing," Peter Stuyvesant said. "On one hand I was tempted—strongly tempted—to lend you whatever support I could. I will grant that my troops and pikemen are a small force, but I thought they might help you to turn the tide. On the other hand, I knew you already had your own organization, and I didn't want to upset your plans by interfering."

He was very clever indeed, Richard thought. "As it turned out," he said, "we required no assistance, although a number of your townsmen—of English descent—volunteered their services and acquitted themselves well in battle."

The flicker in the governor's eyes indicated that he was far more interested in the New Amsterdam volunteers than he let on.

"I would say," Richard went on, "that we owe our victory to fortuitous circumstances. The Indians were carrying equipment totally unfamiliar to them. They had muskets, together with ample supplies of cartridges, but whoever provided them with the firearms made a very serious mistake."

Stuyvesant's eyes narrowed, but he managed to speak calmly. "And what was that error, Sir Richard?" he demanded.

"The donors of the gift," Richard said dryly, "neglected to teach the braves how to use their firearms. There is nothing as useless as a musket in the hands of someone who has no idea how to load or aim it, much less how to shoot it."

His companions guffawed heartily.

"Quite so," Stuyvesant laughed, nothing in his manner indicating he was aware that the joke was at his expense.

The brazen nerve of the man was extraordinary, Richard thought. It was plain Stuyvesant was accepting no responsibility for what had happened and was even pretending that he was completely innocent. Richard decided to drive home the lesson still harder.

"The savages," he said, "will have no opportunity now to learn how to use their muskets. The most significant result of the battle, I believe, is that we confiscated every last musket from them."

Stuyvesant did not lose his poise and smiled politely. "May I ask what you intend to do with the weapons, Major?" he said politely.

Richard's grin was natural and unforced. "As you know, Your Excellency," he said, "the rate of immigration in our American colonies continues unabated. I daresay that the troubles between the Roundheads and the Cavaliers at home are responsible. Whatever the reason, every ship that puts into our ports from England brings new colonists to swell our ranks. Many of them are poor and own no firearms, but the whole civilization of the New World is based on the possession of a musket by every individual, so the weapons will come in very handy, indeed. If we only knew where the Indians acquired them," he continued, his manner as bland as Stuyvesant's, "we'd offer a vote of thanks to the donor. Whoever he may be, he's made a major contribution to the security of the English colonies in the New World." That, he thought, would give the governor pause.

Stuyvesant, however, nodded brightly. "You're very fortunate, indeed," he said, "I almost envy you. In any event, I think the time has come for an understanding to be reached between New Netherland and New England."

"We favor such an understanding, you can be sure, Your Excellency," Richard replied quietly. "The more thoroughly we know and understand each other, the less likelihood that we shall ever come to blows."

"I have been giving the whole question serious thought for some time," Peter Stuyvesant said glibly, "and I've concluded that I should send an invitation to the leaders of the various English colonies, asking them to attend a conference here in New Amsterdam. Out of such a meeting I'm sure will come a binding treaty of friendship."

"I'm sure that our leaders and our colonists would welcome such a conference and would rejoice over such results as Your Excellency has just outlined," Richard said. He knew now that he had won far more than a victory over a band of savage Indian tribes. He had instilled enough fear in Stuyvesant to guarantee that the menace to New England from the Dutch colony would be ended.

Now it no longer mattered whether there was a private agreement between the Dutch and the French regarding the New World colonies. England's possessions were solidly entrenched, and the menace to them from New Netherland was ended. The potential of a threat from New France to the north still existed, but that was minor. France had done little to develop her possessions, and had no settlement much larger than trading posts for furs. Richard had never been much farther north than Massachusetts Bay, but his father-in-law had told him that he very much doubted there were more than one hundred Frenchmen in all of New France. Some day, surely, the French would awaken to the potential of their North American colony, but that day appeared to be far distant still.

The amenities having been observed with Peter Stuyvesant, the four militia leaders rose to take their leave. As they walked to the front door, Stuyvesant contrived to stroll beside Richard, and he asked casually, "I trust Lady Dunstable is well these days?"

Richard had no intention of admitting that he and his wife had not yet been reunited after her stay in New Amsterdam. He replied, "She's quite well, thank you." Something additional was required of him, and he wanted to assure Stuyvesant that he would have to answer for any harm Eliza may have suffered, so he added quietly, "We've had little opportunity as yet to discuss her stay in New Amsterdam. I'm sure we shall do so shortly."

For the first time, Peter Stuyvesant was taken aback. It was one thing to lust after an exceptionally attractive young woman and do his utmost to seduce her. It was another matter entirely to confront a tall, husky young man who happened to be her husband.

Purely in self-defense as they approached the front door of the governor's house, Peter Stuyvesant murmured, "I shall have to see to it that Cardinal Mazarin learns of today's battle and its outcome."

"I wish you would," Richard replied evenly. "I've been hoping to see Laroche while I'm here in order to make certain that his master hears of our victory." Richard already knew of Laroche's probable fate, but he saw no need to let Stuyvesant know.

"Laroche, I'm sorry to say, was found murdered a short time ago," Peter Stuyvesant replied. "It's now necessary to get in touch with Mazarin directly. Do you suppose he'll be pleased or annoyed to hear of your accomplishments today?"

Richard took a deep breath and then replied firmly. "I don't know, Your Excellency, and I'll be damned if I care. There comes a time in the life of every man when he's required to make a choice, a basic choice that affects the rest of his days on earth. I faced such a dilemma, and for better or worse, I cast my lot irrevocably with the English colonists of New Haven. I'm one of them, and I'm very proud of the trust they have in me. Under no circumstances would I dream of letting them down or of neglecting my duty to them."

There! He had gone on record forcefully and openly; there was now no question as to where he stood. He was declaring his independence not only from Peter Stuyvesant, but from the first minister of France as well. Like so many of the militiamen who had fought under his command today, he had become an American. He was loyal to his home, his neighbors, and above all to the way of life represented in these English communities perched so precariously on the edge of an endless wilderness. Regardless of the consequences, he had cast his lot with them, and in so doing had freed himself from Europe.

Richard felt lightheaded when he parted from his colleagues at the bivouac area surrounding Stuyvesant's house, and in high spirits, he called on the MacNeills at the Thorn and Thistle. Mollie and Angus made a great fuss over him, treating him to food and drink and eagerly questioning him about the battle and its outcome.

Then Angus looked at him thoughtfully across the sturdy trestle table that they were sharing. "It may be," he said, "that we have some news for you also. You were reunited with your wife before you set out for this campaign?"

Richard shook his head. Angus exchanged a long look with his wife, and by unspoken consent, Mollie took charge. Speaking with great care, she related how Eliza had come to them for help and how she had been smuggled out of New Amsterdam by Roaring Wolf.

Richard did not interrupt, but when Mollie paused, he said. "I don't understand. Why was she trying to flee? And why was the local constabulary so intent on catching her?"

Although Mollie was on dangerous ground, she knew there was no escape now from candor. Weighing each word, she related how Eliza had been regarded by all of the residents of New Amsterdam as the mistress of Governor Stuyvesant. Richard reddened beneath his tan, but made no comment.

After Eliza had fled to the Thorn and Thistle, Mollie went on, the governor had become set on making a fact out of fiction and, according to Eliza, was so determined to have her as his mistress that he was trying to prevent her from leaving the town.

A white line formed around Richard's mouth, but he confined himself to a succinct, "I see."

Eliza's escape to the land of the Raritan had been successful, Mollie continued, but recently there had been a fresh complication. "Only two days ago," she said, "we heard that the Raritan were attacked by the Wappinger, who were allies of the Dutch governor. The assault was repelled, we know that much, but at what cost to the Raritan we have no idea. So we can't tell you much about Eliza's present welfare."

Richard lost all interest in the food on his plate. "Can you get me a guide," he said, "who will take me to the Raritan as soon as possible?"

Angus was well acquainted with everyone of consequence in New Amsterdam, so he needed only a short time to find a reliable Indian guide, who consented to take Richard to Staten Island in return for payment of a single Dutch guilder. The transaction was made, and Richard astonished his staff and senior officers by bidding them farewell. He explained only that he was embarking on a private venture. He confided the truth to Ezekiel, telling him that he was going to the land of the Raritan to fetch Eliza.

He met the guide at sunset near the fortress at the southern tip of the island, and they set out together in a battered canoe. Richard was required to do his share of the paddling, and in his anxiety to be reunited with his wife at last, he dug the blade powerfully into the salt water. The tiny craft cut through the harbor, and after a long, hard paddle they were able to make out a sandy beach ahead in the dark.

Then there was a quick buzzing sound a short distance overhead, and Richard realized that an arrow had been fired at him. He shouted in the language of the Mohegan, identifying himself and proclaiming his friendship for the Raritan. A hail of arrows greeted his words. In his frustration, he became angry and was on the verge of firing his rifle to show that he meant business. Nothing would deter him from taking his place beside Eliza.

Suddenly a familiar voice sounded from the shore, speaking the language of the Pequot, and he was quick to recognize Roaring Wolf.

Richard identified himself again for his friend's sake, and the hail of arrows halted abruptly. The reluctant guide paddled close enough to shore for Richard to step out of the canoe, then he quickly turned the craft around and sped away. Richard was immediately surrounded by Raritan braves. Roaring Wolf came forward, his usually inexpressive features wreathed in a broad smile as he greeted his friend.

There was much that Richard wanted to know, but he confined himself to questions of primary interest. "Is my wife safe?" he demanded. "Where is she?"

Roaring Wolf assured him that Eliza had become a heroine in the battle with the Wappinger, and he asserted that she was well.

Richard was growing impatient and demanded, "Take me to her!"

The Pequot had the good sense, however, to conduct him first to the hut of Pah-goom. There an impatient Richard was obliged to pause long enough to relate to the chief, haltingly and laboriously through sign language and with the help of Roaring Wolf—who himself could hardly understand the Raritan tongue—a full account of the day's battle and of the victory that he and his militiamen had won. Only then was he free to seek his wife. As he and Roaring Wolf emerged from the hut of the sachem, he saw a small knot of natives gathered nearby, but he paid them scant heed. "Take me now to Eliza," he demanded of the Pequot.

A figure detached itself from the group outside the hut. Richard stared, then stared again. At first glance he was confronting an Indian squaw with braids, wearing moccasins and a dress of soft, ill-fitting doeskin. All at once he realized, however, that this "squaw" was his wife.

Eliza came to him swiftly, smiling but not speaking, and Richard felt no need for words, either, as he swept her into his arms and held her tightly.

The Indians who had accompanied her were embarrassed by the young white couple's display of intimacy. Indians never indulged in such gestures in the presence of outsiders, and the braves and squaws in the group were stunned by the show of deep emotion that they were witnessing.

Richard was oblivious to the proximity of his audience, however, and kissed Eliza hungrily. She knew that by the standards of the Raritan, they were making an exhibition of themselves, but she, too, did not care, and returned his embrace with a passion as great as his own.

At last they drew apart, both of them breathing hard. "I thank God that you're safe and well," Richard said. "I've waited so long for this day. I can scarcely believe it's finally here."

"I've prayed, too, that we'd soon be reunited," Eliza murmured. "Now that it's happening, it's too good to be true."

He gazed down at her lovingly, seriously. "No matter what may happen," he declared, "we shall never be separated again. This I solemnly promise you."

She nodded and was satisfied. Together they were as invincible as they were vulnerable when separated.

In spite of their euphoria at being reunited, they quickly realized they faced a problem for which they had no solution. Apparently it had not occurred to Pah-goom or Roaring Wolf that the couple might want a hut of their own in which to spend the night, so they had nowhere to go in the village where they could be alone. The lodge of the squaws where Eliza's bed of pine boughs was located was forbidden ground for men. Therefore, for want of any place better to go, they sat beside the dying embers of the supper fire, and there they brought each other up to date on all that had happened since they had been separated.

Eliza related how she had been maneuvered into posing as Peter Stuyvesant's mistress. Then she went on to explain what Richard had already learned from Mollie MacNeill—that she had been forced to flee from the governor's lust and fury. She had succeeded brilliantly in her role as a double agent, and it had been her evidence regarding Stuyvesant's gift of firearms to the Indians that had been directly responsible for the raising of the expeditionary force that Richard had led to victory.

Her eyes shining, Eliza listened raptly to her husband's description of the battle and the scene with Peter Stuyvesant that had followed. Then Richard told her how Roaring Wolf had intercepted her letter to Mazarin. She was surprised—even relieved—to learn that Laroche was dead. Roaring Wolf had never said a word to her about the incident.

But in spite of her joy over the triumphs that her husband had achieved, Eliza knew from his manner that he was not being completely frank with her, that he was withholding something.

Richard was undergoing a tormented inner struggle. He knew that if he kept secret his brief affair with Lady Celeste Murette, there would be no way Eliza would ever learn of the relationship. But their marriage would be clouded forever after, and he could not tolerate such a state of affairs. It was essential that he reveal the truth to her, no matter what the cost. He took a deep breath and, mincing no words, told her how he had come to sleep with Lady Celeste.

Eliza made no comment, but was not surprised. As she well knew, she was married to a handsome man whom other women found attractive, and it was obvious to her—although Richard himself did not seem to realize it—that Lady Celeste had tricked him into sharing a bed.

When Richard finished his painful recital, Eliza sighed gently, and then there was a silence that seemed to grow heavier with each passing second.

"I realize that it would be foolish of me to apologize," he said lamely. "What's done is done, and I offer no excuse."

She nodded thoughtfully. "I've heard of Lady Celeste Murette," she said, "in pointed remarks picked up here and there. She occupied my house in New Amsterdam before I moved into it."

His eyes widened. "You mean she was Peter Stuyvesant's mistress?"

She shrugged. "I don't know, and I don't really care," she replied. "What difference does it make?"

Richard wanted to blurt out that Lady Celeste was about to marry her father, but that was unfair to Colonel Adam Burrows, who deserved the privilege of breaking the news to his daughter in whatever manner he deemed appropriate. Therefore Richard made no comment.

Eliza stared at a coal glowing in the dying fire. "In a way," she said, "what's happened served me right. I was determined to succeed in a difficult assignment, and I didn't stop to weigh the cost of our separation. You're a man, and I can hardly blame you for reacting naturally to a situation that was beyond your control."

"I'm grateful to you for thinking it was out of my control," he declared, "but I should have known better and should have curbed my excesses. All I can tell you is that I love only you, Eliza. I hope you will give me the opportunity to prove it."

She laughed softly and reached for his hand. "You're forgiven," she told him. "I just hope that both of us learned a lesson from our separate experiences. It's only by the grace of God that I wasn't unfaithful, too, with Peter Stuyvesant or with some English sea captain whom I was trying to inveigle into accepting Dutch allegiance. Hereafter we'll be together no matter what Cardinal Mazarin may say or do."

Richard's relief was overwhelming, and he slipped an arm around her shoulders. That she forgave his transgressions was all that mattered to him, and the future promised to be bright. Certainly the sly first minister of France was of little concern in this remote corner of the New World, in a territory claimed by the Dutch but stubbornly controlled by Indians who refused to accept the overlordship of Amsterdam.

"Since Laroche is dead, I reckon we'll not only have to write our own letters of resignation from the service of France, but we'll have to find some way to have our correspondence delivered to Cardinal Mazarin in Paris," Richard said.

"We'll find a way, I assure you," Eliza said firmly.

He was heartened by her resolve. It occurred to

him that their separation had not been all to the bad. Eliza had gained a new sense of authority, a new understanding of her own powers, during the time that she had spent alone in New Amsterdam. She had been headstrong and immature when they parted; now she had become a woman who knew her own mind.

They instinctively moved closer together and sat with their shoulders touching and their hands tightly clasped.

"I've dreamed of the night we'd sleep together again," Richard said, "but apparently we'll have to wait until we get home to New Haven. Roaring Wolf will be with us on the trail when we leave here, so it appears we'll never be alone."

Eliza laughed despite herself. "It would be terribly amusing," she said, "if it weren't so sad. I suppose someday we'll recover our sense of humor and be able to laugh about it." They lapsed into silence again. All at once Richard's sixth sense told him someone was coming up behind him. He quietly released his wife's hand and reached for the rifle that lay on the ground beside him.

Eliza was alarmed, but when she peered off into the gloom she was suddenly relieved. "It's Jo-no-ta," she said.

The husky Raritan warrior approached, his face dignified, and folding his arms across his bare chest, he stared first at Eliza and then at her husband. "Jo-no-ta," he declared, "has waited a long time to meet the warrior who claims Eliza, friend of Jo-no-ta, as his squaw."

Eliza thought it would only complicate matters if she explained to Richard that Jo-no-ta had been her admirer. She saw no reason to mention what she regarded as irrelevant, so she translated only what she saw fit.

"As I understand it," Richard said amiably, "you

were jointly responsible for driving off the Wappinger and rendering their surprise attack harmless."

Jo-no-ta nodded solemnly as Eliza translated. "Never has Jo-no-ta seen a squaw with the bravery that Eliza showed that day," he said. "She fought with the skill and courage of a warrior. This is the squaw Jo-no-ta has always wanted as his own squaw."

Eliza was stunned. It appeared that the senior warrior of the Raritan was intent on creating a scene and causing trouble with her husband. She gulped, and translated what the brave had said.

The warrior's comment was so unexpected that Richard was caught totally off guard and could only blink in surprise. "It is sad," Jo-no-ta went on, "that she is already married to a warrior."

Richard smiled steadily.

Eliza, however, had an inkling of what the warrior had in mind and wanted to dissuade him from expressing his thoughts. "I'm sure," she said to him hurriedly, "that the day will come when Jo-no-ta will find a squaw who is right for him among his own people."

The warrior shook his head. Obviously he had already weighed such a possibility and had discarded it. "This is a problem," he said.

Richard wanted to laugh at the situation but was afraid the dignity of the Raritan would be disturbed. As far as he himself was concerned, his mood remained buoyant. He was reunited with his wife, who had forgiven him, and everything else, including the admiration of this savage for her, did not matter.

"It is not possible for a squaw to be married to two braves at the same time," Jo-no-ta declared. "So he who is respected as the greatest warrior of the Raritan and he who is known in his own land as a famous brave must meet in combat for the possession of Eliza."

The idea was ludicrous, but Eliza could not cry out or express her annoyance. She resented being treated like an inanimate object to be awarded to the winner of a trial of strength of some kind, but she knew that Jo-no-ta would have no understanding of what she meant if she tried to explain her feelings to him. She reluctantly translated for Richard, who was so astonished he could only gape at the brave.

"Let Jo-no-ta and the white warrior meet in honorable combat when the sun again rises from the sea," the brave declared. "Let them fight by the rules of honor. May they fight until one or the other is killed. Then he who survives will be the husband of Eliza, and all of the people of the Raritan will recognize that she is his squaw and only his."

Eliza wanted to protest that she was already married and that her wedded state was recognized throughout the civilized world. But she had no opportunity to say a word. Jo-no-ta, devoting his full attention to Richard, bowed stiffly, raised his right arm in farewell, and withdrew again into the shadows.

Richard couldn't help chuckling.

"It isn't funny," Eliza told him. "Jo-no-ta is serious. He intends to meet you in some sort of a duel to the death tomorrow, and I'm to be awarded to the winner as the prize."

Richard saw that she was badly upset and tried to comfort her.

She faced him angrily. "This is serious!" she said. "I know the Raritan, and you don't. We've got to find Roaring Wolf immediately and figure some way out of this insane dilemma!"

Roaring Wolf, as always, was nearby, and no

sooner was his name mentioned than he materialized out of the shadows. He quickly confirmed Eliza's judgment. "Jo-no-ta meant challenge," he said. "He will meet Richard in combat when sun rises tomorrow."

Richard stared at his friend. "But this is madness," he said. "Eliza is already married to me, so what right has this warrior to butt in?"

"He is willing to die. He has right." The Pequot shrugged. "This is old tradition of many tribes. There is nothing that can be done about it. Richard must engage in combat with Jo-no-ta."

Richard's long-drawn sigh indicated his exasperation.

Eliza was furious. "What if Richard refuses?" she asked. "Suppose he fails to appear for this duel or whatever you want to call it?"

Roaring Wolf spread out his hands in a futile attempt to mollify her. "If Richard does not appear, Jo-no-ta will say Richard is coward," he said. "Then all warriors of Raritan will hunt for him, and when they find him they will kill him. Jo-no-ta will wear his scalp."

Eliza didn't know whether to laugh or cry. "I believe," she said to Richard, "that our best plan would be to leave here at once. Tonight."

Roaring Wolf intervened before Richard could reply. "That is not possible," he said. "First we must steal canoe to carry us long distance across water to land Eliza and Richard call New Haven. We must take food, blankets, and weapons to protect us. This cannot be done in one night. When sun rises tomorrow, we will be here in land of Raritan."

Richard did his best to control his anger over the absurd situation. "What you're trying to tell me, Roaring Wolf," he said, "is that whether I like it or not, I've got to accept this brave's challenge and meet him in some primitive form of combat, or I'm going to lose both my wife and my life."

The Pequot nodded solemnly.

Richard turned to Eliza and shrugged. "At the very least," he said, "we will have seen each other before the end comes. If I have no choice, then I must do the best I'm able under the circumstances."

"I'll appeal to Pah-goom," Eliza cried. "Surely he'll stop this fight before it starts."

"Pah-goom cannot prevent fight," Roaring Wolf said quietly. "No sachem has power to change laws by which people have lived since days of the ancestors."

"Just what is expected of me?" Richard wanted to know.

Seeing the deep concern on Eliza's face, Roaring Wolf wanted to make light of the situation, but knew he would be doing his friend a disservice unless he spoke truthfully.

Therefore, choosing his words carefully, he explained that the duel would take place, in all probability, on a flat stretch of beach. The two combatants would be clad only in loincloths, they would carry no weapons, and there would be no rules. Each would be free to maul the other as he saw fit in order to achieve victory. During the fight, Roaring Wolf added reluctantly, Eliza would be required to sit in a prominent place where any member of the tribe could look at her. She would be dressed as a bride, and should Jo-no-ta be victorious, he would claim her instantly.

"I think," she murmured, "that I'm having a nightmare, and I don't seem capable of waking up."

Richard had listened attentively, and now he nodded grimly. He accepted the reality of a situation that was unthinkable according to the tenets of his civilization. He knew now that he had no choice. He had to meet and fight the burly warrior of the Raritan, risking his own life in order to preserve it, and thereby maintain the marriage that meant even more to him than life itself.

IX

A T the insistence of Roaring Wolf, who was convinced it was useless for any human being to rail against the fate that the gods had decreed, Eliza returned to the lodge of squaws for a few hours of rest. Meantime the Pequot took Richard with him to the warrior lodge where he himself had a bed. There he insisted that Richard get as much sleep as he possibly could.

Richard tried to face the unexpected crisis in his life with equanimity. He had thought his troubles were over when he had won a decisive victory over the Indians. Now, through no fault of his own, through no fault of Eliza's, he was being required to fight a duel to the death against Jo-no-ta, a so-called Indian ally. He had no alternative, so he had to do his best. If he faltered, his own life could be snuffed out, and Eliza would be forced to remain on this remote island for the rest of her life as the squaw of a demanding savage.

These thoughts circulating in his head, Richard at last dropped off into a deep sleep. He awoke at daybreak, and was relieved that he felt rested. He went down to the beach to wash. When he emerged from the water, he found Roaring Wolf waiting patiently for him. The Pequot silently handed him a loincloth of buckskin, and as Richard donned it, he knew his ordeal was imminent. He was handed a piece of freshly baked corn bread, which he refused, and he sniffed at the contents of a gourd and then drank his fill, draining the container. Not until later did he learn that he had drunk the heated blood of a bull buffalo, which was supposed to endow him with greater strength. Then, to his amazement, Roaring Wolf picked up a greasy lump of a foul-smelling substance, which he began to smear on the young colonist's body. The odor was faintly rancid, and the thought occurred to Richard that he was probably being coated with animal fat of some kind to make it more difficult for his opponent to grasp and hold him in a wrestling match.

"Very well, I'm ready," he said.

Roaring Wolf fell in beside him, and together they walked up the beach. Although it was still early morning and the sun was just appearing on the horizon of the sea to the east, it seemed that the entire Raritan tribe had gathered for the rare spectacle that awaited them. Pipe-smoking elders mingled with medicine men, and the more active warriors of the nation rested on their haunches and exchanged occasional words in low tones. The squaws of the Raritan were present, too, chattering at one another, and there were small children and dogs everywhere, or so it seemed. Richard's heart stopped beating for a moment when he caught sight of Eliza, seated on the top of a large rock that overlooked an expanse of beach. She was attired in a short dress of doeskin that had been sun-bleached white and decorated with a design executed in dyed porcupine quills. Similar quills protruded from the two braids of her hair, which hung down over her shoulders, and her lips and cheeks had been stained with a red berry juice, making them bright. Apparently she was attired in the costume of a bride of the Raritan. She sat gravely with her arms folded across her breast. When she saw Richard approach, she started to rise, but Roaring Wolf gestured at her violently, and she subsided. She had been warned that she was not permitted to show favoritism, even though she was already married to the white man; and although the rule made no sense to her, she was willing to take Roaring Wolf's word that it was far better for her and Richard if she obeyed the warning scrupulously.

The conversation stopped, and everyone in the tribe examined Richard with considerable interest. Most of the Raritan were seeing him for the first time. They inspected him with thorough candor, looking particularly hard at the muscles in his arms and legs and at the width of his shoulders, trying to judge his qualities as a fighting man by the way he moved.

Ordinarily Richard would have been amused by their scrutiny, but with his life at stake he saw everything from a different perspective. He had no idea what was expected of him, so he halted, folded his arms across his chest and, looking up at Eliza on the top of the rock, winked and grinned boldly. A few of the Raritan squaws seemed to appreciate the gesture, but most continued to look stone-faced as they regarded him. He cared nothing about them or their opinions. He read the expression in Eliza's eyes, knew that she loved him, and was grateful.

The crowd stirred, and Richard followed the direction of their gaze. Coming toward him now was Jo-no-ta, also clad in a loincloth and heavily greased. The brave moved lightly on the balls of his feet, and Richard, gauging him swiftly, knew it was going to be an extremely difficult battle. His opponent looked strong as well as agile and had the advantage of being familiar with Indian wrestling. Jo-no-ta halted about ten or fifteen yards from his opponent and turned his back. He conversed with no one.

Then Pah-goom appeared, wearing a large and cumbersome headdress that appeared to be the symbol of his exalted rank. He seemed to be in high spirits, and after greeting Eliza with an amiable wave, he seated himself at the base of the rock on which she was perched and clapped his hands together. This, it seemed, was the signal that the fight was to begin.

Richard was further warned by Roaring Wolf, who hissed to him in a low tone, "Make ready *now* for your enemy!"

Richard studied Jo-no-ta, who was advancing toward him slowly, cautiously. The brave was about four inches shorter than Richard, and his arms and legs were not as long, but he had the distinct advantage of greater weight. Richard estimated that his opponent outweighed him by at least forty to fifty pounds, and none of that weight was fat. Muscles rippled in the warrior's shoulders, and he was remarkably light on his feet as he crept pantherlike toward his white foe.

Richard braced himself, not knowing precisely what to expect, but anticipating that he would somehow be able to tolerate the shock of initial contact. He expected Jo-no-ta to hurl himself forward and try to bear him to the ground. Therefore Richard planted his feet apart and waited for just such an assault.

To his surprise, however, Jo-no-ta resorted to totally unorthodox tactics, suddenly and viciously launching a kick with his bare right foot. Richard barely managed to leap clear of the unexpected blow, which nonetheless threw him off-balance. It was obvious that Indians did not observe the European methods of sportsmanship that guided white men in their combat. This, Richard told himself, he should have known from the outset and should have been prepared to handle. But he had been caught off guard, and consequently he was annoyed with himself and angry at his opponent.

Ordinarily in a duel of any kind he was cool and calm, using his mind as well as his physical prowess to achieve victory. In this instance, however, his poise deserted him, and he reacted instinctively, lunging forward and lashing out with his fists at the brave.

Although Richard did not know it, he had chosen the best of all possible means of fighting a warrior. English boys learned early to use their fists, usually at the age of six or seven years. Similarly, Indians became familiar with wrestling from the day they began to walk; but fistfighting was unknown to them, and they had no experience in or knowledge of the art.

Richard landed a bruising left on Jo-no-ta's cheekbone, then drove his right fist hard into the pit of the warrior's stomach. The Indian gasped, doubled over, and groped in vain for his foe, trying to obtain a wrestling hold.

Richard kept his distance and continued to use his fists, putting his full force behind every blow, which he drove with fury from his shoulders. Lefts and rights peppered the brave's head, face, and torso, and he began to rock groggily under the steady barrage.

At last it occurred to Richard that he had been fortunate enough to choose a method of fighting with which his opponent had no familiarity. His confidence increasing, he stepped up the tempo and varied his longer punches with short vicious jabs.

The audience, openly partisan, was dismayed. Making no pretense of hiding their favoritism, the Raritan had obviously expected their champion to make short work of his opponent. To their astonishment, however, Jo-no-ta was taking a drubbing, and every time Richard landed a solid blow the spectators responded with moans and groans.

Suddenly, however, one voice rose above the hubbub.

Eliza totally forgot Roaring Wolf's admonition that she was expected to remain neutral, and she began to scream Richard's name in approval, shouting it again and again.

Gradually the spectators, who did not know what the cheer meant, took up the cry, and the beach echoed with the sound. "Rich-ard! Rich-ard! Rich-ard!"

Richard grinned in satisfaction. He was unexpectedly winning what appeared so far to be a surprisingly easy victory, and although he knew better than to rejoice prematurely, his apprehensions about the outcome were greatly diminished.

Blood poured from Jo-no-ta's nose, one eye was so puffed and swollen that he had difficulty in keeping it open, and a hard left jab to his mouth had split his lip. Only his extraordinary stamina enabled him to stay on his feet and continue to take punishment. His eyes were glazed and he staggered, but he would not drop to the ground even though he had no adequate means of defending himself against the punches that rained on him.

Had this been a boxing match with another Englishman, Richard would have appealed to the officials in charge to call a halt for his opponent's sake, but there were no officials supervising this bout, which was a fight to the death.

At last Jo-no-ta sank to one knee and shook his head repeatedly as he tried in vain to clear it.

Flexing his bruised, aching fingers, Richard let his hands drop to his sides.

All at once Jo-no-ta called on his hidden reserves of strength and hurled himself sideways at his opponent. One moment he seemed on the verge of collapse, and the next he was fighting like a demon. Caught totally by surprise, Richard lost his balance and crashed to the hard sand of the beach with his foe on top of him.

Jo-no-ta knew wrestling holds that were new and strange to Richard, who would ordinarily have found them impossible to break. But the warrior had been seriously weakened and lacked the strength to capitalize on this advantage. Nevertheless, he managed to keep Richard flat on his back and to sit astride him, straddling his chest.

Richard well realized that the advantage he had enjoyed so far would soon be dissipated unless he continued to employ the tactics that had brought victory so near. Summoning his strength, Richard dug his heels into the sand, arched his lower back, and managed to roll sideways, throwing Jo-no-ta onto the sand. He continued to punch with abandon at the warrior, concentrating on Jo-no-ta's already battered face.

The punishment was already more severe than even an Indian brave in superb physical condition could tolerate, and Jo-no-ta ultimately slid to the ground and lay still, breathing deeply.

Richard propped himself on one knee preparatory to hauling himself to his feet. Then he realized that Pah-goom was standing over him, offering him a stone knife, with which, Richard assumed, he was to finish off Jo-no-ta.

Jo-no-ta stared up at Richard, and the spectators grew deathly quiet in order to hear what they assumed would be his last words.

"Rich-ard has won his battle against Jo-no-ta," he said. "Take the stone knife now and drive it deep into my heart so that my spirit will depart from my body and join the spirits of my ancestors."

Richard stood and surveyed the crowd. Eliza, with tears of relief in her eyes, looked down at him with love and pride from the top of the rock.

Roaring Wolf made no attempt to conceal his joy. The Raritan, however, reflected the attitude of Pah-goom, who awaited the thrust of the stone knife that would end the life of his best warrior.

But Richard had other ideas. "Jo-no-ta," he said, speaking loudly and slowly, "has fought bravely and well. My people do not believe in killing for the sake of killing. Jo-no-ta has earned the right to live, and he shall live." The crowd stared at him, uncomprehending.

Grasping the knife firmly, Richard bent down and drove the shaft into the sand with such force that he buried it to the hilt. Then he stood erect again and folded his arms across his chest in Indian fashion.

Jo-no-ta seemed mortified. His wooden expression gave way to one of humiliation. He struggled slowly and painfully to his feet and, his head down, walked off into the woods.

Roaring Wolf immediately took off after him.

"Rich-ard," Pah-goom said loudly to his people, "has proved that he is a great warrior. He has beaten the champion of the Raritan. He deserves the prize of Eliza." He paused and peered up toward the top of the rock before again devoting his attention to the young white man. "Rich-ard becomes now the blood brother of all Raritan."

The sachem drew the stone dagger from the sand, nicked the top of one finger with it, then handed the weapon to Richard, indicating that he was to do the same. Not knowing what would happen in the ritual, Richard did as he was bidden. Pah-goom mixed their blood in the palms of their right hands, then raised his own palm to his mouth.

Now Richard understood. His blood and that of the Raritan had been mingled, and he was expected to consume it. He raised his own hand and licked the salty substance from his palm.

To his astonishment, the entire tribe roared with approval. An impromptu dance started, with warriors and squaws forming in a circle around him, gyrating wildly as they leaped and pranced.

Then Eliza was led down from her observation point at the peak of the rock and was thrust into the circle, too.

Immediately aware of her presence, Richard encircled her shoulders with a protective arm. The dancing became wilder, more insistent, and drums began to throb. Soon the dancers were keeping time to the insidious, primitive beat, and it seemed as if the entire tribe had joined in the festivities.

At last Pah-goom called a halt and gave instructions so rapidly that Eliza could not follow what was being said. She took advantage of their moment of relative privacy.

"I thank the Almighty that you are all right," Eliza said. "You'll never know how concerned I was for you."

"I was a mite worried myself," Richard replied, "but I appear to have done the right thing by getting involved in a fistfight. Come to think of it, I've never heard of an Indian who has fought with his fists."

The warriors surrounded Richard, separating him from Eliza, and insisted on escorting him back to the village. There his loincloth was stripped from him, and much to his wife's secret amusement, the squaws of the tribe drenched him with crocks of water to which flower petals had been added; some of the water missed him, other crock-fuls almost drowned him, but that did not matter— the tribe was enjoying a glorious ritual. Next Richard was attired in trousers decorated with dyed porcupine quills, and the war paint of the Raritan was smeared on his torso and cheeks.

Pah-goom made a long, rambling speech, the gist being that Richard and Eliza had now been adopted into the tribe, and for the rest of their days would be regarded as full-fledged Raritan. They had earned the honor separately, and the members of the tribe lined up to welcome them with handclasps.

It was long after dark when the festivities came to an end. By then the Raritan had become conscious of the plight of the two white people in their midst. A hut was provided for them, and at long last they had the privacy they had craved.

They made love as if to fit a lifetime into one night, discovering anew each time the miracle of their union, and at last the endless days and nights of their long separation faded into their memories. They were together again and nothing else mattered.

No work was done on the island for the next few days. No brave went hunting, no squaw picked up a needle or set foot in the fields. Instead, large quantities of fish were roasted in the coals of a huge cooking fire, sides of venison were turned on spits over the open flames, and steaming stews of vegetables were prepared in earthenware pots. Neither Richard nor Eliza had ever witnessed such a prodigal feast.

The Raritan treated both of them with the respect due to a chief, and the young couple were grateful to have the chance to make up for lost time together. However, after a week of enforced idleness and feasting, they grew eager to return to New Haven. One morning Richard communicated this desire to Roaring Wolf, who promptly disappeared. The squaws cooked a breakfast of corn bread and fish, and after Richard and Eliza had eaten, they went to the hut of Pah-goom to say good-bye.

A half hour later, when they returned to gather their belongings, they were surprised to find Jo-no-ta standing patiently before their hut. Roaring Wolf was there, too, and he stepped forward and drew Richard aside.

"Jo-no-ta does not understand ways of white man," the Pequot said. "Roaring Wolf try to explain that Richard is not like Indian, that Richard does not want to kill Jo-no-ta; but Jo-no-ta is stubborn and does not believe Roaring Wolf."

Richard looked at the Raritan Indian brave, who was staring at the ground, his hands at his sides. Well accustomed to the strange behavior of Indians, Richard immediately knew what he had to do, and spoke to Eliza.

"Tell Jo-no-ta that I do not wish to kill him, but that as a blood brother of the Raritan, I want him to help me as a brother would help a brother. I want him to lead us safely to the waters of the Great Bay."

Eliza translated to the brave. As soon as he understood what was required of him, his face brightened. He beckoned Richard and Eliza to follow him.

The couple exchanged a glance and said nothing as they walked down to the water's edge. There a long war canoe awaited them, and Roaring Wolf looked it over appreciatively. Jo-no-ta disappeared, but returned in a matter of minutes with an escort of sixteen Raritan braves.

"We do not wish to risk losing our brother and

our sister to the Dutch, the Wappinger, or our other enemies," Jo-no-ta told them. "We will take them all the way back to their own people."

The generous gesture could not be rejected without hurting the warrior's feelings and those of his colleagues, so Richard and Eliza, still in Indian attire, climbed into the canoe, sitting amidship, with Roaring Wolf beside them. The craft shoved off and the brawny warriors paddled in unison, propelling the boat swiftly across the water.

The braves were tireless, or so it seemed, and paddled for hour after hour without rest. They crossed the harbor and headed up the East River toward the Great Bay, and did not go ashore until late in the afternoon, when they made camp for the night. Several went hunting, returning with some plump geese, which they roasted, and that night the entire party dined in the open.

The braves insisted on setting up sentry outposts, and Eliza slept better than she had in many weeks, knowing that she was protected by her "brothers" of the Raritan as well as by her husband.

The journey was resumed at dawn the next day, and continued without incident until the fourth day, when in midafternoon they rounded a point of land and entered the familiar waters of New Haven harbor.

The appearance of a war canoe filled with strange Indians was so extraordinary that a considerable crowd gathered on shore. Ezekiel Clayton, taking no chances, hastily mustered from among the dockworkers a squad of his militia, and Adam Burrows hurried to the scene from his office.

The crowd gaped in amazement as a squaw and a tall warrior stepped ashore, and the Colonel was struck speechless when he recognized them as his daughter and son-in-law.

Eliza embraced and kissed him, Richard wrung

his hand, and the colonel shook his head in quiet astonishment. "I must say," he declared, "that you two are unique. You, Eliza, provided us with the means of uniting the colonies in a campaign, and you, Richard, led our troops to victory. Now you appear in our midst as members of a strange tribe. I swear, we never know what to expect next from you."

It was the colonel, however, who provided the biggest surprise of the day, announcing that he and his new wife would expect the young couple for supper that evening.

Ezekiel Clayton took charge of the visiting Raritan, making them at home by having tents erected for them on the New Haven Green. Meanwhile, a thoughtful Eliza and Richard retired to their own dwelling for the first time in months.

Eliza remained silent as she bathed and dressed in a costume more appropriate for a civilized colonial woman than the doeskin dress of an Indian squaw. She applied cosmetics lightly to her face, and as she fastened an earring, she remarked quietly, "You neglected to tell me that Papa is married."

"I didn't neglect to tell you," Richard replied, "I deliberately refrained, feeling it was his place, not mine, to tell you of his romance. As to his marriage, I'm also surprised. All I know is that he wasn't married when I led the militia off to the New Amsterdam campaign. Obviously they've had a ceremony since that time."

Eliza appeared to be preoccupied with putting her second earring in place. "And what was his wife's name before she became Mistress Burrows?" she asked quietly.

Richard took a deep breath. "Lady Celeste Murette," he said.

His wife's expression remained unchanged, but her complexion paled slightly, although she wished to indicate no surprise. "The woman with whom you had your affair," she said flatly.

He was so embarrassed he could only nod.

"Of course you know she lived with Peter Stuyvesant for some time before she came here to New Haven?"

"I know," Richard said. "You told me. What are you getting at?"

She didn't want to be evasive, but changed her mind in the name of family peace. She decided to judge Celeste for herself before she revealed any more than was necessary. "Oh, I heard her name mentioned now and again while I was in New Amsterdam," she replied vaguely. She prevented further discussion of the matter by announcing that she was ready to leave.

Richard was increasingly uncomfortable as they walked to Colonel Burrows's house. At last he could no longer stand the silence. "I would have mentioned your father's romance to you had I known he actually would be married during our absence," he said. "I realize that this must be a nasty shock to you."

Eliza shrugged. "My state of mind will depend entirely on my judgment of Papa's bride," she replied. "And for whatever this may be worth, I promise I won't think any the less of her because of your unfortunate association with her."

He murmured his thanks and felt slightly relieved, but still apprehensive.

When they reached their destination, Celeste greeted them at the door and was very much in command of the situation. She needed no introduction to Eliza, so she embraced the other woman lightly, then raised her hand impersonally for Richard to kiss. "I'm sorry we didn't wait to marry until you two returned to New Haven," she said, "but on the spur of the moment Adam and I decided to be married, and we couldn't resist going through with the ceremony then and there. I hope you're not too upset with us."

Eliza proved equal to the occasion. "Not at all," she replied. "I wish both of you great happiness, all the happiness that I wish for Richard and me."

Her father, who had been concerned about her reaction to his news, looked very much relieved.

Celeste played the role of hostess to perfection, serving everyone glasses of sack herself. The elaborate meal was a culinary triumph and consisted of dish after dish that was new to both Eliza and Richard. All had been made according to Celeste's instructions, and it was revealed that she had spent several hours in the kitchen with Mrs. Miller, the cook-housekeeper, supervising the preparation of the meal. Wine flowed freely, and the supper was a great success.

Then, while the men remained at the table to drink brandy, smoke pipefuls of tobacco, and discuss the full details of the New Amsterdam campaign, the women withdrew to the small sitting room that Celeste had claimed as her own.

Celeste felt in control of the situation and of herself as she showed her stepdaughter—who was only a year or two her junior—to a seat. The atmosphere at the table had been convivial. Controversial and embarrassing topics had been avoided, and everyone had been duly impressed with her hospitality. She could ask for little more. A serving maid brought them cups of steaming, fragrant tea, and as they sat opposite each other, Celeste said, "I hope you and I will become fast friends."

Eliza smiled faintly. "That would be in the best interests of everyone concerned."

Celeste wondered if there was a hidden meaning to her words, but decided not to probe. "Your father," she said, "is very fond of you."

"So he's always been," Eliza replied. "I'm equally fond of him, and I'm determined to let nothing hurt him."

Celeste's eyes widened. "So am I, I assure you," she said emphatically.

Eliza sipped her tea and found it to her liking. "He'd be dreadfully upset and hurt," she said softly, "if he knew of your relationship with my husband."

Celeste was taken aback. "You amaze me," she said. "I'm astonished that you know about it."

Eliza had no intention of revealing that Richard had volunteered the information to her. Their closeness was strictly their own business, so she saw no need to reveal such things to Celeste, of all women. Eliza glanced around the room, noting the changes the other woman had made in the brief time she had been mistress of the house.

Celeste was disconcerted, but tried not to show it. "The painting over the hearth," she said, "has been in my family for generations. The Cavalier on this wall happens to have been an old friend."

Eliza glanced up at the painting and then observed quietly, "He bears a striking resemblance to Peter Stuyvesant."

Uncertain of how much Eliza knew, Celeste instantly became cautious. "Do you think so?" she asked vaguely.

Eliza smiled. "There's no question of it," she replied. "Put ten pounds on him and add a touch of color to his face, and I'd say he's the very image of Governor Stuyvesant."

Celeste looked at the painting as if seeing it for the first time. "I never looked at it that way," she murmured, "but it's possible that you're quite right."

Eliza decided to drop her subtlety. "I'm surprised you didn't notice the similarity yourself," she said. "But perhaps you were too close to Governor Stuyvesant."

Celeste took refuge in innocence, and bristled. "I'm not sure I understand your meaning."

"Come now," Eliza told her, "there's no need for subterfuge between us. You forget that I lived for many weeks in New Amsterdam, and I occupied the house that you had vacated when I arrived."

Celeste inwardly retreated, although she continued to look poised and confident on the surface. "You seem to have gone to a great deal of trouble to learn about me," she said.

"Not at all," Eliza replied sweetly. "I didn't know until this afternoon that you were married to my father. I'm not deaf, dumb, and blind, so I did pick up various tidbits about my predecessor in New Amsterdam. Not only that, but you had left items of clothing there. There was a green dress hanging in a wardrobe of the little house, and a purple negligee that you left in Governor Stuyvesant's house."

There was no longer any doubt in the mind of Celeste Burrows. Her new stepdaughter definitely knew, not only about her affair with Richard, but also that she had been the mistress of Peter Stuyvesant. She immediately launched a vigorous counterattack.

"I trust *you* took care," she said, "not to leave any intimate apparel in Stuyvesant's house."

Eliza smiled, but made no reply.

Celeste had expected a strong reaction and was surprised when none was forthcoming. She shifted the basis of her attack somewhat. "It appears," she said, "that you and I are tarred with the same brush."

Eliza shook her head slowly. "Not exactly," she said. "I'm not criticizing you for your conduct with Governor Stuyvesant. You were a single woman then. In fact, you hadn't even met my father, and what you did was strictly your own business."

Celeste inclined her head to indicate her thanks for the generosity of the gesture.

"You're mistaken, though, if you think of me as your successor," Eliza went on. "I was married to Richard when I was in New Amsterdam, and not for one moment did I lose sight of our bond. I assure you that at no time was I the mistress of Peter Stuyvesant or of anyone else."

"That might be rather difficult to prove," Celeste said, still struggling to find an effective weapon.

"I have no need to prove it," Eliza replied brigthly. "But if you're still on good terms with Peter Stuyvesant, I'm sure he'll corroborate what I've told you. I myself wouldn't dare go back to New Amsterdam while he's still there for fear that he'll try to detain me. He failed the last time, but he just might be more successful if I were to become careless."

Celeste didn't quite know what to reply.

Eliza had gained the upper hand and fully intended to keep it. "As to your relationship with Richard," she said, "that's another matter entirely. Granted, *you* were single and didn't feel responsible to anyone for your conduct, but you knew when you inveigled him into bed that *he* was married."

Celeste managed to laugh, although the sound was harsher than she would have liked. "You make me sound like the aggressor in my affair with Richard," she said.

"Exactly so," Eliza replied succinctly. "I was of two minds on the matter until I saw you tonight and had an opportunity to judge for myself. You see, I know Richard, and although I don't know you, I'm thoroughly familiar with your type. You chased after him deliberately in the hope that he'd fall in love with you. I'm certain it was calculated on your part so Richard would assume the responsibility was all his. I know Richard too well to believe he was an aggressive adulterer. I'm not blaming you, mind you, but I'm taking pains to point out to you that I am thoroughly familiar with what you did and why you did it. Your gamble failed, and that's when you decided to marry my father instead."

Celeste had the uncanny feeling that her new stepdaughter had the ability to read her mind. But she could not admit the truth and started to protest vigorously.

Eliza raised a hand to silence her. "Please, my dear, there's no need to put on a false front for my benefit. I've known for years that my father is a splendid catch. He's quite well-to-do by colonial standards, his rank in the militia makes him more or less the first citizen of New Haven, and by marrying him you've acquired both social position and financial security."

"I needed neither, I can assure you," Celeste said in a strangled voice.

"I won't argue the matter with you," Eliza replied cheerfully. "Let's just say that the facts speak for themselves. I haven't brought up these matters in order to hurt you or embarrass you. I give you my solemn word on that."

Celeste drew in a long, sharp breath. "Then may I ask just why you're raking up the past?"

"My reasons should be self-evident," Eliza said. "I wish you every happiness because I so badly want my father to be happy. He's worked very hard all his life, and he's been lonely for many years. What's more, it wasn't easy for him to bring up a daughter single-handedly on the frontier. Believe me, he deserves all the happiness he can crowd into the years he has left on this earth."

"Then we're in complete agreement," Celeste said, starting to recover her aplomb. "All I want is his happiness, too."

"I hope so," Eliza said slowly. "I hope it with all my heart and all my soul. I don't believe in confrontations when they're unnecessary, and I'm not the sort of woman to hold threats over someone else's head, but I want to make my own position plain to you. For whatever his reasons, my father elected to marry you. His future happiness lies in your hands alone."

"Quite true," Celeste interjected.

Eliza ignored the interruption. "Be true to the trust you've accepted," Eliza told her flatly, "and I'm willing to forget your past. Cause my father unhappiness of any kind, in any way, and I warn you solemnly that I'll reveal every unsavory thing that I know about you. I'm sorry to put it so bluntly, but at least you know now where I stand."

They rose with unspoken accord, and each woman took the other's measure.

Celeste realized that the daughter of the man she had married was no dewy-eyed innocent or easy mark. In spite of her lack of experience, Eliza Dunstable was wise and a good judge of character, and it would be difficult to fool her. More than that, as she herself had indicated, it would be dangerous indeed.

For her part, Eliza had formed her own firm conclusions about her new stepmother. She could not deny that Celeste was lovely—as attractive as any woman in New Haven. What was more, she was wise in the ways of men and the world. She had not denied Eliza's account of her affair with Richard; Eliza felt certain that the woman had been responsible for it.

Eliza smiled and held out a hand. "I'm willing to

be friends," she said. "In fact, I'd like it very much."

A smile spread slowly across the face of Celeste Murette Burrows. "It will make life so much simpler for everyone concerned if you and I are friends," she said. "Especially in a community of this size. You have nothing to fear from me." She clasped Eliza's hand, and the bond was sealed.

Eliza entertained misgivings about the tenuous agreement she had just made, but she kept them to herself. She would watch and wait.

Celeste knew, too, that they had merely called a fragile truce and had not actually ended their feud. Whether Adam's blond daughter represented a constant threat to her or whether she could succeed in lessening Eliza's mistrust remained to be seen. She had faced far more menacing adversaries in the past, and in one way or another had rendered them harmless. So she knew of no reason she could not do so again—if it should prove necessary. She, too, was willing to watch and wait.

When Adam and Richard finished their own conversation and joined their wives, they found both women laughing and chatting together in apparent harmony. They were discussing the material that Celeste had in mind for new draperies for the parlor, and both seemed immersed in the subject.

Adam was delighted. He had been far more worried than he had been willing to admit even to himself about his daughter's reaction to his marriage to so young a bride. The mere fact that Celeste and Eliza seemed to be speaking so easily was a great relief to him.

Richard had been even more concerned for reasons of his own. He had been certain that his wife would hate the woman with whom he had been unfaithful, and he had envisioned untold complications. Finding the two women sitting together amicably, in seeming rapport, was totally bewildering. He had to accept the situation even though he didn't understand it.

At least Eliza had forgiven him and bore no grudge against Celeste, so he had to be grateful.

X

THE Louvre, the Paris home of the kings of France, dominated the right bank of the River Seine, where it sat in the midst of a garden so vast that hundreds of men were required to care for the flowers, remove the weeds, and trim the grass. Now, however, everything was covered with snow.

Many of the nobles who were obliged to attend the court of the boy monarch, Louis XIV, hated the place in winter, and their opinion was shared by most of the government officials who worked there. The palace was cold, drafty, and dark, the stone walls made the atmosphere damp regardless of the weather, and most of the rooms were far too small and cramped for the uses for which they were designated.

Cardinal Mazarin, however, did not share the opinion of the court, and although he was aware of the dislike of the nobles for the place, he chose to ignore their complaints. He not only remembered the days when Cardinal Richelieu had made the palace his headquarters, but he himself liked it for the same reasons. It was centrally located, near to the bankers and the financiers whose support the government needed. The palace itself might be a little old and dilapidated, but it was sufficiently large that an entire regiment of king's musketeers could be quartered there, and this provided ample protection for the monarch and his first minister.

Mazarin also knew that when both he and the boy king stayed at the Louvre, they were highly visible to the residents of the city. Parisians were mercurial—difficult people to govern and control—and the knowledge that their monarch and the cardinal were sharing whatever tribulations the city might be suffering from one day to the next had a soothing effect on the people.

Not that Mazarin was exactly suffering. On the contrary; his own living and working quarters took up nearly an entire wing of the palace. His bed-chamber—and it was rumored the cardinal never slept alone—was hung entirely in red velvet and was exceeded in splendor only by his private dining room, where the woodwork, ceiling, and walls were covered all over with a riot of hunting and dining scenes. A dinner of twenty courses there was not unusual, and the table itself was wider than many Paris streets. In fact, it was frequently said that the Boy King Louis was only the third most powerful person in France—after Mazarin and Mazarin's chef.

However, the offices where Mazarin received visitors were relatively humble. The priests who served as the cardinal's secretaries sat at orderly rows of desks in an outer chamber, and the inner sanctum was almost bare. A crucifix hung on one wall, and a blue and gold lily-banner of France decorated another. The cardinal worked at a simple table, which he kept free of papers. His visitors were required to sit facing a set of floor-to-ceiling windows that fronted the south, which meant that the light shone in their eyes when the weather was fair. A crystal bell reposed on the desk and was used to summon subordinates. No one—not even the young king—dared to enter Mazarin's inner sanctum without first having been summoned.

The cardinal sat still, making no movement except for a slight, incessant gesture with one hand that caused the quill pen he held to tap ceaselessly against the edge of his desk. This was a sure sign that he was upset.

He had good reason for being unhappy: Not only were his enemies at court plotting against him and gaining strength, but his New World policy was also in complete disarray. On his desk lay two sheets of paper. One was a brief report from Governor Peter Stuyvesant of New Netherland to the effect that the faithful Laroche had been murdered by a person or persons unknown. Next to this disturbing news was the final report that Mazarin had received from Laroche himself. In it the loyal spymaster had reported on the most recent of Stuyvesant's moves, his giving quantities of muskets to the Indian tribes of New England.

Stuyvesant, in Cardinal Mazarin's opinion, was guilty of stupidity, the worst crime a ruler could commit. Obviously, what had been done needed to be undone, and the entire New World situation had to be brought under control rapidly. Mazarin sat deep in thought. Once he made up his mind, he nodded to himself, picked up the bell from his desk, and rang it vigorously. A young, gray-robed priest hurried into the room.

"You rang, Your Eminence?" the man said unnecessarily.

The cardinal wasted no words. Motioning the priest to a chair, he handed him the two sheets of paper.

"Write a letter, if you will, to Peter Stuyvesant. I'll leave the exact details of composition to you.

Let him know that I'm very annoyed with him for giving firearms to the savages, an act that is sure to cause us all great harm. Be forceful, if you will; you can't be too abrupt for my taste."

The priest busied himself scribbling some notes, then looked up. "What future instructions do you have for the governor, Your Eminence?" he asked.

Mazarin's lips formed in thin, straight lines. "None," he said.

The secretary looked confused.

"One does not dismiss the director-general of a foreign colony from one's service," the Cardinal explained. "Such conduct would not be seemly. However, for all practical purposes, I am finished with Stuyvesant and will let him stew in his own Dutch juice. His colony cannot survive for long as a Dutch entity without my support, which I am now withdrawing. I've decided to let the inevitable happen. Within the next decade, New Amsterdam will be taken by the British. As it is, I cannot intervene without creating a multitude of problems for France. If our settlements to the north were better established, we would have some recourse. Perhaps another opportunity may arise in the future. Until then, the British are welcome to New Netherland."

The young priest was capable of grasping only one subject at a time. "What of Governor Stuyvesant, Your Eminence? What will become of him?"

Mazarin glanced out of the window at the snow-covered gardens. "Stuyvesant," he said, "will remain the director-general of New Netherland. He'll wither on the vine until he rots. The Dutch are giving him inadequate support, and he'll discover in time that he's receiving no further aid from us. I prefer to let him discover that fact for himself."

"This is harsh punishment, Your Eminence."

"That," Mazarin said, "is exactly what he deserves. Now be good enough to tell the Lord Viscount Butler that I will see him."

The priest hurried back to the outer office and immediately dispatched a messenger to find the English lord who had arrived the previous day from the court-in-exile of young Charles II and had been waiting since that time for a private audience with the first minister.

In spite of the size of the Louvre, it was possible, if one knew which servants to question, to find anyone of consequence within a very short time. So Lord Butler was quickly located and conducted to Cardinal Mazarin's inner office.

It was clear at a glance that Lord Butler was a Cavalier. He wore a plumed, broad-brimmed hat jauntily above a breastplate of gleaming silver, over which a collar of exquisite lace showed. His breeches were cut loosely, his high boots were turned down at the calves, and his silver spurs jangled as he strode in. Even his walk was self-confident, arrogant. He obviously knew he was good-looking and was well aware that he held a special place in the world. He belonged to a minority that had been favored for generations, and he was bewildered by the political events that had thrown him into exile.

Like so many of his fellow nobles, he would do anything to see to it that young King Charles II regained the throne from which his father, Charles I, had been driven. "To accomplish the restoration, I would make a pact with the devil himself," he had said. And it occurred to him now, as he stood before the gilt double doors of Mazarin's office, that his pact with the first minister of France was not far from that.

He removed his hat with a flourish as he was ushered into the room. He bowed deeply and his spurs jangled as he clicked his heels. "Your humble servant, Your Eminence," he said in a booming voice. "I bring you greetings from His Majesty and from the Queen Mother."

"Be sure to give them my warmest regards, won't you?" the cardinal replied mildly. He had little in common with the athletic, virile Englishman, yet his own manner was such that he remained master of the situation.

Lord Butler seated himself on a hard, straight-backed wooden chair without having been invited to sit, and looked expectantly at the first minister. Like so many of his class, Lord Butler was blunt and didn't believe in wasting time.

Neither did Mazarin. "I have a mission for you," he said. "A mission that will require delicacy, tact —and above all, secrecy."

Lord Butler nodded, but refrained from comment until he could learn what was expected of him.

"Affairs in the New World are not progressing well," Mazarin told him. "My principal intelligence agent has been killed, or so I've been informed by Governor Stuyvesant of New Netherland. My agents in America are rudderless, so to speak. They require instructions and guidance."

Lord Butler raised a thick eyebrow. "Surely you don't intend to send me to America as your principal spy?" he asked bluntly.

The cardinal shook his head, not desiring to explain that the tasks he had just mentioned were beyond the capabilities of Lord Butler. "No," he said, "I will want you to notify various persons that I wish to see them at their earliest convenience. If necessary, depending on their circumstances, you'll be authorized to invent seemingly valid reasons for them to come to France for personal talks with me."

Lord Butler shrugged. "It doesn't sound like too difficult an assignment," he said.

"It is, and it isn't," Mazarin told him. "I shall want you to avoid New Amsterdam—and Peter Stuyvesant—at all costs."

"I see," Butler said, although he really didn't. He frowned and nodded slowly. "I'm none too familiar with the New World and its ways," he said. "I know nothing about Peter Stuyvesant. Why on earth should I avoid him?"

Mazarin shrugged. He saw no reason to burden Lord Butler with political details yet. One of the reasons for this assignment was, in fact, to test Lord Butler's ability. "Stuyvesant made a major mistake. I'm terminating France's relationship with him, although I prefer that he not be told that formally."

"I see," Lord Butler repeated.

Mazarin laced his fingers and leaned back in his chair. "I presume you're familiar with Lady Celeste Murette?"

Lord Butler grinned broadly. "I don't know what you mean by 'familiar,' Your Eminence, but I can tell you I was acquainted with her at the court of the late King Charles. I had no reason to become intimate with her, but she's a gorgeous wench, if you'll forgive the observation. I should like nothing better than to become more familiar with her."

"Her morals," the cardinal said crisply, "are strictly her own concern and God's. My principal concern is the business of France, and in this instance, the restoration of the young Stuart king to the throne of England, because he is the ally of my country and because France will benefit greatly when he wears the crown. I trust I make myself clear?"

"You do, Your Eminence," Butler assured him.

"Therefore," Mazarin concluded, "you will enjoy your relationship with Lady Celeste Murette—whatever it may be—in private. What matters to me is that you inform her, on my behalf, that it is imperative that she come to France as soon as possible to see me."

The nobleman nodded, unaware of the developments in Celeste's life that would make it difficult for her to comply with the cardinal's request.

"I presume," Mazarin went on, "that you were also acquainted, at the court of the late King Charles, with Lady Dawn Shepherd?"

Lord Butler looked startled. "Yes, I knew her quite well. Don't tell me that she's also in your employ, Your Eminence!"

"How I wish she were!" the cardinal replied. Then he sighed, readying Lord Butler for his test of loyalty. "She eluded my representatives when she went off to the New World. She was scheduled to be recruited on my behalf, but the plans went astray, for whatever reasons. I know virtually nothing about the matter. But if you can locate Lady Dawn, I will be much indebted to you for any information you can relay regarding her present whereabouts and status."

The cardinal knew very well that Lady Dawn—if she was still alive—was residing in New Haven; he had received a letter from Lady Celeste telling him that much months ago. However, if Laroche, before his demise, had relayed the cardinal's execution order to Lady Celeste, there was a good chance that Lady Dawn was dead. Either way, Mazarin couldn't be sure—and that was one situation he would not tolerate. According to Mazarin's agents, Lord Butler had enjoyed an intimate friendship with Lady Dawn—or Mimi Clayton, as she was now called—and if he would go so far as to betray her, perhaps he could be of further use in the cardinal's employ.

Lord Butler grinned slyly. "I shall find out what I can," he promised. He refrained from mentioning that he had indeed enjoyed a very close relationship with Lady Dawn. It seemed apparent to Lord Butler that Mazarin was not acquainted with the inner gossip of the Stuart court, or he would have known that Butler had been a close friend of Lady Dawn's father, the earl of Sturbridge, and had been her first lover.

"There is another couple I want you to contact for me," the cardinal said. "I'm sure you know Sir Richard Dunstable."

Butler marveled privately at the network of aristocratic English subjects who were in the employ of the first minister of France. He wouldn't have dreamed it possible. "We had a passing acquaintance when he was the king's forester," he said. "But he spent very little time at court, so I don't think anyone there knew him well."

Mazarin nodded and said briskly, "All you need to know for your purposes is that I want to interview Dunstable and his wife here. You'll find them living in New Haven, although it's possible that Lady Dunstable may be in New Amsterdam. If she is, you're authorized to get in touch with her through an emissary, but under no circumstances go there yourself."

"And that's the extent of my mission?" The nobleman was surprised and slightly disappointed.

The cardinal nodded. "My treasurer will give you the funds necessary for your expenses," he said. "You'll be expected to make your own travel arrangements from now on. In the event that you encounter difficulties, I'll have to ask you to rely on your own initiative and ingenuity, which I have been assured you possess in no small degree."

"Very well, Your Eminence." His lordship had hoped for greater intrigue—perhaps a kidnapping, murder, or theft.

Mazarin peered at him for a moment, then smiled at him mirthlessly. "If I read your mind correctly," he said, "you're disappointed because you expected to be given a task of importance, and instead you're being sent on what appears to be no more than a messenger's errand."

"You are right," Lord Butler replied bluntly.

"And you are mistaken," the cardinal told him, "badly mistaken. I know of no mission more important to the future of France—*and* to young Charles—in the New World than the task I have just given you. Succeed, and there's a strong hope that we can seriously weaken our Roundhead friends. Fail, and your young Charles may never sit on the throne."

As he was ordered to avoid New Amsterdam, Lord Butler sailed to Boston as soon as the weather permitted, and there began his task of tracing the representatives of the English nobility whom Cardinal Mazarin wanted to see. He could obtain no information on the whereabouts of Lady Dawn Shepherd, and it was difficult for him to strike a rapport with any of the local officials because of their Roundhead sympathies. He soon discovered, however, that everyone in Boston knew of Richard Dunstable, who appeared to have dropped his title. He had commanded the combined troops of the English colonies in a campaign against a number of Indian tribes recently, and had won a stunning victory. Lord Butler wasted no more time in Boston and set out without delay for New Haven. An experienced soldier, he made the hard journey without complaint, although he disliked the vast wilderness of the New World. European in his thinking and habits, he found America too large and too primitive for his taste.

When he reached New Haven he was directed to Richard's office at the Burrows and Clayton warehouse and was conducted into the presence of the man he had come so far to see.

Richard knew Lord Butler by reputation as a distinguished and courageous commander of a regiment of Cavalier horsemen in the recent British civil war that unfortunately had resulted in the triumph of the Roundheads. Consequently he welcomed the visitor warmly.

"I understand, Sir Richard, that we share certain viewpoints and hopes," the nobleman declared.

Richard shrugged. "That well may be, milord, but I no longer am known as Sir Richard. I much prefer the title I've won through my own efforts, that of Major Dunstable."

"Of course, Major. Please call me John," Lord Butler answered suavely. "Be that as it may, we are both dedicated to the restoration of young Charles to the throne, and with good reason, because our own lands have been confiscated by the Roundheads. Only with Charles as king will we recover our fortunes and our standing."

Richard's smile faded slowly. "This may seem very odd to you, John," he said, "but I'll be honest with you. I was a confirmed, dedicated Cavalier when I first came to the colonies; however, the New World has had an unexpected effect on me. I've established roots here—deep, secure roots. I no longer care about recovering my manor house and estate in Lincolnshire, and to be frank with you, I don't care if I ever set foot in England again. Naturally I favor the restoration of young King Charles, but the affairs of the colonies are far more important to me, and I know of nothing of greater significance right now than the unity of the colonies in military and civil affairs."

Lord Butler was surprised by the other man's stand, which he himself regarded as parochial and shortsighted. He was not prepared, however, to argue the relative merits of the Cavalier cause as opposed to that of the colonies.

"I daresay your marriage has played a major part in influencing you," he said. "I look forward to meeting Mistress Dunstable."

He was virtually asking for an invitation, so Richard promptly asked him to come home to dinner with him. Lord Butler agreed instantly, telling himself that in spite of Mazarin's warning, his task on this side of the Atlantic seemed very simple.

He and Richard walked the short distance to the Dunstable house. On introduction, the viscount was immediately struck by Eliza's blond beauty. Lord Butler would have found it difficult to believe that this wholesome young couple secretly worked for Cardinal Mazarin were it not for the fact that he himself worked for the first minister of France. He had learned that nothing connected with Mazarin should surprise him.

At the dinner table, Lord Butler waited for his chance to bring up the subject that had brought him so far from home, but no natural conversational turn presented itself. Finally he decided to make his own opportunity. "Do you ever cross the Atlantic?" he inquired of the young couple.

"We made a brief voyage to England and France about a year ago," Richard replied.

"But," Eliza added, "we have no reason to go there again. We've no legitimate business in the Old World."

"I wouldn't be too sure of that," Lord Butler said quietly.

They stared at him in intense silence, and it was immediately apparent to them that Lord Butler was not precisely what he seemed.

"You might find it vastly interesting and worth your while to make another voyage," he said. "You explained to me that you're sinking roots here in

America, Major, but at the same time I doubt very much that you'd reject an offer of many thousands of pounds for the estate you inherited. First it will have to be regained from the Roundheads who confiscated it from you, of course, and for that we'll need a royal decree from young King Charles, written and signed in London, and corroborated and authenticated by a friendly Parliament."

Richard and Eliza exchanged a glance, but both remained warily silent.

Lord Butler took a bite of the apple pie he had been served, a dessert unlike any he had ever before eaten, and he found it delicious. "You'll find it very advantageous, I believe, to pay a brief visit to England and, while you're about it, to cross the channel. You know Paris?"

Both shook their heads. "A fascinating city," Butler went on, "filled with good, loyal Cavalier friends. You both have a personal friend in Paris, I believe."

Richard smiled self-deprecatingly. "I think you must be mistaken, John. Eliza and I don't know anyone in Paris."

The nobleman lowered his voice. "Ah, but you do," he said. "You have a very powerful friend and ally there, and what's more, he's eager to see you and to renew his, ah, friendship with you."

Richard stared at him, wondering if it were possible that this distinguished Cavalier officer could be representing the first minister of France.

Eliza, quicker and more agile than her husband, immediately took up the challenge. "I know of only one powerful personage in Paris who might fit your description, Lord Butler," she said.

She was mentioning no names, and Lord Butler was grateful for her discretion. A serving maid waited on them, there was a cook in the kitchen, and a handyman was somewhere around the place, too, so it would not be wise to mention Cardinal Mazarin's name aloud. "I think," he said, "that we undoubtedly have the same person in mind, Mistress Dunstable."

It was incredible, Eliza thought, that the long arm of Mazarin should reach across the Atlantic to them. She folded her hands under the edge of the table, her grip so hard that her knuckles turned white.

Richard faced the issue squarely, without flinching. "I take it," he said, "that you're authorized to act as a spokesman for a highly placed official of the French government."

"You might say," Lord Butler replied, "that I'm authorized by him to deliver messages and to receive them on his behalf."

"In that case," Richard said, his voice becoming harsh, "you'll be good enough, I'm sure, to inform him that we will have nothing further to do with him, his schemes, or his country."

He was so firm in his declaration that the nobleman was stunned. This was not the response he had anticipated, so he did not quite know how to react.

"My wife and I," Richard went on, "are British subjects who acknowledge young Charles as our king. We are also citizens of New Haven. We own property here, I work here, and we regard this community—in which my wife was raised—as our home. I have been honored with the field command of the colony's militia. These loyalties come ahead of all others, and we're not going to be trapped again by Cardinal Mazarin. You can tell him what I said, and in just those words."

Lord Butler hastily revised his opinion of his host's discretion. "If you insist," he said, "I shall repeat to him what you've just now said to me, but I don't think it's wise. He exerts a great influence, far greater than you know, on young King Charles and the royal court. It would be too bad if the king were restored to his throne and you failed to recover your property in Lincolnshire."

"I couldn't be any poorer than I was the day the Roundheads took my ancestors' estate from me," Richard declared. "I just finished telling you I no longer regard Lincolnshire as my home. You may tell Mazarin anything you damn well please!"

He was far more strident than Eliza would have been, but she was proud of him and hoped that that would be the end of the matter.

Lord Butler seemed to accept the pronouncement with good grace. "I expect to be spending the summer here in your town," he said, "so I won't accept your word today as final. For your own good, think seriously about the offer I brought you. Then, before I leave, give me your final word in the matter."

The visit of a nobleman of Lord Butler's rank to New Haven was sufficiently unusual to cause a stir in social circles, and it was inevitable that the hostesses of the town should become excited. Celeste Burrows remembered Lord Butler from the court of the late king and informed her husband that she wanted to give a reception in his honor.

Adam Burrows was willing, pleased as always to fulfill his wife's wishes, and he heartily agreed, so invitations were sent to everyone of consequence in the colony. The weather was unseasonably hot, so the party was held on the shady lawn.

Lord Butler, who knew nothing of Adam Burrows's relationship to Eliza and Richard Dunstable, was pleased to accept the invitation as the guest of honor. At the very least, he thought, he might have the opportunity to speak to the stubborn young Dunstables again and to urge them to reconsider their adamant rejection of Cardinal Mazarin.

Arriving before the other guests, Butler was astonished when he saw the radiantly seductive Celeste Burrows waiting to greet him.

"What a wonderful surprise!" he told her.

She smiled at him and then at her proud husband, who stood beside her. "I knew you'd be amazed, John," she said. "I couldn't resist the temptation to surprise you."

"This is fortuitous," Butler replied, and only because of Colonel Burrows's presence did he refrain from adding, *Far more fortuitous than you know.*

Butler bided his time, watching for an opportunity to speak with Celeste in private. While awaiting the arrival of the other guests, he sipped a glass of punch—a concoction with a potent base of rum distilled locally from molasses carried to New Haven from the West Indies in the holds of Burrows and Clayton ships. A further surprise was in store for Lord Butler, and he gaped when he saw the lovely Lady Dawn Shepherd appear on the arm of Ezekiel Clayton. She was presented to him as Mistress Clayton, and he looked hard at her, a quizzical smile on his lips. "I believe we already know each other, isn't that right, Mimi?"

She had been dreading the confrontation with him and had forced herself to attend the reception. No one in New Haven knew of or even suspected her onetime relationship with the viscount.

"I wondered if you'd remember me, John," she replied bravely, and somehow managed to smile.

He bowed gallantly over her hand and kissed it. "As if anyone who ever knew you could forget you, Mimi," he replied, holding her hand a moment longer than was necessary.

Ezekiel Clayton nodded in agreement. "My wife," he said, "has that effect on people."

As other guests arrived, Lord Butler renewed his acquaintance with Richard and Eliza and met a score or more of other leading members of New

Haven Colony's society. He was fortunate, he told himself repeatedly: With no effort on his own part, he had succeeded in locating Lady Dawn *and* Lady Celeste.

Mimi made a point of seeking him out after the last of the guests had arrived and he had had ample opportunity to exchange amenities with them. She put a hand lightly on his arm, and they walked together across the elm-shaded lawn toward a rustic bench located at the far end of the garden.

"You have no idea how much I dreaded seeing you again, John," Mimi told him.

He glanced at her and chuckled. "Am I such an ogre, then?"

She shook her head. "My past was well and truly buried, and in my mind at least, it was temporarily forgotten," she replied. "Seeing you again brings to life a time I'd prefer not to remember."

Lord Butler raised a patrician eyebrow. "Do you have such horrid memories of me, Mimi?" he asked.

She shook her head. "Not of you, John, but of me. I grieve for the naive and foolish young girl who threw herself at you and who succumbed to you. She no longer exists, you see, and I prefer that she remain where she belongs—dead in the past."

"I see," he replied. "Surely," he said, "you must learn to give me some credit for being a gentleman."

A look of relief swept over her face. "You have no idea how glad I am," she said. "No one here, including my husband, his family, or our dear friends the Dunstables, has any notion of my relationship with you."

"As far as I'm concerned," he replied, "what was private in the past shall remain private. You have nothing more to fear from me now than you ever had, Mimi. I'd be untrue to the memory of what we once meant to each other if I acted otherwise."

She looked hard and long at him, a suggestion of tears in her large, limpid eyes. "I'm grateful to you for this, John, more grateful than you'll know."

"But I *will* be happy to report your presence in New Haven when I cross the Atlantic again," he told her.

"Report it? To whom?" she asked.

He smiled. "There's a rather prominent gentleman who has professed an interest in your whereabouts and activities," he said.

To his astonishment, Mimi became alarmed. "Who?" she demanded fiercely.

Surprised by her vehemence, he blinked at her. "Let's say," he declared, "that the gentleman in question is prominent in the affairs of France."

The color suddenly drained from Mimi's face, leaving her chalk-white. She stared at him for a moment, her eyes filled with horror. Then quickly she picked up her skirts, gathered them around her, and fled across the yard.

Finding her conduct inexplicable to say the least, Lord Butler watched intently as Mimi hurried to her husband, who stood with Richard and Eliza Dunstable, sipping punch. She spoke to them earnestly, rapidly, and at length.

Richard replied, apparently saying something to soothe her. Then, without hesitation, he strode across the lawn and approached the nobleman.

"Do I understand correctly, John," he asked in a low, tightly controlled voice, "that Cardinal Mazarin is interested in Lady Dawn's whereabouts?"

He was openly aggressive, so strident that Lord Butler was somewhat confused. "I gleaned," he said, "that our mutual friend in Paris had plans for Mimi, but they hadn't materialized as yet."

Richard planted his feet apart and put his hands

on his hips. "Thank you for your candor," he said. "Now let me be equally blunt with you. I know nothing of Mazarin's plans for Mimi. But I do know that all she has asked is to be left here in peace. If you reveal her whereabouts to Mazarin, there's a good chance you'll be signing her death warrant."

The nobleman moistened his lips, which felt very parched. "Surely you exaggerate," he said.

"You don't know the violence Cardinal Mazarin is capable of," Richard replied. "I've dealt with the first minister for what feels like a very long time, and believe me, I know it well. I do not exaggerate, and I tell you flatly that Mimi's life is in your hands."

"You create a difficult problem for me, Major Dunstable," Butler said.

Richard looked at him in tight-lipped silence. "I despise threats, John, just as I have no use for bullies. But allow me to make myself very plain. Rather than run the risk of watching Mimi meet a seemingly accidental death arranged by unscrupulous French agents, I would gladly kill in her behalf."

Lord Butler was stunned by his intensity.

"I was very close to her at one time, and I am in her debt," Richard said. "This is how I choose to repay it." He eyed Butler menacingly.

The nobleman somehow managed to smile. "I appreciate your confidence, and I take your words to heart, sir," he said. He paused, then added with a smile, "As it happens, I was once close to Mimi, too, and perhaps this gives me the opportunity to pay my debt to her."

Richard didn't understand what he meant. Lord Butler had no intention of explaining, because he would be forced to reveal secrets that he had indicated to Mimi he would keep private. Rather than expose her past actions now, he preferred to hold that information for a moment when he needed leverage, when its divulgence would be of greater benefit.

"I'll make you a deal, John," Richard said. "If you'll keep Mimi's whereabouts to yourself, my wife and I will make the voyage that you recently discussed with us and will pay a call on a certain busy gentleman—but only if and when we receive a written request from him personally."

Butler smiled. He could not believe his luck. "You have struck a fair bargain, Major Dunstable," he said. "I'll gladly hold you to your word."

Richard looked at him steadily and said in a low, even voice, "I'll expect you to keep your word also, John."

They simultaneously extended their hands, and their agreement was sealed with a firm grip. There was much that was being left unsaid; certainly, if Butler violated his oath and revealed Mimi's whereabouts to Cardinal Mazarin, he knew that Richard Dunstable would not rest until he kept his vow and killed the man who had deliberately placed her life in jeopardy.

But even so, Butler had no intention of keeping his word. He would simply wait until he was out of Dunstable's reach. Then Mimi could be exposed without placing his own life in jeopardy. Surely Cardinal Mazarin would offer him protection from Dunstable in return for the information regarding Mimi Clayton's whereabouts—as well as in return for managing to persuade Richard and Eliza to travel to France to meet with the cardinal.

What struck Butler as odd, however, was the nature and depth of New World friendships. It was astonishing to him that the Dunstables were willing to make this major sacrifice for the sake of a friend's safety. Lord Butler had never enjoyed such loyalty from any of his acquaintances; but on the other hand, neither had he been willing to offer selfless gestures to anyone he knew.

For the first time, the nobleman began to understand why Richard was willing to give up his title, his large property, and his ancestral home in Lincolnshire in return for life in the New World. There was more to America, more to Americans than met the casual eye of a visitor to the shores of this huge, barbaric land.

Having already accomplished half his mission, Lord Butler was in a relaxed and affable frame of mind as he drifted back to his hosts and chatted at length with them; but not until the party was well under way and most of the company had consumed several cups of the potent punch did he find the opportunity to speak in private with Celeste Burrows. Seeing her briefly alone as she returned to the lawn from a visit to the kitchen outbuilding where various foods were being prepared, he went to her quickly. "I want a word with you," he told her in low tones.

Not losing her composure, Celeste nodded and replied without looking directly at him. "Walk beside me, then, and take care, sir, to remain in full view of my husband and my guests, particularly my husband. I know you, John, and my husband has a jealous nature. I have no intention of placing my future in jeopardy or of creating an unpleasant scene."

He had to admire her cool, calm demeanor, and he knew she was right. Adam Burrows was her senior by more than a quarter of a century, and when a husband was that much older than his wife, he was vulnerable to suspicion and jealousy.

They crossed the lawn together, ostensibly strolling, and took care to leave an open space between them. "You've done well for yourself, I see," Lord Butler said.

"As you well know, John, or should know," she answered crisply, "I always make it my business to look out for my own best interests. I'm married to a man who adores me. I'm the first lady of the most prominent commercial colony in all of New England. My future is permanently assured." Celeste glanced up at him and her voice hardened. "And I don't intend to allow anything or anyone to jeopardize my position. It takes one opportunist to recognize another, and believe me, dear John, I know you. Not only by your past, but by your whole present attitude. I give you warning: Don't tamper with me, or I'll— But I *do* so love New Haven," she said sweetly—and loudly—as another couple strolled toward them arm in arm.

He smiled at her, his equanimity unruffled, and waited until the other couple had passed. "You always were cold and ruthless, Celeste," he said, "and your sojourn here in America hasn't softened you or your disposition."

"Should it have?" she responded.

"Speaking for myself, I neither know nor care," Butler replied. "You can either live happily ever after, or you can go hang; either is fine with me. But my likes and dislikes are unimportant. I haven't come to the New World completely as my own master."

She studied him out of the corners of her eyes. "Oh?" she said softly.

"We have a mutual friend," he said, "in Paris. He has expressed a strong desire to see you at your earliest convenience."

"You're joking," Celeste said flatly.

"I may have a taste for levity," Lord Butler declared, "but there's one subject about which I never joke. I find no humor in the man or in anything connected with him. All I know is that the primary purpose of my journey across the Atlantic has been to find you and tell you that your presence in France is urgently requested."

Celeste obviously was furiously angry and controlled herself only with great effort. When she spoke again, her voice quivered, but her tone was low, and a casual passerby would have thought that she was chatting about trivialities with one of her guests. "Mazarin," she said, "may be a great and powerful man. The court of young Charles may turn itself inside out for him, as I've heard suggested. The king of Naples and the Holy Roman Emperor may tremble in their boots when his name is mentioned. But I regret to say that he has delusions of grandeur."

Lord Butler tried to interrupt.

Celeste gave him no opportunity. "How would it be humanly possible for me to leave my home and my husband in order to travel to Paris?" she demanded. "What could I possibly say to Adam? What excuse could I give him that would seem valid? By going off to Paris I'd be destroying the very things in this world that I prize most—my marriage, my home, and above all, my lifelong security. The rulers of Europe may jump when Mazarin snaps his fingers, but frankly, dear John, I can't afford to jump, and that's final." She turned to him, smiling blandly. Only her tightly clenched fists indicated the continuing depth of her fury.

Lord Butler shrugged. "You're an old hand at this game," he said. "In fact, I actually believe you're more experienced than I am. I needn't tell you how dangerous our friend in Paris can be when his demands are refused or when his orders are not followed. I've been hearing a great deal about the violence in the New World and the cheapness of lives here. I need scarcely tell you that our friend in Paris places an even lower value on human life than do the English colonials."

Her sigh indicated petulance and more than a touch of exasperation.

"Be sensible," he told her. "You know our Parisian friend always gets precisely what he wants in the way that he wants it."

"Don't misunderstand me," Celeste said, and he was astonished by her almost sugary tone. "I'd love to see the cardinal and to talk to him for as long as he's free to receive me, but he'll have to find some valid way to send for me. I'd leave New Haven and my husband only if my marriage would remain solid and secure. You can tell Mazarin for me that I'm not defying him, and I'm not opposing his will. I'm merely looking out for myself, and I fully intend, now as always, to protect my own interests."

XI

L ORD Butler, though not overly fond of New Haven society, was in no particular hurry to return to Paris. Partly responsible for this change in attitude was the unlimited hunting he was enjoying in the wilderness around New Haven—or at least that was what he said publicly. But undoubtedly more important was a message he had received from Mazarin, saying the cardinal was "for the moment obliged to remain outside of Paris." Rumors told a slightly different story: Mazarin was in temporary exile, apparently the victim of a court conspiracy that was already coming unglued. Butler had no doubts that Mazarin, as long as he was alive, would find a way back to power, so the viscount bided his time safely in New Haven.

However, as the long New England winter settled in, and then dragged on and on, Butler grew impatient to leave. Early in the spring he sailed unobtrusively in a Burrows and Clayton brig for the West Indies and disembarked in Martinique. There he lingered for several days, and then he engaged passage for France on board a vessel that flew the lily banner. He reached Brest after a short, uneventful crossing and immediately rode on to Paris, where Cardinal Mazarin, as Butler had expected, was back in control as if nothing had happened.

The first minister saw him at once and listened in silence as Butler related the status of Lady Celeste and delivered her message word for word to the cardinal. Mazarin was pleased that Butler was not reluctant to reveal that Lady Dawn Shepherd was living in New Haven as Mimi Clayton—though he was annoyed she was still alive—and he inquired at length about the activities of Richard and Eliza Dunstable.

"Above all," the cardinal said, "I want to know one thing about Richard Dunstable. Where do you believe his first loyalties lie?"

"I had no chance to question him about his feelings regarding France, Your Eminence," the English nobleman replied, "but he said he would come here only if you invited him personally, in writing. I certainly don't think he likes the idea; he seems too much involved in the affairs of the colony in which he's living. He's the field commander of the New Haven militia, you must realize. And he was the commander in chief of the expedition that defeated the Indian tribes that had gathered in New Amsterdam under the urging of Governor Stuyvesant to oppose the English colonies."

"You'd not be inclined to say then that he'd be loyal with regard to France?"

Lord Butler pondered the question for a time. "I'd be surprised if he failed to put the New Haven interests ahead of all others. After all, his wife is a native of New Haven, and his own future is tied up there."

Mazarin listened without further comment. "And your opinion of Lady Dawn?" he inquired, changing the subject.

"She appears to be content with her lot, Your Eminence. She used to be lively and always restless, but she's much calmer now and seems far more subdued. I'd say that if she needed taming, she has been tamed."

The cardinal nodded and then asked, "And Lady Celeste?"

Lord Butler laughed. "No one will ever succeed in taming her, I'm sure," he declared.

The first minister twisted the magnificent sapphire ring on his finger and appeared lost in thought. "Be good enough to stay in Paris," he said. "I may have further need of your services in the near future. In the meantime, say nothing to any of your fellow Englishmen of the mission you've just performed. I'm never sure which of them we can trust, and they're inclined to confide in each other a bit too freely for my taste."

Always one to act swiftly once he made up his mind, Cardinal Mazarin pondered the problem for some time, then nodded to himself, chuckled in satisfaction, and called in a priest, to whom he began to dictate quickly.

A little more than two months later, the residents of New Haven, particularly those who knew the sea, were surprised when a French merchantman, more nearly resembling an unarmed war frigate than a commercial vessel, put into the harbor. A further surprise was in store when her master came ashore and asked for Adam Burrows, to whom he handed a letter.

Adam turned over the square of heavy paper in his hands and examined the ornate seal at some length. Obviously this was no ordinary letter.

He sat down at his desk and broke the seal. The writer was none other than Cardinal Mazarin, the first minister of France, who extended an invitation to Colonel Burrows to visit Paris at his convenience

340

to discuss a trade agreement that, Mazarin declared, would be beneficial to New Haven and the firm of Burrows and Clayton, as well as to France. Mistress Burrows was generously included in the invitation.

In a separate portion of the communication, Mazarin suggested that inasmuch as the deal he envisaged would, if mutually satisfactory, last for many years, it might be wise if Colonel Burrows were accompanied by the representatives of the younger generation in his company and their wives also.

Adam was overwhelmed. When he showed the letter to Celeste at the dinner table she feigned surprise, but actually marveled at the extraordinary cleverness of Cardinal Mazarin. It was immediately obvious to her that the cardinal very much wanted to see her and had found a way to bring her to France without in any way arousing her husband's suspicion of the role she had played in the past for France or of any current connection she might have with Mazarin.

Similarly, she knew that Richard and Eliza were being called to a meeting with the first minister.

What worried her more than anything was that Ezekiel and Mimi Clayton had been tacitly included in the invitation. Aware of Mazarin's interest in Mimi, Celeste felt somewhat queasy. She had grown almost to like Mimi and was grateful to the woman for not interfering with her marriage to Adam. Since she and the other English noblewoman had much the same background, Celeste hoped they would, at some point, become easy friends. She was not absolutely certain why Mimi was being summoned, but she had an uncomfortable feeling that the journey might not be too safe for her. However, it was impossible for Celeste to voice her suspicions without giving away her own position. Therefore she said nothing to anyone, but promised herself she would keep her eyes and ears open. If any harm befell Mimi Clayton while in France and if Celeste herself became suspect as a French agent, her whole position in New Haven would crumble instantly.

Adam Burrows discussed Mazarin's offer at length with Tom Clayton, and ultimately the senior partners called in Richard and Ezekiel. All four agreed on one essential point: Pending such time as they learned details, they saw a considerable opportunity for the company and for New Haven looming ahead. The offer of a deal had not been made by a French merchant firm, but by the master of all France, and consequently, the firm of Burrows and Clayton could become wealthy beyond the partners' wildest dreams if the terms were right. It was decided that the invitation should be accepted.

'Celeste, knowing the reasons behind the invitation, pretended great pleasure, but was actually more than a little apprehensive. She knew from long experience that when Mazarin made a gift, the recipient paid for it in full, and she felt certain there were innumerable hidden strings attached to the offer.

Mimi Clayton was terrified at the thought of being within Mazarin's sphere of influence, but Ezekiel prevailed upon his wife to cast aside her fears. He assured her that he and Richard would permit no harm to befall her, and that Mazarin was not such a fool as to attack a guest of the government. Mimi permitted herself to be swayed. After all, since her rescue from Horace Laing's estate, no threats or attempts on her life had surfaced. Possibly her usefulness to the cardinal's cause was long past.

Richard and Eliza were of two minds. To the best of their knowledge, the business offer was only half legitimate, and for that reason, they were apprehensive about dealing with Mazarin. They could not forget that he had tricked them once, subsequently forcing them to enter his employ, and they were afraid of any hidden motives that might emerge after they reached France. But, like Mimi, they knew they would be wrong if they permitted their fears to stand in the way of the journey. After all, Richard reminded himself, he had made a deal with Butler, and though the letter was not addressed directly to Eliza and him, its intent was clear enough. So they agreed to the proposal of Adam that they join him and Celeste and the Claytons on the largest of the company's brigs for a voyage to France in the immediate future.

It was midsummer and the skies were clear, and the ship that carried the party from New Haven benefited from strong following winds, so they made excellent time and reached the fortress town of Le Havre de Grâce in seven weeks. The arrival of the British colonials, including three ladies, created something of a stir; the French harbormaster and his staff extended themselves in their courtesies, and the party was welcomed everywhere with such warmth that it was obvious Cardinal Mazarin had issued orders that the English colonists were to be well taken care of.

To Adam's surprise, an official open coach, pulled by a team of six magnificent matched bay horses, was made available for the journey to Paris. Stops were made on the road at inns of stature, and again the proprietors and their staffs went out of their way to make the group welcome. When only twenty-four hours from Paris, they were joined by a dashing young Frenchman who announced that he was an emissary from Cardinal Mazarin. His name was Monsieur Rochas, and he was a nephew, he declared, of the duc de Vendôme.

Rochas rode his mount beside the carriage. When they reached Paris, yet another surprise awaited the group. Their young guide conducted them to the palace of the duc de Vendôme, located only a short distance from the Louvre, and there they were made at home. Each of the three couples was promptly shown to a large suite that included sitting rooms and a dining room as well as handsome bedchambers and dressing rooms. The palace was fully staffed, and in addition to a host of butlers and chambermaids scurrying in and out of the rooms, personal body maids were assigned to Celeste, Eliza, and Mimi. Celeste and Mimi had been accustomed to such luxuries in England during the reign of Charles I, but the experience was new to Eliza Dunstable. In spite of her apprehension over the coming meetings with the first minister, she was deeply impressed.

The couples had twenty-four hours in which to rest and become acquainted with Paris. The city was the grandest and largest in Europe, and as the nerve center of a great empire, it teemed with life.

"There are more beautiful women here wearing more beautiful clothes than I ever in my life imagined I'd see," Eliza announced after she and Richard had made a tour of the city in a small coach provided by Rochas.

"I always thought London a great and very special city," Mimi confessed, "but I must say I don't think any place on earth has the verve and glamour of Paris."

That afternoon, Rochas told them that they would be received in an audience with the young king, his mother, and his first minister the following morning.

The women wore their best gowns for the occasion, and Richard, after viewing the results, felt certain that they would outshine any of the renowned beauties at the French court. The party arrived promptly for the audience, and two musketeer officers escorted them through a bewildering labyrinth of corridors to a huge audience chamber. Eliza marveled at the large, sparkling chandeliers, in which hundreds of the most expensive French tapers were burning. At the far end of the hall on a raised dais were two thrones. The new arrivals approached these chairs, walking on rich rugs that had been gifts to Henri IV and his son, Louis XIII, from the sultans of Turkey.

Monsieur Rochas was on hand and presented the newcomers. The boy king, Louis XIV, sat squirming slightly on his throne, and paid scant attention to the new arrivals. He was far more interested in exchanging surreptitious signals with two other children of about his age, boys who were stationed behind uniformed courtiers, powdered great ladies, and scores of civilian ministers and other officials.

The other throne was occupied by the official regent of France, young King Louis's mother, Queen Anne of Austria, who compensated for her plain, almost homely features with a gorgeous gown of watered silk and a huge fortune in jewels that blazed on her breast, ears, wrists, and fingers. She took particular note of the women and studied each of them at length. Eliza felt she had never been subjected to such sharp scrutiny, even by the Raritan Indians.

Cardinal Mazarin was nowhere in sight. Apparently he had just been informed of the arrival of the colonials from New Haven and was now on his way from his office to make a rare appearance in the audience chamber.

As he entered the throne room, the atmosphere changed suddenly and dramatically. Courtiers and officers who had been conversing in low undertones, paying scant heed to the proceedings, suddenly fell silent and were alert and attentive. King Louis looked frightened, and knowing he'd be punished for slovenliness unless he behaved like a king, he stopped fidgeting and sat upright on his throne, trying as best a young boy could to look majestic.

Even the Queen Mother, Anne, came to life and smiled beatifically.

The cardinal bowed deeply to her, nodded half-respectfully, half-familiarly to the young king, and immediately went about the business that was of interest to him.

"Colonel Burrows," he said in excellent though accented English, "I'm your servant, sir, and I'm delighted you saw fit to answer my invitation. I assure you that you won't regret it."

He paid no attention whatever to Celeste or the other members of the party, and Richard marveled silently. One would have thought from the cardinal's behavior that he had never set eyes on Richard and Eliza.

Briskly dispensing with formalities, Mazarin summoned two officials out of the throng. One, it developed, was the royal treasurer, and the other was the minister of trade. Both were already familiar with the plans he had in mind and were anticipating the arrival of Colonel Burrows and his party. Without further ado, Adam, Richard, and Ezekiel accompanied the officials to a private chamber where they could begin their discussions. Mazarin made it clear that after an agreement was reached, he would see the visitors again.

While the men were engaged in the business that ostensibly had brought the party to France, the young ladies would be kept occupied by visits to the leading dressmakers of the French capital, supposedly the most accomplished and ingenious seamstresses in the world. It was apparent that Mazarin was overlooking nothing that would add to the comfort and happiness of his guests.

Guides were appointed for each of the ladies, who were separated and taken their own ways. Celeste Burrows, however, did not leave the Louvre; instead, her escort took her to a concealed back staircase and led her up a narrow flight of steps. She was conducted through an anteroom where priests were too busy at writing tables to bother to glance in her direction. She was taken past them to an inner chamber, and the door was closed behind her.

She found herself facing Cardinal Mazarin. He smiled faintly as he extended his hand. She sank to the floor in a graceful curtsy as she kissed his ring.

"You don't appear in the least surprised to find yourself in my presence," he declared.

She grinned impudently. "Hardly, Your Eminence," she said. "I knew what you had in mind the moment I read your invitation to my husband, and I must congratulate you on your extraordinary cleverness. You chose a method of bringing us to France—enabling you to confer in private with me —that did not arouse the slightest suspicion on anyone's part."

"I have done a great deal more than that," the first minister observed quietly. "I anticipate making a trade arrangement with your husband that will prove highly profitable and beneficial for France." He waved her to a chair.

She sat opposite him, her hands folded in her lap.

"You're looking well," Mazarin commented. "In fact, you're lovelier than ever."

Celeste was not surprised by the comment and declined her head. "It's very kind of you to say so, Your Eminence," she replied. "I've been feeling better ever since I left New Amsterdam. I must admit that Peter Stuyvesant was not good for my disposition."

"Stuyvesant," he declared, "is an opinionated, overbearing fool, and I intend to ignore him for as long as he remains the Dutch director-general in New Netherland."

"I think that's wise," Celeste replied. She knew that the loss of the cardinal's support would be the most severe punishment Peter Stuyvesant could suffer. His vanity would be hurt, and politically he was so vulnerable that no other blow he could receive would smart so badly or cripple his career so completely.

"You know that Laroche was murdered? His death was a grave misfortune," Mazarin went on. "Our cause has suffered greatly since his death. No one has been in charge to coordinate our agents in the English and Dutch colonies. More's the pity." Mazarin clucked.

Celeste shook her head cautiously, previous experience with Mazarin having taught her that she must beware when he became confidential.

"Well, no matter now. I have given great thought to the appointment of a successor to Laroche," the first minister told her. "I've analyzed the problem from every possible angle, and one candidate stood out above all the others. In fact, the choice was so obvious, I'm surprised that I didn't think of the person much earlier."

She had no idea what he was talking about.

He quickly realized the fact. "I have decided," he said mirthfully, "to give the appointment to you."

Celeste was stunned, and she simultaneously felt a stab of deep dismay, which she instinctively took pains to conceal.

"Your wages will be doubled," the cardinal said, "and you'll be given bonuses for special assignments as well."

"One moment, Your Eminence," she said. "I hope you're not forgetting I'm now a married woman."

"Indeed, I'm keeping it very much in mind, and it makes you far more attractive for the post. Being married to the first citizen of New Haven Colony, who commands the local militia and owns and operates a large and successful shipping company, you have the perfect cover for the position I'm entrusting to you. No one will ever suspect that you're in the employ of France, or that you're my principal spymaster for all of North America."

She forced a smile, but felt anything but elated.

"You don't seem pleased by your promotion," he observed mildly.

"I'm married to a man who loves me very much," Celeste said, "and who takes wonderful care of me. I never again have to worry about money or how to live. All I must do is protect my marriage at all costs, and this I'm prepared to do." Gathering courage as well as strength, she took a deep breath, then added, "I accept the assignment from you provisionally, Your Eminence. If it places my marriage in jeopardy for a single moment, I must refuse the post."

Mazarin laced his fingers together. "You're in no position to refuse," he replied adamantly. "On the contrary, you'll do as I instruct you, and you won't argue about your assignment." The cardinal paused and looked straight at her. She felt her stomach drop, and all of a sudden she was dizzy and faintly sick.

"I have sufficient evidence to ruin your credibility and destroy you, should I care to use it. Naturally, I vastly prefer to have you active on behalf of France, serving her well. Do this, and your secrets will remain safe with me. Your future depends, henceforth, on how well and how diligently you serve France."

The bottom had fallen out of Celeste's world, and she had no recourse. As she had anticipated in her nightmares, she was helpless, forced to accede to Mazarin's wishes and to do his bidding.

"I dislike threats," the cardinal said. "As you know, that isn't my method. Do as you're bidden, and you'll find I will continue to be most benign."

She swallowed her resentment and despair. "I know, Your Eminence," she murmured.

"And that," he said, "brings up a matter of considerable interest. I wrote to you many months ago via Laroche to eliminate Lady Dawn Shepherd, but she still lives and flourishes. How does it happen that my orders were not obeyed?"

"I never received your instructions, Your Eminence," she said. "Laroche must have died before he could transmit them to me."

Mazarin prided himself on his ability to distinguish truth from falsehoods when dealing with subordinates, and as nearly as he could determine, Celeste was telling the truth. "Well, then," he said mildly, "you shall have ample opportunity now to rectify our lapse of communication."

She took a deep breath. "I have accepted the position of spymaster, Your Eminence, but that does not mean that I'm willing to be an assassin. I must tell you frankly that there are things I cannot do, and I would find it impossible to murder Lady Dawn."

"Ah, you've become fond of her, I take it?"

"To an extent, that's true," she said, "but it's even more true that her life and mine are intertwined in scores of ways, and I would be incapable of acting as your executioner without inviting suspicion."

The cardinal shrugged. "Very well," he said, "I

suspected something like that might be the case, so I included her in my invitation to visit France."

Celeste was horrified. Someone would have to tell Mimi to be on her guard.

Mazarin seemed to read her mind. "The situation," he said, "provides us with a splendid test of your loyalties. Rest assured, I shall judge you accordingly."

She revised her plans hastily. She would be obliged now to remain silent even if Mimi were to lose her life. Mazarin was giving her no choice.

"What is your opinion of Richard Dunstable and his wife?" the first minister demanded suddenly, trying to catch her off guard and thereby enhance the possibility of a guileless response.

"I think very highly of both of them," she replied at once.

He nodded and appeared pleased. "That corroborates my own opinion," he said. "Mistress Dunstable is more of a realist than I had first thought, and from what Laroche wrote to me before his unfortunate demise, she performed admirably as Peter Stuyvesant's mistress."

Celeste well knew that Eliza had perpetrated a great deception and had not been Peter Stuyvesant's mistress, but she had no intention of correcting Mazarin's view. She merely nodded.

"As for Dunstable," he said, "Laroche could find no evidence to the effect that he was responsible for rescuing Lady Dawn in Virginia. Do you know anything to the contrary?"

"No, I do not," she replied firmly.

"I hear that he served the English colonies well in putting down a major Indian rebellion; but he also did France a great service at the same time, even though he doesn't realize it. I think he's still useful to us—especially in light of a new plan I've been developing—and I know his wife will prove most useful."

Celeste began to worry. "I think it would be an error," she said, "for them to learn that you've chosen me as the successor to Laroche, Your Eminence."

"In case you don't know it," she said, "Eliza Dunstable is my husband's daughter."

He smiled, shook his head, and lied. "I did not know that." He pondered briefly. "But I think that's all to the good. You'll have frequent excuses for contact with each other, which will be necessary in your new assignment, and you can meet often without causing the slightest concern on the part of even the most zealously loyal English patriot."

"Suppose," she said slowly, "that Richard and Eliza should turn out to be more patriotic in their feelings for New Haven than you have assumed. Suppose their patriotism is greater than their willingness to serve France?"

Mazarin remained completely calm. "If that should prove to be the case," he said, "it would be your duty as spymaster to take proper steps to remedy the situation."

She knew what he meant, but couldn't help asking, "Proper steps?"

"Don't act naive," he replied firmly. "You've been an agent on my payroll for six years. You know the penalty that must be paid by those who think first of themselves rather than of France. You're aware of the need for undeviating loyalty. If they fail to live up to our necessary standards, it will be your duty to eliminate them. And if you can't do it yourself, you'll just have to find someone else to do it for you. It's all the same to me."

Celeste swallowed hard and knew she could not protest again. She had appeared squeamish in her refusal to kill Mimi Clayton, and she could not let

Mazarin see that she might be lenient, too, in her dealings with the Dunstables.

"I shall see the Dunstables first thing tomorrow and give them instructions regarding their new assignment. You can reveal your identity to them whenever you please."

"How?" she demanded.

He reached into a small purse that dangled from his waist and removed an object, which he handed to her. She held it in the palm of her hand and found herself looking at a small ring of gold with a handsome violet-colored stone inlaid with a gold lily.

"That ring," the cardinal said, "is to be the symbol of your new position. You can tell your husband that you bought it from a Paris jeweler today, and neither he nor anyone else will know the difference."

She nodded, aware that the first minister left nothing to chance. He handed her a small sheaf of papers. "Here," he said, "is a complete list of the French agents who work in North America. Memorize the list, then destroy it, if it is your wish, or keep it concealed where you know it will be safe. It's vitally important, so be sure you protect it accordingly."

She took the list reluctantly, handling it as though it were red-hot. "I'll commit the names to memory," she said. "I want nothing on paper."

The cardinal smiled. "In that case," he told her, "you also won't want the incriminating evidence of my newest scheme to gain possession of the colonies of North America. Read this paper, which will explain my plan, and then burn it."

She reached very slowly for the second sheet of paper that he extended to her.

"Never fear, Celeste,'" he said, "you shall have ample time to yourself while in Paris. I'll see to it that your husband is kept occupied, and that nothing interferes with your learning your duties." He rose to his feet abruptly, indicating that the interview had come to an end.

The escort who would take Celeste to a dressmaker awaited her, and her head spun as she joined the guide. She had been backed into a corner, and no escape was possible. She not only knew that Mimi Clayton was in grave danger, but she realized that her own situation was precarious in the extreme. There was no way of predicting how Richard and Eliza would react when they found out that she was the successor to Laroche and, even though married to Adam Burrows, was acting as the French spymaster for all of North America.

Colonel Burrows was amazed, and his two young colleagues were equally astonished by the breadth of the offer made to them by the French minister of trade. The situation outlined by the minister and the royal treasurer was simple: The French island-colonies in the West Indies were thriving, particularly Martinique and Guadeloupe, where sugarcane was just starting to be raised profitably and in large quantities. Similarly, these Caribbean islands were rich in logwood and other natural materials used in making cloth dyes. What these colonies lacked was a network of markets relatively near at hand. France had only recently started to develop its holdings on the North American mainland, and it would be at least a generation, the minister of trade said, before New France would be a trade center of any importance.

Therefore, the natural trading partner for the French West Indian colonies would be the British colonies in North America. Cardinal Mazarin was just beginning to invest money in a French merchant fleet of consequence, so for the time being, the British colonials would have to be relied upon for the vessels so necessary for the establishment and growth of trade.

In order to encourage such business, France was willing to pay generous subsidies to a shipping company that would devote most of its effort to such trade. After examining the records of a number of concerns in Boston, Providence Plantations, and elsewhere, the trade minister had determined that Burrows and Clayton of New Haven was by far the best natural trading partner that France could obtain.

So if Burrows and Clayton were willing, France would enter into an agreement with them. All that remained to be determined were the size and specific details of the subsidy and a regular schedule under which the firm's ships would be visiting Martinique, Guadeloupe, and the other French possessions in the Caribbean.

Colonel Burrows masked his elation, and both Richard and Ezekiel remained equally controlled. Only when they were alone again after the meeting and were making their way back to their own quarters on the Place Vendôme were they able to speak freely.

"As I see it," a delighted Adam Burrows declared, "we will double our annual income, at the very least. Depending on the size of the subsidy we can squeeze out of Mazarin, we can even triple our profits—not including what it will cost us to buy another three or four new ships."

"It's almost too good to be true," Richard said.

"They're not doing us any favors, to be sure," his father-in-law replied. "Their representatives were surprisingly blunt. They're being generous simply because they need us. They don't like us any more than we like them, but business is business, and they're acting accordingly."

"I think we should do the same," Ezekiel declared. "Business *is* business, and be damned to our low opinion of the French!"

"Do you agree?" Adam asked his son-in-law.

Richard frowned. "I suggest that we modify that position somewhat," he said. "I think we should wait until the French make a firm, irrevocable offer, and that we then examine it point by point. I don't trust them, and I want to study the entire offer very closely before I commit myself to it."

"Now that you explain it that way," a somewhat chastised Ezekiel said, "I'm afraid I see it your way."

"So do I," Adam Burrows declared. "We'll neither agree nor disagree with the proposals being made, but we'll wait until the offer is complete. Then we'll look for possible flaws in it."

When they returned to the palace of the duc de Vendôme, they discovered their wives in high good humor. All three of the young women had ordered dresses made from incomparable Italian silk, far superior to any fabric made elsewhere in Europe. If Celeste's gaiety was somewhat forced, she was a sufficiently accomplished actress that no one was aware of her true feelings.

Monsieur Rochas appeared and suggested that they might enjoy an outing to the Bois de Boulogne, a royal hunting preserve just outside the city. He also pointed out that they could obtain a splendid supper for very little money at an inn located on the edge of the Bois.

Richard was secretly amused that the young nobleman should think that a group of New Englanders would be attracted by a ride in the woods. Apparently he had no idea of the extent of the wilderness of North America, where there was nothing but trees for mile after countless mile. However, the prospect of just getting out of the city for a respite

was so appealing that Richard heartily agreed with
the others. They set out on horseback from the
Vendôme stables, with the women riding sidesaddle.

Richard had never seen a city, London included,
with streets so congested with traffic. Farmers were
heading home with their unsold produce in open
carts drawn by donkeys, while fishmongers pushed
smaller handcarts and offered their remaining wares
at bargain prices to passersby. Larger carts, containing bewildering arrays of merchandise, ranging from
exquisite wardrobes and cabinets to bolts of cloth
and other handcrafted goods, blocked traffic at every
corner.

In addition, there were huge carriages of state
used by members of the high nobility. These cumbersome vehicles, often pulled by spirited teams of four
horses, were far larger than those seen across the
English Channel. They more nearly resembled par-
lors on wheels than carriages, and they sometimes
filled an entire road from one side to the other. The
worst of the congestion, however, was caused by individual horseback riders, particularly the young
gallants and the military. Mounted musketeers, their
blue capes flapping, imperiously galloped their way
past slower vehicles and even forced the huge carriages to slow their paces. Officers from a half
dozen other elite regiments copied the musketeers,
and the civilian gentry, refusing to be outdone in
éclat, were equally reckless.

The net result was chaos. The streams of vehicles
and individual riders stubbornly refused to give way
to each other at intersections, which resulted in all
traffic being halted for several blocks in every
direction. Tempers became frayed, drivers climbed
to the ground and exchanged punches as well as
curses, and very often riders were forced to settle
their differences on the field of honor.

The English colonials, who had never seen anything like this traffic, were both astounded and amused by the spectacle. They were in no hurry to reach the Bois, so they stared in wonder at the Parisians, who so thoroughly lost their tempers with one another.

Richard was by far the most accomplished horseman of the group, and Eliza and Ezekiel were almost as skilled. Colonel Burrows was far more at home on the deck of a merchant ship, however, and he rode slowly, sitting firmly in his saddle. Mimi was a fairly proficient horsewoman, though a lack of practice in recent years made her a rather rusty rider. Celeste Burrows was the most awkward member of the group, although she managed to keep her seat and presented a charming picture.

At last traffic thinned, and the group approached the Bois de Boulogne, where another surprise awaited the colonials. These woods in no way resembled the wilderness with which they were familiar. Here the trees were planted in neat rows, and their symmetry was obvious. Scores of workers kept the ground clear of fallen leaves and twigs, so the paths beneath the hooves of the party's mounts were clean and unobstructed.

Richard, himself not long ago a king's forester, had forgotten it was possible for a woods to be so formal. Something seemed lacking, and at last he realized that there was no earthy scent of rotting vegetation, the sure sign of good health in the wilderness of North America.

The members of the party conversed with one another as their horses walked along sedately. Adam and Ezekiel were in the lead, Monsieur Rochas, Celeste, and Mimi rode behind them, and Richard and Eliza brought up the rear. They were taking their time as they made their way toward the place where they would dine, and no one objected. The woods were redolent with the sweet but sharp scent of pines, and the Americans felt more at home than they had anywhere in Paris. At one point, Richard noted rather idly, Monsieur Rochas had disappeared, but he attached little significance to that fact. He assumed the Frenchman had gone into the woods to relieve himself, or perhaps had ridden ahead to make sure that their table was reserved at the inn.

Suddenly, however, to Richard's astonishment and dismay, a group of five mounted men, all of them masked and carrying long, double-edged swords, halted the group and formed a semicircle around them. Richard, Ezekiel, and Adam immediately drew their own swords.

"Ladies and gentlemen," the leader said, speaking surprisingly good English, "we regret any inconvenience we may be causing you. We apologize in advance for it."

Adam Burrows refused to be cowed. "If this is a robbery," he shouted, waving his own sword, "be damned to you! You'll have to kill me before you take a penny from my purse."

The assailants edged slightly closer, gripping their blades firmly.

Finally the leader replied. "You misunderstand us, sir," he declared. "We have no interest in your money."

"If this is a joke then, we are not amused," Ezekiel said, enraged by the incident.

The leader of the group made no reply, his manner insolent, his menacing eyes glowing behind the mask that covered the lower part of his face. He studied each of the ladies in turn. Then, suddenly, he pointed his blade at Mimi Clayton. "There," he said to his subordinates in a low voice that nevertheless carried. "There is the one we seek."

Richard was stunned, but now he knew that this was no chance meeting. He vividly recalled having rescued Mimi from the dungeon of the French agent Horace Laing in Virginia, and he knew that, for whatever reason, Mimi was still in danger.

He reacted swiftly and coolly, his mind alert and sharp, as it always was in moments of great peril. Using his horse's neck as a screen, he drew one of the pair of pistols he habitually carried, and surreptitiously passed it to Eliza.

Eliza, too, was prepared for an emergency and reacted deftly. She nodded almost imperceptibly as she took the pistol, a quick smile indicating that she knew what Richard required of her.

Although she was riding sidesaddle, which gave her minimal control of her mount, she managed to spur forward unexpectedly. At the same time, she cocked and raised her pistol, quickly took aim at the masked leader of the band, and pulled the trigger. The shot was so unexpected, so startling that it seemed to echo and reverberate even more loudly than it actually did.

The assailants were stunned by the sudden counterattack. Apparently they had been assured they would encounter no resistance. When they did, they quickly lost nerve and began to back off warily. This was precisely the diversion Richard had wanted. His wife had narrowly missed the leader of the group, but the man was nevertheless shaken and appeared to have lost control of his subordinates.

Richard, with cocked pistol in his hand, spurred forward directly at the leader. "Throw down your blade and surrender, sir," he directed in an authoritative voice. "You are my prisoner."

The leader saw the muzzle of a pistol pointing straight at him, and instantly knew he stood no chance, as he was armed only with a sword.

Richard could have killed the man, but that was not his intention. If the leader died and his men disbanded, he would never learn the meaning of the assault or the extent of the danger Mimi Clayton faced. Therefore, he menacingly aimed his pistol between the man's eyes, but did not pull the trigger.

The colonist's intentions frightened the leader, who quickly threw down his sword. Richard gestured to Eliza, who rode her mount over to the brigand, reached out to him, and roughly tore back the man's mask. To the utter amazement of the entire group, they found themselves face to face with a dismayed and deeply embarrassed Lord Butler.

Celeste Burrows understood the situation instantly. After her refusal to act as Mazarin's assassin, Butler had been charged by the cardinal with the responsibility of murdering Mimi Clayton. He had deliberately chosen this occasion in the Bois, where he and his henchmen would be unobserved as they did away with Mimi after separating her from the others in the party.

Mimi also recognized she was in dire peril, and was quick to put two and two together. Butler, her former lover, was, like Horace Laing, a discontent Cavalier, and probably was also financed by the French. She looked around, then instinctively moved behind Ezekiel and Adam.

Richard gazed coldly at Lord Butler. "You, *sir*," he said, "have a great deal of explaining to do."

"Go to the devil, Dunstable," Butler retorted.

Richard did not lose his equanimity. "If you value your life, you'll talk," he said.

Even as he spoke, Richard noticed that the other four members of the assault party had quietly disengaged themselves and were retreating from the scene. They withdrew farther and farther, and as soon as they were out of pistol range, they turned and galloped away.

Richard listened to the receding hoofbeats and knew what had to be done. "Colonel," he said, "you and Ezekiel return with your wives at once to

Paris. We'll not be dining at any country inn to-night. It may be a trifle late by the time we get back to the city, but I'd rather be a little hungry and have all of us alive."

Ezekiel started to object. "What's this about my wife being threatened? Is this connected to what happened to her in Virginia?"

Richard silenced him. "Leave this matter to me," he replied, "and I'll explain everything later. I know how to handle it."

Adam Burrows also objected and began to present his arguments.

Celeste, however, cut him short. "Please, my dear," she said, "listen to Richard, and do as he suggests. He has Mimi's welfare very much in mind."

Not only was she more than willing to leave the problem to Richard, but she was relieved as well because she would not be present at the scene. She was very much conscious of her own awkward position. If she were not on hand, however, Cardinal Mazarin could not point a finger of blame at her in the event that developments in the matter were not to his liking.

Colonel Burrows heeded his wife's request and promptly asked Richard, "What will you and Eliza be doing?"

Richard continued to watch Lord Butler closely and kept his pistol trained on the nobleman. "We have a little business that will detain us temporarily, but we'll catch up with you either on the road or in Paris. Don't worry about us."

The assurance he offered was good enough for Adam Burrows. He was confused and upset by the strange incident, but his trust in his daughter's and son-in-law's competence was complete, so he was willing to leave the disposition of the matter in their hands. He said something in an undertone to Celeste and Mimi, and they immediately turned and started back in the direction from which they had come. Ezekiel accompanied them reluctantly. Adam, bringing up the rear, had a final word with Richard.

"Don't take any needless risks," he called. "Remember, we're in a foreign land."

Lord Butler waited until the quartet no longer were within earshot, then he said dryly, "Colonel Burrows has given you good advice, Dunstable. You'd be well advised to take it. You are not in New Haven now, and you're not even in England."

"I'm well aware that this is France," Richard replied, "and that Cardinal Mazarin pulls the strings here. Be that as it may, you'll now tell me the meaning of this inexcusable attack."

The nobleman smiled. "Your curiosity is insatiable," he said, "and that's unfortunate, because I have no intention of providing any answers for you."

Richard knew he faced a blank wall, and that unless he could persuade Butler to speak freely, the danger to Mimi well might not be lessened. But he knew of no way he could force the recalcitrant nobleman to speak.

While he pondered the problem, Eliza spoke up. "It's rather obvious," she said, "that his lordship is in the employ of Cardinal Mazarin and that he was instructed to do away with Mimi. He happened to choose a method that was too evident and a technique that completely lacked subtlety." She raised an eyebrow as she glanced at the nobleman. "His Eminence won't be pleased with you," she said archly.

The goaded Lord Butler rose to the bait. "In that case," he said, "His Eminence should give unwanted assignments to his French bullyboys and not to me."

He had tacitly admitted he had been acting under orders, and Eliza nodded. "I see no great mystery here, Richie," she said. "Mazarin has spun one of his webs, and his lordship was caught in it. He wasn't the first to be trapped, nor will he be the last."

Lord Butler glowered at her. "You know a great deal," he said. "Far more than is good for you, perhaps."

She shrugged, but made no comment.

Richard scowled at the nobleman. "Whatever dirty work Mazarin requires you to do is his business and is irrelevant to us. I wish to keep it that way. I just want to make certain once and for all that Mimi Clayton stays safe. And I already warned you once."

Lord Butler laughed harshly. "You and your wife have made certain that my hands are tied behind my back, haven't you? Your interference has effectively removed me from taking any action in this matter, so I alone will have to face Mazarin's wrath. You two aren't blameless, you know. You've taken his gold, just as I have, and don't pretend to me that you haven't. We'll say no more about the matter. We'll part company here and go our separate ways."

"Not so fast," Richard cautioned him. "For Mimi's sake, I'd like a full and frank confession from you."

"For a supposedly experienced agent, Dunstable, you play childish games." Lord Butler looked him up and down contemptuously. "You're still an English nobleman, and for that reason I don't believe that you—or your wife—would fire at an unarmed man. Therefore I shall bid both of you a pleasant, if rather abrupt, good day." He wheeled his horse around and rode off, increasing his gait very rapidly to a full gallop.

Richard faced an immediate dilemma and well knew it. Butler was right, to be sure: He could not and would not fire his pistol at the fleeing man, and he knew Eliza felt similarly inhibited. He could try to follow Lord Butler, and perhaps could catch and corner him, but he realized that Eliza, obliged to follow sidesaddle, would fall far behind. He couldn't take the risk of allowing her to make her way alone through these hostile French woods.

Consequently, and with great regret, he allowed his quarry to escape. This, indeed, he reminded himself, was not New Haven, and he had to behave circumspectly.

He and Eliza analyzed the situation as best they could as they rode back to Paris. "At first glance," Richard said, "it appears as though the attempt to abduct and probably kill Mimi was a crude act crudely performed, but on closer examination I think it was very clever."

"Indeed it was," his wife replied. "Had you and I not interfered when we did, Butler and his men could have disappeared with Mimi. Either she would have vanished, or her body would have been found in a day or two with her throat slit, and it would have been impossible to point the finger of blame at anyone."

"Exactly the point I'm trying to make," Richard said. "The French government could have feigned innocence and washed its hands of the matter. Apparently Mazarin never forgets, and we're going to have to take a great many precautions to ensure that Mimi is safe during the rest of our stay here and on our journey home."

It occurred to Eliza that he was giving no thought to her safety or his own, and perhaps that was foolhardy. Cardinal Mazarin was certain to react strongly when he discovered that his plans had gone awry because of their interference.

When they reached the palace of the duc de Vendôme, they discovered that the other members of the party had already gathered in the dining room for a late supper of cold meats and bread. Richard was very much relieved, thinking that here, of all places, Mimi would remain unmolested. He was learning more about the treacherous techniques employed by the first minister of France, and he knew that Mazarin would not want anything to happen to a guest of France under the roof of a high-ranking nobleman.

Richard tried to devise some plans to protect Mimi for the duration of their stay without making her a prisoner in their host's palace. His friends stared at him with tense, paled expressions.

Ezekiel broke the tension. "It isn't Mimi who is in danger," he said. "It's you."

Richard could only gape at him.

Lord Butler had lost no time, his father-in-law explained. "Not a quarter of an hour before you and Eliza came back, we were visited by a man who claimed to be Butler's second. Butler has challenged you to a duel, to be fought at dawn tomorrow."

"We accepted the challenge on your behalf," Ezekiel said. "Perhaps we shouldn't have."

"And just in case you don't remember," Celeste added, "Butler had the reputation of being the deadliest swordsman at the court of King Charles. Obviously he intends to silence you before you can spread the story of tonight's activities."

Richard was awake long before dawn after sleeping poorly. He quietly left the four-poster bed in order not to disturb Eliza, and went off to his dressing room to wash, shave, and prepare for the duel. When he returned to the bedchamber, the bed was empty, but before he could say anything, Eliza called to him from the adjoining sitting room.

Her appearance astonished him. She was dressed in a man's clothing, complete in every detail: She wore a shirt and, over it, a tight-fitting leather jerkin; her trousers were tucked into the tops of high boots; and by piling her pale blond hair beneath a broad-brimmed Cavalier hat, she resembled a young and exceptionally good-looking man. "Why the masquerade?" Richard asked, trying very hard not to smile at her, in spite of everything that was threatening to happen.

She responded carefully, telling him only what she thought he needed to know. "I intend to go with you," she said. "I will be your second."

"But Ezekiel is accompanying me as my second," he said.

"Then you'll have two of us," she declared stubbornly. "From what I know of the laws of dueling, there's nothing to prevent you from being escorted by two seconds."

"But why are you coming with me?" he insisted, bewildered by her behavior.

She shrugged. "Call it concern, if you wish," she said. "We're strangers in France, and I'll worry less if I'm with you and see the duel with my own eyes."

He would not protest further, and secretly was pleased to have her accompany him. She had been a great emotional support during his combat with the Raritan Indian Jo-no-ta. He could use that sort of backing again today.

Obviously Ezekiel knew of Eliza's plan, for he awaited the couple in the courtyard and had three horses saddled and ready. They mounted in silence, with cloaks wrapped around them to protect them from the early morning chill. They rode through the deserted streets to the River Seine, the hooves of their horses clattering on the cobblestones.

A short distance past the Louvre were gardens, less formal than the Tuileries, and it was here, near the edge of the river, that Lord Butler, his second, and a surgeon, all garbed in black, awaited the arrival of the colonials. Monsieur Rochas also was there, in the self-appointed role of referee. His presence, which was a complete surprise to Richard and Eliza, convinced them that he was an active party in the overall conspiracy hatched by Cardinal Mazarin. They tied their horses to trees at the edge of a lawn and entered the grounds, with Richard in the lead and Ezekiel and Eliza close behind him. Eliza hid her features beneath the brim of her hat, which she had pulled down over her eyes.

Monsieur Rochas wasted no time. "We understand that grave differences exist between John, Lord Butler, and Sir Richard Dunstable. I call upon you gentlemen to reconcile your differences in order to avoid bloodshed. Are you willing to do so?"

"I most certainly am not," Lord Butler declared loudly.

Richard was obliged to follow his opponent's lead. "Nor am I," he declared.

"Very well, gentlemen," Monsieur Rochas said, "you are obliged to fight till one or the other of you draws blood. The shedding of blood will wash away any differences that exist between you, and your feud will be terminated. Let me stress that it is not necessary or even desirable to inflict a mortal wound," the referee went on. "A mere scratch is sufficient for the purposes of salvaging honor. Again, do I make myself clear?"

Both men nodded. "You will retire now to opposite sides of the clearing."

They retreated accordingly, and their seconds were summoned by the referee, with Ezekiel responding on behalf of his principal. Inasmuch as Lord Butler had issued the challenge, his opponent was entitled to his choice of swords, and Monsieur Rochas extended a silk-lined box containing two identical, perfectly balanced blades. There was no difference between them, as Ezekiel discovered after testing first one and then the other, so it didn't matter which of them he selected. He took one, returned with it to Richard's side, and handed it to him. Richard removed his cloak and then his doublet. He slowly rolled up the sleeves of his shirt, shivering slightly in the damp morning air beside the river. There was a slight fog, not enough to interfere with vision, and dawn was just breaking, making the twin towers of Notre Dame Cathedral stand out in increasingly bold relief against the sky.

Testing his sword, Richard was relatively satisfied with it. His preference would have been a duel fought with pistols. After swishing it experimentally, he returned the sword to his side.

"Be very careful, my dearest one," Eliza whispered. "I shall be keeping watch for you."

He had no idea what she meant, but felt the need to reassure her. "Don't worry about me," he said softly. "I can take care of myself."

"You may approach, gentlemen," Monsieur Rochas called out.

Richard grinned at Eliza, hoping to dissipate the look of concern he saw in her eyes; then he turned and walked steadily to the center of the lawn. There he came face to face with Lord Butler, whose gaze was impersonal and steady. He bore almost no resemblance to the horseman of the previous evening, who had been both frightened and threatening. He knew what he was doing and was coldly confident that he would emerge victorious from the combat.

"You are both familiar with the rules of swordplay, gentlemen," Monsieur Rochas declared, "so there is no need for me to recite them for you. You may begin when I give the signal. I urge you to stop immediately when I call for a halt. I trust I'm understood."

Both principals nodded. The referee extended his sword between them and held it at arm's length.

Richard took his stance, flexing his knees slightly, and then saluted his opponent. Equally punctilious, Lord Butler did the same.

Monsieur Rochas withdrew his own blade. The two principals spoke simultaneously: *"En garde!"*

The duel was under way, and Eliza, drawing in her breath sharply, riveted her attention on her husband's face. The principals crossed swords experimentally, testing each other; then suddenly, Lord Butler lunged.

Only because he had expected his opponent to try to seize the initiative was Richard able to deflect the blow. But he knew from the speed and drive of the thrust that he was going to have his hands full. He was deadly accurate with musket, pistol, or throwing knives, and there were few marksmen anywhere who were his equal, but as a swordsman he was relatively inexperienced and clumsy.

Certainly he knew that he was no match for the nobleman who was his foe and who had cleverly maneuvered him into fighting this duel. Lord Butler handled himself with consummate ease, and his sword appeared to be an extension of his arm. He wielded it with the grace and total self-confidence of one who has spent countless hours at practice with blades.

As Richard again adopted a defensive stance and awaited his opponent's next thrust, his eyes met Lord Butler's, and a slow chill crept up his spine. Only now did he fully realize the odds against him, and it dawned on him that his opponent would not be satisfied with inflicting a mere scratch. He could read in the other's eyes that Lord Butler aimed to kill him because he knew too much. By allowing the nobleman to leave the Bois de Boulogne the previous night, Richard had signed his own death warrant, which Ezekiel had then sealed for Richard by stupidly accepting the challenge to a duel.

It was too late now for regrets and recriminations, however, and Richard knew he had to do his best in order to prolong his life from one second to the next. He deeply regretted the impulse that had allowed him to grant Eliza permission to accompany him here in disguise; now she would witness his ultimate disgrace and inevitable death.

Lord Butler lunged, fully expecting to find his target. At the last possible moment, Richard again deflected the blow, but was thrown so badly off balance that he could not possibly counter the move with a thrust of his own.

Richard knew he could not afford the time for humiliation any more than he could run the risk of being angry with himself for having fallen into such a transparent trap. The realization emerged frighteningly now at the back of his mind that once Lord Butler had disposed of him, Eliza would be next on the list, vulnerable and ripe for murder.

There appeared to be nothing he could do. His opponent was a far superior swordsman and was icily determined to exterminate him.

Slowly Richard retreated, parrying and deflecting one wicked thrust after another, each of them aimed at a vital place. That he had escaped so far and was still alive was a testimony to his quick reflexes and keen eyesight rather than his prowess in swordplay. But at any moment, he knew, he was going to lose his life, and the others on the bank of the Seine were also well aware of it. Monsieur Rochas, who had apparently known what to expect, watched the progress of the duel with equanimity, as did Lord Butler's second, and only the physician seemed to be concerned.

Richard knew from the expression in his opponent's cold eyes, from the set of his jaw, that he was impatient to end the fight. Butler's strokes became firmer, his thrusts more unpredictable and more difficult to avoid. Then, as the nobleman was preparing to launch yet another thrust, a pistol shot sounded. Lord Butler dropped his sword and clasped his shoulder in pain and astonishment. Richard saw a crimson spot appear and spread on the white linen of his foe's shirt.

Then he gaped in amazement at his wife. Eliza stood with her cloak thrown back and her hat lying on the ground beside her, and her long blond hair was streaming down her shoulders. It was obvious, too, from the fit of her coat that she was very much a woman. Tucked in her belt was the still smoking pistol she had used to end the duel so abruptly. In her right hand was another loaded weapon.

Her eyes blazing, she spoke loudly and clearly. "I intervened, Lord Butler, to prevent the cold-blooded murder of my husband. I'm thankful that I sensed you were up to no good. Richie, you allowed yourself to be led into a vicious trap that would have ended your life. I thank the Almighty that I sensed that Lord Butler somehow intended to trick you. That's why I insisted on coming with you."

The physician, rendered speechless by the unexpected outcome of the duel, rushed into the clearing to attend the wound in Lord Butler's shoulder.

Monsieur Rochas meanwhile turned and faced the woman indignantly. "Your interference in an affair of honor is unprecedented, madame," he said. "You have made a laughingstock of the participants."

Her smile was icy as she faced him. "You are mistaken, monsieur," she replied. "Actually, this is one duel that will never be spoken about in any way. I'm sure you—of all people—will see to it that not a word is said about it." She raised the pistol and pointed it at him accusingly. "Because, monsieur, you share in Lord Butler's guilt. Just as you led us into a trap in the Bois last night, so you intended to participate this morning in the murder of my husband. You won't want that fact repeated, I'm sure, so you'll see to it that nothing is said about the outcome of this duel."

Rochas fought for his voice and finally found it. "If you would be good enough, madame, to stop pointing that weapon at me."

Richard recovered his equilibrium sufficiently to come to his wife's side, and he handed his borrowed sword to Ezekiel. Putting an arm around Eliza and kissing her soundly, he took the pistol from her hand. "Sorry this makes you apprehensive, Monsieur Rochas," he said, "but perhaps you can understand now how I felt facing a swordsman as deadly as Lord Butler. I'm afraid that every word my wife said is true. I urge you to go home and forget that this incident ever took place." He turned to face a very pale Lord Butler, whose shoulder was being bandaged by the physician in an effort to stanch the flow of blood.

"As for you, John, Lord Butler," Richard said, "you may consider yourself fortunate you're still alive. Believe me, if I'd been wielding the pistol that my wife fired, I'd have shot to kill."

The nobleman tried to reply, but seemed to have lost his power of speech.

"If I were you," Richard said to him, "I'd leave Paris, and I wouldn't come back as long as we remain here. I give you fair warning, sir: Don't return —ever—to the New World. If you do, I swear I'll shoot you on sight without a moment's regret."

Lord Butler drew himself up to his full height even though the gesture cost him considerable pain. "You fail to understand the delicacy of my position," he said.

"Not at all," Richard replied. "I have a far

greater understanding of it than you can possibly imagine. I would be inclined to sympathize with you if you hadn't tried to kill first Mimi Clayton and then me, after professing friendship with us on your sojourn in the New World. So just keep in mind what I say to you, sir. Don't ever set foot in the North American colonies again, or your life will be ended as abruptly as you tried to end mine."

He turned away, his arm still encircling Eliza, and he led her to their waiting mounts. They were followed by Ezekiel, who stared hard at the group they were leaving behind. Not until they were mounted, however, and were riding back to the palace of the duc de Vendôme did Ezekiel express his thoughts.

"I always thought that France was a civilized country," Ezekiel said, "but since last night I've been shocked twice. I realized, I guess, just as fast as Eliza did, what was waiting for you in that duel, Richie, but I knew of no way to stop it. I feel so responsible, having accepted the challenge in your behalf. I was paralyzed, more or less, and then, all of a sudden, Eliza acted."

Richard chuckled quietly and then addressed his wife. "I'm in *your* debt now, my dear," he said, "and I reckon I will be for the rest of my days. If it weren't for your intervention, you'd be a widow by now."

Eliza was determined to relieve the somber tenor of the conversation. "I had to do something," she replied, "I don't look in the least attractive dressed in black."

Richard chuckled and shook his head, then reached over and tousled her hair. Her spirit was unique, and he loved her for it. The crowded events of the previous evening and of this morning finally began to take shape in his mind, and all at once he halted. The others drew their mounts up, too, and

Eliza looked at him questioningly. "I was intending to go back to the Place Vendôme for breakfast," he said, "but I've changed my mind. You and I are going to pay a call on Mazarin and get to the root of our difficulties."

"That's a splendid idea, and I agree heartily," Eliza said, "but we'll have to go back first, all the same. I'm not dressed for a visit to His Eminence, and since it's unlikely that he's had his own breakfast yet, we may as well eat and take our time going to the Louvre."

Richard grinned and nodded. So much had happened already this morning that he had to remind himself it was still early in the day. Most Parisians were not yet awake.

Richard made himself inconspicuous by dressing as much as possible like the flocks of courtiers he had noticed around the Louvre. Eliza was far too attractive to remain unnoticed, but even she appeared relatively unexceptional, with only a hint of cosmetics on her face, her blond hair piled high on her head, and her dress modest. They went to the Louvre after they had eaten breakfast, and there the captain of the musketeer guards remembered them from the day they had been presented to young King Louis, so they were admitted without question when they asked to see the first minister.

A musketeer escorted them to the cardinal's suite, where they were conducted to an anteroom to wait until Cardinal Mazarin was free. Apparently they were early, because no other visitors were waiting to see him.

After only a few minutes, a priest appeared at the entrance and conducted them down the corridor to Mazarin's private office. There the cardinal, in a splendid crimson robe, awaited them with a smile. He extended his hand, but Richard neither shook it nor kissed his ring. Instead he bowed just deeply enough to be civil and then seated himself without further ado. Eliza followed her husband's lead.

If Mazarin was aware of the snub, he did not indicate it, and he laughed as he resumed his own seat. "You've been the two busiest people in Paris, I think, in the past twenty-four hours," he told them. "You appear to have developed a habit of countering the best-devised plans of my representatives."

"Sorry if we've upset Your Eminence's schemes," Richard said, "but we object rather strenuously to attempts on my life, just as we also violently oppose attempts to abduct and murder our good friends."

"You're being overly hasty," Mazarin replied. "You're jumping to conclusions."

Richard was stone-faced as he returned the first minister's gaze. "We're aware of the plot against Mimi Clayton," he said flatly. "And this morning my wife thwarted the conspiracy to take my own life. I don't like such activities, and I won't stand for them."

Mazarin grinned, and his entire manner changed. He relaxed, leaned back, and laced his fingers together. "You're quite right, of course," he said. "Lord Butler is far too impetuous, far too inclined to act without thinking a project through to its conclusion, so I see no reason to dissemble with you by trying to protect him. You have every right to be annoyed with him."

"And with you, Your Eminence?" Richard asked.

Mazarin continued to take his ease, still smiling. "I deserve your anger and contempt," he said. "The attempt on Lady Dawn was slipshod, and the plan to kill you was crude and amateurish. No, I don't blame you in the least for being very much annoyed."

Eliza marveled at the cardinal's lack of scruples. Undoubtedly Lord Butler had been acting on Mazarin's instructions, but listening to the cardinal now, she had the distinct impression that he was absolving himself, wiping his hands clean of the matter, as if nothing had happened.

But the first minister had still another surprise in store for her. His manner completely candid, he went on, "Naturally, Lord Butler wasn't in a position of ultimate responsibility. He was being used as a means to an end, and his clumsiness saved your life, just as his ineptitude preserved the life of Lady Dawn. I won't dissemble with you. The orders emanated from me, and I take full responsibility for all that happened, even though I was ignorant of the details. Let me say that my ignorance was deliberate because I preferred not to know."

Richard blinked at him in disbelief, and Eliza, equally stunned, was the first to recover. "Do I gather," she asked incredulously, "that Your Eminence admits being behind the plots to kill Richard and to abduct and murder Mimi?"

"Your language is somewhat blunter than I would use in explaining my role," Mazarin said. "I must say, however, that I do accept full blame, without conditions."

Richard could only glare at him, too upset and angry to reply.

Mazarin still retained his composure. "I've made it an inviolable rule," he said, "always to admit my errors freely and to correct them without delay. I admit to you that I was very much in the wrong, and I'm glad I have the chance to set some new courses."

"What new courses? I don't know what you're talking about," Richard said stiffly.

"No, of course you don't," the cardinal said. "I have long wanted to be rid of Lady Dawn because she found out far too much about my operations in the New World. Only since she has been in France and I've had the chance to have her studied by some of my best operatives have I realized that my fears regarding her were groundless. She appears to have no interest whatever in matters of state-craft and politics."

"That's correct," Richard replied, and Eliza nodded assent. "She cares nothing about the struggle for New World dominance that France, Britain, and a number of other powers are playing."

"What's more," the cardinal continued, "I failed to appreciate properly the talents that both of you display in such abundance. As for you, Mistress Dunstable, I have come to appreciate that you perpetrated a remarkable feat in New Amsterdam by convincing the whole community you were the mistress of Peter Stuyvesant when, in reality, you were not."

"May I ask how you discovered that?" an intrigued Eliza wanted to know.

The cardinal smiled. "I have sources of information that I regard as impeccable," he said, and turned to Richard. "You've also performed ably, Master Dunstable, and you've served France far better than you know. Between the two of you, you first exposed Stuyvesant as the person who was supplying the Indians with firearms—some of which, you may be interested to know, have been used against our traders in New France—and then you nullified that stupid policy by decisively defeating his Indian allies."

Richard inclined his head in a gesture of thanks, but was far from mollified.

"I began to think about you both in earnest this morning," the cardinal said, "when the results of Lord Butler's duel were brought to me. Obviously I underrated you; obviously I gave you insufficient credit for the talents you've so consistently displayed. I shall not make that mistake again."

"If you're telling me," Richard said with just a trace of irony in his voice, "that no further attempts will be made on my life, my wife's, or Mimi Clayton's, I'm grateful to you, Your Eminence. I thank you for making it possible for me to sleep more easily."

Mazarine ignored his sarcasm. "Of course I intend to avail myself more fully of your services and Mistress Dunstable's," he declared. "In return, you have my pledge that you won't be molested again, nor will Lady Dawn."

Eliza could keep silent no longer. "Suppose we were to inform you, Your Eminence, that your offer is insufficient to persuade us to continue our work for you. It may surprise you to know that we've had our fill of acting as French agents, and that we want nothing more than immediate release from your service."

The cardinal was neither surprised nor dismayed. "I daresay it's very normal for you to feel the way you do," he declared. "However, I happen to be in need of your services. In fact, my need is far greater and far more urgent than you realize. Consequently, I shall retain both of you for as many more months as necessary."

Richard bristled. "And if we refuse, Your Eminence?"

Mazarin smiled and shook his head. "You won't do that," he said, "because if you leave me, I shall be forced to reveal to Oliver Cromwell and his Parliament in England, as well as to the leaders of every English colony in the New World, that you have both been serving faithfully in my employ. You'll become pariahs in every English colony in North America, as well as in England herself."

Richard realized that his hope for escape from Mazarin's service had been both premature and unrealistic. He should have known better, he told himself. It was clear that Mazarin had made up his mind to keep both him and Eliza in his employ indefinitely.

"Let us review the situation. Then, perhaps, you'll gain a better understanding of why I need you," the first minister said, as if speaking to children. "For all practical purposes, the Swedes and the Dutch have too small a stake in the New World to be serious contenders for domination. Spain, to be sure, has developed vast holdings in Central and South America, as well as in the West Indies. But aside from some tenuous settlements on the Pacific coast, with which we are not concerned, and in the Floridas, she hasn't exhibited any real desire to enter into a contest for North America. Besides, the situation in Spain itself is upset, and the country is weak militarily."

"That leaves England and France as the major contenders," Richard said. "That has been the case really for a number of years."

"Quite so," Mazarin replied, pleased with his pupil's perception. "And as of the present moment, the English seem to be holding all the advantages. They've established many flourishing colonies on a frontier more than one thousand miles long. English immigrants are pouring into those colonies and making them more secure. They've established themselves economically, and thanks to your efforts with their troops, they've flexed their military muscle as well. They appear to be in the New World to stay."

Richard and Eliza exchanged a wary look, as if they didn't believe Mazarin was giving up so easily.

Their reaction was not lost on the cardinal. "Now," he said, his tone changing, becoming intensely serious, "let us examine the situation of France. We have sent explorers through half the continent, and so far we have substantial land claims both to the north and to the west of the English colonies. But to date, our people have manifested very little interest in these endeavors, and the growth of New France has been painstakingly slow. I intend to reverse that situation and to increase immigration appreciably, but it will be many years before our efforts match those of the British. In the meantime, thanks to Governor Stuyvesant's bungling, New Netherland will fall into the hands of the Roundheads like a ripe apple dropping from a tree. Our task of gaining the upper hand has become far more difficult."

Richard could not help observing, "I'd say the task has become well nigh impossible."

"Not quite," Mazarin said with a gentle smile. "And I am determined not to give up so easily. On the contrary, I've concocted a new plan for the acquisition of the colonies of England by France, and if I place the right people in charge, frankly, I don't see how my scheme can fail."

Here was real news, the vital information Richard wanted. Only with difficulty did he curb his astonishment, pretending to be more or less indifferent. Eliza, he was delighted to observe, was reacting in the same unconcerned manner.

"That which you are about to learn," Mazarin said, "I tell you in the greatest of confidence. It's a symbol of the trust that I place in you that I make you privy to one of France's most important state secrets."

Richard nodded, but made no comment.

"Are you familiar with an island called Bermuda?" the first minister asked.

Richard had to stop and ponder before he was able to reply. "I think I know of the place," he said. "It was claimed by the British a good many years ago, but they did nothing about it, really, until recently. Several small settlements have been established there. The most productive was founded by shipwrecked sailors, who later moved on to Virginia, I believe. Other than that, I don't recall anything of interest about the place."

Eliza had been listening carefully, and she now added a few observations of her own. "Bermuda is only a week's voyage from the Virginia mainland. I've noticed it on my father's charts. But I can't imagine of what possible interest it could be to France. It certainly doesn't produce furs or timber!"

"New France," the first minister replied succinctly, "supplies us with all the furs and timber we require or want. Bermuda has a far different value. As you've so ably pointed out, Mistress Dunstable, it is about a thousand miles from the British colonies on the North American mainland. I am no military man, mind you, so I listen carefully to the advice of our generals and our admirals. However, looking at Bermuda on a map gave me some irresistible ideas."

Richard braced himself, certain that he knew what was coming next.

"Let us suppose," Mazarin went on genially, "that in addition to our hold on New France—which is fairly secure—let us, for the sake of argument, say that France also somehow gains possession of the island of Bermuda." He paused and added with a smile, "That island, if heavily fortified, could well become a thorn in the side of the British colonies in North America."

Richard's worst fears were confirmed. "I see what you mean," he said thoughtfully. "If your forces were to occupy Bermuda, you could apply pressure on England's colonies—for instance, from New France to the north and Bermuda to the south. You could use Bermuda as a natural base for your warships to interrupt the colonies' West Indies trade, and also as a large bivouac area for as vast an army as you cared to send to the New World."

"You are very quick," Mazarin said in admiration. "You start to understand my overall strategy."

"It's both sound and clever," Richard had to admit.

Mazarin nodded. "I had hoped," he said, "to use New Netherland in the same way. But I was mistaken. My scheme failed because the colony already had far too many English residents, and even more important, because Governor Stuyvesant's vanity and greed interfered with his common sense. Therefore, I intend to use Bermuda as I had hoped to use New Netherland. Only this time I will not fail. Because, you see, this time I *will* have your help, won't I?" There was an uneasy silence for a moment, but Mazarin simply smiled and did not wait for an answer. "Whether that help is reluctant or not is up to you, but I am sure you will find it in your best interest to cooperate fully."

It occurred to Eliza that the more she and Richard learned of Mazarin's plans, the more tightly bound they were to the French cause. They had already been told too much for their own good, as far as she was concerned. She felt hot and extremely uncomfortable.

The cardinal rose from his chair and walked to the floor-to-ceiling windows facing Richard and Eliza. He pulled back the draperies and stared out, seemingly lost in thought, his gray hair sparkling in the morning light. He addressed them without turning around. "I have spoken to you frankly and have told you of my plans in detail because you two will play key roles in making my wishes come to pass. Again, I must apologize for my, ah, indiscretion and the behavior of Lord Viscount Butler, since he cannot apologize for himself." The cardinal turned and smiled, and beckoned them to the window. "Please, come and look."

Richard and Eliza rose and approached the window. As they did, the cardinal stepped aside, and suddenly Richard and Eliza knew exactly what Mazarin really was.

Below the window, twisting slowly from a gibbet, hung Lord Butler. The dead white face stared up at them blankly.

Eliza gasped and stiffened, and Richard put his arm around her and led her back to her chair.

Mazarin pulled the curtain closed and sat down again. He smiled, shrugged his shoulders, then took two purses from his belt and dropped them on the desk in front of his guests. Richard knew at once from the sound the little pouches made that they were filled with gold. Eliza stared at them as if they contained poison.

Richard knew they had no choice. If he and Eliza refused the money, they undoubtedly would end up like Lord Butler. If, on the other hand, they accepted it, they were committing themselves to continue in the service of France, whose interests were directly opposed to those of the English colonies that represented their own future.

Mazarin took their silence as assent. "Go on about your business normally," he told them. "As of this very day, the shipping company of Burrows and Clayton is being awarded a very lucrative contract by the French government. It is so satisfactory, in fact, that your colleagues who came with you to France from New Haven will soon forget the unpleasant experience they suffered yesterday in the Bois."

His mind working rapidly, Richard realized that even Adam Burrows would be beholden in the future to the first minister of France. Mazarin, it appeared, was expert at binding people to him with invisible silken bands that, somehow, were too strong to break.

"In due time," the cardinal said, "you will be instructed regarding your specific conduct by your new superior in my service. As you may or may not know, Laroche met an unfortunate end, so I have found it necessary to replace him. The individual who will act as my personal representative will have identification that you will recognize instantly. A gold ring with an amethyst stone inlaid with a fleur-de-lis. All you will need to do is to follow the orders of the person who possesses it."

Richard was tempted to demand, "Is that all?" but somehow managed to refrain. He and Eliza had been trapped again, and there was no way they could escape French service. It appeared that they would be saddled with such a debt for a long time to come.

They were glum and silent when they took their leave of the cardinal. His joviality seemed to compound the depression that swept over them. When they emerged from the Louvre, Eliza sighed deeply. "I was hoping," she said, "that you'd throw your purse of gold in Mazarin's face when he gave it to you. I'd certainly have followed your example, but I realize that that was one thing you couldn't possibly do."

"I was tempted—strongly tempted," Richard replied, "but I couldn't see making a hollow gesture that would cause only trouble for us."

"I know, I know," Eliza replied with a sigh. "I know exactly what Mazarin would have done. He'd have called in the king's musketeer guards, and we would have ended up alongside Lord Butler."

"Correct," Richard said. "We would have signed our death warrants for certain."

When the couple reached the palace on the Place Vendôme, they found Adam Burrows and Ezekiel and Mimi Clayton in a handsome parlor of the suite that the colonists were occupying. Both of the men were ecstatic.

"We've just come from a final meeting with the minister of trade and the royal treasurer," Adam said, exhibiting a large document, "and we've signed an unbelievable agreement. We are now the largest seafaring mercantile representative of France in the New World. All trade with Martinique, Guadeloupe, and the other French islands of the West Indies will be directed through us, and our ships will even carry to France large quantities of furs and timbers from France's northern colonies."

"The contract," Ezekiel added, a tinge of wonder in his voice, "is as good or better than even a French shipping firm could have obtained. Our luck has been so good that I don't understand it."

Richard and Eliza exchanged surreptitious glances. They understood all too well why the contract was so favorable, but they were not in a position to explain.

"We have some news of our own for you," Richard said. "We've just come from the Louvre, and we've been told by the highest authority that the French government deeply regrets any fright or inconvenience you were caused in the attack yesterday. They assured us it will not happen again, and if you wish, they'll offer a formal apology."

"That won't be in the least necessary," murmured Mimi Clayton. "All I ask is to be allowed to live my life in peace."

That was all Eliza wanted, too, and she envied the woman whose tranquility had been assured by the first minister of France himself.

Ezekiel and Mimi went off to their own quarters, and Richard wasted no time as he asked, "Where is Celeste?"

"She had some fittings at the dressmaker's, I believe," Adam replied.

"It's just as well," Eliza said, "because we have to talk with you, Papa."

Richard took the lead in telling his father-in-law in full detail about the duel that morning, their subsequent meeting with Cardinal Mazarin, and the fate of Lord Butler. He left out nothing pertinent, but when he neglected to mention one or another detail, Eliza promptly supplied it.

Colonel Burrows sat very still, listening intently, his face registering surprise only when Lord Butler's execution was related. When they were finished, he looked at his daughter, then at his son-in-law, and said, "I'm pleased for Mimi's sake that she isn't going to be molested in the future. I think you're wise not to tell her the reasons that the French first wanted to be rid of her and why the first minister changed his mind. I think for the sake of whatever peace she can enjoy, the less she knows, the better."

Richard nodded and was glad his father-in-law approved.

Eliza knew her father well enough to realize that his failure to mention their own predicament or Mazarin's long-range plan was not accidental. "You disapprove of the part we're being forced to play, Papa?"

Adam shrugged and shook his head. "No, I don't object," he said. "And frankly, I don't see what good it would do if I did protest. You're helpless and must do Mazarin's bidding. I'm equally helpless and can only stand aside and observe."

"What are your thoughts on the matter?" Richard wanted to know.

"I see no real change in your situation," Adam replied. "You were forced previously to serve the cause of France, and you did, deviating from that service only when the interests of New Haven and the other New England colonies were at stake. Certainly I can appreciate your strong desire to be free of the French obligation, but it appears to be your destiny to continue. Try to look at the bright side of the picture."

"Is there a bright side?" Eliza asked bitterly.

"Of course!" her father assured her. "First off, we'll learn the identity of the new French spymaster in North America. That's terribly important. Then, when you're given your assignments in the scheme involving the capture of Bermuda, you'll learn a great deal more specific information about that plan, which New Haven should find very useful. So don't despair, and don't lose heart. Your situation seems worse now than it really is. You just need some time to get used to the idea."

Richard and Eliza did their best to be consoled by his words, but it was difficult to look forward with any real hope to the future.

That afternoon, after Celeste had returned to the Vendôme palace, they received word that the first minister of France wanted to bid farewell to them in person. Carriages were provided, and the entire group was taken to the Louvre.

Cardinal Mazarin was his most charming during the quarter of an hour that he spent with his guests. He showed a great knowledge of shipping, which impressed the men, and he treated the women with deference and appreciation.

Richard was privately surprised, though he told himself that he shouldn't have been. The cardinal behaved naturally with him and Eliza and was totally at ease. Nothing in his manner suggested what had happened earlier in the day.

That evening the minister of trade hosted a private banquet in his own home in honor of the colonials. They were treated to an endless array of perfectly prepared French dishes. Mimi and Eliza found the meal irresistible, and only Celeste had the strength to refuse more than a token quantity of the many foods that were served.

That banquet ended the visit to Paris, and the following morning the visitors departed by carriage for Le Havre de Grâce, where their ship awaited them for the voyage home. Richard and Eliza were sorry they had come to France and were anxious to put the country behind them, but they knew that there was no hiding from what appeared to be their inescapable fate.

Adam Burrows was highly pleased with the results of the journey, symbolized by the full hold containing merchandise that had been made in France and was being sent to the English North American colonies for sale. Bolts of cloth predominated, but there were also such items as glassware, glazed pottery, and finely crafted furniture.

Adam was content with life itself, and for good reason. After spending years alone, he had a young, exceptionally attractive wife who appeared to be devoted to him, and his business was booming. The contract with the French government made his shipping firm the most important in all of the English colonies, and because of this agreement with the French, his previous income would more than double.

The brig encountered rough seas in the English Channel, and was blown northward off her course, straying so far that the southern coast of England was cleary visible on the horizon. The sight of their native land affected Richard and Mimi Clayton strangely. They knew that as Cavaliers they were not welcome in England and would be placed under arrest by the Roundheads if they tried to go ashore. This realization reconfirmed their already strong conviction that their home was in the New World, and no longer in the land of their birth.

The inclement weather persisted, developing into a full-fledged gale that followed the ship into the open Atlantic. Richard, somewhat to his surprise, was immune to seasickness, as was Eliza, who had grown up on board one or another of her father's ships. Celeste and Mimi were less fortunate, however, and both were confined to their beds for several days until the raging seas became calmer and the howling winds subsided.

Thereafter the voyage went smoothly, and the tranquility of the passengers remained undisturbed. Then, when they were less than a week's voyage from New Haven, the world suddenly fell apart for Richard and Eliza.

On that morning Adam, aided by Ezekiel, was checking his cargo manifest, and Mimi volunteered her services to them as secretary. So, while they busied themselves in the hold, Celeste asked Richard and Eliza to join her in Adam's cabin for tea.

A crew member brought the tea as they sat around a small table, and Celeste held her cup in a rather strange way, making her little finger very conspicuous. Eliza could not help noting that Celeste was wearing a strange ring, and her attention was drawn to it.

Eliza swallowed an involuntary gasp. The ring was gold, and she saw a fleur-de-lis, the symbol of French royalty, inlaid on the amethyst stone.

Aware of his wife's discomfort, Richard stared at Celeste's finger, too, and was thunderstruck. Perhaps it was a coincidence that she was wearing such a ring, however, and it was possible that she had no idea of its significance.

Celeste was keenly aware of their interest, and removing the ring from her finger, she slid it across the table to them.

Eliza had no desire to touch it. Richard picked it up and saw that the fleur-de-lis was impeccably crafted; obviously the ring had been made by a master goldsmith. "I had no idea that you had acquired such a ring," he said carefully. "It's very unusual."

A faint smile touched the corners of Celeste's full mouth. "Yes, isn't it?" she agreed.

Eliza found her voice. "You acquired it in Paris?"

"I did, indeed," Celeste replied, and her smile broadened.

"Was it a gift from my father?" Eliza persisted.

Celeste shook her head. "No," she said. "As a matter of fact, it was presented to me by a mutual friend, someone we all know." She did not identify the donor.

Richard stiffened. Although he could scarcely believe it, Celeste Burrows appeared to be referring to Cardinal Mazarin. If that were the case, it was she who had received the appointment as the French spymaster for North America!

"I can't believe it. I—I can't believe it," Eliza whispered.

Richard shook his head as if to clear it, but made no comment.

"I'm glad we understand each other," Celeste said slowly and distinctly. Reaching for her ring, she retrieved it and dropped it into a small purse she carried at her waist.

Eliza recovered her voice, if not her equilibrium. "Has my father seen the ring?" she asked hoarsely.

Celeste shook her head. "There's no need for him to be aware of it," she said. "It's intended to be seen only by those for whom it bears a special significance. After we reach New Haven," she concluded, "I'll give you full instructions on what your duties will entail."

Richard and Eliza sat in frozen silence and could only nod. Their duty compelled them to carry the shocking news to Adam as rapidly as they could. But Eliza, knowing her father, realized that the truth about his deceptive young wife would crush and utterly destroy him.

She had no right to inflict such grievous harm on him. On the other hand, the safety of the New England colonies depended on his learning that his worst enemy in the New World—the worst enemy of everyone in the English colonies—was his own lovely wife.

WATCH FOR THE NEXT
EXCITING INSTALLMENT

IN THE THUNDERING
SAGA OF
RICHARD AND ELIZA
DUNSTABLE!

THE AMERICAN
PATRIOT SERIES